Phinn neve[...]

who was so intrepid, intelligent, or beautiful. He ambled toward her, and she took a step back. "I'd like to make you an offer."

She stood as straight and assured as if she was in a ballroom, not in a bedroom with nothing between them but a nightgown and a robe. "What?"

"Marry me in truth." He continued to stroll forward and she continued to retreat. Her back hit the tapestry-covered wall. "Augusta, I love you."

"No." She shook her head. Curls escaped the loose braid. He wanted to reach out and run his fingers through her sable hair. "You just said that."

"I can't believe you haven't figured it out." He dragged a hand down his face. Had he been so incompetent in showing his regard for her that she truly didn't know?

Her hands went to her hips. "Why did you not tell me?"

"I just did." His voice echoed in the chamber and he took a breath. Shouting wouldn't help. "You were the one who told me that I didn't love you because I wasn't acting like a man in love. Well, I'm not sure what you were waiting for me to do, but I *do* love you . . ."

Books by Ella Quinn

The Marriage Game

THE SEDUCTION OF LADY PHOEBE
THE SECRET LIFE OF MISS ANNA MARSH
THE TEMPTATION OF LADY SERENA
DESIRING LADY CARO
ENTICING MISS EUGÉNIE VILLARET
A KISS FOR LADY MARY
LADY BERESFORD'S LOVER
MISS FEATHERTON'S CHRISTMAS PRINCE

The Worthingtons

THREE WEEKS TO WED
WHEN A MARQUIS CHOOSES A BRIDE
IT STARTED WITH A KISS
THE MARQUIS AND I
YOU NEVER FORGET YOUR FIRST EARL
BELIEVE IN ME

Novellas

MADELEINE'S CHRISTMAS WISH
THE SECOND TIME AROUND
I'LL ALWAYS LOVE YOU

Published by Kensington Publishing Corporation

BELIEVE *In* ME

ZEBRA BOOKS
KENSINGTON PUBLISHING CORP.
www.kensingtonbooks.com

ZEBRA BOOKS are published by

Kensington Publishing Corp.
119 West 40th Street
New York, NY 10018

All Kensington titles, imprints, and distributed lines are available at special quantity discounts for bulk purchases for sales promotion, premiums, fund-raising, educational, or institutional use.

Special book excerpts or customized printings can also be created to fit specific needs. For details, write or phone the office of the Kensington Sales Manager: Attn.: Sales Department. Kensington Publishing Corp., 119 West 40th Street, New York, NY 10018. Phone: 1-800-221-2647.

Zebra and the Z logo Reg. U.S. Pat. & TM Off.

First Printing: March 2019
ISBN-13: 978-1-4201-4520-5
ISBN-10: 1-4201-4520-7

ISBN-13: 978-1-4201-4521-2 (eBook)
ISBN-10: 1-4201-4521-5 (eBook)

10 9 8 7 6 5 4 3 2 1

Printed in the United States of America

*This book is for my granddaughters Josephine and Vivienne
and to every girl or woman who has had
to fight to achieve her goals*

ACKNOWLEDGMENTS

Anyone involved in publishing knows it takes a team effort to get a book from that inkling in an author's head to the printed or digital page. I'd like to thank my beta readers, Jenna, Doreen, and Margaret for their comments and suggestions. My agents, Deidre Knight and Janna Bonikowski for helping me think through parts of this book and helping me to keep it from sounding like a travel guide.

My wonderful editor, John Scognamiglio, who loves my books enough to contract them for Kensington. The Kensington team, Vida, Jane, and Lauren who do such a tremendous job of publicity. And to the copyeditors who find all the niggling mistakes I never am able to see.

I had lots of help from all sorts of people for helping me with names. Thank you to Kelly Ann Woodford and Tracey De Neal for Constance, Antigony Helen Kratsa reminding me I could use Grace, Brianna Cook for Theodore, Sharon Williams Abraham and Jo Payne-Pierce for Hugo, and Karen Feist for Zephyr.

Thanks also to Rupert Baker of the Royal Society for informing me that women were not allowed to attend the lectures, but that the Royal Institute did allow them to attend. Thus saving my scene.

Whenever possible, I try to use the names of hotels and other places that were in operation at the time. So, thank you to Daniela Hirschl at the Hotel Stephanie, the oldest holstery in Munich, for providing me with the name of the hotel in 1818 and the name of the owner at the time. Likewise, thanks to Sven Rupp for providing me the name of the owner of the Thorbäu in 1818.

Last, but certainly not least, to my readers. Without you, none of this would be worth it. Thank you from the bottom of my heart for loving my stories!

I love to hear from my readers, so feel free to contact me on my website or on Facebook if you have questions. Those links and my newsletter link can be found at www.ellaquinnauthor.com.

On to the next book!

Ella

Chapter One

Worthington House, Berkeley Square, Mayfair. March 1818.

"*Italy!*" Her brother's bellow could probably be heard all over the town house and in Berkeley Square. Possibly even farther.

From her position on the sofa, Lady Augusta Vivers stifled a sigh. She refused to allow her posture to sag or disappointment to show on her countenance. She had known her campaign to be allowed to attend university was not going to be easy. Perhaps she should have started her scheme earlier. Or given her brother a hint to temper his shock.

"It is not as if Padua is some unknown place in South America or Africa," she pointed out calmly.

"Where on earth did you come up with such an . . . idea?" Her mother paled a bit and her faint voice pierced the deadened air.

"I wish to further my studies." Augusta fought to keep the exasperation from her tone. Why else would she want to go to university? Not only that, but traveling there and living in Italy for a time would allow her to see a little of the world she had been studying. "As educated as Miss Tallerton and Mr. Winters are, they long ago exhausted the limits of what they can teach me. Which is the reason I have been corresponding with professors in Europe and taking lessons from visiting scholars, hoping to learn more. It is no longer enough." In fact, her thirst for knowledge had grown to the point that she needed to attend university as much as she needed food or air. "Yet it has become clear that the only way I am going to succeed is by studying with experts. For that, I must attend university."

"But, my dear"—her mother paused for a moment as if to gather her thoughts—"do you not wish to wed?"

Of course she did. Just. Not. Now. "I do not recall anyone asking Charlie if he was forsaking marriage simply because he wished to attend Oxford." She wished Grace's brother, properly called the Earl of Stanwood was here. He'd be able to help. Augusta turned her gaze back to Matt. As her guardian and Earl of Worthington, he was the final decision maker. "If I were a boy you would allow me to go."

"You're fair and far off there, my girl." He raked his fingers through his hair. "I might consider Paris, but Italy is too far away. If anything were to happen"—this time he wiped his hand down his face—"we would not be able to get to you in time. I doubt if there is even an English consul or vice-consul there."

She was glad she'd prepared for this point of contest. "The closest consul is in Venice. Only about twenty-two miles to the east."

"Augusta." Grace's gentle voice was a sharp contrast to Matt's exasperated tone. "Is there not a university that will accept women closer than Italy?"

Augusta shifted on the sofa so that she faced her sister-in-law, next to her, and smiled. "There was one in

Holland, but it was reduced to a school, like Eton, and is just now attempting to regain its status as a university." Trying to ignore the worried look in Mama's eyes, and the tick in Matt's jaw, Augusta focused on Grace, who appeared to be the only helpful person present. She might also be able to persuade Matt. "Padua is also the only university that has an excellent reputation and will award a degree to a female."

Her sister-in-law nodded. "I see."

"My dear." The corners of Mama's lips tipped up weakly. "You did not answer the question about marriage."

"I see no reason to rush into matrimony. Grace did not wed until she was four and twenty." After thinking she could never marry because she had guardianship of her brothers and sisters. Everyone agreed that Matt convincing her he could be trusted with guardianship had been the best thing for all her sisters and brothers and sisters by marriage.

As there was nothing to be said to that, silence fell again. The only comforting thought was that Matt had not actually said no.

The room was so quiet she could hear the birds chirping outside, and the thumps of children running a floor above. The muffled sound of someone coming down the corridor had them all turning their heads.

A knock came, and Walter Carpenter, age seventeen, another of Grace's brothers and Augusta's best friend, poked his head in the study and glanced at them all. "Not a good time? I'll just take myself away."

"Wait right there." Matt's commanding voice stopped Walter's retreat. "What do you know about Augusta's plans to attend university?"

"I . . . er . . ." Walter slid her a quick sidelong glance. "Only that she's been planning it for several months."

One of Matt's brows rose. "It's not as if she's doing anything untoward. Don't we all support ladies being educated?"

Augusta flashed Walter a grateful smile. Her mother groaned, Grace's lips twitched, and Matt slapped his palm against his head.

Mama's husband, Richard, Viscount Wolverton, who had been lounging against the fireplace, straightened. "When does the term begin?"

"Not until September." Did his question mean he might support Augusta's desire to go to Padua? "I brought it up now because I have done all I can do without final permission, and there is the month it will take to travel to Padua."

"September," Mama chirped brightly, a relieved look on her face.

Oh, no. Augusta was not going to allow them to end the conversation. "My other point in mentioning it now is to save you from the expense of a Season for me." Of all the girls in the family, Augusta was sure she was the only one who did not care if she formally came out. "If I am going to attend university, there is no need for me to be on the Marriage Mart."

"I think it's too late for that," Matt grumbled.

Augusta barely kept her jaw from dropping.

"What he means"—Grace held out her hands to Augusta, taking her fingers in a reassuring grip—"is that most of your gowns have already been ordered. Aside from that, if Matt and your mother agree that you should attend university, you will benefit from having been out."

"Yes, indeed, my dear," Mama said quickly. Augusta had the feeling her mother was praying she would decide to marry and forget about continuing her studies. "Grace is absolutely correct. Acquiring a bit of Town bronze is essential for one's . . . one's development."

Augusta scanned the other faces in the room. None of them looked happy. If she refused, they would not take it well. There was no reason she could not continue with her plans and arguments for university while she was attending social events. "Very well. I agree to a Season." Augusta speared her brother Matt with a narrow-eyed look. "That does not mean I have given up my intention to attend university."

His lips thinned as he nodded. "We will continue the discussion later."

"You should know"—she took a breath—"I have contacted Cousin Prudence Brunning and asked if she would be willing to be my chaperone."

Matt's dark brows drew together. "Who?"

"You would not remember her," Mama said with an airy flutter of her hand. "She is the daughter of Martha Vivers, who married George Paine, a rector. Prudence is a year or so younger than you and a widow. Her husband was in the Life Guards and died at Waterloo."

"Indeed." Augusta was glad her mother remembered Cousin Prudence. "When he was in Spain and Portugal she traveled with him. Therefore she is used to foreign places." By this time Matt was staring at Augusta as if she had grown another head. "She also speaks Italian, Portuguese, and Spanish."

"Naturally, why else would you contact her?" He closed his eyes for a moment as if in pain. "You've given me a great deal to think about."

Augusta squeezed Grace's hand and rose. "Thank you for listening to me."

A series of nods and tight smiles answered her. When she reached the corridor, Walter had been joined by her twin sisters by marriage, Alice and Eleanor Carpenter, age fifteen, and Augusta's birth sister, Madeline Vivers, also fifteen.

Alice put a finger to her lips as Eleanor grabbed Augusta's hand.

"Come," Madeline whispered. "We can hear them talk from the antechamber in the other room."

They hurried her into a seldom-used parlor and opened a door to what reminded Augusta more of a butler's pantry. Except instead of dishware and silver, the shelves were filled with ledgers, paper, pens, and bottles of ink. How had she not known this was here?

"You must be very quiet," one of the twins said softly.

"Matt, you cannot possibly be considering allowing her to travel to Italy!" Mama's voice came clearly through the door. "It would have been kinder of you to have told her no."

There was a clink of crystal and a few moments of silence, before Matt responded, "In my opinion, she deserves the opportunity to follow her desire for more education."

"Yes, but not in Italy." Mama sounded almost frantic.

"Patience, calm yourself," Richard said. "If Worthington allows her to go, you know as well as I do that he'll ensure she is well protected."

"Matt," Mama said again. "Do you not remember what happened to Caro Huntley?"

"Who is Caro Huntley?" Madeline whispered. Augusta and the others shrugged.

"Who is Caro Huntley?" Richard asked.

"The former Lady Caroline Martindale, a friend of mine," Grace responded. "She was living in Venice with her godmother when a Venetian nobleman decided she should marry him. Huntley wed her to save her from him."

"I am sure *she* thought she was safe," Mama pointed out.

Augusta wanted to groan. Leave it to her mother to remember a story like that. Well, she would make good and sure she was not trapped into marriage. At least not before she had her diploma.

"Come, my love," Richard said. "Let's leave poor Worthington to try to figure this out. Let me know if you need any help."

"Thank you. I will," Matt said.

The door to Grace's study closed. Without warning the door to the antechamber flew open, and the twins tumbled into the room. Augusta would have fallen as well if Madeline hadn't been in the way and stopped her descent.

Matt eyed them as the girls picked themselves up from the floor. "I trust you heard everything, or is there any part of the conversation you would like to have repeated?"

"I'd like to hear more about Caro Huntley," Alice said.

"Not now, sweetheart." Grace's eyes sparkled with laughter. "Augusta, we will continue to look at ways for you to continue your studies." Her sister-in-law rose. "Come. It will be time for tea shortly, and Charlie should be here soon."

"Matt?" Madeline asked. "How did you know we were listening?"

"You're not as quiet as you think." He lightly tugged one of her braids. "Go on. I'll see you in the morning room."

For the second time that day, Augusta left the study. "I suppose it could have been worse."

Walter fell into step beside her. "He could have refused to listen."

"My mother is going to be a problem. She will probably throw every gentleman she finds into my path."

"Not everyone." Walter grinned. "They have to be eligible."

"There will still be too many of them." Why couldn't her mother simply accept that she wanted more from life? "At least I'll be prepared."

At a warehouse near the London docks, Lord Phineas Carter-Woods surveyed the numerous boxes he'd brought back with him from Mexico. "The ones marked in red will go to Elsworth." That was the bulk of them. At some point he'd have to visit the estate he had been bequeathed. "Have the rest sent to my brother's house in Grosvenor Square, and make sure they aren't put in the attic."

"Yes, my lord." Boman, Phinn's secretary, part-time amanuensis, general factotum, and friend, signaled to one of two carters waiting for instructions. "Have you decided when we're leaving again?"

That was going to be tricky. "I hope to be on our way to Europe in a month, but I've promised my brother I'll look around for a wife. We'll take it as it comes, shall we?"

"What you mean to say"—Boman gave Phinn a stern look—"is that you haven't told his lordship that you're not staying in England."

"Let's just say that I have not had time to divulge all my plans." Boman was right. Phinn would have to tell his brother, the Marquis of Dorchester, about his intent to leave England again. If only Dorchester and his wife could've managed to have a son or two instead of four daughters, they wouldn't be trying to make Phinn marry.

Although, whatever gave them the idea he could do better, he didn't know.

"He isn't going to be happy."

That was putting it mildly. Phinn had decided not to tell his brother he was leaving again until just before he departed. "I'll stay for the Season. Once he perceives that I have not found a suitable wife, he'll be glad to see me go again."

"What happens if some young lady catches your eye?"

Good Lord! Boman too? "Why is everyone suddenly trying to put a leg-shackle on me?"

"I'm just saying it could happen." He shrugged. "You almost got caught by that señorita in Mexico City."

"Not because I wanted her." Phinn ran his finger under his cravat. "For that escape, I can only thank your sharp eyes." If Boman hadn't seen the lady slip something into Phinn's drink, he might have been asleep instead of hiding on the window ledge when she'd sneaked into his room. Thank God English ladies were not so devious. "The less said about that, the better." The last trunk was loaded onto the coach. "We must go to Dorchester House and settle in." Phinn would rather have remained at the hotel, but his brother was insistent he live with him. "There will be no time tomorrow. My brother has made an appointment with me to see Weston, his tailor." He looked at his worn leather breeches with chagrin. "Apparently, I do not have sufficient clothing to pass myself off as an eligible *parti.*"

Phinn climbed into the coach followed by Boman, who settled on the backward-facing seat and said, "Have you decided to hire a proper valet?"

The carriage rolled through the narrow streets. "I don't like the idea of hiring a man, then letting him go in a month or two."

"We can take him with us. Europe isn't the Far East

or Mexico. You'll need someone who knows how to take care of your kit."

"I suppose you're right." Glancing out the window, Phinn marveled at how societies never changed much. There were always the poor living in squalor and the rich who didn't seem to care. "You were able to assist before, but you'll be too busy preparing for the next trip."

"You keep saying that." Boman's tone was as dry as parts of Mexico. "And we haven't even set foot in your brother's house yet."

It wasn't that he didn't love his brother, but Phinn would have been happy to have visited for a week and left again. Not that it would have been possible. He had a paper to deliver at the Royal Institution, letters to write, travel documents to acquire, and a host of other details to which to attend. Unfortunately, other than the paper, he'd have to leave most of it to Boman while Phinn danced, literally, to his sister-in-law's tune, and his family's scheme to get him married.

"Do you have the charms?" He didn't know if they'd work. It might all be a hum. After four daughters, his brother was becoming desperate to secure the succession, and as Dorchester's eye had turned to Phinn, he needed all the help he could get. It was probably ridiculous of him to trust a Haitian witch's magic, but anything was worth a try.

Chapter Two

Augusta, her elder sister Louisa, the Duchess of Rothwell, her step-sister, Charlotte, the Marchioness of Kenilworth, and their mutual friend and cousin, Dotty, the Marchioness of Merton left the modiste's shop where Augusta had had fittings on gowns that had been designed purely on her measurements. What followed could only be described as an extravagant indulgence of shopping that lasted most of the day before they retired to Charlotte's town house. They had just been served tea and sustenance consisting of biscuits, bread, cheese, and plum tarts.

"I must not have been paying any attention at all when you three came out." Augusta reached out and stroked Collette, her sister's Chartreux cat.

"You were still in the schoolroom," Dotty pointed out.

"With a nose in a book." Louisa unobtrusively gave Abby, Charlotte's Great Dane, a piece of cheese.

Charlotte swallowed her sip of tea. "I understand that you have no intention of marrying this Season, but I would not tell that to any of the gentlemen you meet."

"Why not?" Augusta did not like prevarication. If she made the impression her sisters and Dotty had, it would be dishonest to lead a gentleman on. "I would not wish to give anyone false hope."

"You also do not want to become a challenge." Charlotte's dry tone caused Louisa to hold her napkin to her lips while her shoulders shook.

What was so funny? "I don't understand."

"Men, as a rule," Dotty said, "find anything unattainable to be particularly enticing."

That was not something Augusta wanted to hear or had even considered. Yet, now that she thought about it, Bentley had hung around Louisa for her entire Season, even after everyone and his dog knew she would not marry him. And Harrington had done the same thing with Charlotte. Although, she had gone back and forth about him until she'd met Kenilworth. Still, they'd both managed to wed other men. "What did you do?"

"When I was trying to discourage gentlemen," Louisa said, "Grace told me to be kind but to not show them any partiality."

"Unfortunately"—Charlotte grimaced—"that doesn't always work."

"Never be caught alone with a gentleman." Dotty's tone was serious, but her eyes twinkled. "It ended well in my case and Charlotte's, but not if you wish to avoid marriage this Season."

"I must arrange to never be alone at entertainments." Perhaps Augusta could make friends with other ladies she'd meet at Lady Bellamny's party. "I'll also not attempt to save a gentleman from someone else's trap or get kidnapped."

"That should do it," Louisa said, as Dotty and Charlotte laughed. "You can always call upon us and our husbands."

Kind, but noncommittal. How hard could that be?

From what she had seen at the country assemblies, most men would rather talk about themselves. She would simply let them.

Phinn arrived at his brother's house as the boxes he'd sent were delivered. Based upon the other times he'd visited, he assumed he'd be put in the green room in the front of the house. Fortunately, there was a small, little-used chamber next to it.

"Saddock," Phinn said as the butler, who had served his father and now served his brother, bowed. "Be a good fellow and have the boxes put in the room next to mine."

"Very good, my lord. You will find his lordship and her ladyship in the morning room about to partake of tea."

"Excellent, I'm feeling a bit peckish." He strode to the back of the house before Saddock could mention announcing him.

As he neared the morning room, Phinn heard his brother and sister-in-law, Helen, mention his name. He approached more slowly, silencing his steps.

"Have you made a list of eligible ladies yet?" His brother's tone had an underlying layer of mirth he didn't appreciate.

A moment or two passed before Helen responded. He could almost feel her narrowing her eyes at Dorchester. "Not yet. Lady Bellamny's party for young ladies is this evening. I shall leave you and Phineas to become reacquainted while I am at the entertainment."

"I am not sure a young lady is . . . Oh, how should I put this—adequate for the position."

"I should think any lady who will put up with a gentleman who might decide to run off and sail to who-knows-where would be appropriate." Her tone was tart and unquestionably cutting.

"He did promise that if he found a lady to marry, he would stop traveling." *That's it, Chess, stick up for your brother.*

"He said the same thing before he hied off to Mexico and wherever else he traveled." No improvement in her tone at all.

"Helen, that is not being fair. You know as well as I do that my father sent him to Mexico."

"He could be like a normal gentleman and remain in Britain."

Behind him, heavy steps sounded, and a clock chimed the hour. Phinn rapped on the open door and stepped in. "Greetings, I come bearing gifts." He glanced around as if unaware that only his brother and Helen were in the room. "Where are my nieces?"

As if acid hadn't been dripping from her lips, Helen hurried toward him. "Phineas, I am so glad to see you again." She glanced at the package wrapped in oilcloth. "Would you like to take a seat on the sofa, and place your bundle on the table?"

"Excellent suggestion." He bowed before bussing her proffered cheek.

The butler entered, followed by a footman carrying the tea tray.

"You are just in time." She sank onto a smaller sofa opposite him and began to pour. "The girls will be down in a minute."

As if on cue, high-pitched voices could be heard in the corridor. His four nieces entered, followed by their nurse.

"Uncle Phinn, is it really you?" Emma, the eldest at seven, stood in front of him. She would be the only one who remembered him. Cicely had been only three when he'd departed.

"It is." He hugged her as she flung her arms around his neck. "Come now, allow me to say good day to Cicely." The little girl with blond hair and big blue eyes, like her mother, approached him carefully. He bent over and held out his arms. She allowed him to pick her up, and soon Anne, age four, and Rosanna, age two, were on the sofa with him. "Emma, would you be good enough to open the package on the table? I believe you will find dolls for each of you. They were made in Mexico." He glanced at his brother and Helen. "I brought cocoa for you."

"How very kind." Helen smiled tightly as Emma handed her a locked silver casket before giving her sisters the cloth dolls wearing brightly colored gowns.

"Uncle Phinn." Cicely tugged on his arm. "Why do the dolls all have black hair?"

"Because that is the most common hair color in Mexico."

"Do they really wear these clothes?" Emma held up her doll and inspected the muslin shirt, embroidered vest, and colorful red skirt. "They are very different from ours."

"These are Aztec Indian ladies." Or rather what the Europeans *wished* the Aztecs would wear. Helen would have barred the dolls from the house if they'd come draped in the single cloth the Indians were partial to. "The Spanish ladies wear clothing such as yours."

"I wear this." Anne held the doll up to her nurse. "Make it, please."

"I'll see what I can do, my lady. Now"—Nurse gathered the girls with a gesture—"it is time we returned to the nursery to put your presents away before we go for our walk."

"I would really like them to stay." Desperate was more like it. "I want to get to know them better."

Helen glanced at him as if she knew what he was

trying to do. "Now that you are home again, you will have plenty of time to come to know your nieces." She nodded to the nurse, who had stopped. "You may go." Shortly after the girls left, she rose. "I shall leave the two of you alone."

Phinn and his brother both stood until she left, then resumed their seats.

Perdition! He had to tell Dorchester that he was leaving again, but how to do it? Particularly after Helen had reminded him that Phinn never stayed home. It wasn't that he'd lied, he just had never promised.

"Well"—his brother went to a side table and poured two glasses of wine—"I suppose we should discuss your search for a wife."

"Do you have anyone in mind?" Not that Phinn thought his brother would try to play matchmaker. He took the glass, taking a grateful sip of claret. His sister-in-law was a different matter entirely.

"No. No." Dorchester gazed at the goblet as he twirled it. "I believe Helen is going to a soirée where she might form some ideas." He looked at Phinn. "I don't suppose you have any thoughts."

"None at all." How could he? He'd only been back just over a day. The conversation dropped. If only he could find a way to tell his brother he really did not wish to marry yet. "I will not wed a lady for whom I do not have a strong affection." That should limit his choices—to precisely naught.

"No," his brother agreed quickly. "I would not wish you to feel as if you were sacrificing yourself."

Which, of course, was exactly what Phinn *was* doing. "I would like to set a time limit on this search for a wife." In any event, he had to have a firm date to depart the country. "I anticipate I will have met all the eligible ladies in a matter of a month, six weeks at the most.

Unless, that is, some lady arrives in the middle of the Season." He took another sip of wine. After this conversation, he'd have his secretary bring him a bottle of brandy. "If I do not find a female who attaches my affections"—*good God, I sound like an idiot*—"I would like to take a short trip to Europe. I promise I will return by autumn to try again."

Dorchester drained half his glass of wine before staring at Phinn for several moments. Finally his brother sighed. "I know you don't want to wed. And I know you think I'm being unfair." Phinn opened his mouth, but Dorchester held up a hand. "Allow me to finish, before you lie to us both. You must agree that the succession appears to be at risk." Phinn wondered if Boman had been able to place the charms in his brother's and sister-in-law's bedchambers. "We will continue to try to produce a son, but I need you to do your part and marry."

"I do understand." Phinn couldn't just tell his brother no. He raked his fingers through his hair. "I swear to you that I will do my absolute best to find a woman to wed this Season. I will still ask you to agree that if, after a reasonable time, I am unable to do what you ask, I be allowed to visit France. I will not travel far." He wouldn't have to in order to study the churches and other buildings he'd only seen in paintings. "As it is, I can accomplish a great deal without going farther than Paris. I wouldn't have made the journey to Mexico if Europe had been an option." He didn't know why he found it necessary to emphasize that. Unless his sister-in-law's irritability concerning his travel was getting on his nerves. "I'll also pray that you and Helen have a boy the next time."

His brother rubbed the back of his neck, but his lips twitched as well, probably at the vision of Phinn's head bowed and hands together in pious supplication. "I agree. If you haven't found a lady to marry by the time the Season is half over, you can travel to Europe on the condition you present yourself in September, ready to try again."

Free! Thank the Fates, he was free. "I shall try to find a wife."

"I know you will." His brother shook his head. "Although, to be honest, it would astonish me if you managed to find a bride before you found Notre Dame."

As impressive as Notre Dame must be, Phinn truly wanted to find a way to gain entrance to the Hôtel de Cluny, said to be the oldest architecturally fascinating building in Paris. Still, he was a bit surprised that his brother understood. "Thank you."

"On the contrary, it is I who must thank you." Dorchester took another sip of wine. "It is I whose duty it is to produce an heir. I should not have to rely on my younger brother."

"That is one thing over which we have no control." *Those damn charms had better work.* Could he manage to put off marriage until they had their next child? Whenever that would occur.

"Fortunately"—his brother grimaced—"I have been told that, even though we must provide a girl her dowry, they are much less expensive than too many sons. Still, I must have at least one."

"As I said, I shall do my utmost." Phinn started to stand.

"I have arranged appointments for you beginning tomorrow at eleven o'clock." A faint grin showed on Dorchester's face. "You must dress the part of an eligible gentleman as well as act the part."

Phinn had known he'd need a new wardrobe. If he

was honest, his clothing did look a bit worn. Standing, he inclined his head. "I am at your service."

"My valet shall hire a valet for you." His brother drained his glass and set it down.

"I would prefer to have Boman involved in the selection." That way Phinn would be assured the man would not object to overseas travel. "He knows who will suit me."

Dorchester raised one brow as if he knew Phinn was up to something. "As you wish."

A few minutes later, Phinn found Boman. "Were you able to discover where to place the charms?"

"You were right. They belonged in both rooms." Phinn wondered how his secretary had come across that piece of information, but wasn't sure he truly wished to know. "I was able to secure them between the headboard and mattress on both beds."

"Excellent." He smiled to himself. By this time next year, with any luck at all, his brother would have his heir, and he wouldn't have to marry.

"How long do we remain in England?" Boman had lowered his voice.

"Six weeks at the most. I think a month should suffice." That would give Phinn enough time to inspect all the ladies and reject them. There could not possibly be a young lady who was interested in anything but fashion and her own come out. Or who was knowledgeable beyond anything she had been told to learn.

Chapter Three

By the time Augusta arrived home late that afternoon, several packages from Madame Lisette's were waiting for her.

"I've rarely seen such beautiful gowns, my lady." Gobert held up a muslin gown the color of blue ice with embroidery on the hem and sleeves. "They arrived just in time for your first event."

Gobert, an experienced lady's maid about five years older than Augusta, had been recommended by Bolton, Grace's lady's maid, last year before they left Town to return to the country. Over the course of Gobert's employment, she had made it clear that she would be happy to accompany Augusta wherever she wished to take her.

"Madame Lisette is said to be an artist," Augusta said as Gobert held up another gown that reminded Augusta of the sun when it was covered by clouds. She liked her garments even better than the ones her sisters wore a few Seasons ago. "To create these without even having set eyes on me, I think she must be."

"They certainly suit you." Gobert unwrapped an evening gown in pink with a band of pearls on the sleeves and scattered over the bodice. "Would you like the pink for this evening?"

"Yes, please." Augusta had received word that Dotty's sister, Henrietta Stern, had arrived in Town that day and wondered if she would be present this evening. Not that Augusta knew Henrietta well, but at least she'd know someone. And they had got on well the few times they had met. "With the silver spangled shawl?"

"That will do nicely, my lady."

Later that evening she entered Lady Bellamny's house escorted by her mother and sister Louisa.

"Your grace, Patience." Her ladyship squeezed Louisa's hand and bussed Mama's cheek. "Lady Augusta. How are you?" Lady Bellamny's shrewd gaze made Augusta feel as if she was once again being inspected.

"I am well, ma'am." Augusta curtseyed. "It is nice to see you again."

"And you." Without another word, her ladyship greeted the next pair of women.

"My dears," Mama said, "I see some ladies with whom I wish to speak. I shall see you later in the evening."

She was soon swallowed by a mix of brightly colored and pale gowns.

"I don't know how you got away without her making some comment," Louisa said with feeling. "Charlotte and I did not."

"I've met her several times before when I visited Mama." Augusta grinned at her sister. "I think she has already said everything she had to say." She scanned the drawing room for anyone she knew. "Look, there are Dotty and Henrietta."

"I didn't know her sister had arrived." Louisa took Augusta's arm and headed toward their friends.

"Yes, late this afternoon. I wrote, hoping she would attend this evening." Their friends were standing with four other women. "Who are the other ladies?"

"Viscountess Featherton; her daughter Meg, in the red gown, is the Marchioness of Hawksworth. The younger lady must be Georgiana Featherton, who is just out. The lady with the very pale blond hair is Caro, Countess of Huntley, and the one next to her with the mahogany hair is Lady Dorie Calthorp, Huntley's sister. This is her second Season."

So that was the former Lady Caro. She was extremely beautiful. She also appeared to be very happy. "Dorie is an unusual name."

Louisa stopped to introduce her to another lady. "Eugénie, I'd like to introduce my sister, Lady Augusta Vivers. Augusta, this is Viscountess Wivenly."

The woman had dark brown hair and a creamy complexion. Much like Madame Lisette. "*Enchantée.*" Viscountess Wivenly's brown eyes sparkled with welcome. "It appears we are all escorting our sisters." She drew a young woman forward with lighter brown hair and eyes that reminded Augusta of sapphires. "I would like to introduce my sister by marriage, Lady Adeline Wivenly. Adeline, please meet the Duchess of Rothwell and her sister, Lady Augusta Vivers."

Lady Adeline sank into a graceful curtsey. "Your grace." She rose and took the hand Augusta held out. "I'm very glad to meet you, my lady."

Louisa and Lady Wivenly had begun talking. "I am glad to meet you as well, Lady Adeline. Is your sister-in-law French?"

"Yes." Glancing at the lady, she smiled fondly. "She is a cousin by marriage as well. My uncle married her mother when Eugénie was young. She was raised in Saint Thomas in the Danish West Indies."

"She is very striking." And elegant. She made almost every woman here look slightly dowdy somehow.

Lady Adeline chuckled lightly. "She is all that and charming, but she has a wicked temper when it comes to any kind of injustice. And she keeps my brother in line. Something not even my parents have been able to do." She linked her arm with Augusta's. "I'll introduce you to some other ladies making their come out."

"And I shall introduce you to my friend, Miss Stern." Augusta guided Lady Adeline to where Henrietta stood and performed the introductions.

A few moments later, they were introduced to Dorie, who detested her real name Dorcas—that answered that question—and the others Louisa had pointed out earlier.

Augusta was glad when Lady Dorie suggested they address each other by first names in private. It appeared as if their sisters were doing the same thing.

"What are you hoping to find in a husband?" Dorie asked each of them.

Adeline shrugged one shoulder. "A gentleman who is not like my brother was before he married."

"I do not understand," Augusta said.

Adeline's lips formed a thin line. "He was a rake."

"In that case, I completely agree." Augusta wondered what Lady Wively did to keep him in line.

"My gentleman must be able to make me want to laugh and kiss him at the same time," Georgiana said. "I would not mind if he were a bit like my brother. Featherton. Kit is the epitome of a gentleman."

"A man who is kind to me and others, and that I love," Henrietta said.

"What about you, Dorie?" Augusta asked.

"I only know that I'll recognize him when I see him." Dorie heaved a sigh. "It must run in the family. Neither my mother or sister married in their first or second Seasons. What about you, Augusta?"

She bit down on her bottom lip. Should she tell them she was not looking for a husband? They might be as shocked as her mother had been. If that was the case, she would have no friends. Yet, she was fairly positive that Henrietta might be surprised, but not disapproving. After all, she knew how much Augusta loved to learn new things, and she had mentioned the idea once. Then again, it might be best if she wanted their help in avoiding any traps. She took a breath. They would either like her or not. "I have decided to attend university before searching for a husband."

"*University?*" Adeline said in a hushed tone. "But where?"

The other two ladies' eyes had widened. Henrietta just arched a brow. "So, you are going through with it?"

"Yes." Augusta nodded. "In Padua, Italy. If I am allowed to attend." She told them about the plans she had made thus far. "Baron Philipp von Neumann, who works for Prince Esterházy, has been communicating with Professor Giuseppe Angeloni in Padua. I have also been exchanging letters with the professor. He is convinced that I will be admitted." The other ladies, who had leaned toward her so that she would not have to raise her voice, nodded. "One of the problems is my mother. She would dearly like to see me wed or at least attracted enough to a gentleman that I will not wish to leave England."

Dorie's eyes widened even further. "Is she your guardian?"

"No. My brother, the Earl of Worthington, is my guardian."

Before they could continue their conversation, Mama came up with another lady. "Lady Dorchester, I would like you to meet my second eldest daughter, Lady Augusta." Mama smiled in a way Augusta did not quite trust. "Augusta, this is the Marchioness of Dorchester."

"It is a pleasure to meet you, my lady." Augusta curtseyed. The woman could not possibly be old enough to have a daughter her age. "Do you have a sister out as well?"

"I am delighted to meet you as well." Her ladyship turned to Mama. "She is just as lovely as you said." Lady Dorchester glanced at Augusta. "No, my sisters are all married and my daughters are still much too young. Is it true that you are knowledgeable in languages and geography?"

Something was definitely going on. But what? Her ladyship did not look old enough to have a grown son either. "Yes. They are my passion." Augusta debated mentioning her plan to attend university, but decided not to say anything with her mother present. "I wish to travel someday."

Her ladyship's green eyes brightened as if a candle had been lit behind them. "If you marry the right gentleman, I am sure he will take you to Europe."

Unlikely at best. Augusta hurriedly introduced the rest of the young ladies. There was a scheme afoot and she did not want to be caught in it.

When Dorchester entered the parlor, Phinn put down the newssheet he'd been reading and waited.

A piece of paper was all but hidden in his brother's fist. "Would you like to go with me to fetch Helen from the soirée?"

Why in the name of all things holy would Dorchester think Phinn would want to do that? It took a few moments for him to formulate a response. "I thought she took the town coach."

"Er, she did. But she sent it back because . . . because she knew what time the event ended." His brother's fingers tightened around the paper. "I thought it would be nice to fetch her myself. I've heard many gentlemen do."

Many men were also looking for wives, and almost every young lady on the Marriage Mart would be present. Fortunately, he'd already untied his cravat. Phinn pretended he was stifling a yawn. "I'd have to change, and I really need to find my bed. It's been a long couple of days, and an even longer sea passage."

"I'll see you in the morning, then." Poor Chess looked as if he'd failed at the only task he'd been given.

"Until morning." Phinn stood, stretched, and rubbed his face. "Good night."

He walked with slow steps to the stairs and climbed them heavily. He'd already convinced his brother he could leave, but Helen was a different matter. He had absolutely no doubt at all that she had found at least one lady she wanted him to meet. Not being delusional, Phinn knew the introduction would take place, yet the longer he put it off the better. Still, he damn sure wasn't going to be trapped in a house with all the eligible young ladies in Town. He might never get out!

Phinn entered his room, pulling off his cravat as he did.

"Good evening." Boman put down a book and stood.

"What the devil are you doing here? I thought you'd be sleeping by now." Phinn threw his cravat over a chair and started on his waistcoat.

"Your brother's valet tracked me down and insisted I go over a list of valets. I assume, since he was more than a little put out, you rejected his advice."

"I rejected his absolute decision over a servant who would be working for me. You know what I want. It was your idea for the valet to travel with us. Ergo, you get to hire him." He shrugged off his jacket. "Where is your room? It had damn well better not be where the servants are housed."

"I'm in the room next to his lordship's secretary. It's not large, but it's bigger than what I've been used to lately."

That was as good as could be expected. Boman was gentry, after all. At least as far as Phinn was concerned. His mother had been a vicar's daughter who married a wealthy merchant. Phinn had met Boman when they'd attended Eton. After that, they'd gone to Oxford together. It was only because his father had refused to finance Boman's travel that he was working for Phinn. Although, Boman no longer needed the position. Before they'd left Mexico, he'd received a letter informing him that one of his mother's great-uncles had been so pleased he was behaving like a gentleman and not a merchant, he'd left him a comfortable independence. "As long as you are satisfied . . ."

"I am." His secretary gave a rueful grin. "One can't fool an English servant when it comes to where one's place in life is. As far as they are concerned, my father's status is all that matters."

"They'd better treat you as a gentleman or Dorchester will hear about it." Phinn removed his breeches. Required attire for dinner with his sister-in-law. "Is there anything else? If not, I'm going to bed."

"Not a thing." His secretary yawned. "His lordship's valet will be in to help you dress in the morning."

He hadn't liked the servant when the man was his father's valet. It was a good thing Phinn didn't have a weapon on him. He picked up a small, and completely useless, pillow. "Go before I throw this at you."

Boman laughed as he ducked through the door. "Good night, my lord."

"Cawker." Phinn heard his secretary's chuckle from down the corridor.

Having had no trouble at all falling asleep, he woke when the bed curtains were drawn vigorously back, flooding the bed with light.

"Good morning, my lord." Pickerell, Dorchester's valet, sniffed.

"Good morning, Pickle." Knowing it would irritate him, Phinn used the name he'd called the man as a child.

Alas, the old prig refused to be baited. "Would you like me to shave you, my lord?"

Pickle was the last person Phinn would allow to touch him with a sharp instrument. "No, I'm used to doing for myself. Thank you for asking."

"Heathenish ways," the servant muttered just loud enough for him to hear. "Very well. I shall return in a half hour to dress you."

A half hour later, he was sitting in a chair, fully dressed, when Pickle entered the room. Phinn stood and pulled down his jacket. "I waited so that you would not wonder where I'd gone."

Before the valet bowed, he could have sworn he'd seen a look of distaste on the man's face. "Very good, my lord."

His brother would probably hear about his lack of refinement, or clothing that a gentleman could don by himself.

Phinn could almost taste his morning cup of tea. As he approached the breakfast room, he heard Helen speaking. "I do not understand why you could not have brought Phineas last night."

"You would not have wanted me to rouse him from his sleep, would you?"

He struggled not to laugh. Most of the time it appeared his brother was under the cat's paw, but then there were times like this.

Several moments later she sighed. "No, I suppose not. I had so wished I could have introduced him to Lady Augusta, Lord Worthington's sister. She is perfect for him. I know it."

There was a clink of a cup being set down. "What makes you say that?"

"She is highly educated, and has an interest in languages and geography." Other than the sound of tea being poured, the room fell silent for a moment. "Lady Wolverton, her mother, assures me she is not at all a bluestocking. She is extremely lovely and well mannered. She is also well versed on any subject mentioned."

Languages and geography? Phinn scoffed to himself. She probably knew some French and Italian, and thought maps had pretty colors.

"She sounds exactly the type of lady Phinn would like," his brother said in a noncommittal tone.

"Next week when the Season begins," Helen continued, "her mother is giving Lady Augusta a ball at Rothwell House. Phineas will have evening clothes by then, and I shall introduce him to her."

Phinn wanted to groan. Well, it had to happen sooner than later. And the sooner he met the lady, the sooner he could dismiss her. How many more females would his sister-in-law throw his way? Probably dozens. This was going to be a very long several weeks.

Chapter Four

Sunlight streamed through the windows as Augusta was leaving the breakfast room when Walter rushed up. He grabbed her hand and started pulling her along with him. "You have to come with me now."

"I don't understand." He hadn't acted like this for a few years now. "What is it?"

He gave her a sly grin. "You'll see."

Thorton opened the front door as she and Walter approached. "My lady, Mr. Carpenter."

Not even the butler's disapproval could dim Walter's mood. They stepped out onto the stairs and Augusta stopped.

A robin's egg blue, high-perched phaeton, trimmed in gold, with two gray horses harnessed to it, stood on the street in front of them. Jones, her groom, was grinning from ear to ear while Durant, her footman, stood next to the carriage.

"Is it mine?" She could barely believe it. Charlotte and Louisa had shared a phaeton during their Season. But Augusta had never dreamed she would have one.

"It's not for me," Walter scoffed. "Besides, who else in this family likes that color blue as much as you do?"

"Oh, my." She walked slowly toward the vehicle, afraid it might disappear like Cinderella's carriage. "It is beautiful."

"It's not as high as most of them," he pointed out. "And it's more stable."

"Who bought it for me?" Not Matt. He would have mentioned it.

"Lord Wolverton's groom brought it around, my lady," Durant said.

The scent of new leather and horse wafted in the air as she paused beside the wheeler. Reaching out, she stroked her velvet nose. "They are lovely."

"Prettiest mares I've ever seen." Jones rubbed the other horse's nose as it softly blew into his hand and snorted. "And that's saying a lot."

It was, indeed. Jones had trained as a jockey until he grew too large. She walked around the equipage. "I think we need to go for a ride." Augusta glanced at her brother. "Do you want to come with me?"

"Don't I just!" Walter almost did a jig.

"Durant, please walk them while I change." She strode to the house as quickly as she could, just stopping herself from running up the stairs.

"Gobert," Augusta called as she entered her bedchamber. "I need a carriage gown."

"It's out, my lady. Durant told me your mother and stepfather bought you a carriage."

Her new blue carriage gown with darker blue piping lay upon the bed. In no time at all she was dressed and donning her bonnet.

"Have a good time, my lady."

"I will. Thank you."

Less than two minutes later, she was seated, threading the ribbons through her fingers.

Walter pointed to the top of the town house. "All

the children are looking. You'll have to give them rides later."

Augusta waved at her younger brothers and sisters. "Yes, after their lessons." She would make them draw numbers from a bowl. It was not fair to go by age. The youngest was always last. "Let's go around the Park, then we can drive to Grosvenor Square and show our sisters and Dotty my new carriage."

They entered through Grosvenor Gate near a row of chestnut trees that were just furling their leaves. Large trees also lined the Circle and Rotten Row. It was not long before Augusta saw Lady Dorie, one of the ladies she had met last evening, riding a bay gelding and followed by her groom.

She saw Augusta immediately and trotted over. "Good morning. It is good to see I am not the only lady who enjoys early outings. I find it settles me for the rest of the day."

"In my house it is not unusual." Her sister used to ride just after dawn. "I'd like to introduce my brother by marriage: Mr. Carpenter. Walter, Lady Dorie Calthorp."

"Good morning, Mr. Carpenter." Suddenly a look of recognition appeared on Dorie's face. "I believe you have met my youngest brother, Harold."

"I have." Walter nodded. "I should have made the connection right away. It's nice to meet you."

"It is a pleasure to finally meet you." She turned to Augusta. "He helped poor Harold out of a fix. I will be forever grateful." Dorie's gaze shifted to the phaeton. "That is a beautiful carriage. Do you know who made it?"

"I have not the slightest idea. If you wish to know I could ask my stepfather." Augusta grinned. "It was waiting for me after breakfast. Walter tells me that it is not as high as the usual high-perched phaeton. I suspect my mother had something to do with the change in design."

"But, what a lovely surprise." Dorie walked her horse around the carriage. "Your stepfather has excellent taste in cattle."

"Oh, I am extremely pleased with them." Even though Augusta had a strong suspicion the rig and horses were meant to make her wish to remain in England, she could still enjoy them while she was here.

They moved along the carriage path together, but before long, Dorie said, "I'll leave you to it. I still have some fidgets I need to run out. If you would like, I shall contact the others, and we can join the Promenade this afternoon." She pulled a face. "We will most likely have to walk."

"I think that is probable." Augusta laughed. "Although, my sister-in-law has a huge landau we could take. She had it built so it was large enough for all the children."

"Very well." Dorie shuddered. "You have convinced me that strolling is not so bad. I shall see you later today."

Once she'd ridden off, Augusta glanced at Walter. She had missed him terribly when he'd gone off to school. "Why did I not know you had met her brother? I've never heard you mention a Harold."

"But you have heard Phillip mention Harry. He is actually more of his friend than mine, but I look out for them both."

Phillip Carpenter was their youngest brother who had started at Eton last year. "Speaking of that, what did you do?"

"Some of the older boys were picking on Phillip and Harry." Walter shrugged. "It's a rite of passage of sorts.

I was with two chums and happened to see what was going on. We interceded. It did not occur again."

Interceded. A word used around ladies for the pummeling the miscreants had received. Grace had been none too happy when Matt had given the boys boxing lessons. Apparently, he had known what he was about. "I'm glad you were there to help."

"It's what one does." Walter shrugged again. He seemed uncomfortable speaking about the incident. "Charlie did the same for me."

That was not surprising. Charlie took care of everyone. She was glad Matt and Charlie, and now Walter, were there as examples of how a gentleman should act.

Augusta turned back to the horses. Although they were so perfectly behaved, they practically needed no direction at all. Once they reached the gate, she drove to Grosvenor's Square, pulling up in front of Rothwell House.

Two footmen ran out. One went to the horses' heads and the other came to help her down. "My lady, her Grace is in the square."

"Thank you. We shall find her."

"Just look for—"

"Yes, I know. A huge group of people."

"Just so, my lady."

Walter came around and held out his arm. "It will be fun to see how much our nieces and nephews have grown."

"In less than a week?" The moment each of her sisters and Dotty had arrived in Town they'd come to Worthington House with the children.

It did not take long at all to spot them. Louisa, Charlotte, and Dotty were sitting on a blanket with the children—four in total—and were surrounded by nursery maids, footmen, three Great Danes, Abby, Althea, and Millie and three Chartreux cats, Chloe, Collette and Cyril. The dogs were following the children as they toddled around. Charlotte's son, little Hugo, Earl of Reith, had apparently gone too far from the group and was being herded back by Charlotte's Great Dane, Abby. A nursemaid had picked up Constance, Hugo's twin sister. The other two dogs were performing similar guard duties for Dotty's and Louisa's children.

"Goodness, what a menagerie." Augusta laughed as her sisters and Dotty rose to greet her. "The Great Danes I expected to see, but the cats are a surprise."

"What are you doing out in the middle of the square?" Walter asked, as he stroked one of the cats. "I expected to find you walking."

"It was not planned." Louisa bounced her daughter Alexandria. "I came out with Alexandria. Naturally, Millie could not be separated from her. Then Chloe decided she wanted to be with me. Charlotte was already here, then Dotty joined us."

Not far away, a familiar-looking lady was accompanied by four children; one of them looked to be about the same age as Augusta's two-year-old nieces and nephew. "Is that Lady Dorchester?"

Charlotte glanced in the direction Augusta was looking. "Yes, but who is the gentleman with her?"

A few moments later, Lady Dorchester presented her brother-in-law, Lord Phineas Carter-Woods, and four little girls. His lordship gave Augusta a sharp gray-eyed look when they were introduced, but said only what was proper, and exhibited no notice in her at all after that.

His build—tall, with broad shoulders—reminded her of Matt and her sisters' husbands. His hair was much shorter than the current fashion. If Lady Dorchester was trying to marry him off—after all, she had not yet had a son—she would probably not have too much trouble. He was very handsome, in a rugged sort of way. Still, she would have to send him to a tailor. The shabby clothing he wore was not a good recommendation.

"My uncle just came back from Mexico," Emma, the oldest one offered.

Anne held up a brightly clothed cloth doll. "He brought us dolls."

Mexico? Augusta glanced at Lord Phineas again. He was browner than anyone else. His color must have been caused by the sun while on board the ship. Well, of course it was. Weeks exposed to the elements would roughen anyone's skin.

Not for the first time, Augusta wished she could travel. Yet, she'd be lucky to be able to attend university in Italy. Still, this was an opportunity to discover more about the Aztecs and their language. If his lordship had been interested enough to learn any of it. "Did you happen to learn Nahuatl while you were there?"

Chapter Five

That was the last question Phinn expected to receive from a young lady. His jaw began to drop and he clamped it shut.

Nahuatl?

What business did a gently bred English female have knowing anything about Aztec language? This must be the well-read young female he'd heard Helen talking about.

"I did. It was necessary to speak the language in order to discover the information I wished to know about their buildings." The young lady's—what the devil was her name?—eyes shone like the sun behind stained glass windows. What an amazing color they were. Just like lapis. "Did you know that some of the Aztec language has seeped into English?"

"Yes, tomato and chocolate are examples." She looked at him as though he was an idiot. "I am able to keep up with the language by reading the Aztec poetry, but I have not had an opportunity to speak it lately. I believe it is important to continue to practice a language in order not to lose it."

Well-read she might be, but there was no way she

could have learned Nahuatl. It was time to give her a bit of a set-down for exaggerating her skills. Speaking in Nahuatl he said, "God give me strength."

"Only you have the power to change," she shot back in the same language.

Good God! She really did speak it. "How did you learn Nahuatl?"

A smug smile hovered for a moment on her lips. "Mr. John Marsden taught me." Her words were clipped and cool. "He was visiting our local vicar last year."

"In that case, you know as much of the Aztec language as anyone in the country and most of Europe know."

She inclined her head graciously, and murmured in Nahuatl, "You are not a navel after all."

Phinn couldn't help but to laugh at her reference. Nahuatl was nothing if not descriptive. "I do try not to be a waste of space." Lady Augusta. That's what her name was! "I would be happy to speak with you at your convenience."

Again she gazed at him, but this time it was clear she was wondering if he was serious. He'd probably sounded like a condescending coxcomb before. "Thank you. I shall hold you to your offer."

Someone heaved a sigh, and he noticed the young man introduced as Walter Carpenter. "You should know, sir, that my sister speaks and reads at least seven modern languages, some ancient languages, and reads a few others." He gave Phinn a steady look. "I wouldn't underestimate her if I were you."

"Indeed." Phinn gave a short nod. "I believe she has already taught me that lesson." Wishing to resume his conversation with her, he glanced at Lady Augusta, but she was speaking with the duchess, who looked very much like her, and pointing to Rothwell House. In front of the house stood a high-perched phaeton and two of the sweetest goers he'd ever seen.

"It's beautiful, Augusta!" the duchess exclaimed.

The rest of the ladies rose and allowed the nursemaids to take charge of the toddlers.

"You will look like a fairy-tale princess when you drive them," Emma opined.

Phinn trailed after the ladies and small children—who were clearly intent on inspecting the pair and attached equipage.

Helen placed her hand on his arm, holding him back. "What did you think of Lady Augusta?"

"I found her frighteningly intelligent." And beautiful. He'd like to see her dressed in the short piece of embroidered cloth most of the Aztec ladies wore. "Did you plan this rendezvous?"

"Not really. I saw Lady Augusta drive by and stop at Rothwell House. I knew the duchess and other ladies were out here with their children, and decided it would be the perfect time for you to meet her." They had almost joined the rest of the group. "Is she too intelligent for you?"

"Not at all." She was too bright for Polite Society, and it was a pity she would not have an outlet for her clever mind. "In fact, she is a possibility." That ought to keep Helen from further matchmaking.

He joined the others in admiring the carriage and horses. The phaeton was well made and as sturdy as one could make a sporting carriage. The horses must have set someone back several guineas. Listening to the conversation, he learned that the duchess and both her friends drove as well.

Lady Augusta had just finished giving the pair carrots, when the duchess's little one began to fuss. The large Great Dane who had accompanied the child licked her cheek, then glanced at the duchess reproachfully.

"I must take Alexandria in. It is time for her nap."

Lady Augusta hugged her sister, then went around to

the street side of the carriage, where her brother waited to help her up. If it had been a footman, Phinn might have assumed the duty. Still, he had to give Helen her due. Lady Augusta was turning out to be a fascinating female.

He shook himself. The idea was *not* to be attracted to a lady. Not if he wanted to depart in a few weeks. Yet, he found himself watching as Lady Augusta expertly feathered the turn out of the square. What other talents did she have?

His sister-in-law nudged him. "You should have asked for a dance at her come out ball."

"I forgot all about it." Although, he might have remembered if he'd had any intention of doing so.

"Well"—Helen huffed—"there is always Almack's on Wednesday. You can ask one of the patronesses to give you permission to waltz with her." A small smile touched her lips. "That is a way to any young lady's goodwill." She glanced behind her to where the children were walking with their nursemaids. "Yet, first Dorchester must take you to Weston. It is a shame you are so much broader in the shoulders than he is. Otherwise you could wear one of his jackets."

If his brother had done half the exercise Phinn had over the past three years, they would wear the same size jackets. "He has made an appointment for me at eleven o'clock this morning."

"In that case we had better hurry. It cannot be much before the hour."

He murmured his assent. No wonder his brother simply agreed with her. It was easier than the alternative.

Shortly after returning home, Phinn and Dorchester were on their way to Weston's.

"I understand your new valet was hired this morning," his brother said as they crossed into Bond Street.

"I assume he will go through your clothing and make a list of the items you'll need. Pickerell will, of course, give the man any help he requires."

"And I assume my new valet"—whoever he was—"will be experienced enough that he will not be forced to rely on Pickle's help."

A pained expression crossed his brother's countenance. "You would get on much better with him if you would stop calling him Pickle."

"He doesn't approve of me and never has. I do not know how you tolerate him."

"Well, for one thing, I don't insult him every time I open my mouth," his brother retorted. They walked for a few moments in silence. "It's this marriage business that has you upset."

That wasn't helping. "You may be right. I feel as if there are more things I have to do before I wear a Parson's Noose."

"If it makes you feel any better"—Dorchester slid a glance at Phinn—"I did not think I was ready to wed either. Then I met Helen. Father was discussing arranging a marriage, and I told him if he was set on marrying me off, he could talk to her father."

"I didn't realize you and Helen were a love match." Where had he been when his brother had met her? Oxford. He'd had another year before he finished his studies when Dorchester and Helen had married.

His brother gave a gruff laugh. "It was more of a lust match. At least on my part. Fortunately, it all worked out."

Lust match? What a strange way to put it. Though, Phinn supposed if one could have a love match, one could have a lust match. Yet it seemed to him a marriage based on mutual respect, friendship, and interests would be more productive than pure lust. Then again, passion must play some part in the process.

The thought of Lady Augusta in an embroidered cloth slipped across his mind again.

Hell and damnation! He had to get out of England and soon.

Later that afternoon, Augusta met with Dorie, Henrietta, Georgiana, and Adeline at Merton House in Grosvenor Square. The five of them, accompanied by two footmen and three maids, set off to the Park.

"I think we need a plan for the Season," Georgiana said. "We do not want to be taken unawares. Nor do we wish to become involved with gentlemen who seem eligible but are not." She gave the rest of them a knowing look. "That happened to my sister, Meg, before she met Hawksworth."

"I am sure my brother will know who is a good choice and who is not," Augusta said. Of course, Worthington might not be as concerned this year. She *had* said she was not going to wed. Yet she was sure Merton had requested Matt's help with Henrietta. "I can always ask him."

"My brother, Huntley, said he intended to keep an eye on the gentlemen as well," Dorie added. "He should have done a better job with Littleton."

"Who is Littleton?" Augusta asked.

"No one of importance." Dorie changed her scowl into a gay smile. "My, it is a beautiful day."

"I am glad I can count on the help of your relatives." Adeline blew out a breath. "I am not sure my brother, Wivenly, will be of any assistance at all. Although, he is much better than he was before he married. I wish my father wasn't so busy with the Lords."

Augusta and her friends reached the Park and began strolling along the verge next to the carriage path. The day was pleasantly warm for late March. Snowdrops and purple crocus had begun to poke their heads up in the grass. Buds had appeared on the trees. In another week or so they would all be in leaf. She wondered what Padua was like this time of year.

Several gentlemen drove or rode past them, slowing down to glance over. Augusta supposed she would have to meet them at some point. Thank goodness men could not simply introduce themselves.

She blinked as the handsomest gentleman she had ever seen came up, riding on a black gelding, and stopped. He had curly, sable hair that had been fashionably cut, and eyes the color of new grass. When he smiled a dimple appeared on his right cheek. "Lady Dorie, well-met."

How had he even recognized her when she had been looking at Augusta?

For a mere moment, Dorie closed her eyes and a crease appeared in her forehead. The next second, a bright smile dawned on her face, and she inclined her head. "Lord Littleton, I did not know you were in Town."

"I arrived yesterday." Lord Littleton gave her a wary look. "Have you been in Town long?"

"Long enough." She turned to Augusta and the rest of their friends. "Ladies, on the subject of gentlemen who appear eligible and are not, permit me to introduce Lord Littleton to you." Once they had murmured a greeting, Dorie continued, "My lord, Lady Adeline Wively, Lady Augusta Vivers, Miss Featherton, and Miss Stern."

Smiling again, he executed an elegant bow. "Ladies, it is a pleasure to meet you. I hope you enjoy your time in the Metropolis." The grin faded when he glanced at Dorie. "I hope to see you as well, my lady."

"I suppose that is unavoidable." She dipped a slight curtsey. "Good day to you, my lord."

He touched two fingers to his hat, and rode away at a trot.

"Insufferable man." She drew in a breath and let it out. "Shall we continue our stroll?"

By unspoken accord, they started walking again.

What in Heaven's name was going on between the two of them? Augusta would have asked but did not feel as if she knew Dorie well enough.

"What makes him ineligible?" Georgiana asked.

"He has no desire to marry," Dorie answered. "But he will make a lady think she is his sun, moon, and stars."

She must have fallen in love with him and been disappointed.

"It does not matter." She smiled again. "Look, here comes Lord Turley. He is probably searching for Lord Littleton. They are quite good friends, but Lord Turley *is* eligible."

Lord Turley—his father had died eighteen months ago—was Elizabeth Harrington's brother. Like her he had blond hair and lovely light blue eyes. He also stopped and greeted Dorie. Once again, Dorie made the introductions.

When he rode off, Georgiana's gaze followed him for a few moments. "I must say, he is very handsome. He has newly come into his title, has he not?"

"About a year or so ago." Dorie glanced at Georgiana. "Does his rank matter?"

"Not at all." She grinned. "My sister may have married the heir to a dukedom, but a viscount was good enough for my mother."

"Henrietta, are your parents coming to Town?" Augusta asked.

"Only if I wed." She gave an insouciant shrug. "Papa

said they have no reason to visit the Metropolis. Dotty and Grandmamma are here. That will be enough."

By the time they had finished their stroll, they had met a number of other gentlemen as well. Some they wanted to know and one or two Dorie warned them about.

"Now, back to our plans." Georgiana gathered them into a circle. "We must look out for and stand by each other. If one of us is gone too long, the rest of us will come looking for her. However, it will be better if none of us goes anywhere by herself."

"You are saying that if a gentleman escorts us onto a terrace," Adeline said, "the rest of us will follow shortly thereafter."

"Indeed." Georgiana nodded. "Agreed?" One by one, they all nodded. "Augusta, I believe the first event we are attending, other than Almack's, is your come out ball."

"It is." She wanted to roll her eyes. "My mother planned it before I informed my family I wished to attend university."

"Nevertheless," her friend persisted, "it will be the perfect time to practice."

"We could even think up some scenarios to carry out our duties," Adeline suggested. "Augusta, can you arrange for us to come to Rothwell House so that we can learn where everything is?"

"Of course." Louisa would think this was an excellent idea. "How will that aid us when we will not know the other houses?"

"We will practice slipping away to be found," Adeline said.

"Like the game Sardines." The others looked at Augusta as if they had no idea what she was talking about. "In Sardines, one person hides and the others find her. It is played in Spain."

"Sardines, it is." Henrietta laughed.

"Will you attend Almack's this week?" Augusta thought it would be nice to have friends there with whom she could share the experience.

"I'll be there with Dotty and Merton," Henrietta said.

"My mother, brother, and sister will escort me," Georgiana said.

"Caro and Huntley are bringing me," Dorie responded.

"I will be there with my brother and sister-in-law as well. Wively complained about going, but Eugénie said he could remain home if he wished, and that she would dance with whom she pleased." Adeline giggled. "She says it in such a way that makes one think she doesn't care one way or the other, but my brother hates whenever another gentleman stands up with her. So, he will escort us."

Even though they laughed, Augusta was glad she did not have a brother like Adeline's.

Augusta hoped she and her friends would become as close as her sister and *her* friends had. It looked as if they already were making a beginning. Would they remain friends after she left or would she have to find new ones when she returned?

Chapter Six

"You are amazingly calm," Louisa remarked as her town coach came to a stop in front of Almack's two days later. "Charlotte and I both had an attack of nerves, and my sister-in-law, Lucinda, was almost physically ill."

Augusta took in the plain exterior of the building. Perhaps she was calm because she didn't care. It would be fun to dance, and she fully expected that she would be asked, but the rest of it mattered not at all. She was not intimidated by the patronesses. Lady Jersey had been a friend of Mama's for years, and Princess Esterházy and her husband had assisted Augusta in finding tutors in German literature, the different dialects of Italian, and some of the Slavic languages.

"I find that hard to believe." Very little upset Louisa. The door opened and a footman assisted her to the pavement.

"As do I." Rothwell climbed out of the coach, turning to help Louisa.

"Nevertheless, it is the truth." She took the arm he held out for her, while Augusta took the other.

They passed a large room set with tables she had

been told was the supper room. The ballroom's long windows were hung with blue curtains, and a small balcony protruded from above where an orchestra was tuning their instruments.

Mama came up to them as soon as they entered the room, and smiled. "Do not be nervous. You will be fine."

Augusta wanted to roll her eyes. There was absolutely no use in telling her mother that she was not feeling anything other than curiosity. After all, she had heard a great deal about the famous assembly rooms. Nor was there a reason at all to be concerned. She was dressed properly for the event, knew how to dance and behave, and had no desire to form an attachment. Ergo, there was no need to worry.

From across the dance floor, Dorie caught Augusta's eye and smiled. Dorie was speaking with a tall gentleman that looked so much like her he must be her brother, the Earl of Huntley. Augusta spotted Lady Huntley. Of her other friends, only Georgiana was present. Hopefully, Henrietta and Adeline would arrive soon.

A few moments later a gentleman who appeared to be in his late twenties came up to them and bowed. "Rothwell, your grace."

"Ah, yes." Rothwell glanced at Augusta. "My dear, may I introduce Lord Bottomley to you? Bottomley, my sister Lady Augusta Vivers."

"How do you do, my lord." She dipped a curtsey appropriate for a viscount, and held out her hand.

He touched her fingers with his as he bowed. "My evening is better for having made your acquaintance, my lady. May I hope you have a set free?"

"I do indeed." She gave him a polite smile. "If you wish, you may have the next set."

The dance was a Scottish reel, one of her favorites.

He remained with them talking about the weather and people she didn't know until the dance.

After the set, when he returned her to her sister and brother-in-law, two more gentlemen were waiting to be introduced. One stood up with her for a quadrille and the other for a country dance.

Lord Phineas entered with a gentleman she assumed to be his brother—again, there was a strong family resemblance—and Lady Dorchester.

By now the large room was crowded with the select members of Polite Society fortunate enough to have received vouchers. Not far from Augusta, a young lady laughed loudly and was immediately admonished.

Mrs. Drummond-Burrell approached with a gentleman, and Louisa whispered, "You will have to dance with him, but I guarantee you will not like his politics."

"Do you truly think he will even attempt to discuss anything of import?" Augusta murmured. "Thus far, I have not found it to be the case."

Before Louisa could respond, her ladyship curtseyed. "Your graces. Lady Augusta. Please allow me to recommend Lord Lytton to you as a suitable partner for the waltz."

"Thank you, my lady." Augusta dipped a curtsey. "My lord, it is a pleasure to meet you."

"The pleasure is mine." He bowed before holding out his arm and the first chords for the waltz were played.

He danced well—most of the gentlemen appeared to—but as with the others, his conversation was lacking. She would have preferred to spar with him over politics rather than discuss the weather, and how she was enjoying her Season, yet again.

This time, though, when she was returned to Louisa and Rothwell, Lord Phineas was with them. She had no sooner sent her dance partner off when he said, "My lady, do you have a set left?"

She did. It was the last one of her evening. As her sisters had before her, she would return home after supper. Or at supper if Rothwell had his way. He'd complained bitterly about the sustenance to be found at Almack's. "Only if you promise not to discuss the weather."

Shaking her head, Louisa covered her eyes. Rothwell's shoulders quaked.

Lord Phineas cracked a laugh. "I can assure you that I have no opinion on the weather at all. Other than it is much colder than I have been used to."

Rothwell grinned. "I told Worthington she wouldn't be any better than you were, my love." He drew Louisa a little nearer. "Everyone thought Augusta would be quieter and easier because she was always busy with her studies. Yet, this is what happens when you let loose a Vivers lady onto the *ton*."

"I thank the Fates not all young ladies try to hide their intelligence behind trite conversation." Lord Phineas held out his arm. "Shall we dance, my lady?"

Several moments into the set, Augusta was enjoying herself more than she had all evening. Not only was Lord Phineas an excellent partner, but he had her laughing at his stories.

"So, there I was hiding on a narrow ledge over a paved courtyard waiting for the woman to leave my bedchamber." Looking at her he gave a rueful grin. "I suppose I should not tell a young lady that tale."

"Probably not many of them, but I enjoyed it immensely. I assume you took the route from the Canaries to St. Lucia on the way over."

His eyes widened as if she had shocked him. "How do you know about the sailing paths?"

"Geography is one of my passions. Naturally, that would include the trade winds." It always amazed her how so many people expected young ladies to know nothing. "I also know how to navigate by the stars. Although, I have never had an opportunity to put it into practice."

"Now that you mention it, my sister-in-law mentioned that geography was a passion of yours. I was so fascinated that you speak Nahuatl I didn't think to ask you about anything else." They twirled around again before changing positions. "Did not your brother say you spoke several languages?"

"Indeed." Augusta decided not to remind him how many. She had been mastering languages since she was a young child. "I am fascinated by their variances, yet in many ways they are the same. Some languages have many similar words even if the roots of the languages are not the same."

"You said you studied with Mr. Marsden. Have you had the opportunity to train with experts in other languages?"

"I have been fortunate that my family used their connections to find professors and others to help me learn. I was speaking and reading Italian when I was five."

"Fascinating." His gray eyes focused on her in a way she should not encourage.

Talking with him was too easy. He looked as if he would ask another question, and she did not wish to find a gentleman with whom she had a great deal in common. It would make her plans more difficult.

Even though he seemed as if he would not think her strange for wishing to attend university, she must ensure she did not mention her intentions. "Why did you decide to study the Aztec temples?"

"Not just the temples, but the basic structure of their

homes as well." Their eyes met, and his seemed to become warmer. "I developed an aspiration to learn about architecture when my father had a Grecian folly built. I would have liked to travel to Europe and study the medieval churches and other buildings, but because of the war, my family encouraged me to sail to Mexico."

"Did you enjoy your time there?" How exciting it must have been to study buildings that were so different than England's.

"I did." His grin gave him a boyish look. "I was sorry when I had to leave." As they made another turn he caught Lytton looking at them. "By the way, if you ever need an excuse not to dance with the good earl, tell him you are engaged to stand up with me."

"I suppose you mean Lord Lytton." He was the only earl she had danced with this evening. Lord Phineas's offer was kind. She had not enjoyed spending time with the earl.

"Indeed." He came close to rolling his eyes. "Even when he is trying to be interesting, he's a dead bore."

Augusta struggled not to laugh, but a gurgle escaped. "That, sir, is unkind."

"But absolutely true." He glanced at the earl again. "I know of what I speak. We were at school together for eight long years. He only wanted to be my chum because my father was a marquis."

Charlie had mentioned men who attended Oxford solely for the connections. No wonder the earl had been so busy asking her about her family. "What one would call an encroaching mushroom if he were not a peer."

"I think in this case even a peer can be an encroaching mushroom." He gave her a crooked smile, and completely against her will, she became breathless. This would not do at all.

Phinn should have asked Lady Augusta to dance earlier. Perhaps he could have saved her from dancing with the earl. "Exactly." And she was clever. She had very adroitly turned the conversation from her to him. Phinn wanted to know how she was able to learn so much and so quickly. "Do you ever get your languages confused?"

"No, never." She gave her head a little shake. "I have an excellent memory for languages in the written or spoken form. I have been able to quote poems years after I learned them."

If Lady Augusta were a gentleman, she could easily get a position with the Foreign Office. As it was, his first impression had been correct; she'd completely terrify the male population of the *ton*. "Have you ever attempted Egyptian hieroglyphics?"

"I have." She smiled at him as if he was the most fascinating person present, when she was actually the most captivating lady he had ever met. "They are so unusual. I have been able to study tracings and copies, but I would love to be able to travel to Egypt and see real hieroglyphics."

Phinn could have remained in conversation with her all evening and was disappointed that the dance he'd not originally wanted was coming to an end. This must be the fastest half hour he'd ever spent. "Would you like to drive out with me tomorrow for the Grand Strut?"

She tilted her head slightly to one side for a moment. "Yes, but I would like to take my carriage. If you do not mind."

"Not at all." That would save him from having to borrow his brother's curricle. "I shall present myself at Worthington House at five o'clock."

"I shall look forward to it." The dance ended and they

bowed and curtseyed before strolling to where her sister and brother-in-law were waiting.

"Do you mind if we do not remain for supper?" her sister asked.

Lady Augusta paused. "Why do you ask?"

The duchess glanced at her husband. "Rothwell remembered that he disliked weak tea and stale bread."

"I think he remembered that long before now." Lady Augusta chuckled lightly. "I cannot bring myself to blame him."

Phinn wished she was staying so that he could continue to talk with her. "My lady. Your graces." He bowed. "I shall wish you a good evening." He took Lady Augusta's hand. "I'll see you tomorrow."

"Yes, I look forward to our ride. Good evening, my lord."

Wishing he could escape as well, Phinn made his way back to his brother and sister-in-law.

"How was your dance?" Helen asked the instant he arrived.

"I had an excellent time." There was no reason to lie. He and Lady Augusta had laughed and smiled often enough anyone would have known. "I'm driving out with her tomorrow."

His brother cleared his throat. "I suppose that means you'll want to use my curricle."

"No, we are taking hers." Both their brows rose, and he almost laughed.

"Indeed?" Helen remarked, being the first to recover.

"I'm looking forward to it. From what little I saw"— very little—"she is an excellent whip." At least he assumed she would be.

"Yes," Dorchester murmured. "Neither Worthington nor Wolverton have reputations for being stupid men.

If she was given a high-perched phaeton, one must assume she knows how to safely tool it."

"I suppose you are correct, my dear." Helen placed her hand on Dorchester's arm. "Both Lady Kenilworth and the duchess know how to drive a sporting carriage." She glanced at Phinn. "Are there any other ladies with whom you would like to dance?"

"No." After spending time with Lady Augusta, any other female would bore him to death. "To be honest, I am ready to go home."

Unfortunately, Helen was not finished with her inquiries. Once they were seated in the coach, she said, "You and Lady Augusta seemed to have a great deal to discuss, and it was clear the conversation did not revolve around the weather."

"She is remarkable." And unlike any other female Phinn had ever met. "Did you know she is a polyglot?"

The carriage lighting was just bright enough that he could see his sister-in-law's forehead crease and a line form between her brows. "What is a polyglot?"

"She speaks multiple languages. She can also read Egyptian hieroglyphics."

"Are they the squiggly lines carved into the tombs?" Helen sounded as if she was suspicious about something.

"Er, yes." Her eyes narrowed. What the devil was wrong? "It was the written language of the time."

Helen's lips flattened unbecomingly. "Her mother swore to me that Lady Augusta was not a bluestocking."

"Oh." Phinn had to think about that. Most of the ladies he'd met who were known bluestockings were nothing like Lady Augusta. Unlike her, they dressed in boring gowns as if they didn't care how they appeared. Lady Augusta had shimmered in a blue dress that was cut just low enough that the swell of her breasts rose tantalizingly from her bodice. Bluestockings didn't seem to smile much either. He definitely knew none of them had made his cock start to harden. Helen was still awaiting his response. "I do not believe she could properly be called a bluestocking. She is merely very intelligent and has been given the opportunity to use her talents."

Dorchester gave him a look as if to say he knew Phinn was shamming it.

"I suppose . . . well, I suppose you have a point," Helen said, obviously confused.

His brother glanced at the carriage roof and shook his head while Phinn kept his lips firmly pressed together so he wouldn't enrage Helen by laughing.

"I did think you had missed your opportunity to dance with her when Lytton got Clementina Drummond-Burrell to recommend *him* to Lady Augusta for the first waltz."

Obviously, this conversation was not over, and the whole evening was going to be discussed. "Lady Augusta was not impressed by him. I believe she found his conversation lacking."

"I do not know him well, but he is an *earl* looking for a wife."

Phinn supposed that was meant to inform him that he had competition for Augusta.

Lytton could be an earl ten times over, and Phinn doubted Lady Augusta would want the coxcomb.

"As Phinn says, my dear"—Dorchester patted Helen's hand—"I do not believe you have anything about which to be concerned. Lady Augusta appears to be the same type of female as the other ladies in her family. I do not think rank will sway her."

"That is all well and good, but her sister did marry a duke." Helen's tone managed to be both acerbic and sarcastic at the same time. "And her sister by marriage married a marquis."

Phinn agreed with his brother. Still, there was something about Lady Augusta's behavior that made him wonder what it would take to convince her to wed a fellow. And it was those kinds of thoughts that got a fellow who did not wish to wed in trouble. He'd have to walk a fine line between having a pleasant time conversing with Lady Augusta and allowing his feelings to grow.

Chapter Seven

The next afternoon, Phinn arrived at Worthington House promptly at five o'clock prepared to wait. Surprisingly, Augusta, who looked like spring and sunshine in a yellow carriage gown embroidered with flowers and topped with a spencer that hugged her breasts, was pulling on her gloves when he was admitted to the house.

"My lady." He bowed.

"My lord." The butler kept the door open. "Shall we depart?"

Rather than taking his arm, she strode straight to the phaeton, and he had to lengthen his stride to get to the vehicle before she did. "Allow me to help you up."

"Thank you." She held out her hand, obviously expecting him to take it. Instead, he clasped his hands on her waist. His palms warmed against the indentation of her waist and swell of her hips. He sucked in a sharp breath. Short stays then. A man ought to have been warned. This wasn't helping him at all. He wanted to forget the carriage ride, press his body against hers, and plunder.

Lady Augusta had stilled, her breathing grew rapid,

and her eyes widened. Phinn lost no time lifting her to the seat.

What the hell had he been thinking?

Without a word, he went around the phaeton and climbed onto the bench. She gave the pair their office and they started smartly out of the square. As he'd expected, she drove the carriage well. Yet, the way she stared straight ahead made him feel she was ignoring him. Not that he could blame her, but they couldn't go on like this in silence. He debated apologizing to her, but that might make things even more awkward. The other problem with that idea was that he wasn't a bit sorry.

He tried to stick his finger between his neck and cravat, but his gloves were too thick. "You drive extremely well."

Lady Augusta threw him a quick smile. "Thank you. It occurred to me that as am I, you are new to a London Season."

Ah, it was to be small talk. After the attraction that flared between them, he couldn't really blame her. "I am. I didn't spend much time in London before sailing for Mexico. I was more interested in wandering around Scotland and Wales, studying the old castles."

"That must have been fascinating." Her tone was wistful. She probably hadn't even been allowed to go with a group on a hiking trip in the Lake District.

It struck him forcefully how constrained young ladies were in their lives. "It was." They'd reached the Park, and she turned into the gate. "I'd forgotten how crowded it was this time of day."

That made her smile. "I think all of Polite Society is here."

They each nodded to people they knew. Lord Bottomley, riding a fine-looking bay, came up to them. "Lady

Augusta, Carter-Woods, good day." Phinn had known the man in school. He had nothing against Bottomley. Phinn just wished he'd go away.

He and Augusta returned the man's greeting. "I say, Lady Augusta, is this your rig?"

"It is." She was clearly proud of the carriage, as she should be.

"Phinn," Bottomley said, "why don't you get down and hold my horse while I take a ride with Lady Augusta?"

"Why don't I stay exactly where I am," Phinn shot back. "If you wish to drive with Lady Augusta, you may make your own arrangements." He glanced at Augusta, who looked a bit bemused. "Shall we drive on, my lady?"

"Wait," Bottomley said as the carriage moved forward. "I would like to ask if you would accompany me tomorrow."

"Sorry, Bottomley," Phinn replied. "I believe I have another engagement."

For a moment, the other man seemed to be at *point non plus*. Then he urged his horse to a trot, caught up with them, and bellowed, "Not you, you dunderhead. Lady Augusta."

A giggle burst from her lush, deep pink lips.

Ahead of them was a landau carrying four older ladies. "Lord Bottomley," a woman with several large feathers in her hat said. "What are you about, making a scene? Behave yourself." His face flushed bright red. Augusta pressed her lips firmly together, but they were twitching so hard Phinn didn't think she could keep her laughter in for long, and he wondered who the older lady was. Then the woman turned her attention to him. "Lord Phineas, I have not seen you since you were a child."

"Lady Bellamny," Augusta whispered to him.

Now he understood. Her ladyship was one of the

gorgons of the *ton* about whom his brother had warned him. "My lady, a pleasure to see you again."

Lady Bellamny slid a look at Augusta. "Well done." Then her ladyship glanced back at him. "It is plain to see your foreign travel has not hurt *your* manners." She turned her disdainful black gaze on Bottomley. "Unlike some who have not even left England and still cannot remember them."

Augusta turned her head away—probably so that Lady Bellamny couldn't see her silently laughing. Bottomley mumbled something, did his best to bow from his horse, and rode away, no doubt nursing his hurt pride. It was a very satisfactory state of affairs as far as Phinn was concerned. He'd never expected to have such an enjoyable time.

She snapped the reins, the carriage moved forward, and he decided to take advantage of their momentary solitude. "My lady, would you drive with me again to-morrow?"

When she finally glanced at him, her eyes were full of tears. How had he made her cry? He was thinking of a way to console her when, in a shaky voice, she said, "Yes, but only if you do not make me laugh."

Ah, tears of joy. That was a different matter. "You have a great many rules, my lady." Phinn made his voice as prim as possible. "I may not speak of the weather, and I may not make you laugh. What, pray, am I allowed to do?"

"Do you know how to drive?" she asked in a stran-gled voice.

"Of course." What did that have to do with anything?

"Good." She shoved the ribbons in his hand, covered her face with her hands, and succumbed to the mirth she'd been attempting to hold in. It was a full minute, at least, before she regained her countenance and took back the reins. "Thank you."

"My pleasure." She still had not answered his request. "Did I make you laugh too much for you to ride with me again?"

"No." She grinned. "I am having a much better time with you than I expected."

Before he could ask what she meant by that—she really was the most disconcerting female he had ever met—Lytton rode up.

"Lady Augusta. Lord Phineas." The man said Phinn's name as if something sour was in his mouth. Lytton glanced at the phaeton, then at Phinn. "I am surprised you would allow another to drive your new carriage."

"You are mistaken. This is Lady Augusta's phaeton. I am fortunate she allowed me to tool it for a short time."

The man sniffed. "My lady, the reason I stopped is to ask you to stand up with me at Lady Wolverton's ball tomorrow evening for the supper dance."

She quickly schooled her expression into a mask. "I am sorry, my lord, but that set is taken. Lord Phineas has already requested it."

He was more than pleased she had remembered his offer. Smiling smugly, Phinn glanced at his lordship. "Indeed I have."

The man looked as if he'd swallowed a toad. "Do you have a country dance available?"

Augusta gazed innocently up at Lytton. "I have the third set free. I believe it is a cotillion."

"Thank you, my lady. I shall see you then." He inclined his head before riding away.

Phinn wished he could have saved her from dancing with the man at all. In Mexico, if one danced with a lady more than once it was tantamount to a betrothal. And as much as he was coming to like Lady Augusta, that would complicate his life.

Augusta was glad Lord Lytton did not linger. If only she knew enough gentlemen to fill her card. Grace and Mama had warned Augusta that before an entertainment, if she turned a gentleman down, she must find another one to take his place. Not only that, but if a gentleman requested a set she had free during a ball, she would have to accept that too or not dance the rest of the evening. What if she had all her dances scheduled but one, would she then be able to make some excuse? She'd have to ask.

"You should have told him you did not have any sets left," Lord Phineas said.

"If it had been possible, I would have. Do you not know how many rules concerning dancing and comportment there are for young ladies?"

He seemed to consider her question, then shook his head. "I only know of one."

"In that case, I shall tell you." By the time she was done explaining about not dancing with a gentleman, versus standing up with one twice and no more, unless one was betrothed to that gentleman; not laughing too loudly, but always laughing politely when a gentleman thought he was being witty; and the host of other things she had been taught, she thought his eyes would pop out of his head.

"No wonder young ladies all act the same," he said slowly.

"Exactly." Augusta decided to provide what she considered to be the *coup de grâce* to the discussion. "And do you know that a lady is not supposed to show her intelligence at all?"

"Some things my sister-in-law said gave me that idea." His tone was thoughtful. "But you do not hide your intellect."

"I do not. Neither did my sisters or Lady Merton. Our families are very forward thinking." Except for Mama, who had become obsessed with Augusta marrying. "Then again, most gentlemen do not wish to have a real conversation. Ergo, it is easy for me to simply make the appropriate responses while I am thinking of something else."

"Remarkable," he mused. Although, she had the feeling he was talking more to himself than her. Lord Phineas would most likely not give it any more thought. The rules did not affect him, after all.

They had reached Worthington House, and she brought the phaeton to a halt. She would have taken him to his brother's house, but she was not allowed to drive the short distance from Grosvenor Square to Berkeley Square without a groom or another person in the carriage.

"What would happen if some muckworm asked you to dance?"

For a second, she could only stare at him in disbelief. He had actually been analyzing all she had told him. She smiled. "That is easy. If he is someone scurrilous, I would not have been introduced to him. Therefore, I may not stand up with him." She thought back over what she had told him. "I did say I may not dance with a gentleman to whom I have not been introduced."

"Yes. Yes, you did. I just didn't realize that there would not be a situation where someone would, unthinkingly, introduce you to a gentleman you should not know."

"In that event, my brother would step in." And none too politely.

"Yes, of course." He nodded slightly, again as if he were still considering the rules.

"Augusta." Walter was standing next to the carriage. "You do not wish to leave the horses standing too long."

"Oh, yes. Of course." How long had she and Lord Phineas been sitting there? "I must have lost track of time."

"Don't be concerned." Walter snorted. "I never thought to hear an academic discussion about dance partners."

She and Lord Phineas exchanged a glance and smile. "I suppose I should take my leave."

"I should go inside." Yet, she *wanted* to stay here talking with him. Walter came around to her side of the carriage to help her down, and Augusta almost wished it had been Lord Phineas.

Although, she did not wish to repeat the reaction she'd had when he lifted her up. That had been much too disconcerting.

He came around. Taking her fingers in his hand, he pressed a kiss on her knuckles. "Until tomorrow."

Heat raced up her arm in the same fashion as it had affected her torso when he had touched her waist. "Until then." This reaction was much too confusing. She stared at him, turned toward the house, took a step, then whirled back to him. "I must go."

He gave her an odd look. Did he think she was mad? She certainly felt like it. "Yes, I should as well."

Refusing to look back again, Augusta strode to the front door. She was going to Italy. There was no room in her life for strange feelings for a man.

The second she entered the house, she was bombarded by her sisters and Phillip, wanting to know when they could ride in her phaeton. Thank God for the chaos of her family. The last thing she wanted to think about was Lord Phineas.

She held up her hand. "Wait a moment." She could take Mary and Theodora at the same time. Augusta surveyed the children. The two youngest had bonnets hanging from their hands. Mary glanced up hopefully and stuck out her toe. Leather shoes as well. "I shall take Mary and Theo." The twins and Madeline started to protest and Augusta hushed them again. "None of you are ready and they are. I'll take one of you and Phillip when I return, then I'll take the next two. They will only be short rides. You must get ready for dinner soon."

By the time she was done making the trips around Berkeley Square, it was past time to change for dinner. They had all had carriage driving lessons and wanted to take a turn handling the ribbons, but the traffic was heavy and she'd had to promise to take them out early one morning.

After dinner her mother and Richard joined them for tea. Mama sat next to Augusta on the sofa. "I understand you had a lovely carriage ride with Lord Phineas."

"I did." Drat it all, her mother must have spoken to Lady Bellamny. Augusta should have known there was no keeping anything private.

"Excellent." Her mother smiled happily. "Lady Dorchester tells me that Lord Phineas is highly respected. Did you know he is to present papers to the Royal Society *and* the Royal Institution?"

"That does not surprise me." Augusta drained her teacup. She didn't want to think about him. Not his insightful mind or his sparkling silver eyes. Or the way he made her laugh. And definitely not that other thing that happened when they touched.

Mama brought her teacup up to her mouth and gazed at Augusta. "I understand you are going driving with him tomorrow as well."

Where had she heard that? "Ah, yes, and we are to dance the supper set together at my ball." Pretending to yawn, she covered her mouth. "I really must go to bed. Tomorrow will be a busy day." Setting her cup and saucer on the table, she rose. "Good night."

"If you will excuse me." Grace stood. "I wish to look in on the children. Good night."

Mama rose as well. "We should be going. Augusta is correct. Tomorrow will be a hectic day."

Once Augusta, Grace, and Matt had seen Mama and Richard to the door, Grace took Augusta's arm. "If you are sure you do not wish to marry this Season, it would be kinder of you not to raise your mother's expectations."

Drat, drat, drat! How could I not have taken that into consideration?

As much as she enjoyed his company, this was for the best. "I shall limit my time with Lord Phineas."

Grace frowned. "Only if you wish to. You do appear to enjoy his company."

Augusta tried not to sigh. He was the only gentleman, other than Walter, with whom she could have interesting discussions. "I do enjoy his company a great deal, but my mind is set. If at all possible, I wish to attend university."

She said good evening to her sister-in-law and headed toward her bedchamber. Perhaps she and Lord Phineas could meet at another time of the day when they would not be so noticeable.

Chapter Eight

The next afternoon, Phinn once again presented himself at five o'clock. This time he had to ply the large brass knocker before a harried-looking footman answered. "Come in, my lord. I'll find Lady Augusta. We're at sixes and sevens with getting ready for the ball."

Not that he'd ever been in a house when a ball was being got together, but still . . . "You mean to say that Lady Augusta is actually doing things to prepare for the ball?"

The footman looked at him as if he was newly released from Bedlam. "My lord, not only is Lady Augusta preparing, but so is her ladyship, his lordship, Mr. Walter, the rest of the children, and Lord and Lady Wolverton."

It appeared Phinn's domestic education had been sorely neglected. "'Lay on, Macduff,' I shall give what help I am able."

"My name is Franklin, my lord. I don't think we have a Macduff here. But with Lady Merton sending servants over, you never know." The footman turned. "Come with me."

Obviously, the man had not been exposed to Shakespeare, which was a great pity as he'd written his plays for the common man.

"I thought I'd heard the ball was to be at Rothwell House?" In fact, Phinn was certain that's what Helen had said.

"It was until there was an accident of some kind." The footman glanced at him. "Runners have been sent all over Town with messages."

No wonder everyone was in a rush. Phinn found Lady Augusta surrounded by great swathes of different colored silks draped over chairs. The footman had been called away before he was announced.

Her hand was on her forehead as if she was attempting to hold back a headache. Or perhaps she already had one. "Do we really need to do this? The ball is in a few hours. There will not be time to hang the fabric."

"It does not take any time at all," Lady Merton assured Lady Augusta.

Gazing up, her sister the duchess turned around in a circle. "It does need something to tie the rooms together."

It wasn't until then that Phinn noticed doors had been pulled back, allowing almost the whole side of the house to seem like one room. Footmen, being directed by a trio of girls, scurried around with vases full of spring flowers. Walter Carpenter was organizing the placement of large potted palms around the rooms.

"I think the gold is very nice," Lady Wolverton offered.

Her remark drew his attention back to the silk. No. The gold would be too heavy.

"I like the green," Lady Kenilworth opined. "But it will not do for Augusta."

Why wouldn't it do for Lady Augusta? Then he noticed she was dressed for their drive. Had she been attempting to escape for a ride with him and been caught? He studied the green, trying to imagine it on Lady Augusta. Her ladyship was right. It wouldn't do at all, but the yellow and white silk would look well on her.

He cleared his throat, and the ladies turned as one to see who was interrupting. "Good afternoon. Lady Augusta and I were to go for a carriage ride."

Lady Wolverton's eyes narrowed slightly, and her lips pressed together. He'd been on the receiving end of that exact look, but from *his* mother, not Lady Augusta's.

"If I may." He pointed to the fabrics. "I believe the yellow and white would be an excellent idea."

Her beleaguered expression disappeared, and she glanced around the room. "I think Lord Phineas is right. They would be perfect with the different wall coverings and the flowers."

Her grace nodded briskly. "Where are Rothwell and Kenilworth? We will require their help."

"Outside," Walter said. "Helping with the garden decorations."

"I'd be happy to offer my services." Phinn stared at the silk again. "Someone will need to tell me what to do."

"We're finished here." Walter stepped over. "But I've never done this part."

"There are loops on the fabric." Lady Augusta picked up one of the long silk pieces, showing them the almost-invisible loops. "And hooks are on the walls. The difficult part will be weaving the swaths together."

"If we have someone on the ground twisting them as they are handed up to the person on the ladder, that might work." Phinn tried to envision how they'd look.

A footman was sent outside to gather as many ladders as he could, and soon the swaths of yellow and white silk were draped along the upper walls.

"I have to admit," Augusta said an hour later as she surveyed their work, "it does look better."

The brilliant smile she gave him made him want to gather her in his arms and kiss her. For some peculiar reason, he was not nearly as bothered about that thought as he should be.

"Thank you for your suggestion. It was perfect."

"My pleasure." Lord Phineas sketched a short bow.

Augusta's brothers and her brothers-in-law, as well as Merton, stood outside the French windows to the drawing room looking very pleased with themselves.

"The lanterns are up," Matt said. "There is not a dark spot in the garden."

"Precisely what we wanted." Grace along with Mary and Theo entered the drawing room. "Thank you, my love."

"I live to serve." A wicked look entered Matt's eyes as he gazed at Grace, and Augusta wondered what that was about.

"It looks like we're finished here as well," Walter said. "I'm hungry. Dinner should be soon. Are we changing?"

Lord Phineas had sidled up to Augusta. "Dinner?"

"We eat early with the children. They do not do well with Town hours." She had to smile at that. *The children* were growing rapidly. "None of us do."

"There is no need to change," Grace said. "We will have to dress for the ball afterward."

"Would you like to dine with us?" Augusta kept her voice low.

"I would be delighted, but I must visit my tailor for a final fitting of my evening kit if I am not to look shabby at your ball."

That was disappointing but understandable. She held out her hand. "Thank you for your help, and not being upset about missing our carriage ride."

He took her fingers in his and bowed. "How could I have been offended when you appeared as if you were under siege?"

As it had before, his touch started her blood racing.

Still, Augusta could not help but laugh. "That is exactly how I felt. I shall see you this evening."

"I'm looking forward to it." The corners of his eyes creased. "I believe I shall also take pride in having my work admired." When he returned her hand to her, Augusta felt the loss. How strange. "I'll see myself out."

It was not until she was dressing that she recalled her gown for this evening was in the same yellow and white as the decorations. No wonder she had liked his idea so much. Not only that, but the flowers that had been embroidered on the yellow overdress were the same colors as the flowers for the ball.

Her younger sisters burst into the room followed by Grace and Mama.

"Ooooh," Madeline and the twins said at the same time. "You match the ballroom!"

"It is not a ballroom." Theo frowned at the girls. "It is just made to look like one."

"I think you are very pretty." Mary stood on her tiptoes and kissed Augusta's cheek.

Mama gave her a long strand of pearls that Gobert looped around Augusta's neck, and Grace gave her pearl earrings.

Perhaps this evening would be fun after all.

A few hours later, Augusta was in the receiving line when Lord Phineas greeted her again. "I must have been prescient."

"Indeed. I had not even thought about my gown when we were discussing the decorations."

He chuckled softly. "That doesn't surprise me. You looked as if you were trying to decide whom to murder first." Lord Phineas leaned a little closer. "You will be the most beautiful lady in the room tonight."

"Thank you." Augusta appreciated the compliment even if she had heard it several times already. When he said it, it sounded different. More sincere. "I shall see you later."

Charlie, Grace's brother, the Earl of Stanwood, who had arrived just as they were sitting down to dinner and had received a lot of good-hearted teasing about missing all the work, led her out for her first dance.

When she had asked him to stand up with her, he had given her a searching look. "Are you sure there isn't another gentleman you wish to have dance with you?"

"No, I did not want to single out any of the gentlemen and told everyone who asked that I already had a partner."

"Very well, then. I would be honored."

Unfortunately, the rest of the gentlemen with whom she stood up had no more conversation than they'd had at Almack's. Then again, she should not complain. That left her free to begin planning her journey to Italy in early summer. At least when she danced with Lord Phineas, he was stimulating to talk to.

Finally, the gentleman in question strolled up to her and bowed. "My set, I believe."

"It is, indeed." She placed her fingers lightly on his arm. Yet, even that small amount of pressure caused awareness to scurry through her body. The feeling grew even stronger when he placed his hand on her waist. Surely, this wouldn't happen every time they touched.

"Have you been bored to death?" The music started, and they began to twirl.

It was amazing how in tune to her mood he was. "I have been entertaining myself, while pretending to listen."

"I thought that might be the case. Shall I weary you with Aztec architecture?" His eyes twinkled with amusement. "I have been doing an excellent job of it this evening with the other ladies."

"That was not kind of you." Most of the other females would be completely out of their depths.

"Perhaps not, but I could point out that it is not nice of you to pretend to be engrossed in a gentleman's conversation."

"Fair enough." He did have a point. Yet, what harm could her behavior cause? "We shall discuss Aztec architecture in Nahuatl."

"This set will not be nearly long enough." Lord Phineas's grin warmed her.

No, it would not be long enough, but it would be the best dance of the evening.

As Phinn escorted Lady Augusta down to supper with her family, he had the whimsical sensation of taking flight. *If* he were looking for a wife, Augusta—that was much better than Lady Augusta; he did not want that space between them—was exactly the type of lady he would wed. Mayhap he should consider acceding to his brother's wishes and produce an heir sooner rather than later. After all, she was not attached to another gentleman. From what he'd witnessed she found them all tedious in the extreme. She *was* on the Marriage Mart. If she must wed, why should she not marry him?

He already had lustful thoughts about her. Yet even more alluring than her obvious beauty, her mind was a thing of pure magnificence as much or more as her features were. And she reacted to him physically. Though he doubted she understood what the sensations she experienced meant. Nor did it matter. Phinn would be happy to instruct her.

They also had so much in common, they were rapidly becoming close friends. Still more importantly, he could imagine a life with her. They would have babies with rich, sable hair and lapis-blue eyes.

Still, he did not wish to move too quickly. It was early days and marriage was for life. He'd bide his time and see if these feelings he was having for her would last and if he truly wished to wed. Until then, he would make sure he did not raise her expectations.

Helen had already scolded him for arranging another carriage ride so shortly after the first one. It seemed odd to him that something as public and innocuous as an outing during the Promenade could cause talk. She'd also repeated the rules Augusta had explained. There would be no second dances at balls and other entertainments. Until he had made up his mind what he wanted, that was. Then he'd make sure men such as Lytton didn't come near her.

Three tables grouped together had been reserved for them. He held a chair for Augusta before going off with the other gentlemen to select the small dishes they would bring back to the ladies. Thankfully, as Phinn had never been "on the Town" as a young man, his brother had taken the time to explain what was expected of him. No wonder Dorchester had wanted an arranged match. They were much simpler than this courting business.

Luckily, the customs were much less confusing than the Spanish ones he'd had to learn in Mexico.

"What were you discussing with my sister?" Lord Stanwood asked.

"The Aztec buildings." Phinn hoped Augusta liked most of what was on offer. It was her ball, after all. He chose a small mushroom tart. "I studied them when I was in Mexico."

Stanwood pointed to a lobster patty and Phinn took that as well. "That wasn't Spanish you were speaking."

"No, it was the Aztec language. She wished to practice." *What else would she like to eat?*

Her brothers-in-law made grunts of approval. Either that she wished to practice or that he encouraged it, he didn't know.

"She likes the lemon tarts as well," Kenilworth said.

Phinn was reaching for another tart when it occurred to him that Helen wasn't the only one given to matchmaking. He'd have to be careful. He wasn't sure he wished to marry yet, nor did he want to hurt Augusta's feelings. He enjoyed her company. And even though he was always happier in her company than in anyone else's, that was all it could be for the immediate future. The main problem was that marrying would end any plans he had to go to Europe.

Chapter Nine

Augusta was dressing to go shopping with her friends when a knock sounded on her door.

"I'll get it, my lady." Gobert opened the door, exchanging murmured words with whoever was there. "His lordship wishes to see you before you go out."

She was hardly ever summoned to her brother's study. "I wonder what he wants."

"I couldn't say, my lady." Her dresser placed the final pin in her hair. "Durant wasn't told."

Had Matt made a decision about allowing her to go to Italy? That must be the reason.

A knot formed in her stomach. What if he said no? All her planning would be for naught. Then what would she do with herself? The university in Holland was an option, and it was not at all far from England. She might be allowed to go there. The only problem was that she did not know anyone at the university. Not only that, but it did not have the prestige of Padua. Still, it would be better than nothing.

Please let him say yes, please let him say yes, please let him say yes.

She hurried down the stairs to his office.

When she arrived in the study, Grace was seated on one of the chairs in front of Matt's desk.

She waved to the vacant chair. "Please."

Augusta forced herself to smile as she sank onto the chair and waited.

Pressing his lips together in a thin line, Matt placed his forearms on the desk. "I have received four offers for your hand."

For a moment she was so stunned, she couldn't speak. This was not about university after all. "I don't understand. Who would want to marry me? I have encouraged no one." Yet, apparently that didn't matter. But no, Matt had said *offers.* She was not being forced to wed, and she refused to entertain any gentleman's suit until she had accomplished what she wished to. "Tell them no. I do not wish to marry them."

"Augusta"—Grace's lips began to twitch—"You really should know *who* they are. It could become embarrassing if one of the gentlemen mentioned his request to you."

Taking a breath, Augusta nodded. "Very well. Who are they?"

Matt looked down at a piece of paper on his desk. "Lord Lytton made an argument mostly consisting of how eligible he is and how highly you would be regarded as his countess."

Even if she was looking for a husband, his lordship was the last man she'd marry. "His lordship may find another lady, with my blessing. Just not any of my friends."

Matt's brows drew together. "I would have counseled against him in any event." He glanced at the paper again. "Lord Lancelot Somersby made an impassioned plea that I not deny his suit based on the fact that he is a younger son." Her brother cast his eyes at the ceiling. "And asked that I give you the book of poems he wrote for you." Sliding a journal across his desk, Matt heaved a hard put-upon sigh. "He is convinced that even though he has only seen you from afar—his words not mine—his poetry will convince you he is a perfect mawworm."

"He said he was a mawworm?" That was the oddest thing she had ever heard.

Leaning her elbow on the chair arm, Grace dropped her head into her hands and laughed. "Lord Lancelot said his poetry will convince you he is your perfect mate."

But who was Lord Lancelot? Gradually, an image of a very young man—although older than she—with blond curls, who always wore a medium blue satin jacket and breeches, came to her. "Is he even of age?"

"Yes." Matt groaned. "Barely. He also assured me that his father would approve, but in the event the duke did not, you and he could live comfortably on your dowry."

That was the most ridiculous proposal she had ever heard. Although she tried to maintain her placid demeanor, her lips started to twitch, and soon she was laughing so hard tears started in her eyes. She waved her hand in front of her face. "A book of poetry? To convince me to marry?"

Next to her, Grace went into whoops. Matt attempted a stern look, but the corners of his mouth betrayed him. Augusta did not know how she would look at poor Lord Lancelot and maintain her countenance.

"Shall we move on?" Matt asked, apparently having conquered his jollity. "*If* you were looking for a husband, the next two gentlemen would deserve some consideration, Lord Ailesbury and Mr. Seaton-Smythe."

"They are both very nice," she conceded. "My answer is still no." Matt opened a drawer and placed the paper in it. She waited until she had his attention again to ask, "Have you made a decision whether or not I may attend the University of Padua?"

"Absolutely not." Augusta groaned—this was becoming a family habit—as her mother swept into the study. "I would have thought that by now you would have got over this silly notion you have of attending a university in *Italy*."

"Patience." Matt's tone held a warning note Augusta had never heard him use with her mother. "It is my decision to make."

"You might be her guardian, but I am her mother." Mama blotted her eyes with a handkerchief. "I would never, never forgive you if anything happened to her." She dabbed her nose. "Not only that, but I would do my best to see Richard gained guardianship of Madeline and Theo."

How unfair that would be to the girls! Augusta slowly breathed in and out. Oh, God! Was it right of her to continue to insist she be allowed to go to Italy when it would harm her sisters? Theo would run away and who knew what Madeline was capable of. Augusta's heart lurched. Should she give up her desires for the good of her sisters?

Then it occurred to her, Theo was twelve and Madeline was fifteen. They were old enough to choose their guardian. Therefore, Mama could not make good on her threat.

"Patience, Matt has not made a decision one way or the other." Grace's calm voice seemed to lower the tension in the room. "And you know that if he allowed Augusta to go, she would have all the protection she required and more."

At that last part, her mother's face assumed a militant look. "No."

This was outside of enough! Mama wasn't even pretending she would consider Augusta going. Not only that, but Augusta realized that even if her mother couldn't gain custody of her sisters, she *could* make everyone's life difficult. "What do you have against my attending university?"

Mama's eyes softened. "My decision has nothing to do with your attending university." For a moment Mama appeared confused. "Although I do not understand your desire; if you could attend Oxford, Cambridge, or even St. Andrews, I would not object. In Italy, you would have no one of influence to protect you."

No one of influence. Hmm. That might be arranged. Augusta would contact Baron von Neumann. He had been extremely helpful in facilitating her contact with Professor Angeloni in Padua. "Is that your *only* concern?"

"Yes." Mama rubbed her forehead. "You seem to think it is an insignificant matter, but it is not. As you must realize, this discussion is at an end."

"Very well." Augusta knew her response had been ambiguous at best. "I was preparing to go shopping before I was called down here." She stood and curtseyed. "I shall see you later."

"Augusta." Her mother's voice stopped her as she reached the door. "Either Lord Ailesbury or Mr. Seaton-Smythe would be an excellent choice. Ailesbury is the heir to the Marquis of Alton, and Mr. Seaton-Smythe is the Duke of Lancaster's heir."

She took a deep breath and let it out. "I have no interest in either of them." She glanced at Matt. "Thank you for informing me of the offers."

For some reason tears pricked Augusta's eyes and she blinked them back. She would write the baron immediately. Surely he knew someone who could be a "person of influence" for her in Padua.

She had just placed the hat pin in her bonnet when a soft knock came on her chamber door. "Augusta, it is Grace."

The moment she entered the room, Augusta flew into her sister-in-law's arms. "Why is this so hard?"

"Sweetheart, it is never easy when a lady wishes to do something the rest of the world does not wish her to do."

She stood there for a while in her sister-in-law's comforting embrace. "I suppose not. I thought perhaps Baron von Neumann could help find a sponsor for me."

"Is he the one at the Austrian embassy?"

"Yes. I cannot think of anyone else."

Setting her back, Grace's lips tipped up. "We will call upon Lord and Lady Thornhill. They have traveled all over the world. They might know someone."

The Thornhills were considered odd by some, but their status was such they were allowed to do as they pleased. Other than when she spent time with Phinn, Lady Thornhill's salons were the only place Augusta did not have to hide herself. "That is an excellent idea! If the baron can't help me, she will surely be able to!"

"Tomorrow she is having another salon," Grace said. "We shall attend."

"Thank you so very much." The fear and tension that had gripped Augusta fled. Truly, she had the best sister-in-law anyone could ever have. "You seem to be the only one who understands how much this means to me."

Grace gave a wry smile. "I think Cousin Jane might have a good idea."

"You're right." As a young woman, Jane Carpenter fell in love with Hector Addison. Her father refused to allow them to marry, and Hector was sent to India. Jane defied her father and at the church altar rejected the gentleman her father wanted her to wed. Three years ago, Hector returned and they married.

"Now," Grace said, "put some cold water on your eyes and go shopping. Send the bills to me."

"Am I correct in thinking that Mama cannot take Madeline and Theo away from you and Matt?" That possibility was the one thing that could make her give up her scheme.

"Naturally, no one can predict the future, but first she'd have to convince Richard, and he knows as well as anyone that we could keep this in the courts until they were both married. The only reason Matt was able to move your guardianship along was due to my uncle."

"Thank you." Augusta hugged her sister-in-law again. Somehow, her dream would come true.

After several successful hours of shopping at Phaeton's Bazaar, in Bruton Street, and at Hatchards, Augusta had acquired new gloves, fashionable clocked stockings, several colors of ribbon, four new reticules, and three bonnets. Grace had been right. Shopping did make one feel better. Her friends had had similar luck. The day was pleasantly warm, and the sun was shining. Yesterday's rain seemed to have cleaned not only the air but the streets. Lilacs were in bloom and the trees green with new leaves.

"Shall we take a stroll in the Park?" Henrietta looked at her pin watch. "It is almost five o'clock."

"Not with our packages." Augusta glanced at their servants loaded down with their purchases.

"If I may, my lady." Augusta nodded to acknowledge Durant's query. "If you ladies would like to visit Gunter's, Fred"—he nodded to Henrietta's footman—"and I shall take the parcels to Worthington House and make arrangements for them to be delivered to the various houses."

"What a clever idea." She smiled at him. "Thank you."

One of the maids took out a pencil and marked the packages. Once that was accomplished, the footmen left. The rest of them were finishing their ices when the servants returned. She slipped Durant two guineas. "For ices after we return home. I'm sure Fred will want one as well."

"Thank you, my lady."

Her little group was halfway around the Park when a massive white stallion raced at them as if he was out of control. Other strollers scattered.

"Run!" Augusta yelled as she and her friends dashed behind the trees to keep from being trampled. Durant darted to her. "Stay where you are!"

Before she could even register there was a rider on the beast, Lord Lancelot threw himself to the ground and grabbed her hands. "My lady, you must allow me to address you. I have loved you—"

As she opened her mouth to give him a good set-down, the dunderhead rose in the air and landed several feet away. Lord Phineas stood over the recumbent form of Lord Lancelot with his booted foot planted squarely on the other man's chest, scowling. "You wet-behind-the-ears, knocked-in-the-cradle puppy." Lord Phineas's voice was as hard as stone. "When *I* allow you to rise, you will apologize to Lady Augusta for not only accosting and embarrassing her, but putting her life in danger with your reckless and abominable actions. Then you will go home and tell your father that you are too green to be allowed upon the Town. If I see you again, I shall not be nearly as kind as I am now. In that event, after I give you a little taste of home brew, I'll do myself the pleasure of calling upon your father and telling him what a spectacle you made of yourself." Lord Lancelot's face was red, his eyes were bulging with fear, and his lips moved like a fish. "Do you understand me?"

"Yes." He nodded his head several times. "I do. I-I was—"

"I have no desire to hear excuses from you." Lord Phineas's words were a low, icy, growl.

"Well," Dorie murmured. "I must say, I do not believe I have ever witnessed anything this impressive."

Augusta had to agree. "I am sure I have never seen anything quite like it."

"Only in books." Henrietta stared at the two men.

"Where the hero saves his lady love." Adeline sighed.

Augusta was very sure Lord Phineas did not love her, but he obviously had a chivalrous streak.

"But I love her," Lord Lancelot sputtered.

"You haven't even been introduced." Lord Phineas's tone was so dry she wanted a drink of lemonade. "Yet another reason you should not be allowed in Polite Society." Not permitting the young man to rise by himself, Lord Phineas grabbed Lord Lancelot's cravat and yanked him up. Lord Phineas then took the horse's reins and handed them to her footman. "Escort his lordship and his horse to the Duke of Kendal's house in St. James's Square. I shall ensure Lady Augusta arrives safely home."

Durant glanced at her.

"I'll be fine," she assured him. "If need be, my sister shall provide an escort home."

"Yes, my lady." He gave Lord Lancelot a disgusted look. "Come along, my lord."

It was not until they were walking away that she noticed the crowd that had gathered. A landau with four older ladies, including Lady Bellamny, had stopped. "Disgraceful." Her jet gaze followed Lord Lancelot. "I shall make a point of having a word with his mother." She glanced at Augusta. "He will not be welcome at any event this Season." Her ladyship surveyed the group of people gathered. "You may all depart."

"Thank you, ma'am." She watched as the carriage drove off and the on-lookers scattered.

Lord Phineas bowed. "I am sorry you had to be subjected to that worthless fribble."

"I must thank you for interceding." He did not even look as if he had exerted himself. "To be honest, I was not quite sure what to do."

"That's not surprising." He grinned, and his silver eyes sparkled with laughter. "I don't suppose they have lessons in what to do if an uncontrollable puppy in the shape of a man tries to propose in the middle of the Park."

"No." Augusta laughed. What a way to put the matter. He managed to take a bad situation and make it seem like a farce. "There was no relevant instruction."

"Shall I see you home or do you have sufficient company?" His eyes roamed her features as if to satisfy himself she was well.

"As I said before, I will return to Grosvenor Square with my friends. My sister shall see me home from there. Thank you for your assistance."

"My pleasure." He bowed again before strolling away as if nothing had occurred.

What a remarkable man. It was almost a shame she was not in the market for a husband.

Chapter Ten

Phinn's heart had jumped into his throat when that stupid cawker Lord Lancelot rode straight at Lady Augusta and the others. Fortunately, the women had the presence of mind to get out of the horse's way instead of wasting time going into hysterics.

But when the damned paper-skull leaped off his beast and grabbed her hand, Phinn had wanted nothing more than to plant the man a facer. That, however, would have just created even more of a scene. He'd half expected Lord Lancelot—whoever had given him that name in the first place should have expected trouble—to issue a challenge. Phinn was very glad when the halfling didn't seem to think about it.

He hoped the duke would send his errant offspring where the boy couldn't do any more harm to himself, others, and his family. Come to think of it, the idiot probably needed a profession. Nothing good ever came of allowing a young man to get up to his own devices.

Once Phinn got rid of the stripling and could turn his attention to Lady Augusta, he was amazed to find her unperturbed. He shouldn't have been. In their short acquaintance, she had always appeared perfectly rational. An excellent trait in a lady, especially one so young.

He would have rather remained with her, yet she didn't appear to need him. In keeping with his plan, Phinn never danced twice with Augusta at the same event over the past few weeks. He wished he could say the same about some of the other gentlemen. He chatted with her, but never longer than was proper, unlike Lytton, who appeared to be enamored with the sound of his own voice. Phinn waited for her to notice him as opposed to Bottomley, who raced up to her the moment he entered a room or garden. Seaton-Smythe had begun propping up walls and columns while he watched her every move, and someone had placed a wager at White's that Ailesbury was about to make an offer.

Phinn might have been concerned she was growing attached to one of the other men if not for the same expression of polite attention she wore with all the gentlemen except him. His chest swelled like a rooster's. When they were together, she talked about everything under the sun except for inane matters such as the weather. Very little did not interest her, and she never forgot what he or anyone else said. He'd thought that was great fun when she pointed out mistakes others made . . . until it was his turn. Then it was disconcerting.

After bidding her adieu, Phinn was making his way back to the curricle he'd been driving when a thought stopped him. He'd been very glad she was not panicked, but he did not like the fact she didn't seem to need him.

Giving himself a metaphorical shake, Phinn began walking again. He had to get Augusta out of his mind at least for a while. He was due to present his paper to the Royal Society in less than a week. He'd also been asked to present his findings to the Royal Institution.

Why was he even thinking about getting married? His brother had agreed that if he did not meet a lady he wanted, he could leave. Maybe the problem was what *he* had agreed to without thinking about it. Did his feelings—for lack of a better term—for Augusta mean he had to stay and see whatever it was through?

Part of himself thought this back-and-forth was ridiculous. Europe was waiting, and there was no reason he should not proceed as planned. Unlike many explorers, he had his own funds and was not required to find sponsors. The other part of himself knew if he were to marry, Augusta was exactly the type of lady who would hold his attention. To be truthful, she was the only lady he had ever met who engrossed him beyond a night of carnal pleasure. And he might not meet another lady like her.

In effect, his choices were between giving up a long-held dream and possibly not marrying a woman with whom he'd be happy.

A week later, after giving his paper to the Royal Society, Phinn arrived back at Dorchester House determined to find Boman and discover how the arrangements to depart were coming along. Phinn was no closer to making a decision than he had been earlier. But if he decided to wed, plans could be cancelled if need be. Yet, as he passed his sister-in-law's parlor, he heard a gut-wrenching sob, then another.

Damn him for a fool and an eavesdropper. Phinn did not want to know what could make the indomitable Helen cry.

Just then his brother walked out of the door, a grim look on his face.

Why had he stopped? He should have just gone to his room. "What's wrong? Is Helen ill?"

"Only if being sick at heart could be considered an illness." Dorchester regarded Phinn with a steady gaze. "In not providing me an heir, she feels she has failed me and the family. No matter how I try to persuade her that it is not her fault, she cannot be sanguine." His brother glanced over Phinn's shoulder. "Every once in a while, it becomes too much for her."

Bloody hell-hounds in Perdition! "I understand."

"Do you?" His brother raised a brow. "The fact that there is no next generation to carry on the title is tearing her apart. She has cause for her concern. Her father's title was almost lost due to the lack of an heir. It was nothing short of an act of God that after her father's death and eight daughters her mother gave birth to a son."

If only to lighten his brother's mood, or make himself feel better for planning to run off again, Phinn wanted to make a flippant reply. Yet it would not do. What he considered an unnecessary nuisance was for Dorchester and Helen a very real concern.

"Yes. I do." As much as Phinn would like to go on his merry way, there was his family to think about. What would happen if his brother and sister-in-law did not have a son and he died on his travels? There were cousins. But none of them were up to snuff and would most likely make a shambles of the marquisate. Well, there was nothing for it. However much he wished to wait, he had responsibilities to his family that surpassed his own desires. He would have to wed. "Now if you will excuse me. There are some matters to which I must attend."

Such as reconciling himself to giving up his dream

and working out how to convince Lady Augusta to accept him.

None of the other gentlemen had been successful in their pursuit of her. He had known they would not be. What he didn't understand was how the men thought she'd even think of marrying them.

She *did* like him. Of that he was sure. But was it enough to convince her to marry him? And if not, what was she looking for?

Two weeks later, Phinn didn't know if he was making progress in his courtship or not. They had danced several times, sometimes twice in an evening. Augusta had even allowed him to tool her around in his brother's curricle. They had discussed politics, families, the plight of the poor and what she was doing to help—making him feel as if he should be doing something more.

Once she discovered he owned an estate, they had discussed farming and management. She was as knowledgeable in those subjects as she was in everything else.

There were times he thought they would run out of topics to discuss, but they never did. Yet, he still felt as if she was holding something back. As he was himself. And, although he'd also conversed with other ladies— he had to have something to do while waiting to dance with Augusta—he was certain if he had to marry, she was the only woman he could stand to wake up to each morning.

Except for the muffled sounds of fires being built back up, the house was still quiet when Phinn strode to the stables, excited to give his new bay, Pegasus, a try. The grooms were already awake. An older man he recognized as Ryan, the stable master, stopped his conversation with one of the younger grooms. "I suppose you want to take your new lad out, my lord?"

"That's exactly what I wish to do." Phinn went over to his horse, which came right up to him, and he handed the beast a carrot, then he stroked the horse's neck. "How are you this morning, boy?"

"Right proper gentleman he is," the stable master said. "I'll get him ready for ye."

"I can do it," Phinn offered, only to be given a sour look that informed him he knew better than to do a servant's work. "You know I am capable of saddling my own horse. You taught me."

"Be that as it may, my lord. You shouldn't get in the habit of it." The stable master strode off toward the tack room.

Well, that told him. A few minutes later, he had to admit, Ryan was much faster. Phinn swung into the saddle. "Thank you."

"Go easy with him until you two get to know the other."

For a moment, he felt like a child receiving instruction again. "Don't worry, I shall."

He entered the Park and immediately saw Augusta riding a pretty gray mare. Her sister, the duchess, and a groom accompanied her.

Phinn cantered toward them. "Good morning."

"Good morning to you." Her smile lit the cloudy day, making his heart lighter. "I did not know you rode this early."

He hadn't until he'd discovered *she* did. "I didn't have a hack before. My brother finally dragged me to Tattersalls."

"That was nice of him. Ladies are not allowed to attend the sales." Augusta turned her attention to his horse. "He's a handsome boy. What is his name?"

"Pegasus. There seem to be a lot of things ladies aren't allowed to do."

"Yes." Augusta sighed. "I was told that the Aztec women were equal with the men until the Spanish conquered them."

"You are correct. Yet, there is one thing you can be thankful for," he said, trying to cheer her up. "The Spanish are much worse when it comes to their women than we are."

"I should be happy my family allows me to do as much as I have." Urging her horse into a trot, she threw him a strained smile. "Let's gallop."

A short run wouldn't harm his horse. He took off after her. She reached the end of the path ahead of him. "Thank you for that. It's been a long time since I've been able to ride as fast as I wished."

"She runs like the wind." Her gray mare tossed her head as if she knew she was special. "What do you call her?"

"Zephyr." Reaching down, Augusta stroked the horse's neck. When she glanced at him, her eyes were alight with laughter. "Being able to run as fast as one wishes is one of the benefits of rising early."

They began walking the horses back to where her sister waited. "I am glad you came out this morning."

"I am as well."

Augusta's enticing, dark pink lips captured his attention. He wished they were alone. He'd lift her down from her horse and kiss her until they were both out of breath. "Lady Augusta"—she turned her head toward him—"would you call me Phinn? Only when we are alone, of course." He gave her what he hoped was a boyish grin. "I like it so much better than Lord Phineas, and I feel as if we've become friends."

"Only if you call me Augusta." For a second she

dropped her gaze from his as if she felt shy. He'd never seen her do that before. It was charming. "I feel as if we are good enough friends too."

"Thank you. I shall be careful not to abuse your trust." The duchess was riding toward them. "I think you are about to be told it's time to leave."

She followed his gaze. "I suppose I am. I shall see you later."

As often as he could manage. "I wish you a good day."

"You too." She rode toward her sister, leaving him behind.

What would it be like to wake up with her each morning and have a different kind of ride? The thought of her dark curls spread over a pillow and her sleepy, lustful, lapis-blue eyes gazing at him caused him to have to adjust his position. Phinn remembered what his brother said about a lust match—one could just as well say being in lust—and that being a perfectly good way to begin a marriage.

There was no doubt he wanted Augusta in his bed, and that had nothing to do with mere friendship. He liked everything about her. Perhaps he was wasting time courting her and should simply propose.

An hour later, he strolled into the breakfast room. Before he could take his plate to the sideboard, his sister-in-law said, "We are attending Lady Thornhill's drawing room." Helen glanced up from her newssheet. "She attracts a diverse group of guests. She was also close friends with Lady Worthington's mother."

Meaning the lady was to be forgiven for attracting different sorts of people? Or that Lady Augusta would probably be there. "Very well. What time are we expected?"

"Most guests tend to wander in an out at will. I believe we should leave here around three o'clock. It is not far.

That will give us enough time to converse with anyone we wish before the Promenade."

When they arrived, he was surprised that the butler did no more than lead them to the door of what, at first, appeared to be a huge drawing room. Yet, upon a closer look, he realized that two rooms had been put together by virtue of an open pair of pocket doors.

Beside him, his sister-in-law sighed. "I do not understand why they must wear clothing they found during their travels."

He followed her gaze to a couple he guessed to be in their late forties or early fifties who were dressed in brightly colored and embroidered long robes. "They look like Chinese robes."

"I have no idea." She took a breath. "Come, I shall introduce them."

A few moments later he was greeting Lady Thornhill. "It is a pleasure to finally meet you, Lord Phineas. I have heard you visited Mexico."

Had Augusta told her? "I understand you have toured abroad a good deal as well."

"We have been extremely fortunate in that regard." She waved him to a recently vacated chair. "Please tell me about the Aztecs. I have never been to the Americas."

For the next half hour he explained the culture and buildings of the Indian nation. "I was surprised to see so much of it remained after the Spanish arrived."

She pursed her lips. "It is a travesty that many countries seeking new territories destroy or come close to destroying the indigenous populations and their societies. I was at first surprised that the Chinese kept foreigners out, but I came to understand that they wish to protect themselves."

"I cannot disagree. Had the Aztecs done the same, they would not be under Spanish rule."

Her ladyship rose. "I have kept you long enough. Please, introduce yourself to the other guests. We do not stand on ceremony here." A faint crease formed between her dark brows. "The only exception is that if you wish to meet a young lady, come to me and I will introduce you."

He doubted if there were any young ladies he would wish to meet, but in this gathering it was possible. "Thank you."

He was having a conversation with two French artists when one of them exclaimed, "Ah, the terrifying and beautiful Lady Augusta has arrived."

Phinn raised his quizzing glass. That's what he thought other men would think, but one must depress pretentions. "Terrifying?"

"Ah, *monsieur*, have you ever attempted to flirt with a lady who remembers everything one says?" The man shuddered. "It is *très déconcertant*." The man shrugged lightly. "But one must fall in love with her, one cannot help oneself."

Augusta caught Phinn's gaze and started toward him. When she arrived at his side, Phinn took her hand, raising it to his lips. Pink washed her cheeks, and the corners of her lips tipped up. "I see you have already met Monsieur Boudin?"

"I have." The Frenchman made an exaggerated bow to her, and she inclined her head. Phinn wanted to roll his eyes. "He tells me he is an artist."

She raised one brow. "I suppose we must take his word."

"Mademoiselle, you are cruel. I merely require inspiration. If you would pose for me—"

"The chance of that ever happening is highly unlikely," she said in an arid tone. Augusta placed the tips of her fingers on Phinn's arm, and he felt the warmth of her touch. "Shall we mingle with the other guests?"

"As you wish." He allowed himself to be led off. "I take it you are not enamored of Monsieur Boudin?"

"I thought he was much more charming when I barely knew him." Her tone was even, but there was a hint of something stronger. "He claims to be a painter, yet no one has ever seen him produce even a sketch, even when offered the possibility of a commission."

No wonder Augusta frightened the man. She caught all his lies. This called for a change of subject. "I take it Lady Thornhill usually wears foreign costumes for her drawing rooms."

That made Augusta smile. "She does. My sisters said she even wears them when she gives her ball."

"That would be remarkable." His sister-in-law would disapprove of that even more. "I hope I'm invited."

"I am sure you will be." She paused for a moment. "It is not until later in the Season."

If his brother had his way, he'd still be here, and with luck, he would be betrothed to Augusta. Thus far, he had not found anything about her to dislike, and there were a great many things to like. Life with her would never be boring.

"I take it you plan to be in England for the nonce?" They had arrived at a window seat. She arranged the cushions and took a seat.

Phinn lowered himself onto the chair next to the window. "I suppose I shall."

"It is a shame you cannot study the great cathedrals on the Continent."

He thought so too. Did she wish to travel? Augusta never said she did, but she must. There was a restlessness in her to which a part of him responded. "Someday I will. Would you like to go for a carriage ride with me tomorrow?"

She gave him a cheerless look. "I am promised to

Lord Bottomley tomorrow, Mr. Seaton-Smythe today, and Lord Tillerton the day after tomorrow."

Phinn didn't know why Seaton-Smythe continued to pay court to her. "All that doesn't seem to make you very happy." Although, Phinn was extremely pleased about it. She always enjoyed being with him. "Why do you go?"

"My mother expects it of me." She grimaced. "It would appear odd if I did not."

"You certainly do not wish to appear odd." A month ago he would have thought that was funny, but not any longer. He knew too well how vicious the *ton* could be.

"It is only at an event like this I can be myself."

She still hadn't agreed to a carriage ride with him. "May I take you on a ride in three days?"

"No." She grinned. "But I would be pleased to have you accompany me."

"That is even better." Phinn was glad he had made her smile.

Even more than before, he knew they could be happy together. He would ask Augusta to marry him soon.

Chapter Eleven

A soft breeze rustled through the trees. Augusta gazed after Phinn as he rode out of the Park. Ever since the day he had asked her to call him by his first name, he had ridden at the same time she did. Her groom kept a respectful distance, allowing her and Phinn to ride as fast as they wished and talk about anything and everything. Yet this morning, her sister decided to join her for a ride.

Louisa remained beside Augusta when she started toward Berkeley Square. "My groom can see me home."

"I am sure he can." Surprisingly, Louisa was silent for at least three heartbeats. "You and Lord Phineas appear to be getting on well. I take it you've seen each other since the last time I was with you."

"We are friends." Thankfully, *he* had not asked to marry her. When her sister remained silent, she said, "We have a lot in common."

"You have turned down several proposals. Have you thought about finding a husband?"

"Not yet." She really wished Louisa would not pursue this topic. "I still wish to attend university."

Louisa blew out a puff of air. "I know that Mama said you would not be allowed to travel to Italy."

"Without a sponsor. I am making inquiries." Augusta had sent letters to Baron von Neumann, and he had, indeed, found a family willing to sponsor her.

"Do you truly think that will be enough?" Her sister looked at her as if she'd lost her mind. "Augusta, she is dead set against this idea of yours."

She did not wish to have this discussion. "If Italy is too far, there is a university in Holland I can attend as well."

"If for some reason"—her sister brought one hand up and around in an arc as if encompassing the world—"you cannot attend university, would you look upon Lord Phineas as a possible match?"

"I am quite sure he does not want me as a wife." Yes, they got along well, more than well, and he was very handsome. She liked the way his eyes turned to silver when he was angry or laughing. But he had never given her the idea that he was singling her out for special attention. Oh, he'd danced with her twice some evenings, but so had other men. And unlike the other gentlemen, he had not sent her flowers, or poems, nor given her compliments on her beauty. "I am sure you are seeing what you want to see." Unless their mother had put Louisa up to this. "Or what Mama wishes to see."

"Very well. I shall leave you here." They had reached the corner of Mount Street and Carlos Place. It was a short enough distance for Louisa to ride by herself.

"I'll see you at Mama's garden party today." Augusta did not want to be at odds with her sister.

"Think about what I said." Louisa rode off, but glanced back over her shoulder. "We only want you to be happy."

Augusta did not understand why her mother and sister—and who knew who else—thought marrying and having children before she had an opportunity to attend university would make her happy.

Later that morning, Augusta was once again summoned to Matt's study.

There could not possibly be *more* proposals. She groaned. How many men thought she wished to marry them? Yet what else could it be? Until she had someone to sponsor her in Padua, he could not address her attending university. And the only time he asked her to meet with him in his study was because of offers she had received.

Augusta considered writing him a note, instructing him to tell everyone she was not interested in marriage, and to send her the names. Still, *he* was the one who'd had to sit through the interviews. It was the least she could do to listen to him recount them.

Augusta made her way down the corridor to his study at the back of the house and knocked on the door. "Come."

Entering, she took a seat in a leather chair in front of his desk. The scent of lilacs drifted in through the open windows leading to the garden.

He held up a sheet of paper with three names. At the rate this was going, she would not have anyone with whom to dance. "Who are they this time?"

"Fotheringale, Belmont, and Turner." Matt put the paper down, and his steady gaze seemed to accuse her of wrongdoing. "This did not happen with Louisa, Dotty, or Charlotte."

"Don't look at me as if it is my fault." Augusta could not for her life figure out why so many gentlemen wanted to wed her. "I am polite, but have given no gentleman any possible reason to think I might accept a proposal of marriage from him. I do not even go strolling to have a conversation with a gentleman."

Except for Phinn. They, though, were strictly friends, and she was glad for his companionship. "And the only topic of conversation I have ever discussed with any of them is the weather, themselves, or what they think."

"That's probably it." Her brother heaved a sigh. "Not many men can resist a beautiful lady with a good dowry who allows them to talk about themselves."

She took a few moments to consider what he said. "Mayhap I am being too accommodating. If I was looking for a husband, I would be much harder on the gentlemen. They are obviously taking my indifference in the wrong way."

"The bright side is this cannot continue much longer." Matt's lips pulled up in a sorry excuse for a smile. "There will soon be no eligible gentlemen left who have not asked to marry you."

"Thank you for putting up with this." She was glad she did not have to do it.

"For better or worse, it is my duty." He placed the piece of paper in a drawer. "You will tell me if there is anyone I should not refuse?"

"Yes, of course. There will not be anyone." If there were no more suitable gentlemen, her difficulty with her mother would soon end. Mama could not expect her to wed if there was no one eligible left. "Mama wants me to help her with her party today, and there are some things I must complete before I go."

"At least the weather is cooperating. Have a good time. Grace and I will come by for a while." His forehead creased for a moment. "You do know that she only wants what is best for you?"

"What she *thinks* is best for me," Augusta countered. "Yes, I know."

She went to her brother and bussed his cheek. "You are the kindest of brothers."

"I do my poor best. Go have fun."

Phinn nervously paced his bedchamber. Today was the day he would ask Augusta to marry him. That they were on a first-name basis, where no one could overhear them, should have been reassuring but wasn't. They had not had what could even remotely be considered a romantic moment. They *had* grown closer. And friendship was an excellent basis for a marriage. To use his brother's term, he lusted after her. Creating the heir so desperately needed would be no hardship. In fact, the more he thought of her, the more he wanted to sink into her warmth, kiss her until her lips were swollen and her eyes glazed with passion.

He could not imagine life with Augusta would be at all dull. Perhaps someday, after they had children, and the children were old enough, they could travel to Europe. He still wanted to study the medieval churches and other architecture.

Unlike the other gentlemen who'd proposed to her, Phinn would encourage her to continue her correspondence with professors and knowledgeable people. He was sure no other gentleman could or would promise her that.

He shrugged off the guilt dogging him that he was not speaking to her brother first. That was how one properly made an offer to a lady. Yet from what he'd heard, that hadn't done any of the gentlemen who had already asked her much good. None of them had got past Worthington.

Phinn had been present for many of the wagers at

his club concerning who Augusta would marry, and the drunken ramblings that ensued when the gentlemen had been turned down. He knew approximately how many men had asked for her hand and had received an immediate rejection from her brother.

He'd gently probed a few of the gentlemen concerning their delusions about her, when they were in their cups, but they were largely unintelligible.

Finally, one night, Seaton-Smythe said, "She listens to a man. Never interrupts. Makes him feel special."

Listens? Well, yes, she had to in order to make her erudite comments and clever counterpoints. Yet he would be astonished if any of these gentlemen had that type of conversation with her.

"Makes one feel as if he is the only one who has her attention," Lord Gray, the most recent gentleman to be rejected, had mumbled into his brandy.

"Not even my mistress listens as well as Lady Augusta." The Earl of Tillerton poured himself another glass of wine. "Makes all the appropriate responses, doesn't interrupt one." He took a drink. "Seaton-Smythe's right. Makes a gentleman feel special."

Bloody idiots.

Apparently, only Phinn knew exactly what Augusta had been doing. Ignoring the sapskulls. She was more than clever enough to listen with a small part of her brain while she was doing something else with the other part. Translating ancient Hebrew or something more esoteric.

For a brief second, he thought about disabusing them of their notions about Augusta, but it wouldn't do any good, and it might harm her reputation if the gentlemen knew she had not been paying attention to them at all. The *ton* could be vicious with those who didn't fit the mold in which a person was put. And she had done her best to appear to be exactly what she was not, a demure young lady. Not for the first time Phinn knew he had been right when he'd told his sister-in-law Augusta would terrify these men if they actually knew her.

What he did not comprehend was her brother's swift rejection of all the gentlemen who had proposed. From all accounts, Worthington had not even taken the time to ask her if she would accept the offers. It was almost as if he did not want her to wed. Yet from what Helen had relayed to him about Lady Wolverton's wishes, that didn't make sense. She was determined to see Augusta married. Did Augusta know her brother had rejected so many proposals? That was a ridiculous question. Of course she did. Still, a question Phinn could not quite formulate hovered just out of reach.

Confound it all. Propriety and Worthington be hanged. If Augusta rejected Phinn, he was going to have a reason, and it wouldn't be that she had no attraction to him.

Turning his mind to the task at hand, he took out the piece of paper Helen had given him. She'd visited Lady Wolverton several times and had drawn him a detailed plan of the garden. The area was not wide, but it was long. There were several private paths and a secluded rose bower along the stone wall at the end of one of the paths. He tapped the alcove. That is where he would propose. They would be sufficiently far from the rest of the guests to have a private conversation.

He sent a prayer to whatever deity chose to listen to him that Augusta would accept his offer. Otherwise, he didn't know what he was going to do. There was no other he could imagine waking up to in the morning.

A knock sounded on the door. "Phineas," Helen said. "It is time to depart."

He took one last look in the mirror. It was now or never. "I'm ready."

The moment Phinn arrived at Lady Wolverton's garden party his gaze was immediately drawn to Augusta. How he had found her in the throng of guests, he didn't know. It was as though he was always aware of her and had been for a few weeks.

True to his sister-in-law's drawing, the garden had been designed in a series of beds, paths, and fountains. Roses, underplanted with lavender and edged with boxwood, scented the air. A marble fountain of a woman pouring water from a jug, which had probably originated in Italy, gurgled softly, barely discernible under the voices of those present. Three paths led from the fountain deeper into the garden.

He made his way toward her through the swarm of people, greeting those he knew as he went. Occasionally, one of the matchmaking mamas tried to inveigle him into conversation with their daughters. It was an ill-kept secret that he might be responsible for the next heir. Fortunately, he had become an expert at discussing the weather for a few moments and moving on.

As usual, Augusta was surrounded by her circle of friends. "Ladies." He bowed. "How delightful to see you."

Shortly after they had greeted him, several other gentlemen joined their set, and one by one, they took the ladies off to stroll around the garden until only Phinn and Augusta were left.

Glancing around, he made sure no one was in hearing distance. "Augusta, would you like to walk with me?" After they were betrothed he wouldn't mind seeing more of the garden. But right now he had to make his offer before he lost his chance. They wouldn't be left alone for long. "It is lovely here."

"It is." She placed her fingers on his arm and grinned.

"My sister-in-law's great-grandmother planted it. Then her grandmother, mother, and Grace contributed."

As it usually did, Augusta and Phinn's conversation deepened as they discussed the plantings, their origins, and the design. More than one gentleman caught his eye as dubious brows were raised. Lord Gray snickered behind his hand.

Finally, Phinn and Augusta were on the path to the rose arbor. Plants thick with leaves and blooms muffled the voices. When they arrived, he maneuvered himself so that he was facing her, and dropped to one knee. "Augusta."

"Oh, good Lord!" Shock and something between disappointment and horror appeared on her face. Tears pooled in her eyes. This was not at all the reaction he'd expected. "Not you too!"

She turned on her heel and started back up the path toward the house, then stopped and headed down a side path.

What the devil! For a moment her outburst had him rooted in place. Of all the things she could have said . . . What the hell had gone wrong? Perhaps the better question was why she had reacted so strongly. Had someone hurt her? If any man had laid a hand on her, Phinn would find the blackguard and kill him. On second thought, Worthington would have already seen to the cur's death.

He hastened his steps. "Augusta, wait!" Her shoulders hunched around her ears as if to ward his words away. "Couldn't you have at least let me finish what I had to say?"

She whirled around, almost bumping into him, her face a mask of fury. "Oh, was I wrong? Were you *not* going to ask me to wed you?"

"I was. I am asking you to marry me." He raked his

fingers through his hair, knocking his hat off. "I know you rejected the other fellows, but we are friends. *Good* friends."

"Yes, we are. And I *trusted* you." Her eyes again filled with tears she blinked back. "That is exactly the reason you should not be proposing to me."

He reached out, wanting to comfort her, but she whipped her hands behind her back. She was acting as if he'd betrayed her. God help him, he felt like the worst bounder in England. Yet, he couldn't give up. Not now. "Being friends is an excellent reason to wed."

"Phinn, even if you loved me"—her voice hitched on a sob—"which you do not, I shall not marry this Season. I have been accepted to the University of Padua."

"*University?*" All the air in his body rushed out, as if he'd been punched by Jackson himself, leaving Phinn dizzy and making it hard to speak. "In Padua," he croaked, barely able to get the words out. "*Italy?*"

Her chin firmed, and she nodded.

Suddenly the difference in the way her family was behaving made sense. There was a schism. Worthington supported Augusta's wish, while Lady Wolverton was doing her best to thwart Augusta's dream by getting her married. To Phinn.

Naturally, she wouldn't have told anyone outside her immediate family about wanting to attend university. Well, perhaps her particular female friends. They seemed to look out for one another. He wished she would have told him and was a little hurt that she hadn't. Yet, despite how close they'd become, the fact he was a man might be the reason. Very few people in the *ton* would understand or approve of her goals.

Her hopes of attending the university were not at all unfounded. Padua had admitted a lady. Granted it had been almost two hundred years ago, but it *had* happened, and with the proper pressure the university could do so again, and apparently had.

Hell and damnation! Now what was he to do? How was he to convince her to marry him? There was no way he could compete with studying in Italy. Not for a female of her intellect. For that matter, Phinn wouldn't stay for him either.

Chapter Twelve

"Yes, Italy," Augusta said. Why could Phinn have not approached her brother like the rest of them had? Yet, even if any of the others had asked her directly, rejecting him was still so much harder than with any other gentleman.

She liked him a great deal. Under different circumstances, she might even fall in love with him. . . .

Thinking about all of this was useless. She was going to Padua to study. Once she finished, then she'd marry and not before. If any gentleman could understand her need to attend university, Phinn should. Given time.

He opened his mouth as if to speak. Although it could have been his jaw dropping.

Nevertheless, what she had to say must be said before this went any further. She tried to soften her tone. "I am not stupid. I know that you need a wife to produce an heir. You have four nieces, and the only possible reason Lady Dorchester could have for introducing you to eligible ladies is that she wants you to marry. And the only reason for that is because she has not had a son. Am I wrong?"

"You are the least stupid person of my acquaintance.

And you are correct." Phinn gave her a rueful look before raking his fingers through his hair again. Mussing it enough that she wanted to smooth the parts that were standing up. "If you marry me, we could still travel. I want to study the architecture on the Continent."

That might be what he thought they could do, but it was unlikely. "I know what happens when a lady marries." He looked so hopeful she could barely meet his gaze. "She has babies. Grace has even had two, and she has only been married for three years. And as much as I love my nieces and nephews, having a child would prevent me from doing what I need to do." Phinn stood so still his feet might have grown into the earth, like the plantings around them. "I *am* sorry. You will have to find another lady to give your family its heir."

As she brushed past him he still did not move. At least he understood. Or she hoped he did. She wandered through the garden in no hurry to return to her mother's party. She was sure Mama and Lady Dorchester knew he meant to propose. It might be cowardly, but Augusta did not wish to see either of them when they found out she had rejected him. Perhaps the best course of action was to slip around to the side door and avoid the guests.

A strong hand gripped her arm. Well, she should not have expected Phinn to remain where he was forever. He turned her to face him. She had never seen him look so serious. "You said you know I don't love you. How do you know?"

They were so close she had to lean her head back to meet his gaze. His eyes reminded her of clouds before a storm. She took a breath. How she'd miss his company. Yet, even very intelligent men could be so stupid about some things. "You do not act as if you love me." He opened his lips, and she rushed on. "And no, I am not going to tell you what gentlemen in love do because I do not want you to just start behaving as though you love me." From what she'd heard, that had happened to Elizabeth Harrington. It would not happen to Augusta.

Phinn stepped closer and the warmth of his body called to her. Even if he loved her, nothing could change. She had to go. Seeing the hurt in his face made her heart ache. Augusta made a point of glaring at his fingers. "I am leaving."

He dropped his hand as if it had been burned. "Very well. I suppose I shall see you again before you depart."

"I do not think it can be avoided." She still had the rest of the Season to get through. This, then, was the end of their friendship. Despite what he said, Phinn would never want to talk to her again. Only one of the other gentlemen who had proposed wished to even dance with her. Augusta shoved down the grief welling up inside her. She could not think about that now. She'd said what she had to. That was the end of it.

Taking the path along one side of the garden, she hurried past the kitchen door, down the sidewalk and into the square. She met Grace crossing the square from Worthington House to Stanwood House.

Grace's brows snapped together. "Sweetheart, what is the matter? You look as if you have lost your best friend."

In a way Augusta had. She blinked hard several times to keep the tears at bay. Why did she all of a sudden want to cry? She'd never been a watering pot, or dramatic. This was exhausting. "I thought you were at Mama's party."

"I went back to look in on Elizabeth. She was fussy earlier." Grace took Augusta's arm. "Come with me. Whatever it is, a nice cup of tea and some conversation will help."

She would have to confess everything to Grace. Yet better to her than to anyone else.

A few minutes later they were seated in her study, the tea tray on the table between them. Since they had moved into Worthington House two years ago, this was the room in which all the family discussions took place. Before, it had been Grace's study in Stanwood House.

She handed Augusta a cup. "Now then, what has happened to upset you?"

Rubbing a finger along the rim of the fine bone china, she said, "Phinn, Lord Phineas, proposed, and I told him I would not marry him because I am going to Italy to university. I know Mama said I could not, and she is making it difficult for Matt. Still, there must be some way for me to attend. I received a letter the other day from Baron von Neumann. He knows of a family who he is sure will sponsor me in Padua." Augusta raised her head to look at her sister-in-law. "That was Mama's stipulation, and I have met it."

"You like Lord Phineas a great deal," Grace said. Did she really want Augusta to marry as well?

"Yes, but I want to attend university before I marry. Aside from that"—his admitting he didn't love her, or not telling her she was wrong, which was just as good as an admission, hurt more than she had realized—"he does not love me."

"You are certain?"

"Yes. He said as much."

"I see." Grace sipped her tea for a few moments. Her forehead creased as it did when she was thinking. Finally she set the cup down. "Jane and Hector are going to tour Europe. She asked if you wish to go with them. However, I have not mentioned it because your mother has been so against you attending university, and I thought her objections might extend to traveling to the Continent in general." This was the perfect solution to everything. Augusta wanted to jump up and hug her sister-in-law. "I think now might be a good time to tell your mother about the invitation. If you want to accompany them, there is no saying that they might be able to arrange to be in Padua before the term begins, and deliver you to your sponsors."

"Yes. Yes, of course I wish to go. I cannot believe you are so devious!" Augusta rushed around the table and threw herself into Grace's arms.

"Ah, well." Grace hugged Augusta. "One cannot raise this many children without being a little conniving."

Not to mention the fierce fight Grace had had in gaining guardianship of her brothers and sisters before marrying Matt. "When do I leave?"

"In about a week. Hector has already made all the arrangements. All you need to do is pack and order some sturdier shoes. You will require trunks. Matt will arrange your passport. We shall see if Madame Lisette can make you another carriage gown or two. You'll stay with the Harringtons in Paris for a few weeks. If you need additional traveling garments, they can be obtained there."

Augusta felt her eyes widening. "How long have you known about this?"

"Several days. Enough time to send a letter off by special messenger to Elizabeth Harrington, and receive her answer. She is delighted at the prospect of seeing you."

How had Augusta been so lucky to have her brother marry such a wonderful woman? "Does Matt know?"

Her sister-in-law made a face. "Only as much as he wanted to know. He will not lie to your mother. At this point, he is only aware that you have been invited to go to Paris. I imagine after she finds out you have turned Lord Phineas down, Patience will be happy to see you leave Town for a while." Grace released Augusta from her embrace. "I'll tell Matt everything once you depart Paris."

It was settled then. Augusta was going to Europe, and Jane and Hector would escort her to Padua. Augusta would stay with the family who had agreed to sponsor her. She had to write to Cousin Prudence and notify the baron.

The tension drained from her body. Soon she would attend university, and even her mother could not object. Well, Mama could, but from England.

A knock sounded on the door to Grace's study. "Come."

Thorton entered and bowed. "My lady, Lady Wolverton wishes to speak with Lady Augusta."

"I cannot believe she left her guests to come here." This was not at all good.

"Please send her in and bring more tea." Grace signaled to Augusta to sit beside her. "Remember to remain calm."

"I shall." She hastily picked up her cup and moved it to the other side of the table.

A moment later, Mama swept into the room, her muslin skirts swirling around her legs. One brow was raised and her lips flattened. Augusta had never seen her mother so angry.

"Augusta Catherine Anne Vivers, I cannot believe you lied to poor Lord Phineas. I have told you before you shall *not* attend university in Italy or anywhere else."

At least her mother was not angry about her refusing his suit. She slid a quick glance at Grace, and decided to keep her mouth shut.

"Patience." Grace motioned to the other sofa. "Please have some tea."

"Yes, of course." Mama blinked as if just realizing

there was someone else present. "I apologize for my temper. It has been a trying day." Perfectly composed, Mama sank onto the flowered chintz cushions. "Now, I believe we should discuss Augusta's falsehood. I know you must agree with me that she should not have said what she did."

A fresh tea tray arrived, and Grace poured them each a cup. "How did the subject come up?"

"Lady Dorchester was expecting Lord Phineas to propose." Mama cut Augusta an angry look. "They seemed to get on so well, we all believed she would accept his suit. When Lord Phineas returned from his stroll without Augusta, Lady Dorchester asked what had occurred. He told her that Augusta did not wish to marry because she has been accepted to university and intends to travel to Padua." Mama took a large breath. "Naturally, everyone around us heard him."

Grace's mouth and brows drew down. "That will be all over Town by this evening."

"I do not know what to do," Mama complained. "She has turned down at least ten gentlemen, and now everyone will believe she is a bluestocking. Gossip like this does *not* fade. She will never find a husband!"

"Mama, you said I should not feel bound to wed this Season," Augusta said, keeping her tone calm.

"That is not the point!" her mother snapped. "You already have a reputation of being hard to please, and now you have made it worse." Her mother rubbed her forehead. "This is not something you can overcome with time."

No one spoke for a few moments, and she wondered how her sister-in-law would broach her going to Europe.

"I have an idea." Grace balanced her cup on her lap. "My cousin Jane and her husband are making a trip to Paris." Augusta watched Mama as Grace spoke. There was no change in her expression. "They have asked if Augusta would like to join them. Lady Harrington has also expressed a wish that Augusta visit her."

All perfectly true, just not the whole story. Of course, Grace hadn't mentioned where they might go from Paris. Not only that, but Augusta *had* complied with her mother's demand that someone of consequence sponsor her. An Italian count and countess must have enough status. And her mother would not be able to blame Matt, because he didn't know.

"As it stands, I suppose I have no choice but to agree. It would be much better for her to leave Town for a while." Mama sighed. "Perhaps some time in France will rid her of this ludicrous desire to attend university." She moved from rubbing her forehead to rubbing her temple. "When do they depart?"

"In a week. Hector has arranged for a private yacht to carry them across. The traveling coaches and horses will be waiting for them in Calais." Grace smiled reassuringly at Mama. "He has been planning this for some time. They will have a fairly large retinue, and he will not stint on comfort or safety. Augusta will be well chaperoned. I'll also send her maid, footman, and groom with her."

She was about to add that Cousin Prudence would be there as well, but thought it better to allow Grace to handle Mama.

Mama rose gracefully from the sofa, her tea untouched. "Very well, I shall not object. Augusta"—her mother gave her a disgruntled look—"I will see you before you depart."

"Yes, Mama." Augusta managed to make her voice sound meek when she wanted to shout with joy.

Once the door closed and her mother's steps could no longer be heard, she breathed a sigh of relief. "She really is furious. Should I cry off from my entertainments this week?"

"She is indeed, but her anger will not last long." Grace drank the rest of her tea. "No. You are not in disgrace, and we do not need more talk. I shall look over the invitations and decide which events you will attend. I fully suspect news of your journey to Europe will get out shortly." She grinned. "In fact, I would be very much surprised if your mother does not mention your travel plans when she returns to her garden party. Once that happens, no one will expect you to be gadding around Town as you have been doing."

The elation of the coming trip dissipated, and Augusta began to feel a twinge of regret for disappointing her mother. "I am sorry to have caused so much trouble."

"Sweetheart, you are no trouble at all. You simply wish for something different than your mother wants for you." Grace put her arm around Augusta. "Everything will work out just as it is meant to. I have reason to believe it always does."

If only she could be as sanguine. "Will Jane and Hector think I am odd to wish to attend university?"

"Maybe a little." Grace patted Augusta's back. "It is not something a well-bred young lady normally wishes to do, but I'll speak with Jane. Once she understands, she will support you. After all, she defied my family and stood by me."

"And Hector has traveled the world."

"He has. More importantly, he, like Dotty's father, is a true Radical. His travels have convinced him that all men and women should be able to have a say in government."

Matt strolled into the study. "I just spoke with Patience. She said Augusta would join Jane and Hector."

Matt glanced at Augusta. "Based on the talk that has started at Stanwood House, that's probably a good idea."

"Talk?" Grace raised a brow.

"Lady Thornhill and Lord Phineas are attempting to turn the conversation, but he made the mistake of blurting out that Augusta wished to attend university."

She hung her head. Her mother had been correct. She was going to be branded a bluestocking, if not worse. "I might not have any invitations to accept."

"I'm certain your mother will do everything she is able to suppress the gossip."

"If you're sure you wish to go, I must send for my solicitor. Hector will have to be given power of attorney over you."

Augusta had been so focused on her desires, she hadn't thought about how her life would change. She would miss her family, but traveling to the Continent, being able to attend university, were dreams come true. She would not give them up. And despite what her mother said, surely the right gentleman would be there when she was ready to wed. That gentleman was just not Phinn.

Chapter Thirteen

"Phineas." Helen's voice stopped him as he tried to surreptitiously depart from Stanwood House. "What has happened? Where is Lady Augusta?"

That's what he wanted to know. Damn, he did not want to answer either of those questions. "Lady Augusta rejected my proposal." That should keep his sister-in-law from asking any further questions. "I do not know where she is."

"But I do not understand." A slight frown turned the corners of Helen's mouth down. "You appear to get on so well."

Apparently, she was not going to let this go. He glanced around. If he kept his voice down, chances were no one would hear him. "Lady Augusta is not going to marry anyone. She has made plans to attend university in Italy."

"University!" Helen practically shrieked. "In Italy!"

He couldn't blame her for her response. After all, he'd done the same thing, but, blast it all, she didn't have to let the whole world know. "Keep your voice down."

"My daughter is not going to Italy." Lady Wolverton's ice-cold tone startled Phinn. Hell and the Devil confound it. He should have kept his mouth shut until he and Helen were in the coach. "And she is certainly not attending university." Her ladyship inclined her head to him. "Please excuse me for a few minutes."

He took his sister-in-law's arm. "We should leave."

"We cannot go anywhere until Lady Wolverton returns." Helen patted his arm. "I have hope that Lady Augusta will soon change her mind."

Except that Phinn didn't want her to be coerced into marrying him. Not only that, but Helen didn't know to take into account that Worthington seemed to be supporting Augusta. Be that as it may, he couldn't very well drag Helen out, and Augusta might need his help. Already groups of ladies were whispering and he had little doubt the topic was her. "Very well. We shall remain until she returns."

It wasn't long before Lady Thornhill came up to him and Helen. "Are you sure you heard correctly, my lord? I do not believe that any of the universities are accepting ladies." She smiled. "Although, I, for one, would applaud any progress in that area."

Of that he had no doubt. Here was his chance to make amends for letting the cat out of the bag, as it were. "I could very well be mistaken, my lady. Once she had refused my suit, I was rather distraught and not listening properly." He tried to come up with a reason for mentioning Italy and university. "She might have been speaking about the fountain that came from Italy."

"That must be it." Lady Thornhill gave him a look of approval. She launched into a discussion about Italian artists, the art schools, and the number of pieces that had been brought to England from that country before the war, effectively stopping the talk about Augusta until Lady Wolverton returned.

Her ladyship came directly to Phinn. "Please excuse me, my lord, but I had not yet been informed that my daughter is indeed traveling to Europe. She will be accompanying Lady Worthington's cousin Mrs. Addison and her husband on a long-planned trip to the Continent, and staying with Lady Harrington in Paris."

"There you are, Lord Phineas," Lady Thornhill said triumphantly. "You mistook what Lady Augusta said."

"Yes, indeed." He tried to give the impression of being relieved and chagrined at the same time. "How stupid of me to think a lady would wish to attend university at all and in Italy at that. My mind was so muddled I made a mull of everything Lady Augusta said after she gently refused my suit." He bowed. "Thank you for correcting me, my lady. I believe I would like to return home."

"Yes, of course." Lady Wolverton inclined her head. "I understand."

This time Helen didn't argue but bussed her ladyship's cheek. "I shall see you soon."

"I look forward to it." Lady Wolverton kissed Helen's cheek as well. "I do wish Worthington would have informed me earlier, but apparently, the invitation was issued only a day or two ago and he has been extremely busy in the Lords."

"Goodness," one of the older ladies in a turban exclaimed. "I have almost forgotten I have a husband, he has spent so much time at Whitehall."

Once again, the conversation turned from Augusta. Phinn was relieved that Lady Thornhill had averted what could have been a scandal. He'd have to be more careful from now on. Still, he'd thought Helen had more discretion than she'd shown. He wanted to chastise her, but did not wish to discuss his failed bid for Augusta's hand.

The problem now was that Phinn was very sure no other lady would do for him. That meant that one way or another he had to convince Augusta to marry him. And the only way to do that was to follow her to Europe. Ergo, he had plans to set into motion.

Without further to-do, he guided his sister-in-law to the hall and out to the front of the house, where their carriage waited. As soon as he arrived home he sent a footman to fetch Boman.

Phinn impatiently paced his bedchamber until his secretary arrived.

Boman entered without knocking. "You look like a caged animal. What's going on?"

"Find out when and on what ship a Mr. Addison is leaving for France. It will be in about a week. I wish to be on that vessel."

Boman frowned. "I thought you were going to find a lady and marry."

"I am." Phinn grinned. "The lady I plan to wed will be on that ship."

His friend's jaw dropped. "Lady Augusta's going to Europe?"

"Yes, and so are we." This felt like the best decision he'd made in a long time.

The next morning, he woke early and was the first one to the breakfast room. His intention was to speak with his brother without Helen present. Fortunately, he did not have long to wait.

"Good morning," Dorchester said, walking through the door as Phinn was deciding what to eat. He still had not got over the amount of food available. Strange how rough travel changed one's perspective. "Or is it? Helen told me Lady Augusta turned you down."

He finished filling his plate and set it on the table. "Did she also tell you that the lady is traveling to Europe next week?"

"I believe something to that effect was mentioned." His brother took a plate and headed to the sideboard.

"I am going to follow her." He sat down, putting the table between him and his brother.

"*What?*" Dorchester spun around so fast, the ham on his plate flew off, landing several feet away. "Follow her to Europe?"

"Er, yes." Phinn poured cups of tea for him and his brother. "I believe the only reason she rejected me is that she wishes to travel. I cannot blame her for that."

Dorchester raised one brow. "A rather unusual ambition for a young lady."

"Why?" Phinn raised his own brow. "There are many ladies on the Continent at the moment."

"Not many who are looking for husbands. At least not the ones they should be looking for."

He had to be careful what he said. Yesterday, his thoughtlessness almost ruined Augusta's reputation. "I cannot think it odd that a lady of any age would turn down an opportunity to travel in the company of relatives."

"Harrumph." Dorchester finished filling his plate, then took his place at the head of the table. "What are you attempting to tell me?"

"I'm going to follow her." Obviously Phinn had not been clear the first time. He drank his tea as his brother gave him a long, steady, and he hoped, firm look.

Finally, Dorchester said, "And your promise to marry and get an heir?"

"A vow I fully intend to keep." Phinn never broke a

promise. "I can wed and bed my lady on the Continent as well as I can in England."

"You are that serious about her?" Dorchester picked up his cup and sipped as if nothing unusual was going on.

"I am." The silence in the room deepened, and Phinn dug into his baked egg.

His brother cocked one brow, giving him a rather dubious look. "And you believe you can change her mind about marrying you?"

"I do." Once Augusta figured out he would not stop her from her travels, at least until she was breeding or gave birth, he was sure she would marry him. After all, they shared a good many common interests. Phinn wasn't sure how he would deal with her wish to attend university, but he'd come up with some compromise.

A slow smile spread across Dorchester's face. "You're in lust."

Phinn thought about it for a moment. He was not only in lust—bedding her would be a pleasure—but he was in awe of her mind as well. For a second, the memory of Augusta mentioning love pricked him. Surely friendship coupled with strong physical desire was enough. Eventually, it would turn into love. It had for his parents and brother.

He gave his brother an answering smile. "I am."

"Well, Helen will not be happy about it, but as long as you promise to start working on your nursery, I'm confident I can bring her about." Dorchester chewed on a piece of toast and swallowed. "There is no need for you to say anything to her."

"I'll be busy making plans to depart. I only have a week." Phinn hoped Boman would be able to find the ship on which Augusta would sail. Surely, one of the shipping offices here would have the information.

"You'd better attend the evening events before you depart. At least until I can make my wife understand how important this is to you."

That would be a bother. Still, every day Boman would report to Phinn on his progress. And there really wasn't much he could do to prepare in the evenings. "Very well. I suppose I can depend on Boman to do most of the work."

"I think you will have to." Dorchester remained silent as they finished their breakfast. "If you require any assistance in arranging the appropriate travel documents or letters of introduction, I'll be happy to oblige."

He could have knocked Phinn over with a feather. "Thank you, I shall." That reminded him, he'd have to visit his banker. "You can tell me who Lady Harrington is, if you know."

"She is the Countess of Harrington," Dorchester answered promptly. "Her husband, the Marquis of Markham's heir, works for Sir Charles Stuart at our embassy in Paris."

"I'd like a letter of introduction to both Sir Charles and Lord Harrington, if possible."

Dorchester nodded. "I'll arrange it."

Finishing his breakfast, Phinn pushed back his chair and stood. "Thank you for understanding."

"Keep your vow, and I'll be the most understanding brother any man could have." Dorchester picked up the newssheet next to his plate.

"I shall." The devil was if Augusta was serious about not marrying until she had attended university, how was Phinn to talk her out of it? Of course, she was so intelligent, she could probably do both, have a baby and attend lectures.

Damn, he'd forgot to mention to Musson, his new

valet, that they were leaving. The man had actually turned out to be a blessing in disguise. Not only was he supremely competent in advising Phinn as to what he required for the Season, he got along with everyone, even Pickle.

Taking the stairs two at a time, Phinn strode into his bedchamber, where his valet was busy directing a maid in cleaning the room.

He waited until the woman left before saying, "We're departing for Europe in a week. However, Lady Dorchester is not to know until my brother has had a chance to speak with her."

"The trunks will be a bit of a problem." His valet cocked his head to one side. "But I believe we can spirit them out of the house without anyone who would inform her knowing. Are they in the attic?"

"Ah, no." Phinn had forgotten all about having only one trunk. It was a small one at that. It certainly wouldn't hold all the clothing he'd purchased since arriving back in England. "The only one I have is in the chamber next to this one."

"In that case"—Musson nodded briskly—"it will be no trouble at all. If you give me leave to purchase the trunks you need, I shall take care of everything."

"Yes, of course." Phinn breathed a sigh of relief. They would make this happen without Helen's being any the wiser. "Organize everything with Boman. I shall see you later today. I believe I have a ball to attend this evening."

"As you wish, my lord." Musson pulled out a pocket-book and began to make notes.

Phinn went to the parlor he'd been given. It was time to ensure he had a dance with Augusta tonight. Sitting at the desk, he pulled out a piece of pressed paper and began to write.

Dear Lady Augusta,
*   Please save a waltz for me this evening at Lady*
Bellamny's ball.

He frowned at what he'd written. It was too demanding. Crumpling the paper up, he threw it into
the fireplace.

Phinn tried three more times. All the attempts were
consigned to the fire.

He would do this in person. After his proposal yesterday, that was likely the best way of convincing her to
dance with him. Glancing at the gold and walnut clock
on the mantel, he saw it was only shortly after eight. A
bit early to make a call, but she *had* said they broke their
fast early because of her brothers and sisters.

He went back to his bedchamber. "Musson, I'll be
out for several hours. Please tell Boman to meet me at
the Seven Stars in Carey Street at ten o'clock."

It wouldn't take him that long to speak with Augusta,
but he wanted all the time she'd give him.

"As you wish, my lord," his valet called from the
dressing room.

He opened the door and looked both ways down
the corridor before venturing out of his room. Now if
he could just avoid Helen for the next few days, all
would be well.

Rather than calling for a coach, or his brother's
gig, Phinn decided to walk. Several minutes later he
knocked on the door at Worthington House. A tall, thin
man with silver hair opened it.

"Please come in, my lord." The butler bowed and behaved as if it was common for visitors to arrive before
noon. "The family is at breakfast. However, I shall
inform her ladyship you are here."

A few moments later, the butler returned and Phinn followed the man a short way down a corridor. "Lord Phineas Carter-Woods."

He was ushered into a long room filled with people, most of them still in the schoolroom. He recognized the two youngest girls, as well as the three older ones. Walter inclined his head but was busy shoveling food into his mouth. At his age, Phinn had done the same. Another boy, younger than Walter, glanced at Phinn. The lad had been helping to decorate that day as well. Worthington was nowhere to be seen. An empty place had been set at Lady Worthington's right hand.

"Lord Phineas." She indicated he should take a seat. "Please join us."

He considered saying he would wait until they were finished, then he caught sight of the uncertain look on Augusta's face. He hated seeing her like that and felt as if a knife had been thrust in his gut and twisted. Despite her refusal, he'd make sure she knew she could always trust him.

"Thank you." He bowed. "I'd be delighted."

Chapter Fourteen

What in Heaven's name was Phinn doing here? And at such an hour? Augusta sincerely hoped he had not come to renew his suit.

Her pondering came to a quick end when Grace said, "Augusta, please perform the introductions."

That's right. Even though he had helped set up for the ball, he had not met her sisters or Phillip. Forcing a smile, she glanced at her sisters, all of whom had sat up straighter and were staring at Phinn. "Ladies, Madeline, Alice, Eleanor, Theodora, and Mary, I would like to make Lord Phineas Carter-Woods known to you." She waited until they had each said good morning. "My lord, these are my sisters, Lady Madeline Vivers, Ladies Alice and Eleanor Carpenter, Lady Theodora Vivers, and Lady Mary Carpenter."

He gave an elegant bow, more suited in a ballroom to a duchess than a breakfast room to children. "Ladies, it is my pleasure."

The twins and Madeline giggled, Theo inclined her head as if she were a duchess—she would never be a silly young lady—and for a moment Augusta expected her sister to say something embarrassing, but Theo kept her counsel. Augusta wondered how she had not noticed her sister's growing maturity.

Mary gave Phinn a searching look as if she might ferret out all his secrets.

"My lord," Augusta continued, "you have already met my brother Walter. Next to him is my brother Phillip Carpenter."

"Good morning," Phinn said, smiling at the boys.

"Good morning, sir," they said at the same time.

The only residents not present were Miss Tallerton, their governess, and Mr. Winters, their tutor. They liked to spend this time coordinating their lessons. Or, more probably, to have some much-needed quiet before the day began.

Augusta resumed her seat, finished her tea, and poured another cup. She wished the younger girls had decided to interrogate Phinn. Unfortunately, they appeared to have picked this year to grow out of putting one to the blush.

He had no sooner sat in the chair next to Grace, when she said, "To what do we owe your visit?"

For a moment his eyes widened, reminding Augusta of a panicked deer. She almost went into whoops but managed to hide her smile. He obviously thought no one would ask until the children were gone. "I came to attempt to persuade Lady Augusta to dance with me at Lady Bellamny's ball this evening." He glanced at her. "If she is attending."

That was surprising. Augusta fought her urge to gape at him. Was this just another way to try to convince her to marry him, or did he truly wish to remain her friend? Not that there was much else he could do. She was leaving, and he had to marry.

She did want to dance this evening. And there was no reason why it could not be with him. "I would be delighted to stand up with you."

"Excellent." The corners of his well-molded lips tilted up. "May I have a waltz, if you have one left?"

Augusta wanted to sigh. She had more than one left. The situation was so dire that her sisters had promised to enlist their husbands and friends to stand up with her. "You may have the second waltz."

"I had hoped for the supper dance." Phinn's tone was low but insistent.

Their eyes clashed. He was not happy, but what did he expect? "We are not staying for supper. There is no need."

Mary fixed an innocent gaze on Phinn. "Augusta is going to Europe in a few days. We do not know how long she will be away."

Well done, Mary.

Augusta wondered what he would say to that.

"Thank you." His smile faded slightly. "I had heard something about that. I suppose most of London has as well." He glanced at her. "May I tempt you into a carriage ride this afternoon?"

"I am sorry to say that Augusta has a full schedule today." Grace smiled at Phinn. "There are a great many things to accomplish and very little time in which to do so."

He must know that. He had spent a good deal of time traveling. Did he think she would leave all the planning to someone else? Or perhaps he did not understand—despite what Mary had said—how long she meant to be gone.

After giving himself an almost imperceptible shake, he grinned ruefully. "Please forgive me. I, of all people, know how much time arrangements for overseas travel can take. Instead of a carriage ride, allow me to offer my services in the event you require any assistance."

Phinn's admission dissipated the tension that had

been growing in the room. Augusta let out the breath she had been holding. The twins and Madeline giggled lightly. Phillip and Walter excused themselves, and Mary and Theo exchanged a look. Augusta did not even want to know what that was about.

Phinn finished eating, drained his teacup, and stood. "Thank you very much for allowing me to share your breakfast." He bowed to her. "I look forward to our dance, my lady."

"I shall accompany you to the door," Augusta said, rising. They were halfway up the corridor when she stopped, forcing him to do the same. "I am sorry about the carriage ride."

He reached out his hand as if to touch her, then dropped it. "Please don't be. I *do* know how much planning goes into a journey." He grinned at her. "Even if you are not making all the preparations, you still have a great deal to do and many decisions to make. I apologize for not thinking of that."

"Well, thank you, again." She would miss him when she was gone, but she was glad he understood. "If we do not see much of each other over the next few days, good luck with your hunt for a wife."

"Your wishes are appreciated." The corner of his mouth cocked up into a crooked smile. "Not that I blame you for having your ambitions, but your leaving has made my search much harder."

"Yes, well." She brushed back a curl from her face. "Perhaps you will find a lady whom you can love."

Taking her hand, he kissed it, and the warmth of his lips radiated up her arm. Good Lord, she'd forgotten neither of them wore gloves. Augusta became acutely aware of the strength in his lightly calloused hands, and removed her fingers from his grip. "I shall see you this evening."

"Until then." He inclined his head before taking his hat and cane from Thorton and strolling out the door.

She stared at Phinn until Thorton closed the door. Perhaps, after this evening, she should eschew entertainments altogether.

"Augusta," Grace said, "you must decide if you'll take Zephyr with you. Hector needs to know."

"I do wish to take her with me." She was leaving so much behind, but not her horse.

"Very well. I'll send him a message. Please be ready to go in a half hour."

"I will." Phinn had more than surprised her this morning. If he loved her—no! She was not going to think about that. Allowing herself to fall in love with him would only lead to heartache.

Phinn strolled out of Worthington House as if he didn't have a care in the world. Yet it was a damn good thing he'd left when he had. The moment Augusta had pushed back the curl that had fallen over her forehead, he'd wanted to touch it, spear his fingers through her hair, drag her to him, and kiss her witless until she agreed to marry him. The more he thought about it, the more he wanted her as his wife.

By the way she had responded when he'd kissed her hand, Phinn had no doubt she felt something for him too. If she was not so determined to travel to Europe—and he knew that despite what her mother said or thought, Augusta had not given up on attending university—he'd be able to convince her to marry him, and in short order. As it was, she would be more of a challenge. Still, all the best things were worth going to a bit of trouble for. He would simply be persistent. Eventually, she'd see that he was the perfect mate for her. Even if it wasn't a love match, it was a lust match. He would make her happier than any other gentleman could.

Pausing, he pulled out his watch. He'd been with Augusta's family longer than he had thought, but not as long as he wanted to be. Still, even on foot, he'd arrive at the tavern in good time for his meeting with Boman. And Phinn needed a good walk to help him keep his head clear. He was much too prone to considering Augusta's lush form, rather than the business at hand. Although, now that he thought about it, she was the business at hand.

He would have rather met his secretary at a coffeehouse, but they were frequented by gentlemen and there was too great a chance of being overheard and having rumors reach Helen's ears. In fact, he hoped he'd be on his way to Dover before she discovered he was gone.

Upon entering the tavern not far from Lincoln's Inn Fields and popular with the legal population in London, he found it to be relatively empty. He took a seat away from the front windows and immediately a neatly dressed young woman approached him.

"Mornin', sir. C'n I get you ale or coffee? Or somethin' to eat?"

He thought about ordering coffee, but decided ale might be a better choice. "An ale, please."

"Be right up." She bustled toward the bar.

Just about the time she brought his ale, Boman entered the tavern. "Make it two."

"Yes, sir." The woman placed a mug on the table and hurried off again.

Boman slid onto the bench across from Phinn, who pushed his tankard of ale toward his secretary. "What have you discovered?"

"For the most part, Mr. Addison makes his own

arrangements. He was with the East India Company for many years and has a lot of friends around the docks." Boman took a draw of ale. "He and his party will make the crossing on a private yacht."

Perdition! There was no hope of getting on the same ship as Augusta. "Where does that leave us?"

"It just so happens"—his secretary grinned—"there is another ship accompanying the *Sarah Elizabeth*. I have booked us on that vessel. The *Catherine*." Boman pulled out a pocketbook, placing it on the table. "Although Mr. Addision makes his own passage arrangements, he has an Indian fellow who does the rest. I approached him about joining his group when we arrive in Calais. The basis being that it is better to travel together. He will ask Mr. Addison. I only gave him my name."

That was better than nothing. "Good work. What else do we need?"

"Horses and a traveling carriage. I'll leave you to find the animals. I have a recommendation as to where to find a carriage. We'll also need linens. Ours are no better than rags."

"Carriage horses and hacks?" Phinn made a mental list.

Boman nodded. "From what I understand, Addison's cattle will depart tomorrow. He had coaches built in France."

"Should we do the same?" Phinn could get his brother to accompany him to Tattersalls for the horses. There was an argument to be made for hiring a team in France, but one never knew what condition the horses would be in.

"It's unnecessary. He has more equipage than we require." His secretary slid the pocketbook across the table. "Here is the rest of what we need."

Phinn read the neat handwriting. Provisions until

they were able to find a market in France. The trunks he'd already arranged. Musson could take care of most of the rest of the list. "Waterproof coats? What happened to ours?"

Raising one brow, Boman said, "Do you want to look like a pauper or a wealthy gentleman? I guarantee you we shall prosper better on the Continent if we don't look like we can't afford our lodgings or meals."

And that was the reason Phinn trusted his secretary to plan the journey. He hoped his valet could find some coats already made. "You have a point. Other than Paris, do we know where we are traveling?"

"Not until Addison approves our attaching ourselves to his party." Boman twisted his mug around on the table. "You do realize that he is likely to tell Lady Augusta we are joining them?"

No. Phinn hadn't considered that at all. When had his mind stopped working? He'd been so focused on Augusta and following her, he hadn't thought of how she would react. She'd comprehend in a moment what he was about, and she wouldn't like it at all. He would have to be much more subtle than to expect to be able to join her group when they first arrived in France. He had to come up with a way to make her want him there, which would require a change of tactics.

Taking out his pocket watch, he looked at it and hoped his brother was still at the house. "It's five days from Calais to Paris."

Boman nodded. "Naturally, if you want to stop along the way it will be longer."

"You're right. I don't want Lady Augusta knowing that I wish to join her party. It might be better if we are already in Paris when she arrives." Yet, there were a few towns he wished to visit, but that wouldn't put him behind schedule. It would surprise him if her group rushed straight to Paris.

"That will shorten our time to prepare. I'll have to speak with Musson."

"Will it be possible to depart in two or three days?" Phinn took a drink of ale. It was actually quite good.

"I'll speak to the agent representing the ship." His secretary paused while he made notes in his pocket-book. "I should have an answer for you by late this afternoon."

"Fair enough." He put some coins on the table. "I'll see you later."

Phinn walked out of the tavern and hailed a hackney. He no longer had time for leisurely strolls. His first stop was to his bank, where he made arrangements to be able to draw funds while in Europe. The second was to the Royal Institution.

As he climbed the steps to the front door, he suffered some pangs of regret that he probably would not be presenting his paper on Aztec antispasmodic medicines. Walking past a servant standing in the hall, he made his way to the secretary's office, knocking on the open door.

"My lord." The secretary, Mr. Cooper, held a letter in one hand and a pen in the other. His sparse, graying hair looked as if a windstorm had hit it. "I am sorry, but I have a catastrophe on my hands."

"I am afraid I am going to add to your problems." Phinn hated cancelling his presentation, yet he couldn't see a way around it. If he remained until the end of the week, he might not arrive in Paris before Augusta did. "I must depart for the Continent earlier than I'd planned."

Taking off his gold-rimmed spectacles, the secretary rubbed his nose. "When do you leave?"

"The day after tomorrow at the latest." Inwardly, he cringed. There was a very good possibility that he'd never be invited to give a paper again.

Cooper peered through his smudged eyeglasses. "Are you available tomorrow afternoon at two o'clock?"

"I am." Phinn would make himself available. "I will have to leave when I finish."

"Yes, of course. One of our presenters is suddenly unable to arrive in time to present his paper. Now he can take your place. Very good. Very good indeed," the secretary muttered to himself, making notes on a large piece of foolscap covering his desk. "Thank you very much for coming by, my lord."

"My pleasure." Turning, he strolled back out into the corridor. That had worked out well. Hopefully, that meant the Fates were with him.

Chapter Fifteen

"My lady," Thorton said. "Is there anything I can do for you?"

Augusta dragged her gaze from the window on the side of the front door, and her mind from Phineas Carter-Woods. He should be gone, but he'd stopped to look at his watch. The man was dangerous. She wasn't quite sure how she knew it, she just did. To make things worse, she had the feeling her brother's butler knew she had been staring at him. "The carriage will be brought around in thirty minutes?"

"It will, my lady. Just as her ladyship said."

"I had better change." Augusta still could not shake the feeling that Phinn was up to something. If only she knew what it was.

When she reached her bedchamber, the yellow carriage gown had been set out and her maid was waiting. "Have you figured out how many trunks we shall need?"

"Yes, my lady. The list is in your reticule." She stood while she was unlaced from one gown and into another. "You have received a letter from your cousin. I recognized her hand."

"Excellent." In the last note, Cousin Prue had agreed to act as Augusta's companion. She picked up the message from her toilet table and popped open the seal.

My dear Augusta,
   I shall arrive by hired coach in the afternoon of the twelfth of May. I cannot tell you how much I am looking forward to our journey.
                    Your devoted cousin,
                    P. B.

"She will be here tomorrow afternoon. I must tell Grace." Augusta began to walk off when a polite but firm hand stopped her.

"My lady, unless you wish to come back, allow me to put your hat on you, and give you your gloves and reticule."

"Yes, of course." Augusta watched in the mirror as Gobert tilted the bonnet just so and tied the ribbon under Augusta's right ear. "I must admit, I am becoming very excited about our trip."

"As am I, my lady." Her maid stepped back. "Now you are ready."

She was in such a rush, she almost ran into Grace. "Oh, there you are. I received a missive from Cousin Prue. She arrives tomorrow afternoon."

"I am so happy she agreed to accompany you." Grace linked arms with Augusta, turning her toward the stairs. "I know that Jane has said she has enough help for little Tommy, but it will be nice for you not to have to rely on her every time you wish to go somewhere."

"And for her not to have to chaperone me all the time." Augusta and Grace made their way down the stairs.

"Thorton," Grace said. "Please tell Mrs. Thorton that Mrs. Brunning will arrive sometime tomorrow afternoon."

Augusta had always wondered how their house-keeper, who was so jolly, had married Thorton who never showed his thoughts.

"Yes, my lady." He bowed. "I shall be happy to relay your message."

Soon she and Grace were in the town coach headed toward Bruton Street and the traveling-trunk shop.

A bell tinkled as they walked in the door. Several different sizes of chests, portmanteaus, hat boxes, and other items were displayed around the shop. A matching set of five trunks sat off to one side, and Augusta wondered if they were for sale. She needed the items almost immediately.

Two men, one of whom reminded her of her brother's valet, were talking. The second man glanced up. "Ladies, I will be with you straightaway."

"Do not rush on our account," Augusta said. She had never bought a traveling trunk, or, indeed, a trunk of any kind and wanted to look around a bit. The more she gazed at the set of black chests, the more she thought she might just purchase them.

Once the valet-looking man left the store, the other man with graying hair came up to her and Grace. "I am Mr. Briggs." He bowed. "How may I assist you?"

"I would like to buy those trunks." Augusta pointed to the set.

"I'm sorry." The clerk's brow puckered. "Unfortunately, the person who just left already purchased them."

That wasn't good. She needed something right away. "Do you have any other trunks that are already made?"

"I regret to say that I do not. Do you require them immediately?"

"Within the next five days." Well, piffle. She and Grace would have to find another store.

Mr. Briggs tapped his chin for a moment before saying, "I have several trunks that only require coverings. It wouldn't take more than three days at the most for them to be completed. You would also be able to select the coverings you wish and the inside accouterments."

Inside accouterments? Augusta had no idea what that could be. "Could you show me what you mean?"

"It would be my pleasure. Follow me please." He led them to the far corner of the shop where various tray-like containers were shelved. "These are placed in the shell of the trunk to allow you to organize the chest the way you wish." He drew one of the trays out. "This, for example, is designed to hold a traveling desk. I also have compartments for various other items."

"That would be extremely useful," Grace remarked as she inspected one of the other trays.

An hour later, Augusta had selected the insides of her new trunks.

"And here are the coverings from which you can choose." In addition to the black cover she had already seen, he showed Augusta several shades of brown. "The trunk will also have brass tacks, if you like."

Selecting trunks was almost as fun as buying gowns. "Could I have black with dark brown straps?"

"Naturally." The man smiled. "You may have anything you wish."

It was not often she was told that. "I would like black with dark brown straps and brass tacks."

"Excellent choice." The man beamed at her. "Is there anything else you would like?"

She had already selected five trunks, two portmanteaus, several hat boxes, and a valise. "That will be all."

Mr. Briggs hurried to the counter and began writing down her purchases. "If you give me the address, I will have them delivered in three days."

Grace made arrangements for the bill and the trunks to be sent to Worthington House.

"Thank you for your custom, my ladies." Mr. Briggs held the door for them.

As they strolled out of the shop onto the pavement, Augusta worried her thumb nail. "I hope that is enough. I must think of Gobert and the others as well."

"I am sure there are some trunks in the attic if you are short," Grace said in a reassuring tone. "Now, let us stop in at Madame Lisette's and see how your travel garments are coming."

Not long after Augusta and Grace returned to Worthington House, Dorie, Henrietta, Adeline, and Georgiana were ushered into Augusta's parlor.

"What on earth happened yesterday?" Henrietta said as she hugged Augusta.

"We wanted to come immediately after the disturbance, but our mothers said to wait until today," Georgiana said, taking her turn to embrace Augusta.

"Europe! This week?" Adeline replaced Georgiana as the others took seats on the two sofas.

"Lady Thornhill saved the day after Lord Phineas made such a mull of it." Dorie bussed Augusta's cheek. "But then he caught on quickly and admitted he had been so disappointed by your refusal that he had not heard you properly, and you did say you would accompany your cousin to France." She cast her gaze to the ceiling. "Naturally, he was believed because you know gentlemen never listen when a lady is speaking."

Augusta was relieved everything had turned out so well. She should have suspected Phinn would recognize he should not have said anything. It was extremely clever, and he was still her friend. She stepped over to the bellpull to order tea, but a knock came on the door and Durant, her footman, entered with a large tray and two teapots.

Her friends waited until she poured and handed around plates of ginger biscuits.

Henrietta picked up a biscuit. "What did occur?"

It was a relief to be able to discuss what happened with her friends.

"As you have gathered, Lord Phineas proposed. I had no idea he had planned to ask me to marry him."

Her friends stared at her as if she had lost her mind.

"Augusta," Dorie said patiently, "you have spent more time with him than with any other gentleman. It was clear he was looking for a wife."

"He did not even ask my brother first." Had Augusta been the only one not to know he wished to wed her?

"Well, speaking with Worthington did not help any of the other gentlemen," Henrietta pointed out in a dry tone. Adeline and Georgiana nodded.

"In any event, I turned him down." There was no need to explain everything she and Phinn had said. Augusta took a sip of tea. "I told him I planned to go to Italy and study." Thinking back over his initial reaction, he had appeared a bit stunned by the news. "I was shocked by his proposal and decided to come back here. Grace saw me, and we had a discussion. That is when she told me Cousin Jane and her husband had decided to travel to Europe."

"Not just France," Dorie said.

"No. We will visit Paris, then move on." Augusta was starting to feel a little guilty about deceiving her mother. "My mama does not know that part."

Georgiana fluttered her fingers. "As long as your brother knows, that is all that matters."

Augusta needed to change the conversation. "You said Lady Thornhill became involved?"

"Yes." Dorie went on to explain in more detail how her ladyship made everyone believe Phinn had misspoken. Then Mama had returned and confirmed Augusta was simply traveling to Paris.

"Are you attending any more entertainments?" Adeline asked.

"I shall attend Lady Bellamny's ball this evening." Augusta hoped that would be the last one. "There is much to do and my cousin who will accompany me as a companion arrives tomorrow."

"If anyone asks us," Dorie said, "we will tell them that your visit to France has been planned for some time, and that Lord Phineas had not bothered to ask permission to address you."

"Thus shocking you so much by his proposal that you felt you must return home." Georgiana put her teacup down. "Are you all right? Is there anything we can do for you?"

"No." Augusta shook her head. "Thank you for coming to see me."

"Do not dare leave before we can get together again." Adeline bussed Augusta's cheek.

She walked them to the front door. She would miss her friends as well.

Later that evening, Augusta entered Lady Bellamny's house on one of Rothwell's arms. Her sister on the other. They greeted Lady Bellamny and made their way to the ballroom.

"Who are you dancing with first?" Louisa asked.

"I do not have a partner." Augusta wished she'd told Phinn he could have it, but she had not wanted him to think she might change her mind.

"Give me a moment," Rothwell said, before strolling

off. He approached a blond gentleman who greeted him. Shortly thereafter, the man nodded, and Rothwell made his way back to Augusta with the gentleman in tow. "Lady Augusta, I believe you have already met Lord Turley."

She could have kissed her brother-in-law. "I have. Good evening, my lord."

The man bowed. "A pleasure. I hear you will be visiting my sister in Paris."

Augusta inclined her head. "That is correct. I am vastly excited about it. I understand she adores the city."

"She does indeed." His lordship smiled. "I received a letter from her yesterday telling me you were to visit. She is looking forward to seeing you again." Rothwell cleared his throat. "My lady, would you do me the honor of standing up with me for the first set?"

"Thank you, my lord." Augusta smiled. "I would be delighted."

Even though Lord Turley danced extremely well, she did not enjoy the set as much as she should have. Now that the clothing and luggage had been arranged, she wanted nothing more than to concentrate on her journey. Fortunately, his lordship was not a demanding conversationalist.

As he escorted her back to her sister, she overheard two matrons talking as they strolled into the room.

"Now that Lady Augusta is departing for France," one lady said, "I shall speak with Helen Dorchester about an entertainment that will bring my Mary to Lord Phineas's notice."

A tick developed below Augusta's eye. She should not be concerned about Phinn. He had to marry, and it could not be to her.

"I feel badly for Patience Wolverton," the other lady commented. "Her first daughter married so well."

A sliver of guilt again speared Augusta that she had hurt her mother. Still, she would wed eventually, and Madeline would be out in another three years.

Augusta strained to hear the other woman's answer, but by then they were too far away. If it was not for her dance with Phinn, she would have asked to go home.

She refused to think about not seeing him again. He would have a wife and children by the time she returned to England. She hoped he'd marry for love. Of all the gentlemen who had offered for her, only one of them had claimed to love her, and Lord Lancelot was the last man she'd wed.

That, of course, reminded her of the masterful way Phinn had handled the lordling. She'd not seen him in Town since.

Lord Littleton approached and bowed. "Lady Augusta, may I hope that you have a set free?"

Well, Dorie might not like the man, but Augusta appreciated him. "I have the second dance free."

"Thank you, my lady."

He spoke a few words to Rothwell before strolling across the room.

That was three sets spoken for.

She enjoyed her dances with Lords Turley and Littleton. Turley answered her questions about Paris, and Littleton asked her questions about herself. But nothing could compare with being in Phinn's arms for the waltz. Best of all, he acted as if nothing horrible had happened between them.

"My presentation to the Royal Institution has been moved up to tomorrow." As he led her through a turn, she was sure she ended up a bit closer to him than before.

"How did that occur? Don't they usually set their schedules in advance?"

"Someone will be late arriving. So they switched our days." His intent silver gaze had butterflies flitting around in her stomach. "I would like you to come."

Unlike the Royal Society, the Royal Institution did allow ladies to sit through the presentations, but should she? And why did he want her there? "If you'd like, I will come."

"Thank you." He grinned. "Perhaps you could give me a ride. I could walk, but I'll have my papers with me, and I must have a word with the secretary at the Royal Society beforehand. I have to be at the Royal Institution at two o'clock."

"You are impossible." Still she laughed lightly. Trying not to believe it would be the last time they were together.

Chapter Sixteen

If it wasn't for his waltz with Augusta, Phinn would have begged off the ball. If he could have arranged it, he would have appeared for the dance, and left immediately afterward. The two main problems with that idea were Augusta and Helen. Both ladies would want to know what he was about.

Thanks to the efficiency of his secretary, valet, and brother, he'd be ready to leave early morning the day after tomorrow, and neither lady could know. If presenting his paper was not so important to him, he could depart in a matter of hours. At this point, he wasn't sure if the Fates were with him or not.

Earlier that day when he'd arrived back at Dorchester House, Musson said he had been successful in buying the only set of luggage the store had ready-made. Boman found a traveling carriage that had been ordered then refused for no reason he could find, and Dorchester had helped negotiate the purchase of six carriage horses and two hacks. He had also taken Phinn to Manton's gun shop, where he purchased a rifle based on a German design. It was much better to not have to be too close to one's enemy. Not that he expected much trouble on the Continent, but one never knew. He also bought two coaching pistols.

Phinn had been in Dorchester's study, where his brother was writing the letters of introduction, when Boman joined them.

After accepting a glass of wine, he said, "If we can be in Dover by evening the day after tomorrow, we can leave on the next tide."

Dorchester put his goblet down. "That soon?"

"Yes, my lord," Boman said. "The wind is beginning to turn and is expected to remain for only a few days."

"Well, it's a good thing you are ready to depart." Dorchester pulled a face. "Although, I suppose it's better that you leave sooner than later. I was able to convince Helen that you are playing least in sight because you wish to be alone to nurse your hurt feelings after being rejected by Lady Augusta."

Boman raised his brows in a query.

"That won't last long." Phinn heaved a sigh. He wouldn't want to be his brother when Helen discovered he'd left. He glanced at his secretary. "She wanted me to accompany her to some sort of event today. Fortunately, Musson warned me."

"Ah, well," his brother said. "That enabled us to finish what needed to be done."

"What are we doing about a groom?" Boman asked.

Blast it to hell! They couldn't leave without at least two grooms and an equal number of coachmen.

"Don't look at me," Dorchester said. "I don't have any to spare." He pulled the bellpull, and a second later his butler entered the room.

"My lord?"

"Where can I find grooms and coachmen in a hurry?"

"Allow me a few minutes and I shall have an answer." Saddock bowed and left the study.

True to his word, he returned five minutes later. "The Everley Employment Agency has the best reputation." He handed Dorchester a piece of paper. "Will there be anything else, my lord?"

Saddock's question reminded Phinn he'd forgotten to mention his presentation. "I'm giving my paper to the Royal Institution tomorrow early afternoon." Phinn couldn't help but to puff his chest out a little and grin. The elation had finally struck.

"That's excellent news!" Boman shook Phinn's hand. "Well done."

"Indeed it is wonderful news." The butler bowed. "Your father would have been proud of you, sir."

"The hell with our father. I'm proud of him." Dorchester poured Phinn another glass of wine. "We will celebrate with champagne tomorrow. What is the topic?"

"It concerns an antispasmodic medicine the Aztecs discovered." Phinn sipped the fine claret. Soon he'd have his choice of French wines. He would have to discover if Augusta liked wine.

After the butler left, his brother handed the note to Phinn, who gave it to his secretary. "Good luck."

Boman rose. "I'll inform you if I have any difficulty."

"Arrange for them to stay in an inn near the stables," Phinn said. "I want them there by tomorrow afternoon at the latest to help load the coach."

"I have already organized a cart to take your trunks to the stable." His secretary began to walk out then stopped. "Shall I have the carriage meet us in the mews at dawn?"

"That's an excellent idea." The clandestine aspect of this adventure appealed to Phinn. "Perhaps I'll climb out the window so as not to be seen."

His brother heaved a sigh. "You will not climb out

the window, nor will you depart from the mews. You shall leave here as befits your station."

"Spoilsport," Phinn retorted.

"It is ever my role," Dorchester grumbled. "Save your heroic larks for your lady. She will likely appreciate them."

Now Phinn had to watch as Augusta danced with a tall, blond gentleman he'd not seen her stand up with before. He turned to his sister-in-law. "Who is that?"

"Lord Turley." Phinn raised a brow, and a pained expression crossed Helen's face as she briefly closed her eyes. "Viscount Turley. Why are you so focused on Lady Augusta when she is leaving?"

Because Phinn wanted Augusta as he'd not wanted another lady. And he hated seeing her with another man. Instead of answering her query, he shrugged.

"Dorchester was right." She smiled at a matron accompanied by a young lady with light brown hair. "She hurt you badly. Well"—she linked her arm with his—"there is only one way for you to get over her. You must find another lady."

Perdition! That wasn't at all what he wanted. Yet, he couldn't very well refuse to be towed along. Before he knew it, he had a partner for every dance.

"You have one more set for which you do not have a partner," Helen said, scanning the ballroom.

"I do not." She glanced at him. "I asked Lady Augusta for the second waltz."

"You are making a fool of yourself. Everyone knows she rejected you."

Rejected was such a harsh word. He much preferred *put him off*. That was much better. She'd put him off until he changed her mind. "It is my decision to make."

"Very well, but be prepared to start looking for a new lady." Not waiting for a response, she glided off.

He had one dance to suffer through before his waltz with Augusta. The lady was one he'd not met before this evening, a Miss Caldwell. Phinn bowed. "Miss Caldwell, shall we?"

"My lord." She curtseyed and took the arm he held out. They were halfway through the set when she said, "Did you know that you follow her with your eyes?"

Damn. He didn't know he was so obvious. "My apologies."

"Another lady could help you get over her." The dance parted them again, and he tried to focus on his partner. Then she laughed. "Oh, dear. Your expression. Not me. I assure you. I am only here because my parents are making me come. I already have a gentleman I wish to wed."

Phinn wondered what his expression had been. He attempted a smile. "That is what my sister-in-law said. That I was making a fool of myself." It occurred to him that if he was making such a quiz of himself, he needed an explanation as to why he would not be in Town after tomorrow. Otherwise, Augusta was sure to find out he'd left the country. "I think I need a few days to myself. A visit to my estate seems to be in order."

"Running away?" Miss Caldwell said.

"You might say that. Then again, I have not been to the country since returning to England. Surely there is an argument to be made."

"I believe you have the right of it. Waiting until after she leaves would make you appear pathetic."

Little did she know. "You are correct, of course."

Several minutes later, he found himself repeating the lie to Augusta.

"I think you would have rather visited Elsworth when

you first returned. It is a shame you were made to come to Town." She searched his eyes, and his chest began to ache.

He held her closer during a turn. "Yet, I would not have wanted to miss meeting you. I've never had a friend as erudite and clever."

"I have enjoyed spending time with you as well." Her eyes met his. And he was trapped in her brilliant blue gaze. "I will admit that I shall miss you."

"I will likely not see you again."

"Oh." Augusta was silent for a few moments. "I have decided not to attend any more evening entertainments."

If only he could kiss her. "Is it horrible for you?"

She gave a rueful laugh. "Other than you, this evening all my dance partners are friends of my sisters and their husbands." They made another turn and her lips tilted up a little in a travesty of a smile. "If I was staying it would be truly terrible."

If she was staying she'd be marrying him. "You will have fun in France."

That was the right thing to say. This time her smile was real. "I am hoping to see the original Oaths of Strasbourg."

"They were written in Old French?" What other facts did she have stuffed in that head of hers?

"Yes." Her smile grew broader. "Of course. I have never before seen an original document. Only copies."

That's what he'd do. When he arrived in Paris, Phinn would arrange for her to view the documents. Even if she was angry at him for following her, she might forgive him if he did that.

"I wish you luck." Luck he'd arrange.

For a second she appeared sad, then she blinked several times. "I shall miss you."

"I'll miss you as well." Devil it, he'd better change the

conversation or they'd both become maudlin. "Everything will work out as it was meant to be."

"That's what Grace said." The dance ended, and she curtseyed as he bowed. "I am going home now. I hope you enjoy yourself in Lincolnshire."

"I'm sure I will." Phinn would enjoy taking her there after they married.

He accompanied Augusta and her family to the hall. Drawing her off to the side, he wished he could kiss her. Their gazes caught briefly, then she lowered her thick, dark lashes. He'd never before noticed how they curled up at the tips.

For several long moments, she seemed determined to study the marble floor. "I suppose this is good-bye."

Raising her hand, he kissed her small, delicate fingers. "Not good-bye. I shall see you tomorrow."

Augusta raised her eyes to his as if she would say something else, then shook her head. "How could I have forgotten? This evening has been more difficult than I thought."

Tomorrow could not come soon enough. Seeing her again could not come soon enough. If only he could offer her what she wanted rather than what he must have.

Before Augusta entered the coach, she turned her head to see Phinn return to the ballroom. She would miss him and his conversation. If only he cared enough for her to wait for her return, but he had a duty to his family.

"You like Lord Phineas a great deal." Louisa's words made Augusta turn toward her sister. "And he likes you."

Likes, not loves. I must remember that. "Yes. He is a good friend."

"He could become more than a friend," Louisa said in a cajoling tone.

"Louisa." Rothwell's low tone rumbled through the coach. "Now is not the time to be matchmaking."

"I merely want Augusta to be happy," she said.

Good Lord. She sounded like Mama. "I shall be happy traveling."

"You could travel with a husband." Louisa sounded so sure of herself. Then again, she always did.

Augusta wanted to pound her head against the coach wall. "Like you and Charlotte and Dotty have?" This was outside of enough. "I thought you agreed that I should go to Europe."

"That was before I knew you were in love."

Augusta wished her sister had not seen Phinn and her say their almost good-byes. If only she'd remembered their appointment tomorrow. "I am not in love!" She could be, but that would not do her any good at all. Phinn wasn't in love with her.

Even in the dim coach light, she could see her sister's chin firm. "I do not believe you."

"Well, it is true. Aside from that I would not be able to travel if I had a baby. Look at you, Charlotte, and Dotty. None of you have even visited Paris."

"That is because we have responsibilities here." Louisa raised a brow. "You and Lord Phineas do not."

That might be true for her, but not for him. Still, one extremely pertinent fact remained: "Louisa, he does not love me. I challenged him about it when he proposed, and he told me as much."

Rothwell's brows shot up. "Are you sure?"

What was that supposed to mean? Augusta scowled at him. "Very sure."

"Would it make a difference if he *did* love you?" Her sister prodded.

"It would make it harder to leave." She could admit that much. "I want something more before I settle down to have babies." Why was that so hard for others to understand? "Still, the fact remains that he does not love me. And he has a duty to marry. Dorchester is relying on him to have the heir."

"For Heaven's sake." Louisa sounded so disgusted Augusta almost laughed. "They only have four children. Lady Dorchester is bound to have a son at some point."

Augusta had to put an end to this conversation. "I am going to Europe, and I do not wish to discuss it any further."

"Very well." Louisa threw up her hands. "Have it your way."

"Good. I shall." That should be the end of that. Although with Louisa one never knew.

A low chuckle emanated from Rothwell. "She is as stubborn as you are, my love."

Augusta hid her smile as her sister crossed her arms in front of her chest. That was one more hurdle she had successfully cleared. She only hoped there would not be any more.

She wished she could depart tomorrow. Unfortunately, she still needed luggage, and her clothing was not quite ready. Not to mention that Cousin Prue had not yet arrived, or that Jane and Hector still had things they had to do.

There was nothing for it; Augusta must be patient and trust that her journey would proceed as intended. As for Phinn, however much she'd grown to care for him, their fates lay down different paths. She'd simply have to put him and their friendship out of her mind.

Chapter Seventeen

The next day Phinn arrived at Worthington House promptly at quarter after the hour. Naturally, Augusta was ready to depart. "I'm glad the rain cleared the air."

"I am as well." As she had the first time they'd gone for a ride, she strode straight to the phaeton. He had a deal of work to do if was to get back in her good graces. "My carriage has a hood that can be raised, but I've never used it."

Lengthening his stride, he skirted the footman and reached the vehicle in time to assist her. He held his arm out to her. She stared at it for several seconds before placing her fingers gingerly on his coat sleeve. "I hope you enjoy the lecture."

"With you giving it, I'm sure I shall." Augusta threw Phinn a quick smile. Once her groom climbed onto the back, she gave the pair the office to start.

"I trust you know the way." The streets were busy with carriages, drays, and other conveyances. Not to mention boys cleaning the way for ladies and gentlemen crossing the roads.

"I studied a map of London this morning and consulted with my brother's coachman before selecting my route. I have never been so close to the river before."

Twenty minutes later they drew up in front of Somerset House.

"You did an excellent job." But he knew she would. Augusta was nothing if not thorough. "I won't be a minute."

Phinn jumped down, strode through the door, bid the footman good day, and went back out to the carriage. He'd had no business at all with the Royal Society, but he had wanted to spend more time with Augusta, and he couldn't very well have asked her to drive him the extremely short distance from Berkeley Square to Albemarle Street.

He climbed back into the phaeton. "On to the Royal Institution." They arrived almost ten minutes before his appointed time. He jumped down and went around the phaeton. Before she could object, he clasped her trim waist and lifted her down. It might be wrong of him, but he enjoyed the way her color heightened and her breath caught as he kept hold of her a little longer than necessary. "I shall ensure you have a place to sit before I begin."

"Thank you." Blushing adorably, she dropped her gaze before taking his arm.

"My lady." Her groom had gone to the heads of the horses. "How long do you think you'll be?"

She glanced at Phinn and he answered. "No more than an hour."

"Right, my lord. I'll just walk back and forth."

"There you are," Dorchester called as Phinn and Augusta attained the door.

Her eyes narrowed suspiciously. "You did not tell me your brother was attending."

"Honestly, I didn't know." What the devil was Dorchester doing here? "I only mentioned it to him in passing yesterday, and we were interrupted. He never said a word either at dinner or this morning."

Her eyes met Phinn's as she studied him long enough to make him want to squirm. "Very well. I trust he will drive you home."

"I don't know that either." Phinn glanced at his brother, who'd joined them. "I thought you had to be at the Lords or somewhere."

"I wouldn't miss this." His brother bowed. "Lady Augusta, I believe I must apologize to you for not informing my brother I could have driven him."

The tension that had bracketed her mouth eased as she curtseyed. "Not at all, my lord."

"I must request that you return him at the end of his presentation. Unfortunately, I need to dash immediately to a committee meeting."

"I am here." Phinn truly disliked when his brother acted like he was an errant child. Or was that what Dorchester was doing? Had he noticed the disgruntled look on Augusta's face?

"Yes, of course you are. I apologize to you as well. This was obviously not well done of me."

"As long as you're here, you may sit with Lady Augusta." The front door opened and Phinn led them in.

"Lord Phineas?" A neatly dressed gentleman with dark hair who was around his age hurried up to him.

"I am." He indicated Augusta and his brother. "These are my guests."

"I am Mr. Turner, one of the secretaries. Come this way, if you please."

He led them to two chairs in the back of a large room with windows lining one side. A fireplace blazed at the other end of the parlor. The chamber was already more than three-quarters full. "If you please?"

Augusta and Dorchester took their seats.

"I'll see you after I'm finished." Phinn followed Mr. Turner to the front of the room.

The secretary introduced Phinn, explaining the change for those members who had not been notified. After which he launched into his topic. Strangely enough, the only person he noticed was Augusta. Perched on her chair, she leaned forward slightly. When her brows drew together as if something he said did not quite make sense, he explained himself, finding that he had indeed needed to add more information.

An hour later, after being congratulated by the gentlemen and few ladies present, he made it to the back of the room.

She took his arm. "You gave an excellent presentation. But I didn't know you wore eyeglasses."

"He does not need them," Dorchester said drily. "They are only to make him appear more serious."

Augusta gave a soft thrill of laughter. "Well, they work. You appeared extremely serious."

"That is not the only reason." Phinn scowled at his brother. "They are helpful if one must change one's appearance slightly."

"I am quite sure I do not wish to hear about *that*." Dorchester bowed. "I shall bid you adieu. Lady Augusta, I wish you a safe journey to the Continent."

"Thank you, my lord." She curtseyed.

Phinn took her arm. "I'm glad he came. It had not occurred to me that you should have had a maid or someone with you."

"I hadn't thought about it either." She grimaced. "But his lordship was good company, after he figured out he did not need to explain anything to me."

"That must have surprised him." He chuckled.

"I rather think it did." She sucked in a breath when he lifted her to the carriage bench.

Once they arrived in France, he'd have to think of similar ways to make her aware of the effect he had on her. That they had on each other.

Much too soon they arrived at Dorchester House and Augusta brought the horses to a halt. "This is good-bye, I suppose."

"Not good-bye." He wanted to gaze into her eyes again, but she would not meet his look. Taking her hand, he kissed her gloved fingers before climbing down. "I shall see you again."

"Someday perhaps."

She started the carriage, but he remained on the pavement until he could no longer see her. The next two weeks were going to be the longest of his life.

"He's still watching you, my lady." Jones's unnecessary comment was not helpful to Augusta's peace of mind.

"I do not wish to know." Neither did she wish to feel sad about not seeing him again. Yet, even if he loved her, he could not wait to marry until she finished university.

Once they arrived home, she went directly to her bedchamber, changed into a day dress, and donned her smock. A professor of ancient history she had met in London, who was now in Edinburgh, had sent her a puzzle. She solved it, then crafted one for him, and readied it to be mailed.

Augusta was about to continue reading a guide book on France she'd purchased, when Gobert rushed into the room. "My lady. I think your cousin has arrived."

Augusta stood at the front door as Cousin Prue gazed out of an old-fashioned traveling coach. The lady herself was anything but old-fashioned. Her sable brown Vivers's hair was still unmarred by gray. Small laugh lines fanned out from her blue eyes.

She waited for a footman to hand her down, shook

out her skirt, glanced up at the open door, and smiled. "You must be Augusta."

"I am indeed." Holding out her hand, she laughed. Cousin Prue was perfect. She was of average height, and reminded Augusta of her sisters and every other Vivers lady she had ever met. Cousin Prue also appeared much younger than her thirty years. Although that might be due to the energy that seemed to surround her. "I thought you were coming by hired coach. Surely this is not it?"

"Dreadful, isn't it?" She took Augusta's hand, then drew her in for a hug. "But at least it was comfortable, which is more than the post chaises are. I don't feel as if my teeth have been rattled from my head."

A tall, angular woman alighted from the carriage. "This is my maid, Button," Prue said. "She has been with me since before my marriage."

"Pleased to meet you," Augusta said. "I'll ask our housekeeper, Mrs. Thorton, to make up a room for you and introduce you to my maid, Gobert." They waited until a footman took a satchel from her cousin's maid before starting up the short walk to the hall where the children and Walter—she really couldn't call him a child any longer—awaited. "How was your journey here?"

"I shall tell you about it if you give me some tea," Cousin Prue replied.

"First you must be introduced to my younger brothers and sisters and Matt and Grace. Oh, and do not trip over the dogs." It never ceased to amaze Augusta how easy it was to literally trip over a Great Dane.

She laughed again when Cousin Prue entered the hall and her jaw dropped. "I'd been told there were a lot of children. But I didn't expect this many." Cousin Prue's eyes narrowed. "You are not all Vivers."

"No." Augusta grinned, thinking about the contrast they made. The Vivers with their dark brown hair and eyes that had been compared to lapis, and the Carpenters, who had golden blond hair and eyes the color of a clear summer sky.

The first one to greet Cousin Prue was Mary. "Good day. I am Lady Mary Carpenter. You must be our Cousin Prudence." Mary took Cousin Prue's hand. "I shall introduce you, then we will have tea in the morning room, and you can meet Grace and Matt."

Once everyone had been made known to their cousin she begged them to call her Prue instead of Prudence. "For I assure you, I am not well named."

The twins and Madeline carried Cousin Prue off, leaving Augusta to walk with Mary. "That was very well done."

Mary smiled broadly. "I have been practicing, so Grace said I could be the one to introduce Prue. She is very nice."

"Yes, I think we will get on well. Where are Grace and Matt?" It was odd they were not here to greet Prue. Come to think of it, neither were the dogs. Daisy had been in the hall when Augusta went out to meet Prue.

"Matt is in the nursery, and Grace went to get him." As if Mary knew what Augusta's next question was, she added, "Duke is with him and Daisy went up when a footman was sent to fetch them."

As if they had been summoned, Grace and Matt, followed by the Great Danes, came down the stairs. "I take it Cousin Prudence is in the morning room?"

Mary glanced down the now-empty corridor. "Yes. She wants to be called Prue."

"Augusta, what do you think of her?" Grace asked.

"I like her a great deal. I think you will as well." At least Augusta hoped her sister and brother would feel the same way she did about Prue.

"She looks like a Vivers," Mary added knowingly.

They entered the morning room to find the rest of the family crowded around Prue. The boys peppered her with questions about the war in Spain.

She was in the middle of answering when the dogs made themselves known by putting their heads under her hands. "Aren't you beautiful?"

Mary introduced Matt and Grace.

"I hope your trip was not too tedious," Grace said as she sank onto one of the two sofas.

"Not at all." Prue's eyes sparkled with good humor. "I love to travel and have been feeling . . . oh, as if I needed to be moving again." She glanced at Grace. "My parents were wonderful after Jonathan died. I do not know what I would have done without them, but it is time for me to make a new life for myself. Augusta's request that I act as her companion came at the perfect time." Prue smiled again. "I may not travel by myself any more than she may."

"Very true." Grace returned Prue's smile.

Less than ten minutes later, tea had been poured, and everyone had plates of Cook's tarts and biscuits. Augusta remembered her cousin hadn't answered her question about the coach. "Prue, how did you come to have the traveling carriage?"

She smiled wickedly. "As you know, I have been with my mother and father, helping them at the rectory. Much to his mother's dismay, the squire's son had decided I would do very well as his wife. Nothing I have been able to say to him would convince him that I am not interested in the position." She chuckled lightly.

"Once his mother discovered I intended to leave, she offered me her traveling coach."

"Oh, dear." Grace laughed. "Does he expect you to return?"

"I am quite sure he does." Prue pulled a face. "He is very worthy and could not conceive of a lady wanting to journey abroad or indeed anywhere at all without benefit of a husband. I will tell you he has berated my father for allowing me to follow the drum." Prue grinned again. "Poor Papa, there was really nothing he could have done to stop me. And I am very glad he did not. For the most part, I had an excellent time."

"I never thought about my sisters' willfulness being a family trait." Matt closed his eyes for a second. "Yet I see that it must be." He finished his tea and set the cup down. "I feel for your father."

"I would not be too sorry for him." She laughed. "If it was not for my mother declaring she would wed him and no other, they wouldn't be married." She held her cup out for more tea. "Now, when do I meet Mr. and Mrs. Addison, who Augusta has told me are also cousins but on the Carpenter side?"

"If you are not too tired, we will have a meeting after dinner with Jane and her husband, Hector, who, as you know, is in charge of the trip."

"I am not tired at all." Prue stroked Daisy, who had leaned against her. "I feel as if I haven't had so much energy in a very long time."

As Augusta poured Prue another cup, Grace explained that when Jane and Hector were young, Jane's father had refused to allow her to marry Hector. She refused to wed the man her father had chosen. Actually stating her objection at the altar, since her father had refused to listen to her earlier. Later she had acted as a companion to Grace's mother after her father died.

When they had all come to Town for Charlotte's come out, Jane and Hector met again and married not long afterward. "She also wished to travel, and he promised to show her Europe."

"I see willfulness is not confined to Vivers ladies," Prue said, giving Matt an arch look.

He ran a hand down his face as the rest of them went into whoops.

Augusta's throat tightened. How she would miss all her brothers and sisters and the dogs. Still, she'd have parts of her family with her, and she would not be gone forever.

It was a shame she could not ask Phinn to wait for her. On the other hand, he needed to find a lady he could love. Obviously, that was not her.

"Well, now." Prue stood. "If someone will show me to my room, I shall wash off the dust and change my gown."

"We'll show you," the twins and Madeline said in chorus.

The rest of the children excused themselves as well and the parlor was suddenly very empty.

Augusta picked up the last ginger biscuit, took a bite, and swallowed. "How do you like her?"

"I agree with you." Grace tugged the bellpull. "She'll make an excellent companion."

After finishing her biscuit, Augusta rose. "I'll go change for dinner."

Saying good-bye to Phinn had been difficult, because no matter what he said, it was good-bye, but with Prue's arrival Augusta felt as if her world had started to right itself again. She'd have so much to occupy her time she wouldn't miss him at all.

Chapter Eighteen

The first rays of the sun streaked the antelucan sky in shades of pink, purple, and gray. Boman had been successful in hiring the coachmen and grooms. Although, he'd had to interview several of them before he found men who didn't mind leaving England immediately and for an indefinite period of time. One of the grooms had left yesterday with their hacks so that they'd be in Dover when Phinn and the rest of his small group arrived.

The luggage was loaded on the roof and boot, and Musson had placed a large basket of food items in the coach.

"Just where do you think you are going?" Helen's angry voice pierced the morning stillness. She stood in the door still dressed in her nightclothes, her hands on her hips, looking more like a fisherman's wife than a marchioness.

Her bedchamber was in the back of the house. How the devil had she known what they were doing?

"I knew I should have left from the mews," Phinn murmured to his brother. They had been in the process of saying farewell when they'd heard her.

"I'll take care of this. You prepare to leave on my signal." Dorchester walked back up the shallow steps to the house. "My love, what are you doing up so early?"

"I was sick." She waved her hand at Phinn. "What is *he* doing?"

"Going to Lincolnshire for a few days." Dorchester's tone was as even as if he'd told the truth. "There is a problem there he must resolve." He drew her into his arms. "You've never been sick before."

Before what? What had Dorchester not told me?

"In the middle of the Season?" Helen glared at Phinn.

He debated lying to her and decided he was better off remaining silent.

"I will see you later." Dorchester made a shooing motion, and Phinn signaled the coachman to start as he climbed into the carriage. His brother looked back at Helen. "Come inside. You do not need to be here if you are feeling poorly."

The coach rumbled down the streets and out of the square.

Phinn placed his hat on the rack above him. "That was a narrow escape."

Boman gazed out the window. "When do you think he'll tell her that you're not, in fact, going to Lincolnshire?"

"Not for a few days, I hope. It is doubtful she'd keep the news to herself. And I don't want Lady Augusta to get wind of it." Dorchester's last words to Helen niggled. "What do you think it meant when my brother said she wasn't usually ill?"

"Her ladyship might be breeding," Musson said as he leaned over and moved the basket farther under the seat.

"Pregnant?" Phinn sat up straighter. "And neither of

them mentioned a word." He caught Boman's eye. "Do you think the charms might be working?"

"Could be." He shrugged. "I don't know much about ladies who are in a delicate condition."

"Charms?" Musson glanced between Phinn and his secretary.

"On the way back from Mexico, I bought charms from a woman in Haiti that are supposed to . . . ah . . . encourage the birth of a boy."

"If you do not mind, my lord," Musson said gravely, "I shall add my prayers to your charms."

Boman's shoulders shook, and Phinn grinned. "Not at all. We need all the help we can get."

With each mile they put between themselves and London, the mood in the coach seemed to lighten. Phinn hadn't realized how constrained he'd felt attending *ton* entertainments and being trotted out for inspection. He now had a much better understanding of how the young ladies must feel. In fact, the only times he'd actually been able to be himself were around Augusta. With her he could discuss the things that he liked and not have a lady's eyes widen in ignorance or panic. He wasn't puffed up enough to think it was awe. He wasn't a peer and prayed he never would be. As far as anyone outside of the family knew—and Helen had been told in no uncertain terms never to mention it— he only had a younger son's meager independence. Ergo, the only reason a lady would find him desirable was to produce the next heir of Dorchester.

He was much better off leaving Town . . . and following Augusta no matter where she traveled. Not only didn't she care if she gave birth to the next Marquis of Dorchester, she did not want children right away. Although, if Helen didn't have a son, that could prove to be a problem. Phinn wondered if he would have to wait either until Augusta had achieved her aspirations, or his sister-in-law had given birth to an heir, before she would agree to marry him.

The carriage slowed to nurse the team. As Phinn would be unable to change horses in France, his brother had insisted he purchase six heavy coach horses, making it easier on the beasts as well as him.

The grooms and coachmen were all former Light Dragoons who thought going back to France without being shot at would be just the thing they were looking for. Dorchester had been quick to donate the extra weapons Phinn needed for the new servants. Now that he thought about it, ever since he'd confessed to his lust for Augusta, his brother had done a great deal to help him make his escape from Town.

Twelve hours after they left Grosvenor Square they arrived at the Ship in Dover. "I hope they have rooms for us," Phinn said as he jumped down from the coach. He and his secretary had stayed there when they'd first returned from Mexico. "I could use a soft bed and a good meal."

"I sent an express to them yesterday." Boman was next out of the coach. "While you're seeing to the rooms, I'll find the captain, and the *Catherine*."

"My lord." Musson exited the carriage more nimbly than Phinn had expected him to. "I shall accompany you and ensure the rooms are satisfactory."

"As you will, Musson." Phinn and Boman exchanged a smile. "My consequence will be much higher with you in charge."

"Indeed, my lord." Phinn's valet entered the inn.

Fortunately, the clerk had received the letter, and had their chambers available. Musson busied himself putting the rooms in order, while Phinn wandered into the bar and ordered an ale.

He had just drained his mug when Boman returned with a gentleman around the same age as he and Phinn. "My lord, this is Captain Rodgers, late of His Majesty's Royal Navy."

"Pleased to meet you, Captain." Phinn held out his hand. "When do we sail?"

A grin cracked the captain's weather-beaten face. "Either within the next two hours or at four in the morning."

The promise of a comfortable bed and a good meal warred with his wish to arrive in France as soon as possible. They were all tired from the long drive, and he didn't know if any of his servants suffered from *mal de mer*. "Let's make it in the morning. I take it you will want to load the horses and coach this evening?"

"Yes, my lord. We can't do that in the dark."

Poor beasts. Phinn hoped they'd be able to rest on the ship. He glanced at his secretary. "We need to find the hacks."

"They're at the inn's stables," Boman said. "I'll get everyone together and meet you at the ship."

As it turned out, only one of their party suffered from seasickness. John Coachman, as he asked to be called, pointed to the groom, Freeman. "Sick on every passage we ever took. No need to worry about 'im, me lord. He just takes to 'is bunk and he's fine." The coachman puckered his brow. "Only problem is, 'e can't get up without casting up his accounts. Least not for a few days. Fair useless, 'e is."

Phinn was tempted to laugh. "Well, it's a good thing we don't have far to sail."

The man's brow cleared. "Right ye are, me lord."

They retired directly after dinner, rose early the next morning, and went to the dory that would carry them out to the ship. The *Catherine* had moved to the outer part of the harbor to make the departure easier.

Shortly after noon the following day, they anchored in Calais.

After the children went to bed, Augusta, Prue, Grace, Jane, Matt, Hector, and Walter convened their meeting in the drawing room.

Hector glanced at Walter, who shrugged. "It's too early for me to retire. I might as well listen to the plans. If I did not have to be right back at school, I'd go with you. I just came down to wish Augusta a good trip."

Matt handed around glasses of wine and his butler appeared with a large platter of cheese, bread, and fruit. Once everyone had settled, he nodded to Hector.

"First allow me to say that I am pleased Prue is able to join us."

"I was delighted to be asked." She inclined her head.

"Very well." He handed a piece of paper to Matt. "These are the hotels we'll visit en route to Paris. Lady Harrington has offered to let us reside with her once we arrive in the city." Hector waited until Matt had perused the note. "The Ship in Dover is well-known and perfectly safe. The Chariot Royal in Calais caters to the English and it is well respected. Naturally, whenever any of the ladies wishes to take a walk, at least one footman will accompany her."

Augusta would have her footman as well as her groom with her.

"Being port towns, Calais and Dover are the most concerning, and we will not be in either place long." Hector made a face. "As long as we don't have to wait for wind. I do not expect there to be any difficulties in the rest of the towns."

Augusta knew the journey from Calais to Paris was approximately five days of easy travel. Naturally, they would want to stop and see the sights along the way.

Hector glanced at his list. "I have sent the carriage horses and our hacks ahead so that they'll be rested and waiting in Calais. The coaches were built in France."

She had already arranged for her riding horse to go. But she'd gone back and forth about her carriage. "May I take my phaeton and pair?"

"I don't have any objections." Hector glanced at her brother. "Worthington?"

"As long as you realize that at some point you might well have to abandon the carriage." He raised a brow. He knew! Before Augusta could stop it, her jaw dropped.

"I am not stupid. I am well aware that you will not remain in Paris with Lady Harrington when Addison continues on."

"Mama?" Augusta's voice was weaker than she would have liked.

"As far as I know, she has not a clue, and I would prefer to keep it that way."

"As would I." Her mother would put a stop to her leaving. "I'll leave them here."

Her brother held up his glass of wine, signaling his approval. "A good decision."

"Prue," Hector said. "Do you have any cattle or carriages you wish to take?"

"Not a one." She took a sip of wine. "Aries, my old gelding, could not make the journey. I shall purchase what I need when we arrive on the Continent." She set the goblet down. "We have not discussed finances, but I wish you to know that I was well provided for and can bear my own expenses."

"Thank you," Jane said. "We will allow you to purchase your own horses and any other personal items. But it will be much easier if we take care of the travel."

Prue pressed her lips together for a second then nodded. "If that is what you wish."

"Well, it is," Hector said. "There are times we will be occupying an entire inn. It would be unnecessarily complicated to figure out your share of that. We are also paying for Augusta's travel, and, I assure you, her family is perfectly able to afford it."

"You have me there." Prue's lips relaxed and she smiled again. "I had not thought of all that."

"If you insist on spending your money," Augusta said, "you may accompany me when I visit the modiste in Paris that has been recommended to me."

"Oh." Prue clapped her hands together and a beatific expression appeared on her face. "To have French gowns again. How wonderful!"

For the second time, Augusta's jaw dropped. "You have been to Paris before?"

"Yes, indeed." Her cousin nodded. "After Napoleon was defeated the first time. But only for a month."

The talk turned to all the sights they must visit while in the city.

"I have been told that Sir Charles and Lady Elizabeth entertain quite frequently," Jane said. "We are sure to be invited to one of their events."

"At least one, my dear." Hector chuckled. "I would expect many more than that."

Augusta had not thought about having to attend balls and other parties while in France. Stupid of her really. "I wonder how I should go about obtaining access to some old treaties I wish to view."

"You must ask Lord Harrington to assist you," Hector said. "If anyone is able to help you it will be him."

"Yes, of course. I should have thought of that." It would make sense that an Englishman or -woman would have to go through the embassy. She would like to ask Louisa what she knew of Lady Harrington's life in Paris. But Louisa would bring up Phinn again, and Augusta did not wish to listen to any more discussion about him. He had left for his estate in the country, and in just a few days she would be far away. Then again, Charlotte or Dotty would know as much as Louisa did about Elizabeth's life in Paris. Augusta would just have to decide which one of them to approach.

Chapter Nineteen

The next morning after breakfast, Augusta called for her footman and headed to Grosvenor Square, walking all the way to Brook Street so that no one in her sister's household could see her. Louisa would not waste a minute crossing to Merton House to discover what Augusta was doing. The door opened as she climbed the steps to Merton House.

"Good morning, my lady." The butler bowed. "Her ladyship will be pleased to see you."

She stifled her laugh at the twinkle in the butler's eyes. Her cousin, Merton, always decried that his butler was not as somber as her brother's butler. "Thank you, Kimble. I can find my way."

"I should hope so, my lady."

Despite herself she let out a peal of laughter. "I wish Thorton was more like you."

Kimble's lips twitched. "It would not serve. We have different roles. Please tell her ladyship I shall bring tea immediately."

"I will." She found Dotty seated at an elegant walnut-burl desk with scroll legs. "Good morning."

Dotty glanced over her shoulder. "Good morning to you." Rising from the chair, she came over and hugged Augusta. "What brings you here?"

"I have some questions about Elizabeth Harrington's life in Paris. You know I will accompany Jane and Hector."

"Yes, I do. Allow me to ring for tea." She started toward the bellpull.

"There is no need. Kimble is bringing it."

"Very well. Please"—she motioned toward the sofa—"have a seat and tell me what you require of me."

"Does she attend a lot of entertainments?" Augusta knew the answer was most likely yes, but it did not hurt to ask.

"They are very busy." Dotty took the sofa facing Augusta. "Not only do Sir Charles and his wife entertain a great deal, but there are other parties to which the senior embassy staff are invited. Elizabeth is required to do her part as well. So, the short answer is yes, she does." Kimble entered with the tea tray. When he left, Dotty said, "I take it you had hoped for a reprieve."

"I did, but now I see that I was being naïve." Augusta sighed softly. "I just do not want a repeat of what occurred here." She took a cup of tea from her cousin. "With so many gentlemen thinking they should marry me."

"I am quite sure Matt will provide Hector with all the necessary information." Dotty tilted her head slightly to one side. "Louisa seems to think Lord Phineas would like to marry you."

"Oh, I know he would." Was this part of the conversation truly necessary? "Unfortunately, he does not love me. Even if I was not set on . . . on enjoying Europe, I could not wed a gentleman who does not love me."

"Nor should you." Dotty placed a biscuit on a plate. "You have not given up your idea to study in Italy."

How in Heaven's name did she know that? "I had no idea I was so transparent."

Dotty chuckled. "Only to those of us who know you well. You can be very single-minded. You do remember when you insisted that Matt have a telescope built like the one Mr. Herschel used so that you could see . . . What is the name of that planet?"

"Uranus," Augusta supplied.

"That's the one." Her cousin took a bite of the lemon biscuit. "Then you made him arrange an introduction to Herschel himself so that you could quiz him about astronomy."

"I did not 'quiz' him. I wanted to learn. He introduced me to his sister, Caroline, who taught me a great deal."

"I have no doubt." Dotty's shoulders shook. "That led to you wanting to learn how to navigate by the stars, so you convinced Hector to find a sea captain who would teach you."

Augusta sighed. "If only I could have gone on just one passage so that I could have put it all into practice."

"Perhaps you will be able to make use of your knowledge on this journey."

Augusta hoped Dotty was right.

"Now that I have satisfied your curiosity concerning Paris, is there anything else?" she asked.

"Not at the moment." Augusta put her cup on the low table between the sofas, then rose. "Grace is planning a small *bon voyage* party, just family and close friends."

Dotty came around and bussed Augusta's cheek. "I'll see you then, but if you have any more questions, please come by or send a note."

"I will." She gave her cousin a hug. "Thank you."

A crease formed on Dotty's brow. "There is one thing Elizabeth did say of which you should be aware. The French men tend to be quite a bit more persistent in pursuing a lady than our English gentlemen."

That was something Augusta had not considered. "I suppose I will have Elizabeth to guide me. What I really wish to do is to study some of the old documents housed in Paris. I have written Elizabeth about gaining access to them."

"I am sure you will have a splendid time."

Augusta gathered her footman and started walking home. She was glad Dotty had warned her about the gentlemen, but what a bother. Somehow Augusta would have to find a way to avoid the entertainments in Paris without seeming churlish.

Phinn was happy to find that his brother had sent a message to Le Chariot Royal, reserving rooms for them. After discovering he intended to travel to Paris, the manager recommended the Hôtel Meurice on Rue Saint-Honoré and offered to send a letter to the hotel with Phinn's requirements.

They spent a day in Calais resting the horses before heading southeast to Paris.

Despite wishing to arrive in good time, he could not resist studying the cathedral's architecture in Amiens. They, or rather he, spent two days asking questions about Robert de Luzarches's design that allowed so much light into the building. Finally he was able to look at some of the original drawings.

Before dark on the sixth day after leaving Calais, they arrived at the Hôtel Meurice. Phinn and Boman were offered glasses of wine in a parlor set aside for guests while Musson made the room arrangements.

Several minutes later, a servant appeared at the door. "My lord, your man has your chamber prepared."

"Thank you," Phinn murmured to his secretary as they climbed the stairs. "I can speak French."

"I think they pride themselves on speaking English to us."

"I suppose it doesn't matter. At this point, all I want is a bath and dinner."

"You've read my mind," Boman said.

Phinn wondered when Augusta would arrive and how long she'd remain in the city. He would have only a short time in which to convince her they should travel together.

The following morning, he and his secretary went to the British Embassy and were immediately shown to Lord Harrington's office.

"Good morning, my lord, sir," a young gentleman said as they walked in. "My lord"—the man bowed— "Lord Harrington will see you now." The man turned to Boman. "Please take a chair. Tea will be up in a moment."

Phinn was ushered into his lordship's office. "My lord." Phinn bowed and handed Harrington the letter his brother had written. "This is from Dorchester."

"Yes, I received a missive from him a few days ago apprising me of your pending arrival. Please have a seat. We are always happy to see our countrymen." As Harrington popped open the seal and perused the note, Phinn surveyed the room. It was bright, and resplendent with plaster work. Long windows lined the outer walls, and small balconies were set outside them. Gold and blue curtains complemented the light blue walls.

At one end of the room, an elaborately carved marble fireplace dominated the wall.

After several moments Harrington raised his head. "Your brother asks that we give you any assistance possible in viewing various cathedrals and their architectural renderings throughout the country."

"Indeed. It is one of my passions." Harrington's secretary entered with a tea tray. "Two sugars and a splash of milk, please."

Harrington drummed his fingers on the walnut desk. "Have you done any work with ancient documents?"

Documents? Not really, but Phinn knew someone who had. He raised his cup to his lips and took a sip before answering. "Why?"

"We have a guest, actually several of them, coming to stay with us for a few weeks. One of them is a lady who is quite intent on viewing the original Oaths of Strasbourg. Unfortunately, the director of the Bibliothèque nationale de France will not allow a woman to view them. He is of the opinion that only those who are doing serious research should be allowed access." Harrington took a drink of tea. "Normally, I would accompany her myself. After all, her request is unusual for a lady, and many would not approve." He rubbed his hand over his chin. "I am not sure I approve. But my wife tells me that I am not being open-minded enough, and that the lady's scholarly tendencies are supported by her family." Phinn waited patiently while the other man drained his cup and poured another. Harrington was obviously having trouble getting to the point. "Well, you see it is a delicate matter. Her being a lady."

Finally, Phinn decided to help the man along. "Would this female be Lady Augusta Vivers?"

Relief swept Harrington's features. "Ah, yes. Yes, indeed. Do you know her?"

"I have had that honor." Phinn placed his cup on a small round table next to him. "It would be my pleasure to escort her to the Bibliothèque." Not only would it make Augusta happy, but it might make her think better of him. Once she recovered from the shock of seeing him in Paris.

"My wife seems to think she is quite bright." Harrington sounded dubious.

"She is one of the most learned and intelligent people I know, man or woman." Bright? Augusta would outshine a diamond, she was so brilliant. "When I was in Mexico, the Spanish told me that when Isabella of Spain died, an extra dent was put in the pillow of her effigy to denote her superior brain. Lady Augusta would have two dents at least."

Harrington gave Phinn a long, considering look before rising. "Excellent." He held out his hand. "Lord Phineas, welcome to Paris. We are planning a small party when Lady Augusta and her group arrive. Sir Charles and Lady Elizabeth entertain a good deal as well. If you leave your direction with my secretary, he will ensure that you are invited to the embassy entertainments."

Phinn shook the man's hand and left the office. *Bright indeed.* He scoffed.

He found Boman having a discussion with Harrington's secretary. "Are you ready to go back to the hotel?"

He took a piece of paper the other man handed him. "I am now. I have a list of the most important sights, recommendations for restaurants and taverns, a tailor, and a hatter. I also gave Mr. Turner our direction."

"One word of warning," Medbury said. "I'd stay away from the Latin Quarter in the fifth and sixth arrondissements. The students are not happy with the king." He grimaced. "They aren't the only ones. There is still support for Napoleon here."

"Thank you." That was one thing Phinn had not heard. Thus far, everyone had been welcoming. "We'll be careful."

When she arrived, he'd make sure Augusta was kept safe as well.

"Worthington, you wanted to see me?" Hector Addison strolled into the study. He'd been expecting to have a conversation about Augusta with his cousin by marriage.

"Yes. I meant to have the power of attorney for Augusta to you before now." The man looked as if he'd aged five years in the past week.

"There is no need to worry. Jane, Prue, and I will take good care of her." He took a seat on one of the leather chairs in front of Worthington's desk.

"Claret?" He'd gone to a small sideboard and held up a glass.

"Don't mind if I do." Hector accepted the goblet.

Worthington slid a sheaf of papers across the desk to Hector. "Here is the power of attorney as well as a settlement agreement that I would require if Augusta were to wed."

Wed! Hector had just taken a sip of wine and had to press his handkerchief to his mouth to keep from spitting it out. "I thought one of the reasons Augusta is accompanying us is because she does not wish to marry yet."

Worthington drank half the wine in his glass. "You know she was supposed to be the easy one?"

"I always thought you were deluding yourself when it came to her." Chuckling, Hector started to take another sip of wine and decided to wait. Who knew what his cousin would say next, and the farewell party was start-ing soon. He did not want to have to go home and change clothes. "She's as smart as a whip, as the Amer-icans would say. No female that clever can be easy to guide."

"I wish I'd thought of that." Worthington drained the glass, and poured another. "You know that Lord Phineas Carter-Woods is interested in Augusta?"

Hector nodded. By now, everyone had heard. "I thought he went up to the Midlands after Lady Bel-lamny's ball."

"That's what he told Augusta. But I have reason to believe that he is in France." That was an interesting piece of news. "Kenilworth saw him depart Dorchester House in a large traveling coach, heading toward Pic-cadilly. I wouldn't have thought much of that, but Merton had made a dash down to his estate in Kent, and on his way back is positive he saw Lord Phineas as he was passing through Canterbury."

"Did you approach Dorchester? He must know where his brother went."

"I sent a note but have not heard from him." Wor-thington glanced at the wine, shook his head, and put it down.

A bit of conversation niggled at Hector, then he re-membered it. "You don't happen to know if Lord Phin-eas has a man by the name of Boman working for him, do you?"

"No. But then I would have no reason to. Why?"

"Just after the garden party incident, a man ap-proached Baiju, my general factotum, asking for a ride to Calais on our ship. Naturally, he said that he'd have to ask my permission, but then he didn't hear from him again."

"I do know that he and Augusta got on extremely well together. If it wasn't for this university idea, she might have accepted him." Worthington grinned. "As long as she could get him to admit he's in love with her."

Hector laughed. "I can't say I'm opposed to love matches."

"No. Neither can I." Worthington looked at the papers. "I just want to ensure that you have everything you might require."

"I thought you supported her desire to attend university." Before he left England, he wanted to make sure he knew exactly what Worthington's thoughts were.

"If it were only that simple." Leaning back in his chair, he blew out a frustrated breath. After a moment, he straightened. "I want her to be happy. We all do. In the upshot, that means marriage and children. I do not think she has given enough consideration to how attending university will harm her chances on the Marriage Mart. If Lord Phineas wants her"—Worthington grimaced—"if he loves her as she is, and she loves him, then in my opinion, she should marry the man."

"Even if it means giving up her dreams?" Hector was sure Augusta would not agree she should be made to. "You do know the *on dit* is that his brother wants him to help ensure there is an heir."

"If they love each other enough, they'll find a way to make it work." Worthington laughed. "Lord knows I did. It will be up to Lord Phineas to work out a way for them both to have what they want. That's probably the only thing I know for a fact."

Hector tapped the documents. "I'll pick these up before I leave today."

"As you wish." Worthington came out from behind his desk. "You're a good friend."

"That's what family is for." Hector shook Worthington's hand. "I'll keep an eye out for Lord Phineas."

Worthington raised a brow. "Another American saying? You're picking up quite a few of them."

"Now that everyone is at peace, I've been dealing with a lot of American ships' captains and agents." Hector opened the door.

"We'll soon have two different ways of speaking English," Worthington said as he ambled into the corridor.

"I think we already do." Hector followed his cousin to the other side of the house where the party would be held. He decided to tell Jane what Augusta's brother had said, but not Prue. She was growing too close to Augusta, and he did not want anyone to influence what might happen between her and Lord Phineas. Of one thing Hector was certain. No one would force her into anything she did not want. Not while he had charge of her.

Chapter Twenty

The farewell party Grace held for Augusta and the rest had been wonderful. It was set in the garden and her family and friends had all been present.

"I shall miss you." Henrietta gave Augusta a package. "It is tea. We all contributed. We thought you might have need of it."

"Thank you." Good tea would probably be in short supply. "If you think of anything you'd like me to send, write to me."

Her friend laughed. "I'm sure there are a great many items I'd like, but they'd all require fittings."

"Perhaps some fabric, if you come across anything we do not have here," Georgiana commented.

"That's an excellent idea." Dorie held up her champagne glass, prompting the rest of the ladies to do so as well. "To a wonderful and educational journey."

Adeline took a sip of champagne. "I only want letters, and I shall write you every week."

"Rothwell and Merton have arranged to have letters sent with the diplomatic post," Augusta said. "If you give your missives to them, they'll take care of it for you."

Her friends agreed that was the most expeditious method. After many wishes for a good journey, embraces exchanged, and teary eyes dabbed, they left.

Early the next morning, Matt and Grace came to Augusta's bedchamber as she donned her gloves. Her maid had already left with the other servants.

"It's not long now." Her brother hugged her. "I've given Hector all the documents you should require, including the information for drawing funds if you should have need of them."

"Thank you." She returned his embrace, then turned to Grace. "I shall write often."

"Well, you will have no excuse not to." She drew Augusta into her arms. "I arranged for a great deal of paper, pens, and ink to be sent with you. And you must give your new travel table a try." She handed Augusta a purse. "This is for whatever you want."

"Thank you for everything." Without Grace none of this would be happening.

"I hope you find what you are looking for. Your happiness is all we want." She wiped one eye. "Now, you must say adieu to the rest of the family."

This was going to be the hardest thing she had done so far. Outside her room the twins and Madeline waited for her. Her brothers were lining the stairs, and the two youngest were at the bottom of the stairs. Mama and Richard stood at the door.

Before stepping into the corridor, Augusta took a breath and blew it out.

"You promise you will be back for our come out," Madeline said. She was flanked by Alice and Eleanor, who nodded.

"Yes." Somehow Augusta would find a way to be in Town for her sisters. "Write to me."

"We will," Alice said, trying to blink back her tears.

But there was no hope for that and soon all three of them were weeping.

Mary and Theo too had tears in their eyes when they hugged Augusta tightly.

"We will miss you," Theo said.

"Both of us," Mary added, as if Theo's meaning wasn't clear.

The girls gave Augusta handkerchiefs with their latest attempts at embroidery. Theo had started doing white work, and Mary had almost mastered the art. "These are lovely."

"We will be able to do much better when you come home." Mary embraced Augusta again.

Charlie, Walter, and Phillip each handed her heavy sacks. "What is in them?"

"We each picked things we thought you'd need on your trip." Charlie grinned. "But you'll have to find out for yourself what they are."

Handing the bags to Durant, she hugged the boys. "You are the best brothers a lady could have."

"You'll show them the way in Padua," Walter whispered in her ear.

"I hope so." Despite her education, she expected university to be a challenge.

Next came Louisa, Charlotte, and Dotty. "We have no gifts for you," Louisa said, hugging Augusta. "Only our best wishes."

Charlotte peeked at the coaches outside piled high with trunks and bags. "We thought you might have enough to carry. I expect you brought all the books you wanted, and I hear the shopping in France is excellent."

"I expect you are right." Augusta hugged Charlotte.

"Write often." Dotty embraced Augusta tightly. "You can depend upon Jane's guidance if you should need it."

"I know. I will." Augusta brushed back tears of her own.

Her mother and Richard were the last to say farewell. Richard patted her shoulder and handed her a small purse. "Put this aside for an emergency. You never know when you will need ready funds."

"Thank you." She hoped she would not need it, but her stepfather had traveled the world and knew more about it than she did.

"I hope you have a wonderful time." Mama kissed Augusta's cheek. "I look forward to your return. I know you will write."

"Of course, I will." It seemed that her mother was the only one who did not realize she would be gone for more than a few months. Or perhaps she simply refused to believe it.

Thorton bowed. "Have a good journey, my lady."

"Thank you, Thorton. I hope to." Durant escorted her to the coach, then took his place next to the coachman.

Before Hector handed her into the coach, she turned and waved at her family, now congregated around the front door. The Great Danes had joined them. Mama turned her head into Richard, and he put his arms around her . . . Mayhap, she did know after all.

Prue was already in the coach with Jane on the forward-facing seat of the comfortable traveling coach, where Augusta joined them. Hector, Nurse and Tommy—Jane, and Hector's two-year-old son —sat on the backward-facing seat. This conveyance would take them to Dover. Once they arrived in Calais, another vehicle awaited them.

As the driver set the coach in motion, Augusta glanced back. Her heart tightened as the children's waving hands faded into a blur, and the family she loved disappeared.

A tear slid down her cheek, and she wiped it away. She was a grown woman off to see the world, to study, something she'd always yearned to do. She should be excited, not sad. It wasn't as if she'd be gone forever. Her journey was no different from the ones young gentlemen made every year. Yet, she expected she would probably learn more than most of them did.

Augusta watched as Tommy's eyes fluttered closed. He spent a good amount of time with his cousins. Would he miss them? "What does the coach in France look like?"

"Coaches, my dear. Much larger than this one." Hector beamed. "I borrowed an idea from the French *diligence,* their version of a stagecoach. They both have three compartments. I shall tell you about the one in which we will travel first. Two of the compartments have seats that can fold down into beds." He pulled out a sheet of paper on a board from a pocket on the side of the carriage, and as he spoke, he drew an image. "There are multiple pockets on the sides for gloves, books, games, or numerous other things." He pointed to the front of the drawing. "Here you can see that the coachman's seat has an oilcloth cover that can be pulled over him in case of rain."

"Sort of like Matt's gig at home?" Augusta asked.

"Exactly the same idea." Hector went back to the sketch. "The benches inside of the main compartment are covered in brown velvet. The rear compartment has leather seats that can be protected with canvas."

"That is where Tommy will ride," Jane added. "If he becomes ill or has an accident of any sort, the canvas can be washed."

"What about the front?" Augusta was intrigued by the planning that had gone into this.

"Velvet as well. That will be used by anyone who needs to sleep or would like time alone. There is a cupboard for linens so that the bed can be easily made up."

She could see herself wishing time alone. "What about the other one?"

"I asked my valet and Jane's maid what they would like." Hector grinned. "We must keep the servants happy. That front section will be for the second coachman and whoever of the grooms or outriders needs to rest. The middle compartment is for the ladies' maids, and the smaller compartment is for my valet and my general factotum."

"Do the middle and last sections have beds as well?" Prue asked.

"Three and two respectively," Hector said. "In effect, it can accommodate all the different needs we could think of."

Although Augusta had heard about the French *diligence,* she had never even seen a drawing of one. "How did you know what the stagecoaches looked like?"

"By traveling to France, of course." She gave him a disgruntled look and he laughed. "I had some business in Paris and saw one leaving for Lyon. I was so intrigued that I made it a point to get a closer look."

"Hector has been planning our journey since Tommy was born." Jane glanced at her sleeping son. "He was simply waiting for a good time for us to depart."

"Then I realized if we waited until everything was perfect, we'd never go." Hector glanced lovingly at Jane.

Mentally, Augusta counted up the number of servants and something wasn't right. "Who is going to help Nurse?"

"Mr. Addison is going to hire nursemaids when we get to France," Nurse said as she shifted the sleeping boy. "I've picked up a bit of French here and there, so it will be good for Tommy and me to learn some of a new language. It will also help when I must buy things."

"The two we had before did not wish to leave England," Jane added. "I gave them excellent references and helped them find new positions."

"If the coaches in France are as comfortable as this one," Prue said, "I shall be extremely grateful. If you'll excuse me, I am going to take a nap."

She closed her eyes and a short time later was snoring softly. Augusta wondered if her cousin could always do that or if she had learned the skill following the drum with her husband during the war. Nurse pulled up a cloth that was hanging loose and attached it to her apron, holding Tommy fast before she closed her eyes. Soon Hector was asleep as well.

Augusta glanced at Jane. "I believe we have been left to our own devices."

"I fear we are surrounded by experienced travelers and another who knows how to take her rest when she is able."

"I'm much too excited to sleep. I suppose at some point I will be able to." Augusta gazed out the window. They were already out of London and would soon reach the toll road. "How many stops have been arranged?"

"We shall change horses every ten miles or so." Jane glanced out the window. "Hector has posted some of his own horses and received permission to use others." She smiled broadly. "I cannot believe I am finally going to Europe."

"Why did you not travel to Paris for your wedding trip?"

Jane shrugged lightly. "Grace and Matt were newly married and had Charlotte and Louisa to chaperone. I decided to continue to help with all you children." Jane gazed softly at Tommy. "Then I became pregnant, and we decided again to wait."

"That seems to always be the way." Which was exactly the reason Augusta did not wish to wed right away.

Jane gazed up at the ceiling, then said, "But we were

wrong. Women have babies all over the world. Some of the ladies I have met have gone to sea with their husbands, and had their children onboard. It is more what our families and our society expect of us that holds us back."

"You're right." That really was the problem. The preconceptions of others. And when one did or wanted to do something outside of those expectations, she, not society, was considered somehow wrong.

"I am proud of you for following your dream." Jane held up one of the flasks of lemonade, and Augusta took it. "Not many young ladies would take the chance or the opportunity."

"Not many ladies have at least part of their family that supports their strange aspirations." She thought of her mother. "It is hard to feel like a disappointment to ones you love."

"It is." Jane took a drink of her lemonade. "Even though I was extraordinarily angry with my father and him with me, I was still sorry I disappointed him." She glanced over at Hector, sleeping soundly. "Still, I have never regretted my decision."

"Did you always feel or know deep in your heart that you and Hector would be together?" Over the past few days, Augusta had missed Phinn more than she liked. She didn't know what she would have done if he'd loved her.

"I cannot say that I did." Jane gazed out the window for several moments. "I simply knew that I would never love another man." She glanced at Augusta. "You will meet the right gentleman for you. And when you do, he will be more concerned about making you happy than anything else."

Until recently, she never thought her wish to attend university would make her ineligible as a wife. That when she was ready a gentleman would simply be waiting for her. Yet, after her mother's garden party, Augusta suspected that a gentleman would have to be extremely forward thinking to accept her as she was. Just like Matt had accepted Grace and all her brothers and sisters, and Grace had accepted Louisa, Madeline, Augusta, and Theo. And made sure they were all one family. Of course, the meeting all of the children had had in the schoolroom that day helped bind them together.

For a while she watched the rolling, green countryside. Sheep and lambs dotted the meadows. Trees and hedgerows always seemed to bloom earlier in Kent than elsewhere. Maybe if she met the right gentleman, a man who loved her for herself, she could have everything she wanted.

Chapter Twenty-One

Phinn took particular care with his cravat. Musson stood by with several extra neckcloths placed carefully over his arm. This was the only part in dressing for which Phinn was actually responsible. And for tonight, it had to be perfect. Though part of him wondered if Augusta would notice the pains he'd taken. She had never given him any indication at all she even found him well-looking.

She and her party had arrived at Harrington House late yesterday. This evening Lady Harrington had planned a soirée. Phinn had received an invitation accompanied by a short note from Lord Harrington that Augusta would attend. Phinn paused in the process of lowering his chin. Just why his lordship had sent the missive was not clear. He thought he'd been careful not letting his intentions toward Augusta be known.

Dipping his chin twice more, he looked at the results.

"Excellent." Musson carefully laid aside the other cravats. "I venture to say it will shortly be copied. What shall we call it?"

We? As if standing there ready to assist with a fresh neckcloth was part of the endeavor. Phinn supposed there could be a "we." His valet was responsible for seeing to the perfect laundering of the neckcloth. "*Trone d'amour* is taken, therefore I suggest 'Gone Hunting.'"

Musson pulled a face. "If I understand your meaning, may I suggest 'Love's Knot'?"

Phinn frowned. "No one said anything about love."

"Of course not, my lord." His valet's back was to him as Musson returned the unused cravats to the clothespress.

After dining with Sir Charles and Lady Elizabeth at their private apartments in the embassy, Phinn would accompany them to Harrington House for a soirée. Despite the numerous entertainments he had attended over the past ten days, waiting for Augusta's party to arrive, he'd missed her. Not only talking with her, which was always a pleasure to be savored, but having her near him. She would have understood and taken part in his joy in the way the stones had been laid to form the great arches of the cathedral in Amiens. But she would also have been happy to stroll along the streets, appreciating the differences and the sameness of the towns on the way to Paris.

He kept thinking it was a great shame he had not kissed her that day in the garden. Yes, he was a gentleman, and gentlemen did not kiss unmarried ladies without a declaration. Still, Phinn wished he'd been able to taste her rosy red lips and stroke the silken skin of her cheeks.

He felt a tug as his valet attached his pocket watch and stuck it into a vest pocket. Glancing into the mirror, he noticed his quizzing glass had been attached as well.

"The sapphire tie pin I believe, my lord."

The stone was close to Augusta's eye color. "I agree."

What would she think of seeing him here? Would she be happily surprised or furious? He wished he knew. She might feel as if he'd tricked her. Which, to be honest, he had. Well, there was one thing she'd be glad about. That was seeing the Oaths of Strasbourg. He had arranged for her to view them tomorrow.

Musson assisted Phinn into his jacket. He donned his topper, picked up his cane, strolled out the door, and into the private parlor where Boman waited. "Shall we depart?"

"I was waiting for you." He rose from the sofa.

One of the hotel town coaches stood outside the front door to take them to the embassy. Just over two hours later, after an excellent dinner, their party arrived at Harrington House.

Only Harrington and his wife stood in the receiving line, and it appeared the Stuarts, Phinn, and Boman were not among the first to arrive. What startled him was the number of people present that he had not already met. He'd been to several entertainments since arriving in Paris.

As had happened in England, he found Augusta almost immediately. He made his way slowly through the other guests. He'd been pleased to discover that without his sister-in-law escorting him around, the matchmaking mothers gave him little thought. He was, after all, merely a younger son.

Augusta was speaking with another lady who had the same dark hair as she did, but was several years older.

Grinning to himself, he sauntered up behind her. "Lady Augusta."

Phinn bowed as Augusta turned to face him, raising a brow. "Are you not a little far from Lincolnshire, my lord?"

"I did say I would see you again." He kept his tone lighthearted, as if she should have expected to see him here.

"You did." She narrowed her eyes slightly. "You also

knew that I thought you meant you would see me when I returned from the Continent. What in Heaven's name are you doing here in Paris?"

"I couldn't very well tell you I was leaving for the Continent. You might have found a way to avoid me." The real question was would she do so now.

"But why?" Augusta shook her head slightly. "This— you make no sense at all. You have to marry, and I am not ready to—"

"Have babies. Yes, I am well aware of that fact." For a second he felt as frustrated as she looked. "Who is the gentleman in the green jacket staring at you?"

"I have no idea. Comte something." Phinn raised a disbelieving brow, and Augusta heaved a sigh. "Oh, very well." She cast her gaze to the ceiling. "He is the Comte de Châlons."

"You've only been here a day, and already you are attracting gentlemen." Phinn surveyed the room, noticing several other men looking at Augusta and him.

"It is not my fault." She cut a disgruntled look at the comte. "There are almost as many single gentlemen here as there were in London. I am trying not to attract more attention than I already have."

"No one, least of all me, said you were." Phinn offered her his arm. "Would you care to stroll around the room? I've met a number of thought-provoking people since arriving. You might wish to know them."

She took his arm as if it was the most normal thing in the world. Or perhaps he was the enemy she knew. After all, he too wished to marry her. "How long have you been here?"

"Just over a week. Did you stop to see the cathedral in Amiens on the way here?"

"Yes, indeed." Her expression brightened and a smile touched her lips. "I take it you did as well."

"I couldn't have resisted if I'd wanted to." He chuckled lightly. "I pestered the priest until he allowed me to see the plans."

A slight frown marred her countenance. "Lord Harrington said that he inquired, but that I am not allowed to view the Oaths of Strasbourg because I am a female and cannot be considered a serious scholar."

"So I was told." Phinn was glad the man had not told her he had agreed to help.

Her gaze flew to his. "But how?"

"He mentioned the problem to me." Phinn tucked her arm more securely in his. "I have made arrangements to accompany you."

"You do not know Old French." Drawing her brows together, she seemed as if she was pondering the difficulty. "It will be boring for you, waiting for me to read it."

He wanted to tell Augusta that making her happy could never bore him. But she wasn't ready to hear that. "It's a library. I'll find something to read."

"If you are sure, then thank you very much." Augusta smiled at him again. "I was afraid I would have a problem finding a scholar to accompany me."

"You need not worry about that." They approached an open French window, and he was tempted to stroll outside with her. "I shall be happy to be your scholar."

Her musical laughter made him feel lighter. It had been too long since he'd heard it. "Oh, dear, we are being rude. Prue—" Augusta glanced around. "She left."

"Actually, we left. She is over there." He pointed to a group of people around Lady Harrington that included his secretary. "Who is she?"

"My cousin, Mrs. Prudence Brunning. Her husband died at Waterloo. She has agreed to be my companion."

Augusta seemed happier, more at ease than she'd

been in England. He wanted to believe it was because of him. "How long do you remain in Paris?"

"A few weeks, I think." She puckered her brow. "My cousin, Hector Addison—oh, he is the one who planned the journey—has some details for our onward travel he must finalize. Have you been invited to many entertainments since you have been here?"

"It is not London, but yes." They had begun strolling once more. "Everyday someone or another is hosting an event." She looked as if she wanted to run away. "I have a suggestion." He wanted to laugh at the appalled look on her face, but smiled instead. "Let's not focus on the evening entertainments and instead decide upon the sights you would like to see and we shall visit them. I bought a guidebook and have found a number of noteworthy buildings and other places."

"That is what I have heard as well." She lowered her eyes, and thick, dark lashes lay against her milky skin. "Thank you again for making it possible for me to see the treaty."

"It seemed extremely unfair to me that they would not allow you in on your own merit." He was not going to mention that another reason for arranging it was so that she'd forgive him if she had been angry.

Augusta halted for a moment and gave him a searching look. "May we go tomorrow? It might sound silly, but for years I have wanted to actually see, smell, and touch the earliest and one of the few existing documents in Old French."

"I completely understand. That is how I felt when I viewed the original plans to the cathedral. In fact, I thought you might wish to view the documents as soon as possible and made an appointment for tomorrow." And had purposefully ensured he had no other obligations in the event she wished to view the treaty. He glanced down at Augusta. Her blue eyes deepened with what he hoped was pleasure. What other types of pleasure would make her eyes that shade? "Afterward, we can visit one of the cafés."

"That would be wonderful! I have heard it is proper for ladies to dine or drink coffee or tea in the cafés and restaurants in France. I wanted to dine or have tea in one on the way here, but Jane wished to wait until she knew that it was acceptable, so it was one of the first things she asked Elizabeth."

"I've seen a number of ladies at restaurants." He'd consult the hotel about which café he should take Augusta.

"There you are." Lady Harrington sailed up to them. "There are several gentlemen who would like to be introduced, Lady Augusta."

She glanced at Phinn as she sucked in a breath. "May I meet them some other time?"

Her tone was so doleful, Phinn wanted to take her away where she could just concentrate on her studies.

"I am afraid you must meet them now." Lady Harrington took Augusta's arm.

She glanced at Phinn, as if asking for his help, and he started to follow them. "I shall come with you."

"No, no," her ladyship said in a hasty tone. "You must mingle."

So much for that. Bowing, he took Augusta's hand and whispered, "I'll come for you at ten tomorrow morning, if that meets your approval."

She graced him with one of her bright smiles. "I shall be ready."

Augusta wanted to protest meeting yet more gentlemen, but she had been too well brought up to argue with Elizabeth. Therefore, she smiled politely as three

Frenchmen and two Englishmen who had just arrived in Paris a day or so ago were made known to her. Fortunately, it was a soirée, and there was no dancing. After a few minutes of conversation, she gave them a shallow curtsey. "If you will excuse me, I must find my cousin."

Phinn was acting like her friend again, and Augusta could almost forget he had proposed to her. He still had not completely answered her question as to why he was here and not in London. Yet, she did not wish to press the issue. It was enough she would have with her one of the very few people with whom she could discuss anything. Not only that, but he had arranged for her to see the treaty she had been looking forward to reading.

When he'd said what he did about the library not being fair to her, his gray eyes had taken on the color of molten silver, and his expression was sincere. The best thing about that statement was Phinn meant it.

She remembered what Jane had said about the right man. If only he did not have to marry and have an heir, and he loved her.

Augusta scanned the room but could not see him. Where had he gone?

She had entered the second drawing room before she found Prue and Jane engaging in a comfortable coze. Phinn was still nowhere to be seen. "If you do not mind, I would like to retire."

"Not at all," Jane said, rising. "I shall come with you. I wish to look in on Tommy." She linked her arm with Augusta's. "How are you enjoying yourself?"

"Honestly?" Jane nodded. "I would have rather been left alone with a good book." One of the not-so-pleasant aspects of traveling such long distances was that she discovered she began feeling ill if she read in a coach. "I do have some good news. Phi—Lord Phineas has arranged for me to see the treaty I wished to read. He will collect me tomorrow morning."

Jane took a few more steps before responding, "Excellent. You should mention it to Prue in the event she must go with you."

"You are right." The library was only a little over a mile. "I assumed we would walk, but in the event we take a town coach, I will need a chaperone."

Augusta hesitated to tell her cousin the rest, but she could not lie by omission. And she did not wish to destroy Jane's trust in her. "He has also asked if I would like to visit a café or restaurant afterward."

"Elizabeth did say it is what everyone does. Therefore, who am I to object?" They started to climb the stairs. "As long as you sit outside, I will not ask that you take Prue."

"Very well." Prue might not like the library, but she had wanted to visit a restaurant as well. "Although I think she would like the treat."

The corners of Jane's eyes crinkled. "You must ask her at breakfast."

The following morning, Phinn arrived while Augusta, Jane, Prue, and Elizabeth were still at the breakfast table. Geoff, Lord Harrington, had gone to the embassy, and Hector was off doing business of some sort.

"Have you broken your fast yet?" Elizabeth asked after Phinn had bowed and bid them good morning.

"I have." He grinned. "But if you have tea, I would dearly love a cup." It was strange how Augusta had never before noticed what a nice smile he had. His teeth were even and none that she could see were missing.

Elizabeth waved him to a chair next to Augusta. "I was told your hotel catered to English visitors."

"They do, but the tea just isn't the same as what I have at home." Pulling out the chair, he lowered himself into it.

She poured him a cup of tea. "Will we walk to the Bibliothèque nationale or take a carriage?"

"The weather is excellent. I see no reason not to have a nice stroll." He took a sip and looked as if he was in Heaven. "I thought you might like to stretch your legs after so many days in a coach."

"Yes, I would. Thank you for thinking of it." She glanced at Prue. "Would you like to accompany us?"

"Thank you for asking, but you do not need me. I would rather visit the modiste Madame Lisette recommended." Prue's gaze stayed on Augusta for a few moments longer. "Unless you wish for me to go."

"I actually think you would be bored." She was just as happy her cousin was not coming. She did not wish to be hurried, and would feel that she must if Prue was waiting for her.

"In that case, we all have our plans for the day," Jane said. She glanced at Phinn. "I have given Lady Augusta permission to go to a café if you dine outside."

"As you wish," he said, inclining his head. "I no way desire to harm her reputation."

"Naturally. Her footman will accompany you as well," Jane added.

"Naturally." Phinn calmly drank his tea.

She should be ecstatic he did not appear to want to be alone with her. They were just friends as they had been before. Yet a strange sense of hurt pinched at her. Augusta drained her cup. She was being ridiculous. She had everything she wanted. "I shall be ready in a few minutes."

Chapter Twenty-Two

Shortly after Augusta left the breakfast room, Phinn rose. "If you will excuse me, I shall wait for Lady Augusta in the hall."

"As you wish," Mrs. Addison said. Yet, there was an undertone in her voice that had him wondering if she knew he wanted to be more than a friend to Augusta. "Have a good time, and thank you for making it possible for Lady Augusta to read the document."

"It is my pleasure." He bowed before leaving the room.

When he gained the hall, a tall footman with dark hair who looked to be in his late twenties stood off to the side waiting. That must be the servant who was to accompany them. He'd have to think of something for the man to do while he was dining with Augusta.

Just as Phinn was about to approach the fellow, light steps could be heard on the upper floor. He turned in time to see Augusta pause at the top of the stairs and caught his breath. Light from the upper windows illuminated her form, the small hat she wore appeared like a halo, and for that moment, she looked like one of the angels in the cathedral. Her rose-colored walking gown, topped by a spencer, hugged her full breasts—spencers must have been designed to torture men—making him shift uncomfortably. Thank the deity he was wearing trousers and not pantaloons.

She caught him gazing at her and smiled. "Oh good. You are ready to depart."

Phinn didn't think he'd ever seen her so happy. How many more documents in Old French could he manage to find?

When Augusta reached the bottom step, he strode forward and held out his arm. "Shall we, my lady?"

She tucked her hand in his arm. "Of course, my lord."

The footman opened the door, and followed them out. They strolled down the rue du Faubourg before turning to go by Place Vendôme, pausing to look at the tower with the bronze statue of Napoleon sitting on a horse atop the column.

"Do you think they will ever succeed in pulling the statue down?" Augusta asked. "They have tried more than once."

"I don't know." What made a man need a tower with a bronze statue of himself on it? "Many people here are still quite fond of him."

She hugged herself as if she was cold, and he wished he could take her in his arms. "I fail to understand how anyone could be enamored of a man who was responsible for the deaths of so many."

"Nor do I, but perhaps we will find someone to explain it to us." He started forward, but she didn't move. "Augusta?"

Her gaze was still on the bronze man and horse. "Oh, yes." She started walking again. "I was caught up in a thought."

"Which thought?" Her head must be full of them. She seemed more distracted here than in England.

"He brought order to a country that was steeped in

chaos. If he had not attempted to conquer the rest of Europe, he might have been a hero to us as well."

Phinn mulled that around for a moment. She had a valid point. "I believe you're correct."

Sighing, she shrugged. "Sadly, I cannot change history."

Several minutes later they reached the Bibliothèque nationale de France and entered a good-sized hall with a marble floor. Doors were situated on the sides, a corridor on either side of the hall led to the back of the building, and stairs led to the upper floors.

"Durant." Augusta turned to the footman. "I shall be at least an hour. Would you like to look around for a bit?"

"No, my lady. I will wait here." A small cloth-bound book appeared in his hands.

"We must find—"

Before she could finish her sentence, a middle-aged man in a dark cloth suit of no particular note addressed them in French, "Good day, I am Monsieur Clement. May I assist you?"

"*Oui*," Phinn responded, continuing in the same language. "I am Lord Phineas Carter-Woods. I have come to look at the Oaths of Strasbourg."

Clement glanced at Augusta. "This is not a place for entertaining a lady."

Phinn gave the man a hard look. He supposed it had been unrealistic of him to think he could merely walk in with her and not have her presence questioned. He drew her forward a little. "Lady Augusta, this is Monsieur Clement"—as if she had not heard the man introduce himself. "Monsieur, this is Lady Augusta Vivers. She is even more knowledgeable about the treaty than I am."

The man scowled disapprovingly. "Is this the young woman about whom Lord Harrington contacted the director?"

"It is. However, when you would not allow her to view the document herself, I offered to escort her. I am a member of the British Royal Society." A lie, but how would anyone know?

"There are no women allowed." The man started to turn his back.

Augusta had not come all this way to have some self-important little man stop her. Phinn moved to grab him, but she kept ahold of his arm—accosting Clement would not help them. Using her best Old French, she said, "Do you speak and read Old French, *monsieur?*"

Stopping, the man faced her, astonishment writ on his heavy features. "What did you say?"

She raised her chin. "I asked you in Old French if you either spoke or read the language."

He glanced at Phinn, whose lips were twitching. "I believe you were informed that she knew the language."

"But how—" Augusta remained as calm as she could as the man struggled with himself. Finally, he signaled for them to follow him. "Do not tell anyone."

A sense of accomplishment and success surged through her. She had never been so excited in her life. *I've won! I am really going to be able to see the treaty! For the first time I am being treated as a scholar.*

This is what attending university will be like. It will complete my dreams.

She glanced at Phinn, whose silver eyes were full of pride as he returned her gaze. He inclined his head, and they followed Clement down a corridor to a large room with a domed ceiling and desks set up in rows.

Taking out a set of keys, he inserted one in the lock

of a small wooden door built into the end of the room. "Choose a place to sit. I will return with the treaty."

Augusta shivered with excitement. She had tried to view *The Song of Roland,* which was housed in England, but no one had had the time or credentials to accompany her. Yet Phinn had the qualifications and he had made the time. "Thank you."

Before he could answer, Monsieur Clement returned holding a worn and aged manuscript, placing it on the table in front of her. "Mademoiselle, I ask that you read the first page to me. I have only heard one other person speaking my original language."

"I would be honored." As she turned the pages to the beginning of the treaty, her hands trembled, and her heart pounded. Augusta could barely believe she was touching the same paper, would be reading the same words, that were touched and read eight hundred years ago. Words that brought an end to war and suffering. She took a breath, but her voice still trembled as she read in Old French. "'For the love of God and for the Christian people, and our common salvation, from this day forward, as God will give me the knowledge and the power, I will defend my brother Charles with my help in everything . . .'"

The writing was better than the copies and, as she read, the language flowed as if it was begging to be used again. Tears sprang to her eyes, but she blinked them back. Elation rose in her as her voice filled the almost-empty room. While she read, Augusta began to envision the men writing the agreements that King Charles the Bald entered into with his brothers in the year 842.

She had expected Clement to leave. Yet, an hour later, when she had finished, he was still there, tears blurring his dark eyes.

He took out a handkerchief and blew his nose. "I

have never heard anything so beautiful. Thank you for insisting you be permitted to read this document." Gathering the manuscript, he rose. "Now, you must be parched. I have wine in my office. Will you allow me to give you and his lordship a glass?"

"Yes. I would love a glass of wine." The privilege was not lost on her. She was being treated as an equal.

After he'd disappeared into the other room, Phinn's thumb caressed her cheek. "You did it."

She covered his thumb with her hand and realized he was wiping tears away. "No, *we* did it. I would never have had an opportunity to change his mind if you had not brought me." Augusta wanted to kiss the palm of his hand, but that would not be prudent. "I have never felt so, so elated."

"Yes." He nodded. "I know. It's like that when one has achieved ones greatest desire." He handed her his handkerchief. "You might want to use this."

She dabbed her eyes then blew her nose. "Thank you. I am indebted to you again today."

"Never." His tone was suddenly sharp, so serious it startled her. "No matter what I do for you, I do not want you to feel as if you owe me for it. I have and will do anything I am able to ease your way."

Once again, Monsieur Clement returned before the conversation could continue. "Mademoiselle, monsieur, please follow me."

He led them to a light-filled room on the same floor and poured glasses of a fine claret. For several minutes he spoke of her reading and his love for his language before saying, "The *Sequence of Saint Eulalia* is the most perfect example of the spelling and sound of Old French. It is in Valenciennes. If you are able to travel there, I will give you a letter for the director, allowing you to read it." He heaved a sigh. "My only regret is that I will not be there to hear you read."

Valenciennes was north of Paris. Would it be possible for her to talk Hector into taking a detour? Augusta finished her wine. "If it is at all possible, I will travel to Valenciennes."

Phinn rose, holding his hand out to her. "Thank you, monsieur."

Clement stood as well. "No, thank you for allowing me to listen."

When Clement kissed her and Phinn on both cheeks, she almost went into whoops at the look on his face. Shortly after that, they entered the hall where Durant was waiting. "Got to read it, my lady?"

"Yes. It was as wonderful as I thought it would be." She linked her arm with Phinn's as they regained the street. "Where are we going to eat? I'm famished."

"Au Chien Qui Fume. I am told it is an excellent restaurant." They headed back the way they had come. "It is not far from here."

"I was so nervous on our way to the library, I did not notice much of the surroundings. It will be nice to take in the views."

As they ambled through the streets, Augusta took time to notice some of the differences in fashion and decided she would visit the modiste as well. A lady with a beautiful silk bonnet adorned with flowers sauntered by. "I just thought of something. If we pass a milliner, I would like to buy bonnets for my sisters. They are fifteen and adore hats." On second thought . . . "Although, it might be better for me to go with my cousins."

"I shall have you know that I shall take umbrage at the suggestion that I do not know anything about fashion." Phinn cut her a look. "I may not be an expert, but I know what I like."

Augusta cast her eyes at the sky. "Very well. You may help me select the hats."

They reached the restaurant without finding a milliner.

"My lady?" Durant said. "There is a tavern across the street that would be more suited to me."

"If you wish." She was about to ask if he needed money, when Phinn handed him several coins.

"Thank you, sir." Augusta watched as he took a table outside.

The *maître d'hôtel* showed them to a round table with two chairs on the wide pavement in front of the main restaurant. Phinn ordered wine. Unlike the tavern across the street, the other people eating, or drinking wine, or whatever was in their cups, looked more fashionable than she did. It was definitely time to visit the dressmaker. "What shall we eat?"

"A waiter will come out and recite today's menu." He held out a chair for her and she sat on the round cane seat.

After the waiter had finished, Augusta said, "*Pommes frites?* Have you had them?"

"I have. They are thinly cut pieces of fried potato. I enjoyed them."

The potatoes sounded tasty. "And steak *au poivre?* I assume there is pepper in it."

"A pepper sauce is served over the steak. It will also have *pommes frites.*"

Three other dishes had been mentioned, but two of them she had eaten at home. "I will have the steak *au poivre* and the salad."

"I'll have the same thing. Would you like wine or tea?"

Augusta would have liked another glass of wine, but she did not dare go home in her altitudes. "Do you think they would have the Vichy water here? I have heard some of the restaurants serve it."

When the waiter returned, Phinn ordered the food, then asked about the water. Augusta was pleased to discover that they did serve it.

Her meal was very good. The sauce was excellent and the *pommes frites* were as delicious as they sounded, crunchy on the outside but soft on the inside. The water had bubbles. Like champagne. But other than that, it tasted somewhat like the spring water at home.

As pleased as she was with luncheon, it was the experience of dining outside at a restaurant that she enjoyed most. Being able to watch people of all sorts walking up and down the street was fascinating. She kept an eye on Durant, but he seemed to be doing well. He was even conversing with some of the others around him. Were they English? Or perhaps Irish. Then again, he could have picked up enough French for simple conversation.

"It's nothing like England, is it?" Phinn said.

"It is not." He had finished his luncheon, and now swirled the wine in his glass. "Even if we had restaurants with tables on the pavement, ladies would not be allowed to give them our custom."

"I can understand the male wish to protect ladies." Raising his brows, he shook his head. "However, I do not comprehend creating whole societies dedicated to the oppression of the female sex."

She had seen the males in her family protect or try to protect the women, but even Merton learned he could not control what Dotty decided was the right thing to do. "Nor do I. Some men treat women as if their ideas or thoughts are a threat to them."

"The gentlemen in your family don't appear to believe that."

"Well, not most of them." Thinking of Dotty and

Merton again made Augusta grin. "It took my cousin Merton some time to come around."

Phinn leaned forward slightly, creating a cozy atmosphere. As if they were the only persons present. "I had heard he was much different before his marriage."

"You could say that." She laughed. "Her father is a Radical. He even believes every man and woman in Britain should be able to vote." His jaw dropped and Augusta laughed again. "Even you are not that forward thinking."

One of his eyes closed slightly as he canted his head. "I'm not so sure about that. Quite frankly, I have never given it much thought. When I inherited my estate and became eligible to vote I was out of the country, so I have not been involved in politics."

"I would like to say universal suffrage will come, but I doubt I will see it in my lifetime."

"Unfortunately, I believe you are correct." Phinn finished his wine.

Tomorrow she'd have a glass.

A church bell pealed, and she glanced at the watch pin. It was almost three o'clock. Augusta had been having such fun, the time had flown. "We should start back."

"Yes, indeed. Especially if I am going to be allowed to squire you around again."

He paid the shot, and signaled to her footman. On the way back to Harrington House they took their time, ambling through the Tuileries, the beautiful and famous gardens designed and planted by Marie de' Medici. *London should have gardens like this that everyone could visit.* "Perhaps the next time we can see the Seine."

Phinn grinned. "Or we could visit Notre Dame."

Augusta smiled. "Or we could do both."

As they strolled she could not remember a time when

she'd had so much fun. Phinn seemed to enjoy himself as well. Could something come of it? Probably not. "You did not completely answer my question about what you are doing in France."

Just then they came upon artists lining the pathway. "They are fascinating."

Augusta stood watching while a pastelist sketched a young woman. "I had heard artists from all over the world come to Paris to study."

Once again, Phinn had managed to evade answering her question about his presence in Paris. This time, by distracting her with street artists. Who were marvelous and something one would never see in London. But what was he trying to hide?

Chapter Twenty-Three

"Artists from all over the word study in Paris and Rome as well." The image of Phinn with Augusta in Rome was so clear and strong, it surely must happen.

"Yes, of course. I shall travel to Rome when I have school holidays." She tugged on his arm. "Look, there is a woman drawing with charcoal. I wonder if she will be able to make her name."

"Most of the well-known female artists come from artistic families." Another area where men were against women. How had he never noticed the differences in England before? When he was with the Spanish in Mexico, he'd thought it was just their culture. He hadn't realized how pervasive the fear of women was. That could be the only reason to keep them from spreading their wings.

"It is the same for women scientists and musicians." They passed out of the gardens and onto the Rue du Faubourg, still talking as if they could change the world.

By God, Augusta deserved the chance to attend university. Phinn didn't think it would teach her much, if anything at all. But she deserved to experience what she wished. She warranted being honored for her knowledge. And the only way that could happen was through a university.

By the time they finally reached Harrington House, it was time for tea.

"Will you join us?" Augusta asked, removing her hat.

"Augusta, dear," Mrs. Addison said, "you have just spent the entire day with Lord Phineas. I am sure he has other things he must do."

He'd rather spend more time with her, but not under the watchful eye of her cousin and Lady Harrington. "Shall I see you at the ball this evening?"

"Yes." Augusta sounded none too happy about it.

Taking her hand, he bowed. "Until this evening."

When he didn't ask for a dance, her brow wrinkled in confusion. "Very well."

Phinn remembered seeing a flower seller near his hotel. Fortunately, the man still had bouquets left when he got there. One of the posies filled with yellow and white flowers reminded him of Augusta in her yellow carriage gown. He handed the vendor a few coins, and strode straight to his rooms where he took off his gloves, took out a sheet of paper from his traveling desk, and sat down at the cherry desk. Using the hotel's pen and ink, he wrote to Augusta.

Dear Lady Augusta,
 Please do me the honor of standing up with me for the first waltz and the supper dance.
 I hope you enjoy the flowers. They remind me of you. The messenger will await your answer.
  Yr. Friend and Servant,
  P. C-W

"Musson," Phinn called.

A second later the man appeared from the dressing room. He handed his valet the flowers and note. "Please have these delivered to Lady Augusta at Harrington House. I want the messenger to wait for her answer."

"Yes, my lord."

Phinn paced the room while he waited. It seemed like hours had passed before a knock sounded on the door. "Come."

"My lord." Musson entered the room holding out a missive. "From the lady."

"Thank you." Taking the note, Phinn turned it over, noticing the precise, firm, but feminine hand. Just like Augusta herself. What caught his attention above all else was the image of an open book on the seal.

He held the message, almost afraid to open it. He'd thought he had a good idea, inviting her in private to dance, instead of in the presence of her cousin. But did she agree? He had been told that normally a young lady would not be the first to see a letter. Yet he knew she had a wide-ranging correspondence that no one monitored. Taking a breath, he popped the seal and shook it out.

> *Dear Phinn,*
> *I would be delighted to stand up with you.*
> *The flowers are lovely. Thank you.*
> *Your Friend,*
> *A. V.*

Letting out the breath, he wondered why he'd been so concerned. As far as Augusta was concerned, they *were* simply friends. Nothing else. The problem was *how* to make her think of him as something more.

Phinn and Boman arrived at the ball not long before the first waltz. Phinn had no desire to stand up with anyone other than Augusta, and with Helen not around to prod him, he didn't have to.

He found Augusta dancing the cotillion with one of the English gentlemen who had flocked to France, giving him what he began to think of as her vacant look. Unfortunately, the fellow appeared extremely pleased with himself as he nattered on.

Devil confound it. The same thing that had occurred in London was going to happen here. Somehow he had to find a way to discourage gentlemen from offering for her. Augusta deserved to enjoy the entertainments without a man offering for her every time she turned around. To the best of Phinn's knowledge, there was no one gentlemen's club the Englishmen frequented. That would make his objective harder.

Spotting her family, he made his way to them before the set ended. "Good evening."

The Addisons and Mrs. Brunning returned his greeting.

"Thank you for arranging Lady Augusta's visit to see the documents," Mrs. Addison said. "She was absolutely delighted with the experience."

Had Augusta not told them she was the one who tipped the scales, as it were? "I did nothing more than facilitate her entry into the building. Lady Augusta was the one who convinced the director to allow her to read the treaty."

The older woman's eyes widened. "She did not tell us that part."

"She is too modest." Phinn decided to say no more. This was Augusta's story to tell. Did she not trust her cousin? She had spoken well about the woman today.

As he conversed with Augusta's family, her dance partner, Lord Reynolds, returned her to her family. "Lady

Augusta," the man gushed, "I greatly enjoyed standing up with you."

Phinn had to stop himself from rolling his eyes; then he caught Addison's look. Her cousin was no more excited about the fribble than Phinn was.

He'd met his lordship shortly after he had arrived in Paris. Reynolds had been traveling on the Continent for the past year, but it was now time for him to return home—and no doubt find a bride. Phinn knew that even if he proposed, again, she wouldn't accept him, but the fact that Reynolds was bound to make an offer irked Phinn to no end.

Fortunately, the music announcing the waltz began. "My lady." Holding out his hand, he bowed to Augusta. "This is our dance."

Her smile lit a fire in his soul, and she placed her small, perfect fingers in his. "It is, my lord."

He steeled himself against the way his body heated when he placed his hands on her waist. How could she not feel something! Then he saw it. The pulse on her neck quickened and her eyes grew darker as he twirled her around the floor. Yet, how was he to convince her she belonged with him?

Augusta did not understand why she felt so warm when she danced with Phinn. She did not have this reaction to anyone else. Perhaps it was because she actually enjoyed the set instead of going through the motions. She glanced up at him. His eyes were like storm clouds. Had the rest of his day not gone well?

"Are you upset about anything?"

"Me?" He seemed startled by the question. "No. I'm fine. Would you like to visit Notre Dame tomorrow? We'll go to a milliner's afterward, and you can purchase hats for your sisters."

That was a wonderful idea. "I would love to. I have

wanted to see the cathedral. If you need someone to take notes, I am happy to act as your amanuensis."

"Excellent." She'd do a good job as well. "Shall I collect you at ten again?" Phinn was keeping up with the conversation, but Augusta thought he seemed distracted. And he was not telling her everything. Although, maybe she should not wish to know what he did when he was not with her. After all, he was a man. Perhaps he had found a lady to whom he would propose. Yet, if he had, why would he want to spend the day with her? Perhaps the lady did not like analyzing the architecture of churches. If that was the case, it wouldn't be a good match. She would make a decision when she met the woman. Surely, Phinn would introduce the lady to his friends.

They spent the rest of that set and the next discussing what they wished to see. At the end of the evening, she still had the unsettling feeling she was missing something. But she no longer thought a lady had distracted him.

The next day they went to the cathedral, where they spent several hours, then to a milliner's. He found a wide-brimmed bonnet that curved down when a ribbon was tied beneath one's chin.

"How do you like this?" He held it up over her head, then pulled a face, making her laugh. "I think you should try it on."

After removing her hat, she donned the other one. "Yes, I think this will do. Now to make it extravagant so that the twins and Madeline will love it." Augusta called to a young woman who seemed to be in her mid-twenties. Recalling the name on the sign out in front, she said, "Good day, are you Madame Belrose?"

"I am her daughter. How may I help you, Madame?"

"I have three sisters who are fifteen years of age and adore beautiful and unusual bonnets. Can you design something for them?"

"Fifteen, you said?" the woman asked. Augusta nodded. "I have a new fabric from the town of Tulle. Perhaps that and silk flowers. But at that age, they must begin to understand that more is not always better." The milliner sketched as she spoke. When she was done, she showed Augusta a hat adorned with a sheer fabric, ribbons, and flowers, but also with more sophistication than what the girls normally wore. "I will show you the fabric."

Tulle turned out to be a fine net fabric. Some of it was plain, but some had small dots, and others were embroidered in gold and silver thread. Her eye was drawn to one with small seed pearls attached to it. Then Madame showed her one with spangles. "That is perfect. The bonnets each need to be in a different color."

The young woman grinned. "But, of course."

"I would also like to buy several ells of tulle." The new fabric would be perfect for her friends. Before they left the shop Augusta had ordered three bonnets, trimmed as Madame had drawn them.

She linked her arm with Phinn's as they left the shop. "Now I must find something for Mary and Theo."

"The terrifying younger two?"

Augusta was ready to chastise him, but his eyes were full of laughter. "Yes. Do you have any ideas?"

"Not at the moment, but I'll think on it." They passed a store window with gowns for younger girls. "Let's look in here."

"Good day, Madame. I am looking for gowns for two girls. . . ." The modiste went over designs and fabrics with Augusta. She drew out the list Grace had provided of the girls' measurements. An hour later, after ordering two gowns that could be worn for dinner as well as special occasions, she and Phinn departed the store.

"Do you have any more shopping to do?" he asked.

"I should get something for everyone, but there are other countries."

"There are indeed." He chuckled. A few minutes later he said, "Is Paris everything you thought it would be?"

"Parts of it are." The parts when she was discovering the city with him were fun and entertaining and just what she liked. It was strange no one else seemed to wish to accompany them. Not even Prue, whose position it was supposed to have been. Then again, Augusta did not pay her cousin, and she really did not need her. In fact, Prue would be *de trop* when Augusta was with Phinn. "I am not as fascinated in the evening entertainments."

"I find myself in total agreement with you." Phinn's tone was as dry as dust. Was that it?

"Then why do you attend?" If she had her way, she'd do something else. "No one is making you."

"To ensure you are having a good time." He glanced down at her. "Even if no one else notices, I can see you are bored to death."

If she could dance every set with him, she would not be bored. "If only more gentlemen had the slightest interest in anything other than themselves."

"Yes, well . . ." He let the sentence hang. They had crossed one of the small bridges crossing the Seine and were in an area called La Rive Gauche. Artists lined the pavement along the river as they had in the park yesterday. "Would you like to have your portrait painted?"

"Perhaps some other time." She glanced around. A number of cafés were in the area. "Right now I am quite peckish."

Phinn let out a bark of laughter. "Never let it be said I keep you from nourishment."

Although the restaurants were busy, they found one with a vacant table outside. The offerings were different from what they had had before, but they still sounded wonderful. But it was growing late, and not only tea, but dinner awaited. In the end, they both chose omelets accompanied by a green salad and crusty bread.

After arriving back at Harrington House, Phinn suggested they visit the Musée du Luxembourg and have luncheon at another restaurant. "We shall be hungry again."

"Do you not wish to go to the Hôtel de Cluny?"

"I do. In fact, I've asked Lord Harrington if he can make the arrangements."

"I hope he's successful."

Three weeks later, Phinn and Augusta had visited the famous house and had exhausted the sights to see in Paris.

"We are going to Versailles tomorrow," Augusta said as she and Phinn walked back to Harrington House.

"I know. Your cousin, Mr. Addison, invited me to accompany your party."

"Did he?" Her brows shot up. That was surprising.

"Do you mind?" Phinn frowned slightly, his tone hesitant.

"Not at all. It is only that Hector has not asked any of the gentlemen to do anything with us. He even requested Lady Harrington not to invite any of them to dinner."

Phinn guided her across the street. "I shall choose to be honored."

"I should say so." Augusta laughed.

She was not laughing an hour later when Hector asked to speak with her privately in Lord Harrington's office.

"I have received three offers for your hand." He sounded as if proposals were the last thing with which he wished to deal.

"You cannot be serious." She had made absolutely sure she did nothing but dance with any gentleman other than Phinn. She bit down on her bottom lip, praying one of the offers wasn't from him. But he would not. He knew she must attend university.

"I wish I was." Hector heaved a sigh. "Your brother warned me this might happen."

She sat on a cane-backed chair, allowing her cousin to occupy the sofa. "Who are they and what did you say?"

"Lord Reynolds, Lord Cloverly, and the Comte de Mortain. I told them all that you were not available to wed."

She wrinkled her nose. "Not available to marry. I suppose that is as good an excuse as any. Did any of them ask for a reason?"

"No." Hector drew his lips down. "I imagine they will make their own assumptions. I can only trust word spreads, putting an end to this foolishness."

Augusta hoped his expectation bore fruit. "Very well then." When she rose, he did as well. "I'll be happy to leave Paris. Maybe the next place we visit, I will not be made to attend balls and such."

He suddenly barked a gruff laugh. "That would be my recommendation."

Chapter Twenty-Four

When Augusta walked into the breakfast room the next morning, she was surprised to see she was the last one down. Everyone, other than Jane and Hector who had begun breaking their fast in their rooms with Tommy, was at the table. "You are all up early."

"I could not sleep another wink." Prue picked up the pot of tea next to her and poured a cup for Augusta. "I loved Versailles the last time I saw it, but that was in the evening. I cannot wait to see the gardens."

She put two sugars and milk in her tea. "Is it as fabulous as everyone says?"

"More so," Elizabeth replied. "I am very glad it was not destroyed during the revolution."

"Indeed." Harrington handed the newssheet he'd been reading to his wife. "The gardens are exquisite."

"I would advise you to eat now. There will be food at Versailles, but you will be lucky to get much of it. There will also be a great many guests."

A footman brought Augusta two soft boiled eggs and fresh toast. "I must admit, I am looking forward to wearing my new gown." She had been surprised to discover she was not limited to pale colors, yet she looked well in white. The modiste Madame Lisette had recommended turned out to be her cousin, Madame Félicité. She had recommended a white silk heavily embroidered with bright spring flowers, seed pearls, and silver thread. It was a court gown, after all. With it Augusta would wear the pearls her mother had given her. "I find it strange to be dressing so elegantly for a daytime event. Then again, I had to do the same when I was presented."

"Day or evening," Elizabeth said, "it is still the French court."

That was true. Augusta dug into her breakfast.

A few hours later, Augusta, Prue, Jane, Hector, Elizabeth, and Harrington stood at the front door while two coaches were brought around the courtyard drive of Harrington House. Each coach had a matched team of four horses. One set in black and the other set in dark bay with white socks. Two footmen rode on platforms built onto the back of the coaches. Six outriders, also in livery, were on horseback. They were all required to make the correct impression, and the jewelry they were wearing was worth a fortune to those less fortunate.

Elizabeth decided the ladies would travel together, leaving the gentlemen to their conversation.

Augusta was about to take her place in the coach, when Harrington pulled out his pocket watch. "I informed Lord Phineas we would depart on the hour. You ladies may leave when you wish. We should have no problem catching up to you." Just as Harrington tucked his watch into his waistcoat pocket, Phinn strolled into the courtyard. "Well met." Harrington inclined his head. "Gentlemen, ladies. We are ready."

As with the other men, Phinn's jacket was velvet and heavily embroidered. The color was Prussian blue with gold thread and flowers around the collar, down the edges, and around the hem. The jacket showed his broad shoulders to perfection. The flowers on his waistcoat matched the jacket, but along the bottom edge of the waistcoat were small peacocks. His breeches were the same color blue. He wore a court sword and carried a *chapeau bras*. As at the English court, gentlemen did not actually wear the hat.

Although Augusta had expected him to wear court dress, she had not expected him to be so handsome. When did that happen? She had spent at least part of every day with him and had never given his looks much thought. Now, she could not stop gazing at him.

"Augusta, dear." Prue touched Augusta's arm. "You are staring."

Heat rose in her cheeks, and her heart began to pound harder, making it hard to breathe. Then Phinn's gaze met hers, and he grinned like he always did. "You"—he kept his eyes on her as he bowed—"all of you look lovely."

"I'd thought I'd left my days of dressing for court behind me," Hector complained. "Although, the courts I attended belonged to Indian princes and pashas."

"You look very handsome, my love." Jane reached up and bussed his cheek. "I shall see you there."

When Augusta finally managed to drag her gaze from Phinn, he offered her his hand. "Allow me."

"Thank you." She placed her fingers lightly on his palm. A tingling started the moment he closed his hand around hers.

Not this again.

The next second she was in the carriage, and he had stepped away. She was not going to think about him anymore. He was just her friend. Nothing more. The paths their lives were taking would not allow them to be together.

Despite the warning Elizabeth had given them, when

they arrived at the Palace of Versailles, the gathering was much larger than Augusta had expected.

Long tables had been set up, and footmen were running back and forth putting platters on them. Smaller tables with chairs dotted the area at the back of the palace, around the garden.

They made their way to where the king and queen sat on a dais under a canopy, and were presented. After that, her party began strolling through the gardens, greeting the people they knew.

Somehow Augusta found herself separated from the others and being escorted through the gardens by the Comte de Châlons.

Drat, she really needed to pay more attention to what she was doing, where she was going, and with whom.

A rose bower stood at the end of the path they were on, which would effectively shelter her and the comte from anyone else's sight. "I must go back."

"You cannot truly wish to return." His tone—she was certain—was meant to be seductive. All it did was raise the hairs on the back of her neck.

"I do, indeed, wish to return." She dropped her hand from his arm and turned to leave. Before she could make her escape, his fingers closed around her arm.

"My lady, I have something I wish to say to you . . . privately."

"I am sure you do," she muttered to herself. How was she going to get out of this bumble-broth without creating a scene?

"I beg your pardon?" He started steering her back down the path toward the bower. "After we have our little talk, I will show you our late queen's favorite palace, the Petit Trianon. You will adore it."

"Let. Me. Go." Augusta jerked her arm trying to loosen his hold. "I do not wish to have a discussion with you."

"Ah, but I cannot." The comte turned to her again, trying to draw her closer. "You are an innocent. This I know. But you need have no fear. I would never harm you, *mon trésor.*"

She dug the heels of her half-boots into the macadam path. Why had she not been paying more attention? Why hadn't she brought her dagger? Not that this gown had a pocket for it.

"Monsieur le Comte." A young man with blond hair and a heavily embroidered blue suit, whom she'd never met, moved his hand to his sword. "Did I not hear the lady say she wishes to leave?"

"I do not believe you are here to save a lady in distress." Sneering derisively at the young man, he pulled her arm. "You are mistaken."

"I do not believe I am." The other man stepped toward them.

"Lady Augusta, I have been looking for you." At the sound of Phinn's voice, Châlons's grip slackened and she broke free.

She had just reached Phinn and taken his arm, when the comte said, "*Messieurs,* you interrupt."

Phinn arched one haughty brow. "I am quite sure I did."

"What right have you?" Ignoring the young man, Châlons focused on Phinn. His brows lowered, and his tone held a dangerous note. Even more disturbing, the comte's hand went to his sword. "I demand you depart immediately."

Phinn covered her fingers with his. "We will be happy to comply." He nodded curtly to both men. "I wish you a good day."

"You will meet me for such an affront." At the same time, Châlons moved as if he would stop her and Phinn from leaving, and the other man closed the distance between them.

"Meet you? As in a duel?" Augusta couldn't hide her shock. The man could not be serious. "They are illegal."

"It's not enforced," Phinn murmured. "Monsieur, perhaps you are unaware that Lady Augusta and I are betrothed."

"Betrothed?" The man shook his head as if he did not understand.

Oh, for the love of God! Augusta blew out a frustrated breath. This was becoming a family habit. First Dotty, then Louisa, and Charlotte. Although Louisa had been the one to declare she and Rothwell were engaged. Unfortunately, Augusta could not very well object at the moment. The last thing she wanted was for Phinn to be killed in a duel.

"*Elle est ma fiancée*," he said patiently, as she did her best to gaze lovingly up at him.

"Come." She tugged on his arm. "We should go back. I have been gone too long."

"As you wish, my dear." They strolled off before the comte could ask any more questions.

Suddenly, the young man was in front of them, staring at her like Lord Lancelot used to do. "I would have been honored to rescue you."

Although the gentleman had addressed her, Phinn answered. "We appreciate your assistance, monsieur."

He took a step forward, but instead of moving out of their way, the man said, "I would have fought a duel for you."

Phinn's arm tightened as if he were preparing to fight, yet when he spoke, his tone was a well-bred drawl. "I am quite sure you would have, however, I beg you will not. The lady is averse to bloodshed on her account."

This time he gave the young man a pointed look, and the gentleman stepped aside then left.

She glanced at Phinn. "Are all young men so dramatic?"

"All young men are in need of a great deal of maturity."

They were almost at the palace before Augusta decided it was safe to speak. "We are not betrothed."

"You may jilt me when we leave Paris." Phinn's tone was even, but he gave her a hard look. "What the deuce were you about, going off with the man?"

"I was trying to think of a way to convince Hector and Jane to allow me to travel to Valenciennes."

"Valenciennes?" Phinn's brow cleared. "Ah. The *Sequence of Saint Eulalia.*"

"Yes." She was pleased she had not had to explain herself. "You must remember that Monsieur Clement said it is the best example of Old French as it was spoken."

"Augusta, I understand how important that is to you." It suddenly occurred to her that he really *did* understand. "But, you must be more aware of what is going on around you." He heaved a sigh. "Do you know what might have happened if Châlons had succeeded in getting you alone?"

"I suppose he would have tried to kiss me, but—"

Phinn stopped strolling. "He might have succeeded in compromising you."

"I suppose you are right." In fact, if it wasn't for Phinn, that is exactly what could have occurred. If only she could pay attention long enough to keep gentlemen from paying attention to her. The problem was, almost every time one of them started speaking, her mind wandered to a more absorbing topic. "I shall have to start carrying my dagger."

"While you're at it you can have shoes specially made with blades in the heels."

"Oh, so that if I stamp on a gentleman's foot it will hurt him." This is what she needed, practical help. "That is an excellent idea. Thank you."

"I wasn't entirely serious." He closed his eyes for a moment, rubbing the spot between them. "If Addison agrees, I will escort you to Valenciennes."

"Oh, Phinn, thank you!" Augusta wanted to throw her arms around him and . . . and kiss him. Where had that thought come from? She gave herself a shake, then smiled at him. "You are the best of friends."

And a friend was all he would ever be. No matter how handsome he had become, or how much she enjoyed his company, and he hers. Phinn did not even wish to remain betrothed to her. He most likely thought of her as the sister he never had. She should think of him like she did Walter or Charlie, but . . . but . . . No! She wasn't going to think about him at all.

Phinn searched through the crowd of guests near the palace until he saw Lord and Lady Harrington. He'd have to have a conversation with them and Addison before the comte got back and told everyone that Phinn and Augusta were betrothed.

It had felt good claiming her as his. Unfortunately, it wasn't what she wanted, and he would never trap her into marriage. Images of them ambling along hand in hand assailed him. For the first time, he could not envision his life without her. Not just in his bed, but going through life's daily chores and traveling with her. Lately, it had been hard to leave her at Harrington House. Phinn wanted to take her home with him.

Did that mean he was falling in love? Dorchester said it snuck up on a man. One day a gentleman was just happy bedding a beautiful, desirable creature, and the next he realized he never wanted to live without her.

Well, blast it all. Phinn hadn't even got to bed Augusta,

and already he could not imagine a time when she was not in his life. But what would he have to do to make her willingly enter into the state of matrimony with him? Not what he had been doing. That was clear.

He had to give her what she wanted, but how could he do that and keep his promise to his brother? Until he figured that out there would be no bedding.

Phinn left Augusta with her cousin and Mrs. Addison while he joined Addison's group. The man raised a brow and Phinn gave a slight nod. They had both seen Châlons steering a completely oblivious Augusta away from the rest of the guests. Fortunately, Addison had agreed Phinn should be the one to fetch her.

"Excuse me, gentlemen," Addison said before following Phinn. "Not that I have anything against the comte. He appears to be a perfectly good man, but Augusta is in my charge. What the devil happened?"

Phinn couldn't help but smile a bit. "She was trying to come up with an argument to convince you to allow her to go to Valenciennes."

The other man's eyes widened. "What the deuce is in Valenciennes?"

"The *Sequence of Saint Eulalia*, of course." He laughed as Addison hung his head and shook it. "It was as we thought. She started thinking about something and stopped paying attention to everything else." Phinn explained he'd found Augusta demanding to return to her party and the comte refusing to let her go. "I daresay, many English gentlemen would do the same." He held that thought for a moment then said, "I don't think it's right, but there it is."

"Is that all?" The look Addison gave Phinn told him he expected there to be more to the story.

"Not precisely." His lacy cravat seemed to tighten. "Châlons objected to my interference and called me out. That was when I told him Lady Augusta and I were betrothed." Addison heaved a sigh. "I told her she could jilt me when we left Paris, but our so-called betrothal should give you some peace."

"Well, if it gets out, that would explain my telling the men who have proposed that she is unavailable." He wiped a hand down his face. "And Worthington thought she'd be the easy one." Yet instead of grumbling, the older man barked a laugh. "What do you suggest we do?"

Unavailable to wed? What did that mean? And what other men? Glancing around, Phinn caught a young man staring at Augusta in the same way Lord Lancelot used to do. "Allow me to escort her to see the Sequence. Naturally, Mrs. Brunning will accompany us, so there will be no issue of propriety. With the travel there and back, and the time it will likely take to get permission to see the document, it will be around ten days before we return."

"Which is when we'll be ready to continue our journey." Addison thoughtfully rubbed his chin. "That will work. With you and Augusta out of sight and mind, as it were, any gossip will, hopefully, die down."

"Not only that, but with the amount of time we'll be traveling, by the time we return to England, it will have been forgotten."

"Unless you do wish to wed her." There was a sly look in his eyes.

"Mr. Addison, in case you have not heard, I have already asked Lady Augusta to marry me, and she was not open to my proposal." Vehemently, not willing to even listen to Phinn's offer.

"I know." He gave Phinn a steady look. "But it doesn't look to me as though your feelings have changed."

The neckcloth tightened. Not only had they not changed, they had become deeper. "The difficulty is that I made a promise to find a wife and get an heir. She is not yet ready to settle down with children."

"That is a problem. But I'll tell you that I will always regret not staying and fighting for Jane. I was damned lucky she didn't marry another man." Addison's brows lowered and he rubbed his chin. "You know, even if you did wed to get an heir, there is no controlling how long it would take." Gazing over Phinn's shoulder, Addison said, "As far as I know, there's no law that says a lady can't attend university and be married at the same time." He patted Phinn on his shoulder. "You collect the ladies and call for the carriages. I'll find Harrison."

What the hell had just happened? Even though Phinn had tried to put the incident with the comte in the best light, he had expected Addison to be at least a little upset. Not try to encourage Phinn to do exactly what he wanted. In fact the only thing stopping him from promising Augusta everything she wanted was his duty to his brother. He could not bring himself to abrogate one vow to take another. Somehow he had to find a way to have Augusta and keep his promise to his brother. Still, what her cousin said made sense. Babies did not necessarily follow marriage. Especially, if one took care.

Chapter Twenty-Five

When their party arrived back at Harrington House, Hector sent Augusta up to consult with the maid about packing for the jaunt to Valenciennes and promptly convened a meeting with Jane, the Harringtons, and Prue. He told them what had happened with Augusta and Lord Phineas at Versailles.

"That was fortuitous," Elizabeth Harrington said as she poured them glasses of wine. "I was running out of gentlemen to throw at her."

"I, for one, don't know that it did much good." Harrington took his goblet of wine. "He never seemed jealous."

"Because he knew Augusta did not care for any of them," his wife pointed out. "She only had a good time dancing with him."

"I must say"—Jane took a sip of wine and swallowed it—"I've felt almost guilty allowing her to run all over Paris with Lord Phineas. Even if I did make her take her footman. She would never have been allowed to do that in London."

"Think about how I feel," Prue added. "I am supposed

to be her companion and have done absolutely nothing but acquire a new, and very fashionable, wardrobe."

Hector set his goblet down. "In London they would have been noticed. I doubt any of our set saw them going to the historical sights."

"I believe you are correct," Elizabeth said. "I would have heard about it from someone."

"Other than allow them to spend time alone"—Jane's lips formed a moue—"I don't know how else to show them they were meant for each other."

"But do we know he loves her?" Harrington asked. "He is not doing anything that was on the list."

Sitting next to him, his wife patted his knee. "Augusta is not a typical young lady. He has done everything *she* wished him to do, and he made it possible for her to see that document."

"He only sent her flowers once." Apparently the man could not give the topic up.

"That is true," Elizabeth said. "But it was an unexpected, singular gesture. Unlike the other gentlemen who bombarded the house with posies she never even noticed."

"I talked to him after he rescued Augusta from the comte." Hector grinned to himself. "The poor devil is torn between his feelings for her and his vow to his brother." This time he couldn't keep his laughter in and it was a few moments before he could continue. "I suggested that babies did not necessarily need to come straightaway. I'm not entirely sure he took my meaning."

Jane glanced at Elizabeth. "Speaking of getting heirs. Have you heard anything about Lady Dorchester? If she was to have an heir, Lord Phineas would be free to follow his heart, and Augusta would have the gentleman she needs."

"I received a letter from Louisa. It appears that Helen Dorchester is breeding again. Unfortunately the birth will not be until around Christmas."

"I don't want them to wait that long," Hector said.

"I am not convinced she has given the matter any thought at all," Elizabeth said.

"Well, she was thinking of something today." Prue gave them all a look. "She couldn't drag her eyes away from him."

"Oh, I think she is attracted to him," Jane said. "I do not believe that she has any idea he loves her."

"Well, that is a problem." Elizabeth drummed her fingers on the arm of the sofa. "I wonder if there is anything more we can do."

"I can give him the list," Harrington suggested.

His wife rolled her eyes. "The only thing that list did was get you into trouble."

He slid her a heated look. "It got me you."

"I shall see if I can come up with something while we're gone." Prue rose. "If you will excuse me, I must see to my own packing."

"I'll send a note around to Lord Phineas telling him to take our main coach. It will be easier for all of you."

"That will make the journey much nicer." Prue gave a little wave and left the room.

The conversation changed to where Hector and his party would travel next.

"I do not wish to go over the Alps." After Jane had discovered that going through the mountains would require disassembling the coaches, she'd been firm on that point.

"I didn't think you would." Much to Hector's disappointment. "I made tentative plans to visit Baden-Baden, then travel on to Munich, Vienna, and Budapest."

Augusta strolled into the room holding a piece of

foolscap. "I have bonnets for Madeline and the twins, gowns for Mary and Theo, and fabric for my friends being delivered." Augusta glanced at Jane. "They can be sent to Grace. I wrote a letter to her. Here are the details." She handed the list to Jane. "Can you arrange to send the packages to England?"

"Of course, dear."

The next morning Augusta hugged Elizabeth, Jane, and Hector, then shook hands with Harrington. "How soon after we return would you like to leave Paris?"

"Almost immediately," Hector said. "Have a good time with your document."

"We will." Augusta smiled. She couldn't believe she was being allowed to travel to see the Sequence. "Lord Phineas sent a note that he received the letter of introduction from Monsieur Clement to the director in Valenciennes. I cannot wait to read it."

In addition to her groom and footman, her cousin sent his coachman. Phinn's grooms and hers would act as outriders and one of his coachmen would second Hector's. They'd collect Phinn and his secretary from their hotel.

Augusta hugged Tommy, Jane, and Hector. "Thank you."

He assisted her into the coach. "Have a good journey."

"I will." Augusta turned to wave at the others. "Other than reading the Oaths of Strasbourg, this is the most thrilling adventure I have ever had."

Hector chuckled. "I'm sure it is."

Prue settled in next to Augusta, and Hector gave the order to depart. She was so excited she could barely sit still. This is what being in Italy would be like when she and her cousin traveled during school holidays. When she would finally be a university student. She must purchase her own carriage. Assuming Matt sent her enough money to buy a vehicle. But that could be addressed later. She should ask Phinn about buying an already made conveyance as he had done.

A few minutes later, they stopped in front of the Hôtel Meurice, and Durant went in to inform Phinn they had arrived. Moments later, his luggage was added to hers. He spoke to her through the window. "I've never seen a private coach built like a diligence. Where do you want us?"

"I thought your valet could travel in the back section with my maid and Button, Prue's maid. You and Mr. Boman may ride with us."

"Excellent." A few moments later Phinn opened the door and settled onto the back-facing bench of the coach. Boman, his secretary, followed. As soon as the carriage started again, Phinn brought out a map. "I thought we could take the route through Noyon and Saint-Quentin if you have no objection."

Augusta drew her finger along the route, bringing to mind what she had read of the towns. "You wish to visit the cathedral and the basilica."

"Yes." He nodded. "They are both said to be fine examples of medieval architecture." He handed her a piece of paper. "My hotel suggested these inns."

"Very well." She read the names. "We shall spend the first night at the Hôtel Coeur de Noyon." She glanced at Prue. "There are two recommendations in Saint-Quentin. We can make our decision when we arrive."

"How long will it take to get to Valenciennes?" Prue asked.

"About two-and-a-half days of easy travel," Augusta responded, handing the map to Phinn. "That will give us time to look at the towns."

"I remembered you said that you cannot read in a coach, so I brought a traveling chess set." He pulled out a box from his valise. "Would you like to play?"

"After we leave the city, I would be delighted." She smiled at him. How thoughtful he was. "A game will help pass the time."

It was not long before they passed through Porte Saint-Martin and were on the other side of the Paris wall.

Ten days later, they returned to Paris.

"Was it as wonderful as you thought it would be?" Jane asked as Phinn helped Augusta down from the carriage.

"It was even better." She waited for Prue before linking arms with Jane. "The director asked me to sing the canticle. He even had a mandolin player to accompany me. I have been thinking that I must purchase a coach when I arrive in Padua."

"We will discuss that once you are settled." Jane glanced back at Phinn. "We are just about to have tea. You're welcome to join us."

"Thank you." He glanced at his secretary.

"I'm going to the hotel," Boman said.

"In that case, I'll see you there later." Phinn followed the ladies to the morning room, where tea was being set out.

Addison fell in next to him. "Augusta is in good spirits."

"She should be. She was treated like royalty."

"There is a young man who's been asking after Augusta. A Viscount Celje. Do you know him?"

The name didn't sound familiar, but the vision of an earnest young man staring hungrily at Augusta crossed his mind. "Medium height, blond hair, about one- or two-and-twenty, and favors blue?"

"That sounds like him."

Perdition! Augusta didn't need another wet-behind-the-ears puppy following her around. "He was attempting to rescue Augusta from the count when I arrived."

Hector nodded. "He's probably just lovestruck. It seems to be occurring a great deal."

"I can't argue with that." As far as Phinn was concerned, it was happening far too often. "Celje's not a French name. What's he doing here?"

"He's been on a Grand Tour." Addison led the way down the corridor.

As long as the man stayed away from Augusta, Phinn wished him a good journey. "Do you plan to attend any events between now and when you depart?"

"Not at the moment." Addison gave Phinn an inscrutable look. "We'd better join the others."

"Indeed." He was a coward for not asking the man if he and Boman could join them when they left Paris.

The next day, Phinn accompanied Augusta shopping and for a final gown-fitting. He had one more restaurant that had been recommended. "Shall we have luncheon before returning?"

"Always." She flashed him a happy grin. "I wonder if the food in the rest of Europe is as wonderful as it has been here."

"I suppose you shall find out." He guided them toward a restaurant with a few empty tables.

Suddenly he was jerked to stop. "What do you mean *I* shall find out? Are you returning to England?"

"No—" He stared at her for a moment. "Are you

saying you want me to accompany you and your family when you leave Paris?"

"I-I . . ." Her forehead wrinkled in thought. "I just assumed you would come with us."

That was exactly what Phinn had wanted to hear but had been afraid to hope for. "I will speak with your cousin when we return."

Her brow smoothed, and she nodded. "Yes. You should do that."

Phinn no longer had any doubt that he wished to spend the rest of his life with Augusta. Nor did he question his feelings. He was in love. Now all he had to do was convince her she loved him.

Part of him thought she must. No matter how much time they spent together, they never ran out of conversation and they continually found things they had in common. And she had just made clear she wanted them to continue to be together. He knew she was as physically attracted to him as he was to her. Yet, she did not recognize her reactions for what they were. Would it help him if she knew? Or would it scare her? She was so convinced she could not marry until she finished university.

Addison's words came back to Phinn.

You know, even if you did wed to get an heir, there is no controlling how long it would take . . . As far as I know, there's no law that says a lady can't attend university and be married.

Chapter Twenty-Six

Two days after Augusta, Phinn, Prue, and Boman returned from Valenciennes, Hector announced they would begin the next part of their journey the following morning. They traveled by easy stages to Strasbourg then on to Baden-Baden, and Stuttgart, and were now in Munich. Soon they'd travel to Vienna.

The day before they were to leave, Augusta and Phinn were having coffee at a café. "I wonder how long it will take us to reach Vienna."

"That depends where we stop and for how long." He covered her hand with his.

He'd never made such an intimate gesture before. What did it mean? Not that it mattered. He had not given any indication that he loved her or that he would break his promise to his brother. Not that she would want him to act dishonorably. "At least we do not have balls and other entertainments to attend."

His forehead creased. "That might change in Vienna."

Hopefully not. Augusta had not liked the French court and could not imagine that the Habsburg court was any better. "Hector will present the introduction on my behalf. It is simply to reinforce Prince Esterházy's assurance that I have been accepted to the university. Although, what can be done from Vienna, I do not know."

"I'm sure they are powerful enough to make happen what they wish." Phinn removed his hand and drained his cup. "He will have to go through our ambassador, Lord Stewart."

She missed the warmth and strength of his hand. "That is true."

"There will also be a good number of our fellow countrymen and -women in Vienna." He signaled to the waiter. "Do you want anything else?"

"No, thank you." What he'd said bothered her. Every time she had to attend evening entertainments, she was bored silly. "Who told you there would be English in Vienna?"

"I overheard it when we were in Paris."

"Well, drat."

Phinn laughed loudly. "We can always tell people we are betrothed."

A pang struck her heart. Augusta was glad he found that amusing. She did not. "I wish to go."

"You haven't finished your coffee." He stood as she did.

"I don't care." She signaled to Durant. "I shall see you at the hotel."

Her footman caught up to her as she strode away from Phinn, and a horrifying feeling came over her. The closer they had got to Italy, the more excited she had become, but now she could not accept the idea that soon he would no longer be in her life.

And she knew exactly what was wrong. She was in love with him. When had that happened and why? She hadn't wanted to fall in love. It was not part of her plans. And worse, that he could laugh about being betrothed just proved what she had thought at Versailles. He was *not* in love with her. After all the time they had spent together, if he was not in love with her by now, he never would be.

Tears pricked her eyes and she blinked hard. Why did this have to happen to her? All she wanted to do was attend university and now she had to fall in love. Even if Phinn did return her affections, it wouldn't change her plans.

She reached the hotel, went straight to her bed-chamber, and tried to take off her bonnet. But the more she pulled on the ribbon, the more mangled it became.

Gently brushing her hand aside, Gobert said, "Let me help you with that, my lady."

"Thank you." The tears were still trying to conquer her, and she fisted her hands. Soon the hat was off and she turned her head. "I wish to be alone for a while."

"I'll return to dress you for dinner."

Drat! Augusta did not wish to go to dinner. Perhaps she could instruct her maid to tell Jane she would dine in her room. That, though, would bring her up to Augusta, and her cousin would want to know why she did not wish to come down. Yet how could she face Phinn, knowing she loved him and he did not love her?

Blast it all. She was supposed to be happy when she fell in love. And she was supposed to fall in love with a gentleman who loved her in return.

She paced while Gobert waited patiently for a response. Augusta could not very well avoid him. *She* was the one who had wanted him to accompany them. Well, blast it all. There was nothing for it. She had to get herself under control.

"Thank you."

Her maid paused, a heavy frown on her normally placid features. "I hesitate to ask, my lady, but *is* something amiss?"

This is what everyone would ask if she did not go down to dinner. "Thank you, but I merely have a slight headache. Please help me out of this gown. I shall take a nap."

"Yes, my lady." Her maid did not sound convinced. Still Gobert did as she was told, and shortly after Augusta lay down on the bed, the door opened and closed.

If she could not convince her maid, how would she convince Jane and Hector? Not to mention Phinn. Augusta absolutely could not let him know how she felt. It would be humiliating if he found out. Not only that, but he would most likely renew his proposal, and, university aside, she could not marry him when he did not love her in return.

If only she had someone she could confide in. Someone who would understand. Unfortunately, that person was always Phinn. She swung her legs over the side of the bed and began to pace again. No, this time it had to be another woman. The question was, should it be Jane or Prue? As much as they both cared for her, Augusta knew they also wanted her to wed. She had got the feeling from Prue that she and her husband were both young when they married and it was their sense of adventure that brought them together. They had liked each other a great deal and their liking had soon grown into love. If she thought Augusta and Phinn could fall in love, her cousin might be more likely to counsel her to marry him if he would agree to allow her to attend university. Yet, unless Lady Dorchester had a son, he was not likely to allow her to put off having a child. Augusta had read there were ways, but nothing she had found told her what they were.

Jane, on the other hand, had refused to marry for less than love. Surely, she would understand. And she had already given Augusta some good advice. Maybe Jane could tell her what to do. Or perhaps she should simply enjoy her friendship with Phinn and try not to think about her feelings for him. Augusta drew a breath and blew it out. When had life become so complicated?

We are friends, we are friends. We are only friends!

If she repeated it enough, she was certain she would start believing it. And when she began university, she would be so busy she would forget all about him.

Except that Hector and Jane had not forgotten each other and they had been apart for years. Nor had Augusta's mother forgotten Richard, and she had been married to her father! And apparently, her father had never got over the death of his first wife.

She blew out another puff of air. All that did not bode well for her future. She rarely, if ever, doubted her actions. Yet, she had no experience being in love. That was the answer. She'd do what she always did when approaching a subject about which she had no experience: research it and find a knowledgeable mentor. But not Jane or Prue. They only knew how ladies felt. Hector was the only gentleman Augusta could ask about why a gentleman fell in love. She would do it as soon as she could arrange to talk to him alone.

Phinn stared at Augusta as she stomped off in anger. What the devil had he said to make her so furious? She hadn't been at all upset when they had pretended to be betrothed before. What about his jest had distressed her now? They'd never even had cross words for each other before. Well, except for the first time they'd met, when he had severely underestimated her, and the time he'd proposed. But then she had been upset because the plans they each had for their lives were impossible to reconcile. He needed to think about this some more. And he must go after her. He could ruminate on his way back to the hotel. From the corner of his eye, he caught a glimpse of young Viscount Celje. Phinn had seen the man several times along the way, but if the viscount was on a Grand Tour, that wouldn't be out of the ordinary. And, although he stared at Augusta with longing in the same fashion Lord Lancelot had, Celje never approached them.

Sharking off the prickling at the back of his neck, Phinn signaled to the waiter. *"Die Rechnung, bitte."*

After settling the bill, he strode down the street. Augusta had been upset in London because everyone and his dog had asked for her hand in marriage, and, due to his circumstances, she had felt betrayed by him. Although to be fair to himself, he'd not known she wished to attend university. She'd gone along with the pretend proposal because she was concerned he would be killed in a duel. Nevertheless, she had made very clear to him they would not wed. Had he made the same joke in France, he was certain she would have thought it humorous. What had changed? Was it that she didn't think it was funny, being in a situation where gentlemen were bothering her so much that they'd have to playact again? If that was the case, he'd expect her to groan and tell him it wasn't amusing. No, something had definitely changed. He just wished he knew what it was.

Phinn entered the rooms—a parlor with a separate dining room—he shared with Augusta's family. Their chambers led to the parlor while his was down the corridor.

Jane, as he'd finally been asked to call her, was reading to Tommy. The instant Phinn entered the room, the little boy ran to him with his arms in the air. "Up."

He lifted the child high over his head and twirled around. Loud giggles filled the room.

"You are extremely good with him." Jane's eyes crinkled when she smiled.

"I enjoy being around him." Children were so easy to please. He lowered Tommy and lifted him again, before setting him on the floor. "Have you seen Augusta?" After being caught using their first names too many times, they'd given up the pretense. "She left the café before I paid the bill."

"Her maid told me that she had a headache and was taking a nap." Jane settled Tommy on the couch again.

"A nap?" He'd never known her to sleep during the day or have a headache. This might be more serious than he thought.

"I thought it was odd as well," Jane said as Tommy wiggled down and toddled over to some brightly painted wooden blocks. "Did anything happen to upset her?"

"You could say that." Even if he couldn't explain *what* exactly occurred. Phinn sat in one of the heavily padded oak chairs. "I made what I thought was a jest, and she became angry."

"Really?" Jane appeared as puzzled as he felt. "I do not think I have ever seen her angry at anyone. Frustrated, yes. Exasperated, absolutely, but angry, no." She drew her brows together. "What on earth did you say?"

"We were talking about Vienna, and I mentioned that Hector would have to meet with the ambassador regarding the letter Prince Esterházy gave her. That led to a discussion of balls she might have to attend." Feeling like he was getting a headache too, Phinn pinched the bridge of his nose. "I said if the gentlemen started proposing again we could always pretend to be betrothed." An image of Augusta blinking rapidly just before she left intruded on his thoughts. Had she started to weep? "She looked like a storm cloud and left."

Jane pressed her lips together, drawing them in as she

did. "Did she?" Finished with the blocks, Tommy ran full tilt back to Jane. She lifted him onto her lap. "If it helps, I do not think you said anything untoward."

"That's comforting. Thank you." Phinn hadn't thought he had, but it was nice that he wasn't the only one.

"I shall look in on her before dinner." Tommy turned and put his arms around Jane's neck, laying his head on her shoulder. "He needs his nap. Perhaps it is as she said, merely a sick head."

"I hope that is the case." Phinn stood as she rose. He wondered what his children with Augusta would look like. He could almost feel them as soft warm bundles in his arms. "I shall see you at dinner."

Opening the door, he held it for Jane. If Augusta did tell her cousin what was wrong, would Jane tell him in return?

That evening Augusta entered the parlor looking particularly beautiful in a white gown trimmed with pink. She smiled at everyone, including him, but there was something not quite right about her gaiety. It seemed false somehow. Phinn attempted to talk to her about what happened, but she waved him off.

"I do not know why I became so upset. It must have been the onset of the headache. Truly, there is no need for you to concern yourself about it. I am perfectly fine."

"I'm glad your nap helped." He surreptitiously searched her features.

"Yes." Augusta might be smiling, but the expression seemed pasted onto her face. "Yes, it did."

Did she think she was fooling him? Sooner or later he'd discover what was going on in that clever head of hers. "I'm glad." He heard the door to the dining room open. "Here is Baiju to call us in to dinner." She shivered when he placed her hand on his arm to escort her. "Augusta?"

A slight blush rose in her cheeks. "It is nothing."

Balderdash. If it was nothing, she wouldn't be acting like this. Perhaps tomorrow he'd discover what was bothering her.

As dinner was ending, Hector said, "I have received our travel documents to continue our journey. Unless anyone has an objection, I thought we could depart in the morning."

The news was unfortunate. It meant Phinn could not be alone with Augusta, but it was not unexpected. In fact, today they had finished the list of places and things they wished to see. Everyone glanced at one another and shook their heads.

"Tomorrow it is."

Jane rose and the ladies followed her out of the room. Durant placed port and brandy on the table, then withdrew.

Baiju spread out a map on the table, then joined them with a pocketbook and pencil in his hand. "As you see, the route is straightforward. Unfortunately, the roads are said to be even worse than in France."

At this rate, Phinn would soon have to replace the wheels and axles on his coach. "How long will it take?"

Hector glanced to his general factotum, who answered, "We have decided to travel by barge. It will be faster and save the coaches." Baiju placed his finger on the map, tracing the Isar river to the Danube. "It will take two barges for our coaches. Yours"—he glanced at Phinn—"will fit with one of ours."

"I've inspected the vessels," Hector said. "We will have one with several staterooms, a large combined parlor and dining area, and a rooftop terrace, as it were."

"It sounds like you are describing the *Zille* boats." He and Augusta had looked at them. Some were exceedingly opulent. From what Addison said, he had arranged one of the larger ones to carry them downstream. Perhaps it was the one she'd loved.

"Exactly." He grinned at Phinn. "It will be a nice break from being bounced around on less-than-desirable highways."

He agreed. It would also give him time to ferret out what was bothering Augusta. He knew whom he had to thank for the idea. "Well done, Baiju."

The man inclined his head. "We have rented the vessel to Budapest."

"Meaning"—Addison gave Phinn a look laden with meaning—"we will not remain long in Vienna. Therefore, make your plans accordingly."

That was one problem solved. It didn't surprise Phinn that Jane had spoken to her husband. He would have been more surprised if she had not.

"Do we know anything about the route from Budapest to Trieste?" Unfortunately, after Budapest, the Danube went in the wrong direction for them.

"It is well maintained, as I am sure you know," Baiju said. "Trieste *is* the most important port in the Austrian empire."

Phinn grinned. "I'm still happy to have my suppositions confirmed."

And he would have days on a vessel where he could find a private place to speak with Augusta. He did not like feeling estranged from her, and sent a prayer to the deity she would confide in him.

Chapter Twenty-Seven

Augusta listened with growing excitement to Jane's description of the *Zille* boat. "You will adore it. There is a roof terrace with a sun awning. Its width surprised me. It is large enough to have an indoor corridor. That is how you reach the staterooms. Those span the width of the boat. And there is room on the bow and stern to sit as well. Hector thinks he will be able to fish from the stern."

"Does it have a bright blue hull?" Augusta was certain she had seen the *Zille* when she and Phinn had been out.

Her cousin nodded. "Yes."

"It is the *Aurelia*. She is named after a saint." A saint who ran away from a marriage to a man she could not like. Perhaps she too wanted love.

"I think it sounds exciting," Prue said. "It is definitely much better than taking the roads."

Augusta agreed. The moment she had seen the barges, she had wanted to travel on one. On a boat, she would be able to read, something that was impossible in a coach. The only problem was she would be in very close proximity to Phinn the whole trip.

"A cook who has trained in France will prepare our meals," Jane continued. "At night, we will tie up to the shore. The captain explained that it is too dangerous to navigate the rivers in the dark." She smiled. "You two will be able to exercise your hacks in the evenings."

"That will be a pleasure." Prue had bought a lovely bay shortly after arriving in Paris. She glanced at Augusta. "Do you agree?"

"I do. Did Mr. Baiju find the barge?" Augusta had called him that since she had met him. All the younger children did as well. He had come from an important family, but something had happened, and when Hector left India, Baiju came with him. She supposed his and Hector's relationship was much like Phinn's and Boman's. Although, for reasons she didn't understand, Baiju never took his meals with them. She had not asked, but she knew enough about the Indian culture to suppose it was because he did not eat meat, and beef was especially repugnant. It would be wonderful to visit India someday. Augusta stifled a sigh. Attending university would have to be enough.

"He did." Jane took a sip of sherry. "He narrowed our choice to three vessels. Hector and I looked at the other two, but"—her forehead wrinkled—"did you call her the *Aurelia*? I forgot to look at the name."

"Yes. She was the prettiest of all the barges, and the largest."

Her cousin blushed. "You know how Hector is about making sure I am comfortable."

"I just think he likes to spoil you." Prue's eyes twinkled, their corners creasing. "Which is something to be happy about." She pulled a silly face. "My husband called me his best soldier. Although, to be fair, he did pamper me when he could."

The gentlemen joined them, Hector going straight to Jane, Phinn to Augusta, and Boman seemed to gravitate to Prue. Now that was interesting.

"Well, my dear." Hector kissed Jane's cheek. "Have you finished extolling the boat's comforts?"

"I was still in the process. Augusta has seen the boat and remembered her name." She tucked her hand in Hector's as he sank onto the sofa next to her. "She was named after a saint."

"The *Aurelia*." Phinn pulled a chair up next to Augusta's. It was so close her skirts touched his leg. "Am I right?"

"You are." She thought about moving her chair over an inch or so, but everyone would notice. "I am surprised you remembered. We looked at so many *Zillen* that day."

"We did, but you liked that one the best. I'm glad we'll be able to sail on her."

"You and Mr. Boman have crossed the Atlantic twice," Jane said. The tea tray arrived and Jane began to pour.

"We have." Phinn smiled as if he was enjoying a fond memory. "This will be a very different experience."

"We didn't dock at night." Mr. Boman chuckled. "Although, you'd be surprised at the number of people who think it's possible."

They all laughed at that, and she decided she liked being next to Phinn too much to try to avoid him.

He leaned close to her and lowered his voice so only she could hear him. "I'm glad you're feeling better."

"So am I." She had the strangest urge to take his hand. This was definitely not going to be easy.

One of the barge captains had told her the speed of the currents in the Isar and the Danube, enabling Augusta to make some quick mental calculations. If they were able to sail for fourteen hours a day, their group would reach Vienna in approximately five or six days. She was tempted to figure the time it would take to reach Padua, but that was madness. It was better to think of being with him for a few days at a time. First she had to reach Vienna where Hector, and possibly she, would meet with Prince von Metternich, the Austrian foreign minister who had become involved in her wish to attend university. She knew that although Professor Angeloni had assured her of a place, something could still go wrong. What she would do if she couldn't attend Padua, Augusta did not know. Actually, she did. She would have no choice but to continue on with Jane and Hector. Or, she could apply to Utrecht.

"Are you thinking about the river travel?" Phinn's smile was tentative. As if he feared upsetting her again.

"Yes." Excitement for the new adventure burbled up inside her. "I hope it will be as fascinating as I think it will be."

"I've heard the scenery is spectacular." He got a misty look in his eyes as if he was seeing it in his mind.

"I think we should all find our coaches," Jane said, rising. "We have an early morning tomorrow."

Phinn took Augusta's hand, holding it in his for several long moments. If only he loved her and could wait for her, and agree not to have children yet. If only she could stop dreaming of the impossible. "I'll see you tomorrow."

"Until then." She removed her fingers from his, trying not to act as if she had been singed by his touch. Even though she had. Perhaps she could find a way to ensure she was always around the others when he was there. At least then she would not be so close to him. Then again, it had not helped this evening. No matter where they were or who they were around, it was as if he managed to make her feel as if they were the only two people in the room.

Augusta woke to find her clothing for the day had already been laid out and the wardrobes were empty. How had she slept through all that?

Gobert bustled back into the bedchamber. "As soon as you are dressed, I can pack the last of your things."

Going behind the screen, she attended to her needs and washed. Her maid took her nightgown from where she had placed it over the screen and put a chemise in its place. The valise she had bought in Paris stood open on a chair. As Gobert performed her duties she put the items she no longer needed in the bag. By the time Augusta was ready, the only things left in the room were her toothbrush and tooth powder.

Jane carried Tommy into the dining room, joining Augusta, who had already broken her fast.

"Let me hold him while you eat," she offered.

"Thank you. He was being fussy with Nurse. He must know we are leaving again. She managed to get an egg down him, but if you can convince him to have a piece of toast . . ." Jane wrinkled her nose. "Do not allow him to soil your gown."

"I won't." Augusta looked at the boy. "Did you hear that? You may not make me dirty." He reached out as she broke off a piece of toast. "Here you are."

"Mmmm, good." Swallowing, he held his chubby little hand out for more.

"He reminds me of Theo at this age."

"Good morning." Phinn strolled into the room and smiled at her. For a second she could imagine him kissing her, before he stroked Tommy's head.

"Good morning." Augusta gave herself a shake. What

would it be like to have children with Phinn? During their travels she had seen him playing with the baby and enjoying it. He would make an excellent father.

For someone else. Not me. I am not ready to have children.

"Oh, no, you don't." He caught Tommy's hand.

She glanced at the child and Phinn. "What did he do?"

"He was about to smear his buttery little hand on your clean gown." He tore off another bit of toast. "Keep your hands on your toast and ask if you would like more. Are we clear?" Holding his hand out for the bread, Tommy nodded enthusiastically. "Somehow I doubt your memory will last past swallowing this piece."

After Tommy finished the last of the toast, Augusta wiped his fingers before handing him back to Jane. Phinn had almost gaped at seeing her with the child in her arms. He'd wanted to wrap his arms around both of them. Not that he thought Tommy would ever be Phinn's with Augusta, but another child could be.

In time. When she was ready for one.

Prue, Boman, and Addison wandered into the dining room, relieving Phinn of the necessity of making conversation when he'd rather think about a life with Augusta.

Guilt stabbed at him. He remembered Helen's pain and despair over not having given birth to a son. But was Addison right? Could Phinn still keep his vow to his brother and put off having children? After all—he glanced at the man in question—Addison was an honorable gentleman and wouldn't suggest anything that would cause Phinn to break his vow. He had promised to try to have a son. But it *did* take some couples years to have children, even when they had come from large families. His parents had not had his brother until they'd been married for almost five years. Even then, they'd only managed to have two living children. Still, he knew Helen wanted him to fill his nursery immediately, though Dorchester had not asked that of Phinn.

And now that he knew he loved Augusta, he could not in good conscience marry another woman. He'd make himself and the unknown lady miserable. He had to have her as his wife. To do that, he had to give her what she wanted—university, and to put off having babies. But he required something too. Lust was no longer enough. He needed her to love him.

She pushed her chair back from the table. "I will be ready to depart in a few minutes."

He would simply have to wear her down. "Would you like to walk with me to the port?"

Augusta stilled, and he wondered if she'd refuse. Was whatever happened yesterday still affecting her? "Yes. I shall meet you back here."

He hurried down to his rooms where his valet waited to finish packing, brushed his teeth, and strode back to the parlor. When he arrived she was opening the door to her bedchamber and talking to someone in the room. She turned and smiled at him, but her eyes were guarded. This was going to take some time. Fortunately, he had a lot of that particular commodity.

Holding out his arm, Phinn said, "Shall we?"

"Of course." She gingerly placed her slender fingers on his jacket.

Before leaving the hotel, they stopped to bid farewell to the landlord and his wife.

"We have so enjoyed staying with you," Augusta said.

"And we have been delighted to host you." The landlady dipped a curtsey. "I wish you a pleasant journey from here."

"Herr Duschl." Phinn gave a short bow. "It has been a pleasure."

"When you return, you shall stay with us." The man bowed.

"By then you will be married, yes?" Frau Duschl nodded her head.

Flushing a deep red, Augusta muttered something unintelligible and hurried out the door.

Phinn drew a breath before saying, "I sincerely hope we will. Thank you and farewell." He caught up with her next to the bakery. "Let's buy some *Butterbrezelen*."

Her breathing was rapid, and instead of answering she headed toward the door. He got to it just in time to open it for her. He had the sinking feeling the landlady had set him back weeks in his campaign to convince her to marry him. Perhaps if he ignored what had been said as if the incident had not occurred, it would help her recover her countenance.

"Good morning, Frau Becker."

"*Grüß Gott. Butterbrezelen* for you?" she asked, using the local Munich dialect.

"Yes, please. Two for us"—he pointed to himself and Augusta—"and eight packed for later." Ever since they had discovered the salted bread in the shape of a knot spread with fresh butter in Strasbourg, *Brezelen* had been one of their favorite treats. He'd miss visiting the bakery. If Vienna didn't have them, he'd have to find another treat.

The baker's wife handed him one of the two *Brezelen*. The other she gave to Augusta. She licked the bits of butter that had oozed out from the slice in the bread, and it was all he could do to not think of her licking him and him returning the favor.

Her eyes closed as if she was in Heaven. "Thank you."

"You're welcome." Phinn was surprised his voice was so steady. The rest of him wasn't. Damn, he had to get control of himself.

The last coach had just been loaded onto the boat when they arrived some twenty minutes later.

"You took your time," Addison said.

Phinn held up the package. "We brought *Butterbrezelen* for everyone."

"You'll be forgiven then." The man grinned. "I'm sure."

He took the bread into the dining area and placed them on the table where Tommy couldn't get into them on his own. They were a favorite treat for the little boy. Then Phinn found his chamber.

It had two windows with curtains on either side of the wooden door. At the other end of the room were more windows with a view of the river. The room was much more spacious than he'd thought it would be. In essence it was a long, wide platform that looked as if a house had been set on top of it. Musson was busy unpacking, prompting Phinn to explore the rest of the boat.

He went through the covered corridor to the stern. Set along the wall as if they were billiard cues were several fishing poles. To one side was a steep, narrow staircase leading to the roof. He climbed up. A waist-high rail ran the length and width of the area set up as a terrace with wicker chairs and two sofas. As Jane had said, the whole space was covered by a canvas awning. Below, a narrow deck ran past the stateroom windows. Phinn strolled to the other end where a ladder had been built in, and climbed down to the bow. As far as he could see, the vessel was clean and in excellent condition.

Augusta stood off to the port side of the bow looking over the river. "Have you looked around yet?"

She turned as if he'd startled her. "Not yet. Have you?"

"I was on the roof." He ambled toward her. "We will like sitting up there."

"I did not react well to what the landlady said."

Pulling her bottom lip between her teeth, she wrung her hands. "I apologize for embarrassing you."

"Your apology is accepted, but I was not embarrassed." Wanting to hold her close, he settled for placing his hands on her shoulders. "I was concerned about you."

"It is nothing. I have been feeling a little out of sorts." Why was she lying? Augusta lifted her shoulders and he let his hands slip off her.

"Perhaps being on the boat will help." He wished she'd confide in him. "I'm told it's relaxing."

"I am sure it will be." She turned her attention back to the river. "Even this, being at the dock, is peaceful."

On the other side of the barge, the crew brought in the gangway. Shortly after that, the lines were cast loose and the boat was under way as two crewmen using long poles pushed them away from shore.

"This is so different from the ship leaving Dover." Augusta glanced over her shoulder, a broad smile on her face and in her eyes.

"It is." He joined her at the rail. "Not nearly as hectic."

Phinn wanted to tell her that everything would be fine. That he would make it right for her. If only she'd tell him what was wrong. If she did not confide in him, and this continued, he'd ask. What he refused to do was allow her to continue to suffer or shut him out of her life. He was beginning to think Dorchester had the right of it when he'd married before falling in love. To be always on tiptoes around her was hell.

Chapter Twenty-Eight

Augusta gripped the rail as if her life depended upon it. As indeed it did if she wanted to remain standing. Whether it had been the landlady's comment about her marrying Phinn or her discovery that she loved him, Augusta did not know. Yet an awareness of him had burst over her, even worse than when she danced with him. His body seemed larger and warmer, and his scent of pure male and a hint of a spice that must be in his soap, more intoxicating. His silver eyes were more alluring. He had always been good-looking—especially in court dress—but she had never before thought him the most handsome gentleman she had ever seen. Still, she could no more act on her newly heightened senses than she could jump over the side of the boat.

If she released the rail, her knees would betray her, then she would start to fall. Phinn would catch her in his strong arms, she would hang on to him and want to kiss him. Naturally, he would want to kiss her—she had seen him look at her lips—and everyone would see them and all her hopes for a love match and university would be ruined.

Augusta was thankful her gloves hid how tightly she

clung to the rail. Why could he not find somewhere else to be? It would be very helpful if she could manage to become ill until they reached Vienna, recover enough to do whatever she had to there, then fall ill again until they reached Trieste. Thus enabling her to avoid him for most of the duration of the journey. Yet, no matter how much she wished that would happen, it was extremely unrealistic. If she were that ill, it was unlikely her family would agree to continue the passage.

Augusta took a deep breath and let it out. In addition to her studies, she had had years of practice hiding her feelings when necessary. Those lessons would be useful now. The only problem was, Phinn knew her too well. He always noticed when she was not minding what was being said. Based on that, she could only assume he would recognize when she was attempting to hide something from him. Drat it all. Why did men—or love, for that matter—have to be so difficult?

"There you are." Prue came up to the rail on Augusta's other side. "I believe I will enjoy this much better than a sea passage."

"We were just saying how lovely and calm it is," Phinn responded. "Augusta will be able to read without becoming sick."

She cut him a look, and he gave her a boyish grin. What was she going to do about him? "I am looking forward to that. I was able to purchase some books in Hungarian and Slovenian."

He looked at her in surprise. "I didn't know there was one Slovenian language."

Wrinkling her nose, she shrugged. "There has been one standard language since the last century. Although parts of the northwest are heavily Germanic. In the south Italian is spoken. Along the borders of Hungary and Croatia, the dialects include those languages as well.

I know a little of the Croatian dialects, so if need be, I am sure I will be able to make out what is being said."

Prue's eyes had grown wide. "Were you able to practice speaking either Hungarian or Croatian?"

"And Slovenian. When Prince Esterházy discovered I wished to learn the language, he had one of his secretaries tutor me in Slovenian. I read to improve my vocabulary. I was only able to learn school-taught Slovenian, and a little of the southern dialect. Charlie"—she glanced at Phinn—"Stanwood, my brother on the Carpenter side, found another student who agreed to tutor me in Croatian when they were on a school holiday. Although there is no standard Croatian, there used to be, and books were written using it."

Phinn studied her as if he had found something new. "That means that you know Croatian, have read the books on the combined language, and are now able to pick out the parts that are not Croatian but another dialect."

"Yes. The only difficulty is that some of the pronunciations are different and I have not heard them. Unfortunately, I doubt I will be able to study the others. Dalmatia is not at all close to where we will be." She brought up the route in her mind. "Although at some point, even if we stay with the original plan of traveling through Zagreb, we must pass through Slovenia to reach Trieste. I hope I shall be able to practice as we travel."

"One would think I would be used to you by now, Augusta, but you continue to amaze me. I have never known such a polyglot." Prue quietly gazed out over the river for a while, before saying, "When we arrive in Vienna and continue on from there, it might be more beneficial if you did not let people know about *all* your language skills."

Augusta could not believe what her cousin had just

said. Why would anyone give up an opportunity to learn? "I do not understand."

"One of the things I discovered was that people will say things they normally would not say when they think another person cannot understand. I have heard that the Austrian court is at least as full of intrigue as the French court. Probably more so. They were not disbanded, as it were."

Augusta did not like it, but . . . "You make a good point. I shall play the typical Englishwoman."

"A grasp of German, French, and Italian?" Phinn had raised his brows in inquiry.

"Indeed. I assume that German will carry us a long way." She would be surprised if it was not spoken in Hungary. Nevertheless, she did not wish to miss the opportunity to use some of her languages. "Perhaps I can use Hungarian at the hotel and restaurants."

"Why not?" he said thoughtfully. "We will probably receive better service if you do."

Augusta laughed, and the cloud that had been hanging over her dissipated. She liked Phinn far too much not to enjoy his company. As long as she did not act on her love, all would be well.

Phinn's heart lightened when Augusta laughed. He'd still keep an eye on her, but her melancholy seemed to have disappeared. He hoped it didn't return. Never in his life had he felt so helpless. She'd been hurting, and he'd not been able to do anything to help her.

He offered her his arm. Then remembered Prue and held out his other arm, even though it would be impossible to walk the narrow corridor or deck with two ladies on his arms. "Would you like to see the rest of the boat?"

Prue chuckled. "I shall decline your escort. There are some things I must see to."

"During this passage I would like to begin learning

some Hungarian and Slovenian," Phinn said. "One never knows when it might be useful."

Augusta chewed her bottom lip. He'd never seen her do that before. "There is only one problem." She gave him a guilty look. "I have never actually taught anyone before."

"Then I shall be your first student." Phinn used a cheerfully confident tone. He was not going to let her wiggle out of this. If she was instructing him, they'd spend more time together.

"Very well." She sounded unsure of herself. "I shall try."

Although he was not as clever as Augusta, Phinn did have a gift for languages, and by the time they docked in Vienna, he had a rudimentary grasp of both Hungarian and Slovenian. Unfortunately, none of the books she'd used mentioned food, and Augusta only knew dishes that would be served at court.

"We will simply have to learn them." The captain and his crew were busy tying up the boat. Phinn glanced around. There were a few passenger barges like theirs, but the rest carried goods for sale, and bars lined the opposite side of the street. "I'm not sure Hector will wish to remain on the boat."

Augusta glanced around. "I see what you mean. I hope we can find a hotel."

The lines released, and once again they were being pushed off. "I'll be right back."

"I am coming with you." She hurried after him.

"If you wish." He took her arm. He was sure there was no danger. Even if there was, she would be safer with him.

A few moments later they found one of the crew members and addressed him in German. "Why did we leave?"

"To make sure we had a space in the city," the man said. Behind them, another passenger barge pushed off as well. "Herr Addison has made reservations for you at the Weißen Rose. It is one of the best hotels in the city." Phinn and Augusta must have looked confused, for the crewman continued, "It will be easier for you when it is time to depart and for us not to be around all the bars. We will remain at the dock near the hotel until it is time for you to sail to Budapest."

"Thank you." Augusta said nothing until they had returned to the bow. "I had started thinking of the boat as home. It seems strange to leave it."

Phinn knew exactly what she meant. "I'll be glad to be back on her as well. Shall we purchase a guidebook tomorrow and discuss which sights we'll see?"

"Yes." She blew out a breath and her brow cleared for a moment before wrinkling again. "I just hope we do not have to go to court."

He almost repeated what he'd said in Munich that had got him in so much trouble, but held his tongue. The chances of them not going to at least a few entertainments was an air castle. The Austrians had been too involved in her quest to attend university. What he would do was stay by her side. People could make of that what they wished. There would be no more strolling off with another gentleman because she was thinking about something else and not paying attention.

The boat sailed under a long bridge connecting the imperial city of Vienna with Leopoldstadt before docking again. Other passenger boats lined the banks. Hostelries and other businesses and buildings stood outside the walls as if spilling out from the city. A little way down the river, fashionably dressed people ambled along a broad, well-kept path lined with trees. This location was much better than the previous one.

"There are no pavements." Augusta's breath caressed his ear, playing havoc with his senses.

Phinn studied the street in front of them. Pedestrians and carriages were all over the street. "How odd. We must be careful when walking."

The coaches and horses were being taken off the other two barges when Addison came up to them. "We will be ready to go to the hotel soon. The grooms and coachmen are seeing to them."

"Where will they be housed?" Phinn had no difficulty with Augusta's cousin making the decisions regarding the beasts and conveyances.

"The coaches will be stored in the building three doors down on the right of the gate. We'll take the horses to the hotel. I've been advised to hire a town coach with a local driver." Addison rubbed his forehead. "I'm told the traffic here is impossible to navigate unless one is trained."

"When will you send word to Lord Stewart?" Augusta asked.

"As soon as we arrive at the inn. I do not wish to be backward in notifying him."

She nodded, but said nothing further. Phinn couldn't blame her. Almost every time she attended entertainments, it was, as far as she was concerned, an unmitigated disaster. A few minutes later, their party had assembled. A wagon and two carriages pulled up in front of them.

"The hotel is in Leopoldstadt. I have arranged transportation for our baggage, what does not remain on the boat, and our servants," Addison said. "Jane and I shall walk. Does anyone wish to wait for the coaches to return?"

"I'd rather take a stroll," Phinn said. "It will give me an opportunity to see some of the city."

Next to him Augusta nodded.

"I shall walk as well." Prue turned to her maid and said a few words he couldn't hear, and the woman scurried off.

"I'm up for a ramble," Boman agreed.

"In that case—" Addison took Tommy from Jane, then steadied her as she stepped up to the gangway and down to the ground.

Not five minutes later, they arrived at the hotel, which appeared to combine two buildings. Flowers decorated the windows, and tables had been set outside in the front. The coaches were there and men hurried inside with the baggage.

"Herr Addison?" A man just over medium height came out to greet them in German.

"I'm Addison." He handed Tommy back to Jane. "Herr Riegert?"

"I am." The landlord nodded. "Please follow me. I will have wine brought for you while your apartments are being prepared."

He glanced at the rest of them, and Addison performed the introductions. "I am honored to have you stay with us."

They were escorted to a leafy courtyard filled with different-sized tables and chairs, where chilled white wine and bread and cheese were brought to them. Addison murmured something to Herr Riegert and they walked back into the hotel hall.

Phinn held Augusta's chair as she gracefully sank into it. "Thank you." She glanced at him. "Do your legs feel a little strange?"

"Ah, no. But I remember the sensation. As if you are still on board the boat instead of dry land."

"I recall it as well," Boman said. "The first time we got to land after being on the ship."

"It will only happen once." He grinned at the face she made. "I can promise I have never heard of anyone suffering it more than that."

"It did not occur after the channel crossing." She

looked down at her lap as if she could tell her limbs to behave. "How long will it last?"

Raising one brow and lowering the other, Prue nodded. "I remember feeling like my legs were still on the ship after we arrived in Portugal. It was terribly disconcerting, but by the next morning the feeling was gone."

"Augusta, dear," Jane said. "I think the only ones not suffering are Prue, Phinn, and Boman."

"That is a relief. I hope we do not have to go anywhere this evening."

She was concerned about looking like a drunken sailor, but Phinn would have kept her steady.

"How is the wine?" Returning, Addison sat in the chair next to Jane and took their son in his arms before bowing to the little boy's demands to be let down.

Just then a large, light brown Great Dane rose from a cushion at the far end of the courtyard and ambled over.

"She looks almost just like Daisy." Augusta's tone was hushed, as if she was afraid of disturbing the dog.

Standing next to her, Tommy, who had most likely spent a fair amount of time around the massive dogs, toddled forward a few steps with his arms out.

"Not Daisy." Before anyone could move, he'd flung his arms around the Dane's neck and received a slobbery kiss for his trouble. "Good dog." Leaning back, he looked the animal in her eyes. "What's your name?"

"Minerva." Herr Riegert strolled forward. "She belonged to a German count. He left her in our keeping but, unfortunately, died before he reached his next destination." He glanced at Tommy, who had plopped down at the dog's feet. Minerva, apparently being careful not to step on the child, leaned up against Augusta, who stroked the dog, giving the beast an occasional hug. Phinn was definitely jealous. "We have been waiting until she, the dog, took more than a passing liking to someone."

Using two fingers, Addison rubbed from the bridge of his nose to the top of his forehead, then, leaned his elbow on the chair arm, covering his face from his mouth to his jaw. "Let us see how this progresses."

"She is extremely well trained," the landlord added. Clearly praying they'd take the Dane.

"How old is she?" Augusta continued to pat the dog.

"Two years. We have her papers." There was a hopeful tone in Herr Riegert's voice.

"I would say she is extraordinarily well behaved." She raised one brow. "Could she, perhaps, be closer to three years of age?"

He shrugged. "I must look at her documents again. The count said she was two."

"How long has he been gone?" Augusta queried.

She had not stopped touching the dog, and Phinn knew they were adding that Great Dane to their party.

"Six months." Herr Riegert stilled. Minerva reached down and licked Tommy's head before granting the same honor to Augusta's cheek. She glanced at Hector. "If she wishes to remain with us, we will take her."

Addison's hand moved from covering the bottom part of his face to covering from his brows to his nose. Pinching the bridge of her nose, Jane chuckled lightly, and the dog buried her large head into Augusta's bosom, gazing up at her.

Phinn stifled a sigh. Hopefully, the dog would like him as much as she liked Augusta. If not, all his hopes and dreams were lost.

Chapter Twenty-Nine

A sense of calm flowed through Augusta as she stroked Minerva. This was one of the things Augusta had missed most, a dog. She could not remember not having a Great Dane in the house. When her father died, Duke had become Matt's dog instead of the family pet. She knew the Dane still loved the rest of them, but Duke seemed to sense that Matt needed him more. Was that the reason this Dane had come to her? Could the dog sense her need to be loved?

Leaning down, she nuzzled Minerva's large head, whispering, "I hope you stay with me."

From the corner of her eye, Augusta saw Jane pat Hector on his back. "Think of it this way. She knows how to care for a dog, and the Dane will be able to wait until we dock at night to go ashore."

"She can sleep with me." Augusta knew she had complicated their travel, but how could she resist? It was as if Minerva had been waiting for her.

"I'll help with the dog duties," Phinn said. He leaned behind her and patted Minerva. "I was raised with dogs."

"All we need now is a Chartreux and it will be as if we had never left home." Jane smiled brightly.

"A Chartreux?" Herr Riegert asked.

"It is an old breed of French cat known for its gray fur and yellow eyes." Augusta was positive the cat could not be found here.

The landlord furrowed his brow. "I shall inquire."

He bowed, then turned and strode inside.

She stared at the retreating landlord. "Do you think he can find a Chartreux?"

"I have no idea, my dear." Jane shrugged. "Vienna is an international city, and the Habsburg Empire is vast." She gazed at the dog for a moment. "To be honest, I would be surprised if Herr Riegert was *unable* to find a kitten."

Phinn straightened, and Minerva moved so that he could stoke her without losing Augusta's attention. "Were they the gray cats your sisters had?"

"Yes." She held back a laugh. That move was pure Great Dane. "They get along with everyone, especially the Danes." She glanced at Hector, who gazed up at the sky as if he was saying a silent prayer. "They travel very well. My sister was even kidnapped with her cat and she behaved extremely well."

"Your sister?" Phinn seemed confused.

"No, the cat." The Dane's tail started to thump.

Hector burst into laughter. "Now that I think about it, I have to admit that when Grace was kidnapped, the Danes being able to stop the carriage she was in played a large part in her rescue, and the cats *have* always been very well behaved." Taking a breath, he shrugged his shoulders and blew out. "I have no objection to four-legged additions to our little family. Tommy will love them."

She glanced down at a sleeping child. The cobblestones were probably warm, but they would cool soon.

"I'll get him." Phinn gently moved the Dane's backside before rising and going to the little boy.

After picking Tommy up, Phinn sat in the chair on the other side of her. Naturally, Minerva moved so that she was between them. But this time she rested her head on Phinn's leg. Did he need help too? No matter what it meant, having the dog grow close to both of them could present a problem when he left.

That night, the dog slept on a pillow next to Augusta's bed.

The following morning after breakfast, Hector pulled Augusta aside. "Phinn and I are going to the embassy. I would like you to come as well."

"Of course." She would have to prepare for the disapproval from whomever they were seeing, probably Lord Stewart. Unlike in London, there was no hiding her intent to attend university. She must meet with either Prince von Metternich or his representative. "When do we leave?"

"It is still early." Hector did not try to hide his concern. "Can you be ready in an hour?"

"Yes." Augusta entered her bedchamber. She would have to dress carefully. Not like a bluestocking, but not like a young lady on the Marriage Mart either. Serious, but at the same time fashionable. Perhaps one of the walking gowns she had bought in Paris?

Gobert was directing one of the hotel maids in cleaning Augusta's room. She waited until the maid dipped a curtsey and left. "I am going to the British Embassy with my cousin. What do you suggest I wear?"

Gobert went to the clothespress, took out the cerulean blue walking dress, and shook it out. "This is darker than what a lady making her come out would wear, yet I believe it will give you the necessary gravity you must project."

The gown was full from the high waist down and had three rows of thick satin ribbon in a color just a shade darker than the blue of the sarsenet near the hem. The neck was high and trimmed with lace. The sleeves had puffs at the shoulder, but were long and trimmed with the same lace.

"You are exactly right." Now for the bonnet. "What do you think about the shallow leghorn bonnet I bought to go with the dress?" The hat had the same blue satin ribbons, but yellow flowers had been added as well.

"That will do nicely, my lady." Gobert gave the gown a hard look. "I shall need to press this. It won't take long."

An hour later, brown leather half-boots and a soft, brown leather reticule completed her costume. Augusta had not spent this amount of time and effort preparing for a ball. Then again, the result of a ball had not absorbed her nearly as much as the outcome of this meeting did.

She walked out of her room into the private parlor. Both men carried letter cases. She knew her cousin had Prince Esterházy's letter to Prince von Metternich; still, she had to ask. "The letter?"

"Safe in my letter pouch. Have you taken care of the dog?"

"Yes, Phinn and Durant took her for a walk this morning. Durant is in charge of her until we return." She just hoped he remembered the German commands the landlord had explained.

Before Hector could offer to escort her, Phinn held out his arm. "Shall we?"

She had expected to feel the tingles she usually got when touching him. Contrarily, she felt safe, as if nothing could harm her.

"It will all be fine," he said, patting her hand.

"It is not as if Lord Stewart can stop me . . . Can he?"

"No. You have impressed Prince Esterházy sufficiently to give you the letter of introduction to Prince von Metternich. I imagine Esterházy has written his own missive as well, which will have arrived well before we did."

They reached the street, which had no pavement for pedestrians, and Phinn drew her closer. She became a bit breathless being that close to him. Fortunately, they did not have far to go.

"His lordship probably has no idea about your plans." Hector turned the corner.

"And there is no reason to tell him," Phinn added.

They were both right. As far as Lord Stewart was concerned, she had a letter of introduction to the foreign minister to the Habsburg Empire, and that was all.

Once they arrived at the embassy, they did not have long to wait. Lord Stewart greeted them warmly. "As a host, I am afraid I cannot compare with Sir Charles and Lady Elizabeth. I am a widower. However, as we have a number of our countrymen here at present, my second's wife has agreed to act as my hostess. There will be a soirée here tomorrow evening. If you would like to attend."

Augusta caught Phinn's eye as her cousin accepted the invitation. He was no happier than she was.

He turned his attention to the ambassador. "We have

a letter of introduction from Prince Esterházy for von Metternich."

"I dislike being the bearer of bad news." The ambassador shook his head. "Unfortunately, Prince von Metternich's father died in April, and he is in Koblenz."

Now what was Augusta to do? The foreign ambassador was to have had the final arrangements for her verified, to include the information on the couple with whom she was to have resided.

"To whom can we give the letter?" Phinn's haughty tone astounded her. "It concerns arrangements that must be made for our travel in Italy."

"I would have offered to send the letter to the ministry." Lord Stewart went around to his desk. "But I see the matter is of some urgency." He scribbled a note. "This should enable you to be admitted to von Metternich's secretary."

"Thank you." Phinn inclined his head. "We shall take our leave of you. I wish you a good day."

"You are very kind. Have a pleasant stay in Vienna, and I shall see you tomorrow evening." His lordship walked them to the entrance of the embassy. "Take care on the streets. They can be perilous."

No sooner did Addison, Augusta, and Phinn walk out than he pulled her up against him and a coach being driven much too quickly sped by with inches to spare. Her heart was beating too erratically to be afraid of the coach. Augusta was afraid she would not be able to pull herself away from him. Fortunately, he slowly set her back from him.

Her senses—she was being ridiculous. Augusta wanted his arms holding her and she should not. She took a shuddering breath. His willingness to encourage her to attend university had to mean he had given up wanting to marry her at all.

From the corner of his eye, Phinn had seen the sporting carriage careening toward them, Augusta in its path. He grabbed her and held her tightly against him. Her heart beat a rapid tattoo against his chest. Damn, if anything had happened to her he'd have murdered that care-for-nothing driver with his bare hands.

He wanted to keep holding her and never let her go, but Addison and Stewart were standing there. Slowly, as if he was moving through water, Phinn eased back from her. "Are you all right?"

"Yes." She nodded but her pulse was still too fast.

"Would you like to go back to the hotel, or shall we carry on?"

"I want to finish this." Her words sounded as if she had pushed them out of her lips through sheer willpower.

"Very well." He placed her hand on his sleeve. "Let's go."

Phinn walked toward the Hofburg Palace with Addison bringing up the rear. Nothing had changed her determination to attend university. Not even all the time they'd spent together had swayed her from her course. The only thing that had changed was him. After almost losing her today, Phinn knew he'd do anything he needed to do to make her happy. Even if it was finding something useful to do around Padua until she finished her studies and would agree to marry him. He wasn't looking forward to the letter he'd have to write his brother.

Although the prince wasn't present, his secretary, Count von Meysenbug, was extremely helpful.

"Prince von Metternich has been called away for most of the year," the man said to Augusta. "However, I received a note from Prince Esterházy extolling your intelligence and dedication to all you put your mind to." The count went to a cabinet and took out a sheaf of papers. "I wrote Professor Giuseppe Angeloni in order to verify that you would be accepted to attend lectures in Padua."

He glanced at Augusta, his round spectacles slipping down on his nose. "You understand that only one lady has been allowed to attend the university in the past two hundred years."

"I am aware of that fact." Her hands tightened around the strings of her reticule.

"You will be pleased to hear that his answers to my questions were positive. Now"—the count took out a sheet of paper—"this is the information about Count and Countess Papafava, the family who has agreed to sponsor you while you are in Padua."

Phinn wondered how the count and countess would feel about a Great Dane being added to their household. He supposed they would find out after they arrived.

"You should write to them as soon as you know the date of your arrival." Count von Meysenbug handed her several documents, which she in turn gave to her cousin.

"Thank you, my lord. I appreciate the trouble you have gone to."

"It was nothing more than writing a few letters at the behest of Prince Esterházy."

Her fingers on the strings relaxed. "If you need to contact me, we are staying at the Weißen Rosen."

"If I hear anything I shall send a messenger." The man bowed. "Enjoy your stay in Vienna. I am sure Lord Stewart has sent your names to the court secretary. I shall do the same."

Phinn slid a glance at Augusta, whose smile had become rigidly polite.

Count von Meysenbug walked them out of the building. "It was a pleasure to meet you, my lady."

After thanking him again, the three of them headed back to the hotel. Phinn made sure that Augusta was always the person closest to a wall in the event another idiot in a carriage was around.

It wasn't until they were back at the hotel that any of them relaxed.

"I wish someone would have told me how dangerous the streets here are." Addison led them to the terrace, where the rest of their party was partaking in luncheon. "I don't know if I want Jane and Tommy to go out now."

"I know what you mean." Phinn glanced at Augusta, who was busy stroking an exuberant Dane. "I think Minerva has decided she belongs to her." Yet, once the dog noticed he was present, he was greeted as well.

They were so close now, he was sure it would not take much to make Augusta fall in love with him.

"I take it all went well?" Jane asked.

Tommy bounced up and down, holding his arms out to Addison.

"Yes." Augusta gave Phinn a grateful look. "Thank you for your help. I am positive that if you had not used your haughty tone, Lord Stewart would have insisted on taking care of everything."

"We have been invited to an embassy entertainment tomorrow evening," Addison said, now holding Tommy. "We still need our traveling documents."

"What did the count give you?" Augusta took the glass of white wine Prue handed to her and gave it to Phinn before taking her own.

Placing the letter case on the table, her cousin took out the documents. "Aside from the letter to your sponsors, we have our passports allowing us to travel freely in the

Austrian Empire." Addison handed Phinn several sheets of paper. "You and Boman are included."

Someone had been hard at work on his behalf, probably his brother. "We should have asked Stewart if we had any correspondence waiting for us."

"But the letters arrived," Jane said. "A runner from the embassy delivered them while you were out."

"There were quite a few," Prue added. "We separated them and put them in stacks in the parlor."

One of the hotel's servants set three more places at the long table and another brought out more food.

"I am too hungry to read them now." Augusta lowered herself onto a chair. "We can see to them after luncheon."

Taking his own chair, Phinn chuckled lightly. "Far be it from me to keep you from a meal."

"Yes." She waved her fork in the air. "That is extremely wise of you."

Minerva lay down between them, hopefully waiting for something to drop. This was definitely going to be interesting. Perhaps Augusta would marry him for the Dane's sake. If he added a cat to their little family, that might help as well.

Chapter Thirty

After luncheon, Augusta went directly to the parlor and found her stack of letters on the heavy walnut table. Shuffling through them, she found a very thick packet with her brother's seal on it. It would take the rest of today and part of tomorrow to answer all of the missives. Hector had said they'd be departing soon. Mayhap she could wait to answer all but the most important until she was back on the boat. There should be a British Consul in Budapest, and there was one in Venice.

Deciding to answer the note from Grace first—Matt may have sealed it, but she would have done the writing—Augusta took the letters to her bedchamber. Sitting down at the small French-style desk, she popped open the seal and found the letter was dated almost a month ago. How quickly time passed when one was traveling.

Dearest Augusta,
I have enclosed notes from all the girls. I do not have to tell you how thrilled Madeline and the twins were to have received their new bonnets. Mary and

Theo were just as pleased with the gowns. There was no need to alter them at all.

Walter has gone on a monthlong hike in the Lake District with several friends. I miss him terribly, but that is part of allowing him to mature. Charlie plans to spend most of his time at Stanwood. Matt and I have visited him with the younger children. Phillip asked to remain a bit longer. As with Walter, this is part of him growing up.

Thank you for sending notes from the places you are visiting. Mary and Theo are keeping account of your travels on a large map that has been put up in the schoolroom. They are also making a list of what they want you to tell them when you return. Much to Matt's dismay, they both expressed a desire to travel as well.

I trust that by the time you receive this letter, you will have good news concerning your university acceptance. Neither Matt nor I have told your mother we do not expect you to return for a few years.

Elizabeth wrote to me saying how much she enjoyed your visit. I expect she will have written more to Louisa and Charlotte. You should receive letters from them and Dotty.

All is well here. May your travels continue to be safe.

> *With much love,*
> *Your sister,*
> *Grace*

The notes from the girls were as Grace said they would be. Walter said he planned to convince Matt to allow him with a group of friends to visit France or Holland next year. Augusta smiled when she read Phillip's short letter asking her if she had ended up traveling to Venice by boat. He had met a fellow whose brother, who had just returned from Germany and Austria, said river travel was easier and safer than traveling by land. He also hoped Matt would think he was old enough to accompany Walter on any Continental travel next year. Charlie wrote Augusta about how his estate, Stanwood, was coming along.

She settled in to answer all their letters. Once she was finished, she would read the ones she'd received from her friends.

More than an hour later, just as she had sanded and sealed the missives, a knock sounded on her door.

"I'll get it, my lady." Gobert went to the door, opening it a crack. A moment later, she closed it. "It is Lord Phineas. He would like to know if you would care to accompany him for an outing."

The sun was shining, and they had yet to see much of the city. Augusta did not relish the streets, but it would be nice to get out. She would have to change. The gown she wore was sadly crushed. She should have donned a day dress when she'd returned to the room. "Tell him I shall be there shortly."

"Yes, my lady." Gobert stuck her head out the door, then went to the wardrobe and took out an emerald-green carriage gown. "His lordship said he hired an open carriage."

Well, that took care of the streets. "How thoughtful of him."

"Yes, my lady. The servants here said walking could be dangerous."

Augusta caught a view of the street. It was filled with people. Still, a carriage ride would be enjoyable.

When she entered the parlor, Phinn was waiting with Minerva, who had a lead attached to her collar. The dog leaned her head just under Augusta's breasts, waiting to be stroked. "Is she coming with us?"

"I thought it would be a good idea to get her used to traveling with us. I don't know how she did before."

"That is an excellent idea."

When they reached the front of the hotel, a landau waited for them. Durant stood on a platform on the back, in full livery. It was the first time he had worn it since leaving Munich. Augusta placed her fingers in Phinn's hand as he helped her up the steps into the carriage. Minerva needed no help climbing in after her and making herself comfortable on the backward-facing seat, her head resting on the side of the coach.

"Hmm." Augusta glanced at Phinn. "I wonder what Hector will make of that?"

Phinn's lips twitched as he looked at the Dane. "Once we start traveling in coaches again, we'll have to make some adjustments." He sat next to her and gave the coachman the office to start. "I thought we could take a tour of the city. Then if there is a place we wish to visit, we may do so."

"I like that idea." They crossed the bridge leading to the inner city and through the gate. She gazed out at the buildings that appeared much larger than in other cities. "Have Jane and Hector decided how long we will remain here?"

"There is a concert at the Gesellschaft der Musikfreunde in five days. We'll leave the day after."

After crossing the bridge into the city, they saw two large parks and circled the palace and then the cathedral before heading back in the direction of the gate and the bridge leading back to the hotel. The driver turned down a side street.

"Where are we going?"

Phinn grinned as if he was hiding something. "Trust me. I have a surprise for you."

She wondered what he could have found in so short a time. Then again, Herr Riegert seemed to know everything there was to know about Vienna. The small street led to a larger boulevard, where they stopped at a town house set in front of a park.

Phinn ushered her to the door as Durant plied the knocker, then handed a card to a butler dressed in black.

"Please enter." The servant bowed. "Madame is expecting you."

The hall was square with a curved staircase rising from one end of it. The lower part of the walls were paneled in dark wood and the upper portions papered in white flowered silk. A prosperous but not aristocratic house. They were led to a parlor in the back of the house and Augusta immediately saw what Phinn wanted to show her. Several Chartreux cats ranging in size from adults to three kittens lounged on tall towers built especially for them.

An elegant blond woman only a few years older than Augusta entered the room. "I am Frau Schmid." She spoke in French-accented German. "I understand you have come from Herr Riegert."

"Yes, we have," Augusta answered in the same language. "I am Lady Augusta Vivers, and this is my friend Lord Phineas Carter-Woods." She and Phinn inclined their heads, as Frau Schmid curtseyed.

"Please have a seat." Frau Schmid indicated a sofa. "Do you drink coffee or would you prefer tea?"

"Coffee, please." Augusta perched on the sofa. The other lady sat, allowing Phinn to take a place next to her.

Once her gaze was drawn from the cats, Augusta could see the tall windows lining two walls. Outside a brick wall at least ten feet high enclosed the garden.

One of the cats jumped down and went through a small flap built into a French window. Why had none of her family thought of that? She'd have to write Louisa about it.

"That is quite clever, yes?" Frau Schmid said. "It was my housekeeper's idea." The coffee came and she poured. Once everyone had a sip, she continued, "I am told you know the Chartreux."

"I do. My sisters have them." One of the kittens jumped down onto the back of the sofa and began walking along it. Phinn grabbed Augusta's cup as the cat came to inspect her. A deep rumble emitted from the small animal. Removing one glove, she began to stroke the kitten. "He is a handsome boy."

"Yes." Frau Schmid smiled indulgently at the cat. "That is Etienne." The cat settled on Augusta's lap. "I believe he has chosen you."

"I had thought a female . . ." Yet they brought their own set of problems. Charlotte and Louisa had to watch their girls closely during certain times of the year.

"Do you want to hold another of the kittens?" Phinn asked.

Etienne bumped his head against her arm and gazed up at her. "No. I think I have found the one for me." Then she thought of Dotty's, or rather Merton's, cat. "I hope he does not choose someone else."

Frau Schmid's light laughter filled the room. "You do know the Chartreux. Etienne has not gone to anyone else."

"That settles it then." Phinn reached over and stroked the cat, who took it as his due, but did not move. "One boy and one girl."

She raised a brow. "You already have a cat?"

"No." Augusta grinned. "A Great Dane. I believe you call them a German mastiff."

"From what I've seen"—he abandoned stroking the cat—"they get on quite well with dogs."

"That is true." Frau Schmid rose. "I have a harness for him. You will have to change it when he grows larger." She went to a bureau, opened a drawer, and took out a red silk harness. "It will be easier for you to take him around with this. He is already used to it."

The cat stood still as Phinn held it up to see just how it went on. Fortunately, the harness was relatively straightforward. A lead was sewn on. A calm had come over Augusta that he hadn't seen before. Having animals was good for her. "May I ask how you happened to have the cats?"

"My grandmother was the first to have them. Her first one was given to her by Madame Pinceloup de la Grange. That was a female. Then she found a male and they had babies." She shrugged. "It went on from there."

"Thank you so much." Augusta looked at him as he picked up the glove she'd cast aside for the kitten.

He bowed to Frau Schmid. "Thank you."

"It is I who should thank you." She smiled. "My husband has said I may keep no more of the babies."

She walked them to the front door, and they said farewell.

Now to get the cat in the carriage with the dog. He hoped Minerva was as gentle with Etienne as she had been with Tommy. Augusta held the kitten with one hand as he helped her into the coach. Minerva turned her attention from the door to the cat. They went nose to nose for a moment, before Minerva lay back down on the bench, and Etienne resumed his place in Augusta's lap. So far, everything appeared as if it would work out well.

Durant gave Phinn a dubious look. "Am I taking the cat and the dog for walks?"

"It should not be a problem," Augusta answered. "We have been told he knows how to walk on a lead."

"If you say so, my lady."

Once the carriage had started forward, Phinn leaned over to Augusta. "You might want to have a word with your cousin about raising Durant's wages."

She glanced at Phinn, and they were so close only two inches separated their lips. Without his conscious consent, his gaze dropped to her mouth and her breath hitched. This was the reaction he wanted from her, but not in a blasted open coach!

When Durant cleared his throat, Phinn hastily straightened, tugging at his cravat. He must have tied the damned thing too tight this morning.

"How are you going to take care of Etienne at night?" Hopefully the question would give them both a chance to regain their countenances.

"They can be trained to use a chamber pot." She continued stroking the kitten. "There is a special lid. I'll draw a picture of it. Perhaps Herr Riegert knows a carpenter."

"I'm sure he will." Phinn's voice was tighter than he'd meant it to be.

First he'd been jealous of the dog; now he wanted to take the cat's place. There had to be some way to bring her around. If he weren't a trusted member of her family's party, he could try to seduce her. But Addison would have no problem sending Phinn on his way.

"Do you think Hector will mind that I now have a cat as well?" A worried look had settled on her face. "He did not seem to yesterday."

"I've no reason to think he will be upset." Phinn had made sure of the fact before he took Augusta to get the cat. Actually, the man had just given him a knowing look. "I'd be more concerned about the couple in Padua."

A stricken look entered her clear, lapis eyes. "Perhaps I should make other arrangements. It was my mother who insisted, but did not think I *could* find a sponsor."

He had no doubt Lady Wolverton was attempting to keep Augusta in England by throwing stones in her path. So far, that hadn't worked well for her ladyship. Still, there was reason to be concerned. Without a sponsor, Augusta would be much more vulnerable, but if she attended as a married lady, he'd be there to protect her.

The coach pulled up in front of the hotel. As for now, he had to give the landlord the fee they had agreed upon, and ask the man to find him a carpenter. A couple with their heads together strolled toward them. *Boman and Prue.* What was going on there? Or was Phinn seeing romance because he wanted Augusta?

Durant opened the door, and Phinn jumped down.

When Augusta stood, Prue hurried up to the carriage. "You got your kitten! How happy I am for you!"

His secretary glanced at him, an amused twinkle in his eyes.

"I did." Augusta's smile was everything he'd hoped to see. "Phinn took me there." Once she reached the street she held up the cat. "His name is Etienne. He and Minerva already get along."

Phinn held his hand out to the dog, and she jumped out of the coach. He placed Augusta's hand on his arm before taking the dog's lead. "Shall we continue this on the terrace?"

"My lady." Durant bowed. "If you give me the cat, I'll take him for a short constitutional."

For a moment, she looked as if she didn't want to give the kitten up. "That is probably for the best."

Once they took their places at the table on the terrace, Prue said, "Do you have any idea if the family in Padua expects me to arrive with you?"

"I do not." Augusta rubbed her forehead. "I have been thinking about the animals as well. I know they will not expect them. I believe it will be better if we find rooms of our own."

She could not, even with her cousin, set up her own household. Phinn wanted to rake his fingers through his hair. But that wasn't something a man did in public. If she weren't so set on attending university, she'd realize it as well. If word ever got back to her family . . . Somehow, between here and Venice, he'd find a way to persuade Augusta to marry him.

Chapter Thirty-One

Jane, Hector, and Tommy joined them, ending the conversation Augusta was going to have with Prue. Neither Jane nor Hector would approve of Augusta having rooms or a house of her own, even with her cousin as a companion.

Phinn had stared at her as if she had lost her mind. Naturally, it would not have done in England, but there was no reason anyone there had to know. She glared at him. His problem with her plans was his problem, not hers. If he loved her he might be able to help in some way. Then again, no. The only thing he could possibly do to assist her would be for them to wed, and she was not getting married. Not yet. Not when he had promised his brother he would try to get an heir, and not when he did not love her.

Etienne had returned and immediately jumped onto her lap. He tapped her arm, reminding her to continue to stroke him. Soon his deep purring calmed her again. Augusta had always liked being with her sisters' cats, but having one's own cat was much better. She didn't have to worry about what he wanted. She slid a sidelong look at Phinn. Unlike other males she knew.

One of the servants brought champagne. What were they celebrating? Drat! Had she missed something?

"So"—Jane held up a thick card—"as you see, we are fortunate to have been invited. At least I think so." She glanced at Augusta.

Apparently she was supposed to say something other than *I am so sorry I was not paying attention.*

"It's an invitation to the last royal ball before the court moves to the summer castle," Phinn whispered.

Oh. "Oh!" No wonder her cousin was waiting for her to reply. She wanted to refuse to attend. These entertainments never turned out well for her. Still, Jane obviously wished to go. And, in Augusta's experience, being surly never achieved what one wanted to achieve. Instead, she smiled politely. "Yes, of course we should attend."

"I am so happy you agree." Jane's smile was kind and warm. "More to your liking, I'm sure, is an invitation to a salon given by Frau Pichler. From the description, I believe it will be much like Lady Thornhill's salons."

"That does sound like fun." At least there was one event Augusta was sure to enjoy. "When are the ball and salon taking place?"

"The salon is tomorrow afternoon, and the ball is the following evening. The night after that is a concert." Jane took a sip of champagne. "The next day we shall return to the boat and sail to Budapest."

"That sounds like an excellent plan." Augusta took a drink of her champagne. How had all this come about?

"Stewart," Phinn said as if he could read her mind. They had become so close, perhaps he could. "He wants to ensure we enjoy Vienna to the fullest."

Sometimes helpful people were anything but. "How kind of him."

The corners of Phinn's lips twitched.

What would they feel like on hers? For a second today she'd thought she would find out.

"Wasn't it?" he said. She thought he would burst out laughing. "Look at it this way, it's only one concert and one ball. There won't be time for anything untoward to occur."

"You're right. We went to three balls in Munich and no one bothered me." Of course, her family and Phinn had kept her by their sides the whole time. Even Boman danced with her. She was probably apprehensive about nothing. They would do the same thing at this ball. "And we will enjoy the salon."

"As long as you are not importuned by some bounder pretending to be a painter." Phinn's tone was a low growl, as if he was already thinking of ways to rid her of such a man.

"I will remind you that I took care of that situation myself without any assistance." Augusta needed to remind him that she was not helpless in all social situations. Merely the ones where she forgot to attend to what was going on.

"You did, and quite effectively." This time when he smiled, her eyes met his molten-silver ones.

She wished he would stop looking at her like that. It made her wish he cared more than he did. She took a gulp of the wine, and the waiter refilled her glass. Minerva settled in next to Phinn. Perhaps Augusta was not going to have a Great Dane after all. She gave herself a shake. Grace always said things work out the way they were meant to. This would as well.

"I see you found a cat," Hector said, holding Tommy back from inspecting the new addition.

"I did." She could not help but give credit to Phinn

as she told the story. "I was amazed that Etienne came straight to me."

Jane tilted her head a bit. "The same thing happened with Charlotte, Louisa, and Merton. The cats picked the person they wished to be with." Jane laughed. "In Merton's case, he did not want the cat at all, but Cyrille was determined he was Merton's cat and nothing could convince him otherwise."

Augusta laughed as well. "He still rides in the carriage with Merton."

If only humans were so sure of their feelings, how much easier love and life would be.

Phinn stroked Minerva's massive head as she leaned against his pantaloons, and he wondered if his valet would complain about the hair. If only Augusta was as easy to please. Had humans ever been like the cat? Selecting a mate by sheer instinct? If so, that certainty had been almost destroyed by society and expectations. And desires. He could not forget that. The desire to go his own way had almost blinded him to meeting Augusta and seeing what could be between them. Her desire to attend university was stopping her from understanding they were stronger together than apart. The problem was he didn't know how to counter her doubts. Except to declare himself again. Yet that was too big of a risk to take. If he was asked to leave the group, he could no longer spend time with her.

First, he had to get through the next few days.

Phinn and Augusta agreed to start early the next morning. Once again, he arranged for the landau. After hearing the story of Merton's cat, Phinn was not surprised to find Etienne had insisted on joining them. Naturally,

Minerva would not be left behind. She most likely thought she'd been abandoned for too long as it was.

They visited the cathedral, which did not allow animals, and a park that did.

Bordering one side of the park was a restaurant set up in the French style with tables outside. "It is almost one o'clock. Shall we have luncheon?"

"Yes, let's. I enjoy the terrace at the hotel, but this is the first city we've visited where we have only dined at our hotel."

"It's the streets." Phinn had kept watch for the crazy driver who almost hit Augusta, but hadn't seen him again. "We do not have the trick of avoiding carriages the way the Viennese do, and Addison is concerned one of us will be injured."

"The streets *are* dangerous to non-natives." She wrinkled her nose. "The parks are nice."

"As is this restaurant." The waiter came over and greeted them. "What do you suggest for today?"

"We specialize in *Wiener backhendl*, a fried chicken cutlet, or a *Wiener schnitzel*. It is prepared in the same way but is made of veal."

"If you take the chicken, I shall have the veal and we can share," Augusta suggested.

"Very well." He glanced at the waiter. "We would like a green salad as well." He turned to Augusta. "Do you want *pommes frites*?"

Grinning, she nodded.

"Yes, we'll have the *pommes frites* as well."

Phinn ordered a dry white wine to go with their meal. "I think the potatoes must be a French import."

"That's not surprising." Augusta sipped her wine. "The idea of a salon is French as well. There were some famous ones during the Congress of Vienna."

"Now that you mention it, there is a definite French atmosphere in Vienna." Even some of the buildings reminded him of France.

"It is very different from Munich, which is very German." A basket of crusty white bread was placed on the table. Also more French than German.

They arrived at the hotel with just enough time to dress for the salon.

Frau Pichler, a well-known author, lived in an elegant apartment not far from Hofburg Palace. As at Lady Thornhill's salons, the rooms were filled with artists, writers, aristocrats, and hangers-on. There was one large terrace, visible from both drawing rooms. Phinn's tension eased. Augusta would be safe here. She gravitated to a group of ladies discussing literature, and he was drawn into a conversation about architecture. One of the men, Joseph Kornhäusel, had some fascinating ideas concerning the contemporary style of neoclassical architecture.

From the corner of Phinn's eye, he saw Augusta move to another group that included Viscount Celje. Several minutes later, she found yet another party with which to speak. The hairs lifted on the back of Phinn's neck as he watched the young gentleman's eyes follow her hungrily.

"That is Pavle Celje, a viscount," Herr Kornhäusel said.

"I beg your pardon?" Phinn had been watching Augusta instead of listening to the conversation.

"The gentleman who has eyes for the lady in blue." Herr Kornhäusel glanced in the direction Phinn had been looking. "His name is Pavle Celje. He has just finished his Grand Tour and his father, Count Celje, is here arranging a match for him."

Phinn hoped his father found the man a wife quickly. The viscount was much too interested in Augusta. Although it was most likely just calf love. "Where are they from?"

"Slovenia. Just north of Ljubljana. They are a wealthy and influential family." That didn't make Phinn happy. It was a good thing Jane wanted to visit Zagreb, thus avoiding that part of Slovenia. "I met him a few years ago when I spoke with his father, Count Celje, about the possibility of designing a palace, but he wanted only small follies, and I require a patron of larger vision. Fortunately, I found one in Prince von Liechtenstein. I am only here to visit my family while the prince is at court."

"You're fortunate." Architectural patrons were not easy to find. Phinn rose. "It's been a pleasure speaking with you."

Herr Kornhäusel bowed. "For me as well. I rarely find such an astute listener. If you ever find yourself in Liechtenstein, I am very easy to find."

"Excuse me, Lord Phineas." An older man bowed. "I understand you and the lady are English."

"Yes. We are." Phinn inclined his head.

"I am Count Celje. My wife and I are attending the embassy soirée this evening, and I wished to introduce myself."

Ah, the father of the spoiled viscount. "A pleasure to meet you. Do you frequent Vienna often?"

The man gave a gruff laugh. "Only when I must. Which is too often for my taste. We are here to collect our son from university." He heaved a sigh. "Janez is bringing several friends home with him, and we want to ensure nothing untoward occurs on the way home. I must also attend to a family matter."

Phinn remembered his university days, and knew what kind of trouble young men could get into and none of his friends' trips home had been nearly as long. "Undoubtedly a wise decision."

"I should find my wife. I look forward to meeting the rest of your party tonight."

Augusta joined Phinn as he strolled toward the terrace. "I was told the gentleman to whom you were speaking is a famous architect."

"Um, yes. He is in the employ of the Prince von Liechtenstein and has invited me to see his buildings if I ever visit that area." Phinn glanced at her. "Where exactly is Liechtenstein? I've heard of it, but I have no idea where it is located."

"South of Lake Constance."

That didn't help. He shook his head.

"South of Stuttgart there is a large lake, Lake Constance. South and east of there lies Liechtenstein. There is no easy way to travel there from here."

"That settles that. I am unlikely to find myself there any time in the near future." Or at all. Although the buildings sounded interesting. "Who was the older gentleman in the green jacket?"

"Count Celje. He and his wife will be at the entertainment this evening." Phinn tucked her hand in his arm. "He's Slovenian."

"His son, Viscount Celje, asked if we were attending the ball tomorrow night." She'd lowered her voice so that only Phinn could hear her. "When I told him I was, he asked for a dance."

Hell and damnation! "What did you say?"

She lifted one shoulder. "I told him I would have to ask my guardian. Hopefully, he will forget, or we'll leave before I have a set free."

Or the puppy would wait for her and pester her to

stand up with him. Phinn would simply have to protect her from any unwanted advances.

When they arrived back at the hotel, a package addressed to Jane awaited them.

"This was sent by the embassy," Herr Riegert said. "I was asked to see that you received it immediately upon your return."

"Thank you." She took the packet. "We shall be down for drinks within the hour."

He smiled at Augusta. "Minerva and your cat have been waiting for your return. They were on the terrace, but are now out with your servant."

"I wonder what that means?" Augusta turned a confused face to Phinn.

"I suppose we'll find out when Durant returns."

In the end, Phinn discovered what'd been going on from Musson. "After Master Tommy went for his nap, the dog and cat curled up together where they had a view of the front door." The valet removed Phinn's coat. "Although *sweet* is not a term I normally use for anything but food, I must agree with Mrs. Gobert that seeing that huge dog cradling the kitten was sweet."

"I'd have liked to have seen that." Phinn changed his pantaloons for breeches, donned a clean shirt, waistcoat, and began to tie his cravat.

"Mayhap they will do it when you are present." Musson eased on Phinn's jacket. "Will the dog be able to climb the stairs to the terrace on the boat?"

That was a good question. Minerva wouldn't stand for being left out. "When the time comes, I'll figure out something."

He walked into the courtyard as Jane handed the ladies small pocketbooks covered in gold leaf with a coat of arms stamped in the center surrounded by rubies. A gold tasseled loop and pencil were attached to each one.

"What are they?" He stood next to Augusta as she opened hers.

"Dance cards," Jane said. "You see the dances for the evening are listed as well as the type of dance and the composer."

He peered more closely. "Are they all waltzes?"

"Well, there are no Scottish country dances," Prue remarked drily.

"The third dance is a polonaise." Augusta pointed at the card.

"Here is a cotillion," Jane added.

"May I?" He held his hand out to Augusta for the dance card.

"Of course." She gave it to him.

After reading the whole list—the damned ball must go until the wee hours of the morning—he wrote his name in the space for the first dance, a waltz. Then handed it to Boman. "Put your name down for a set."

Augusta's brows arched haughtily and her beautiful, deep pink lips opened, but before she had a chance to chastise him, Addison handed Phinn Jane's card. "Excellent idea. Lord Stewart has sent a note around asking that he and a Colonel Whitestone be granted one dance each."

Addison handed Augusta's card back to her. "Don't forget to write their names down." Once all the gentlemen had been added to the cards, he glanced at his wife. "That should take us to midnight. Will you be ready to leave?"

"I shall. It has been an age since I have stayed up that late . . . voluntarily, that is."

He looked at Prue. "Is it too early for you?"

"Not at all. I've been used to country hours."

Durant came in, being pulled straight to Phinn and Augusta by one determined Great Dane and an equally resolute kitten.

"They're happy to see you." The footman removed their leads.

"So I heard." Augusta cuddled the kitten that'd wasted no time in jumping onto her lap.

Minerva's tail thumped against the chairs as she demanded attention from Phinn and Augusta before finally settling in her normal place between their seats. She gave him a comfortable smile as if this domestic situation appealed to her. Even more than before, he could see them with children. Much like the scene he had come upon with her sisters and Lady Merton in the square. Young ones toddling around with the Danes and cats watching over them. How much deeper would her feelings be after another week on the boat?

Soon. She would be his. He could feel it in his bones.

Chapter Thirty-Two

Phinn entered the parlor and Augusta was the only thing he saw. But he had to run the gauntlet of Great Dane and cat before he could get to her. He stroked Minerva's head, making sure she didn't rub against his dark blue breeches. Etienne almost succeeded in rubbing against Phinn's stockings before he gently pushed the kitten away, stroking him as he did. By the time he was done and Durant had taken the animals away, it was time to depart.

Augusta took his arm. "You look quite fine this evening."

Did he tell her how enchanting she was? "So do you."

They arrived at the embassy to find the rooms filling rapidly. Most of the guests appeared to be English, and, fortunately, Phinn knew none of them. Which meant that any gossip from Paris about Augusta and him would not have reached here.

Lord Stewart took it upon himself to perform introductions for Phinn and Augusta while his second, Colonel Whitestone, took the rest of their party off.

All went well until a lady who looked to be in her late forties or early fifties approached them, smiling,

"Lady Augusta, I am Lady Cartridge. I know your mother." Then the woman turned her brown gaze on Phinn. "And I know your mother as well. I am sure she is delighted that you have made such an advantageous match."

Augusta swayed, but her hand was firmly tucked into his arm and he was able to hold her up. At first he couldn't believe the gossip had spread so far and so fast. They must be using carrier pigeons. Then he remembered the letters his mother and sister-in-law were constantly writing, and mail being sent by diplomatic channels, and he wondered why he hadn't thought of this possibility before. "Thank you, my lady. I am indeed fortunate." He would have stopped there, but Augusta had paled alarmingly and seemed to be having difficulty regaining her countenance. He tightened his grip on her. "Lady Augusta and I have a great deal in common and are very happy."

Her ladyship glanced at Augusta, who'd pasted a smile on her face and none too soon. "I heard your mother and Lady Dorchester are thrilled with the match."

Augusta took a shallow breath. "They could not be happier."

Phinn and she would have to discuss this, but Lord Celje came up, escorting an elegant lady some years younger than him. "My lord." He bowed and looked at the lady. "My dear, allow me to introduce Lord Phineas Carter-Woods to you." The lady curtseyed. "Lord Phineas, my wife, Lady Celje."

Phinn bowed and finished the introductions.

Augusta addressed the couple in Slovenian. "It is a pleasure to meet you."

They answered in the same language, and he was happy that he could understand most of it.

"I understand you are traveling to Trieste," Lady Celje said. "I so wish we were going to be at home so that you could break your journey with us. The inns are not as they are here."

"It is a shame. I can tell you from personal experience," Lord Stewart said, "that Lord and Lady Celje have a remarkable castle. I, as well as the colonel and his wife, have stayed with them on occasion."

"We would have loved to visit you," Augusta said.

Several of the other guests wished Phinn and Augusta happy on their betrothal, and Augusta maintained composure. He, on the other hand, was not looking forward to the conversation that was sure to follow. At Versailles, he'd forced himself to agree to let her go. Indeed, he vowed he wouldn't trap her, and he would not. But if there was any way he could keep her with him as his wife, he'd do it.

All the next day, Augusta had waited for Phinn to say something about the talk that had spread about their betrothal. Yet he hadn't said a word. Instead, they spent most of the day at the cathedral. Well, if he wasn't going to say anything, neither was she. The conversation would be awkward at best, and she did not think she could stand another rejection. It was enough that she knew he did not love her. That was probably why he'd not spoken of it.

The following evening, she wore a primrose silk ball gown with an overskirt of tulle that she'd had made in Paris. She'd had her footman remove the animals before they all met in the parlor, and when she saw Phinn, she was glad she had. Dressed in a black jacket and breeches with a waistcoat embroidered in silver and red, on a gray background, Augusta had never seen him look more handsome and elegant. Animal hair would have ruined the effect.

Bowing, he lifted her fingers to his lips. "You look as if you're floating."

Her cheeks heated, and she felt as if she could float. It felt so right taking his arm, as if they truly would have a life together. Just for tonight, and maybe the rest of the journey to Padua, she'd not think about their separate goals. It would break her heart when he left, but surely his family expected him back for the next Season. And she'd have studies that were sure to engross her.

They arrived at the castle before the start of the first dance. The ballroom was over two stories high with painted and gilded arched ceilings. A gallery ran along one end, where the orchestra members were tuning their instruments. Richly embroidered tapestries lined the walls and potted palms were grouped in areas at the bottom of the double-curved staircases and along the sides of the room. As they reached the stairs they were announced.

Shortly after they found a grouping of chairs, and had sent a footman for wine, Viscount Celje strolled up and bowed generally to their party, then to Augusta alone.

"My lady, may I hope you have a dance for me, or should I ask Herr Addison?"

Her smile was tight. They had known this would most likely occur. "I regret that I have no dances left, my lord."

His eyes widened and he glanced at Hector. "How is this possible?"

"Quite easily." She hoped her tone was cold enough to discourage the man. "We will depart after the fifth set."

For a second, Celje appeared shocked, then a polite mask slipped over his face, and he bowed again. "Perhaps another time then."

The music signaling the first dance began, and Phinn held out his arm. "My dance, I believe?"

"It is." Placing her fingers on his strong arm, the tension drained from her body. Having made her decision, she let herself enjoy the freedom of being "betrothed." Last evening none of the unmarried gentlemen had asked to be made known to her, and tonight she could expect the same. Other than the viscount. Perhaps the man hadn't heard. "I knew this ball was a mistake. If only Jane had not wished to come."

"The worst of it is over now." They rose from bowing and curtseying and began to dance. "You can relax. Five sets and we return to the hotel." Phinn's firm tone reassured her. No matter what happened, he'd keep her safe.

"I would love to attend a ball and have fun rather than being made to dance with men with whom I do not wish to dance." She felt as light as a feather in his arms, and she didn't want him to let go of her.

"There will be no more balls for a while." He drew her closer as they made the turn, making her feel as if he wanted her in his arms. "We shall attend the concert tomorrow night and depart the following morning."

"I'll be glad to be back on the boat."

"I shall be as well. Count Celje gave me a list of villages and small towns we should visit for a day or so."

"That sounds like fun." Part of Augusta wished the barge journey could last forever.

The dance ended all too soon, and her next partner was Boman, while Phinn danced with Prue.

* * *

On their last evening in Vienna, they were invited to use the British Embassy's box at the concert hall. Augusta was glad they had stayed for the musical. She'd never heard such an excellent performance. The only events marring the evening were visits by English ladies asking when and where she and Phinn would marry.

Fortunately, Jane came to their rescue. "They have not yet decided."

That, though, reminded Augusta she would have to write to her mother saying she had broken her betrothal and was remaining in Padua. There, she would live in relative anonymity as a student, and her life would be just as she wished it to be. If only she hadn't fallen in love with Phinn.

How long does it take to recover from a broken heart?

The following morning when the boat pushed away from shore, Phinn heaved a sigh of relief. He had never been so happy to leave a city in his life. At the ball, he'd caught the viscount staring at Augusta. Had Celje been following them, or were they simply traveling the same route?

Last night, when the English ladies had queried them on their wedding date, he'd half expected Augusta to roundly deny they were betrothed. Not only had she not demurred, she had yet to say anything to him. And he *knew* she'd not changed her mind about marriage.

"Will you come help?" Augusta touched his sleeve. "We are trying to convince Minerva to go up the stairs." Augusta giggled, filling his heart with joy. He wasn't the only one glad to leave. "Etienne keeps going up the stairs, then looking back down at her as if he is trying to show her how to do it."

This Phinn had to see. "I think I know a way to get her up."

When they arrived at the stern, the Dane was stretched as far as she could go on the steps. One back paw hovered near the first tread, the other was firmly planted on the deck. The cat crouched at the top, gazing down at her as if giving encouragement.

Augusta glanced at him, her eyes full of laughter, and that was all it took for him to go into whoops. Unfortunately, it earned him a disdainful look from the cat and one of reproach from the dog.

"Right then, here we go." Positioning himself behind Minerva, he braced her rear, lifting her so that her back paws could start climbing the steps. Soon her front paws had gained purchase on the roof and the rest followed. He scrambled up after her. "There. Are you happy now?"

The Dane was attempting to wrap herself around him when Augusta arrived. "That was well done. How are you going to get her down?"

"By being in front and giving her encouragement. She wants to be with us too much not to at least try. I just don't want her hurting herself."

Once the animals were settled, Augusta resumed teaching Phinn Slovenian.

"Your Slovenian is coming along very well. You must have a facility for languages." She closed the book.

Not as good as hers. But he had no jealousy. Her mind was one of the reasons he loved her so much. "Either that, or you are an excellent teacher."

Augusta's smile deepened and she linked her arm with his. "I have never told you, but I value our friendship."

Well, that was like the kiss of death. Would she address their "betrothal" now? How many men had watched the woman they loved marry someone else because the lady refused to recognize his intentions for what they were? That was not going to happen to him. Phinn might have to ask permission from her cousin and her footman to kiss her. Durant had been more of a chaperone than had Addison.

Minerva barked.

"I think I need to help her down."

Thank God for dogs.

On their second day in Budapest, Jane was silent as she read one of the letters Hector had brought back from the British consul. "As I suspected, news of Augusta and Phinn's betrothal reached England." She handed Hector a thick packet of papers. "This is from Matt. It is a revised settlement agreement containing Phinn's financial information."

"Blast it all, why couldn't that blasted French count have kept the information to himself?"

"That would have been too much to expect." Jane set the letter aside. "I'll answer Grace when I work out what to say to her."

Prue strode into the room waiving a missive. "My mother received correspondence from Patience Wolverton informing her about the betrothal. She wants to know what I plan to do now that Augusta will wed." Prue dropped into a chair. "This has got out of hand."

"I'm afraid I have to agree." Boman also with a letter in hand took a chair next to Prue's. "My mother wants to know when I'll return to England."

"I do as well," Jane said. "But what are we to do about it? I am positive they are in love with each other, but neither one of them will admit it."

"If Dorchester hadn't made Phinn vow to go about getting an heir"—at this point, Hector would gladly wring the marquis's neck—"this problem could be easily resolved."

"That's not a problem any longer," Boman said. "Phinn received a missive telling him it looks like his sister-in-law could have a son, relieving him of his promise."

"Then what is keeping him from declaring himself to Augusta?" Prue had never sounded so exasperated.

Boman's eyes widened as if he could not believe what she'd just said. "You must be joking. After the way she rejected him, no sane man would willingly put himself through that again."

"What did you expect her to do?" Prue poked Boman in the chest. "He would have destroyed all her plans, and he didn't even love her."

"Well, he's fair mad about her now." He jabbed his finger into the air. "And look where it's got him. Nowhere."

"All you have to do is look at the way Augusta gazes at him to know she loves him too, but she is not going to tell him first, and I don't blame her." Prue took the top off the teapot, glancing into it before going to the bell-pull and jerking it. "How is she supposed to know he's changed his mind about anything?"

As enlightening as this quarrel was, Hector decided to put a stop to it. "The two of you arguing about this isn't going to help anything."

"Someone has to have this discussion," Boman objected. "*They're* not going to."

"It's a shame we don't have bride kidnappings in England," she mumbled.

Jane sat up sharply. "What did you say?"

"Oh, it's nothing." Prue fluttered her fingers. "One of the maids got married not long ago. Before the ceremony, friends kidnapped her, and her groom had to make concessions if he wished to have her as his wife."

"That's our answer," Jane said. Hector thought he knew where his wife was going with this line of thought, but the other two were clearly confused. "Augusta and Phinn love each other. That is clear. But, due to valid reasons of their own, neither one will tell the other." Jane glanced at Hector. "Therefore, it stands to reason that their friends and family must assist them."

He nodded. "Go on."

"We'll kidnap Augusta. Boman, you will tell him that if he wants to marry her, he will have to enter into negotiations for her hand."

"Which include supporting her desire to attend university," Prue added. "And not having children until afterward."

"I can almost guarantee you he'll agree," Boman said. "In fact, he'll probably be happy to get it all out."

"Excellent." Hector opened the door to a quiet knock. "Let's celebrate." He glanced at the hotel's servant. "Two bottles of white wine."

"The only question is when will we have the kidnapping?" Boman asked.

"That we'll have to decide," Jane responded.

Chapter Thirty-Three

They were roughly two days from Trieste and only about seven miles from Ljubljana, where they would spend the night, when Phinn felt more than heard the rumble of horses. "We need to move off to the side."

"I don't have a good feeling about this." Boman glanced over his shoulder at the carriages and held up his hand. "There are too many of them."

Having decided to ride, Augusta and Prue reined in their horses next to them.

"I heard it too," Prue said.

"What is it?" Augusta looked at each of them.

"There are a lot of horsemen coming." The problem was, Phinn didn't know from which direction they were approaching. "It's flat enough here we should be able to see them soon."

"Don't stop," Prue said. "Keep going as if nothing is happening. I'll tell Hector."

Whirling her horse around, she galloped to the first coach; once it started to move again, she came back. "Whatever it is, we stay together."

"You've been through this before. Phinn was pleased

that Augusta didn't sound afraid. This wasn't the first time for him and Boman either.

"Yes, during the war." Her smile was grim. "We were told we'd be safer on this route than the one to Zagreb, but that doesn't mean there are not highwaymen."

"There is supposed to be a town ahead of us." Augusta's voice was firm, but her horse danced, betraying her nervousness.

"Let's go." Boman urged his horse faster. "I just hope we're not running straight into their arms."

They'd reached the outskirts of the village, when a group of horsemen, most of them in uniform, arrived. The leader held up his arm and they came to a halt.

"Good afternoon," Viscount Celje said in German, grinning like a cat that had just caught its prey.

Augusta moved her horse closer to Phinn's, narrowed her eyes, and in the same language said, "You!"

"Yes." He bowed. "I was informed that you were traveling this way. My parents were desolate that they could not invite you to stay with us and requested that I do so. My grandmother is here as well."

"And you required all of these soldiers to extend an invitation." Her tone made clear that not only was it not a question, but she was not at all happy about it.

"Having private soldiers is quite common in this part of Europe." Celje shrugged. "I was pleased my parents extended the invitation. It will allow me to get to know you better."

"Indeed."

Damn, she sounded like her sister the duchess. Phinn's chest swelled with pride.

"I, on the other hand, have no desire to know you better, my lord. Apparently you have not heard that I am already betrothed to the gentleman of my choice." She lifted one brow and gave him her best haughty look. It was very helpful having a sister who was a duchess.

"A pity." The viscount glanced at Phinn as if he'd like to get rid of him. "Nevertheless, it is my parents' invitation."

Next to him one of Celje's men, who looked to be the captain of the guard, said in Slovenian, "She does not seem as delighted as you told your grandmother she would be."

"Be quiet. I don't believe she is in love with him. I've seen them together," Celje answered in the same language.

She exchanged a look with Phinn, and said in Nahuatl, "Did you understand what they said?"

He nodded. "The grandmother is in charge. Do you think Lord and Lady Celje really invited us?"

"Unfortunately, we do not have the answer to that. It's possible. They are very nice and like helping English travelers. I do not trust *his* motives." Augusta was careful not to say anything that would let the viscount know they were talking about him. "The man next to him is doubting his word." She quickly reviewed all their options and none of them were good. "If it wasn't for my cousin, the child, and our personal servants, I would say we ride through them."

"You're right. It's too dangerous." Phinn's eyes as good as said he trusted her decision.

Her throat closed with tears of happiness. Yet this was no time to show them. Men always took tears as a weakness.

"Tell me, what language you are speaking," the viscount demanded.

She opened her eyes wide and gave him an innocent

look. "Why, the dialect from our home county in Northumberland."

Phinn grinned at her. "You don't come from Northumberland."

"Neither do you, but some of the dialects there are based on Danish and few outsiders can understand them."

He shook his head and quietly sniggered. "You are brilliant."

"If you do not wish to partake of our hospitality," the viscount said, "please feel free to ride on. However, my grandmother and parents will no doubt be insulted."

If Lord and Lady Celje had been the ones to extend the offer, they would be insulted. Yet, Augusta could not bring herself to trust the viscount. Still, what harm could he actually cause? She glanced at Phinn. "What do you think?"

"We don't want to insult nobles of the Austrian Empire." He heaved a sigh. "We must find out if the invitation is real."

Augusta raised her chin. "Very well. We will visit your parents' home."

The viscount inclined his head. "My grandmother will be pleased."

"You're mad if you think your grandmother will believe you have a chance with the English lady," the captain of the guard said.

"Don't be a fool. Look at them. They do not look like lovers at all, but like brother and sister."

"My lord." The captain bowed his head. "I will apprise her ladyship she will be having visitors."

Well, drat and blast it all. "I shouldn't have trusted him at all."

"Apparently not," Phinn said drily. "We'll leave in the morning."

Prue brought her horse next to Augusta's and said in Portuguese, "Boman told me what you and Phinn were saying. What did that man just say?"

"He has gone back to the castle to tell the idiot's grandmother we are coming."

"Another English dialect?" Celje asked suspiciously.

Prue gazed at him as if he was a fool. "Naturally. I'm from Hertfordshire. You can't expect me to know Northumberland."

No one must have been paying attention to the coaches, because Hector came up to them on his horse, and using Punjabi asked, "What's going on?"

Augusta told him everything that had happened. "If you want to take Jane and Tommy and go to Trieste, I will understand."

"That's very kind of you," he responded sarcastically. "But neither your brother nor Jane will either agree or understand. We do as Prue said and stay together. Aside from that, his father is a great friend to English travelers. We wouldn't want to insult him."

"That's true." Even though she didn't trust the look in the viscount's eyes, he was no more dangerous than Lord Lancelot had been. She turned to the viscount and spoke in German. "In case you are wondering, that was Punjabi. My guardian spent years in India."

A tick started in Phinn's jaw. Prue looked away, and Boman dropped his face into his hands. Augusta would be lucky if they all didn't break out laughing.

"We have wasted enough time." The viscount gave a signal for his troops to turn around. "Follow me. My grandmother, old woman as she is, will be waiting for us when we arrive."

"I have the distinct feeling he was trying to make us feel sorry for his grandmother and parents," Phinn said, using Nahuatl.

"I agree. I have the feeling she will be our savior."

"I for one am glad our English dialects are so unintelligible." Prue had again used Portuguese. Her lips were pressed tight, but her eyes sparkled. "I'm also very impressed at how you are handling all of this."

Augusta was as well. Looking up she saw the castle was visible from the main road and glanced at Phinn riding next to her. "It looks just like an old castle in a fairy tale."

"The tower has to date from the twelfth century." He sounded as much in awe as she was.

"How do you know?"

"Do you see how it is made into a wide square with several levels?" She nodded. "The family and their men-at-arms would have all lived in it. We have similar towers in England."

She caught sight of a large white building farther inside the wall. "Those buildings must have come later."

No more than twenty minutes later, they entered through a gate that still had a portcullis. She gazed up as they passed under it. "Amazing."

"The whole thing looks to be in wonderful condition." He looked around with fascination.

Augusta grinned. Knowing Phinn, he'd be inspecting every part of the castle before they continued their journey.

The dowager Lady Celje, the viscount's grandmother, met them at the steps to the castle proper. "Welcome." Her ladyship addressed them in French. "We hope you enjoy your stay with us."

The coaches came to a halt behind Augusta and Phinn. He swung down from his horse in one fluid motion then came to lift her down. The instant his hands circled her waist she knew she should have dismounted herself. Frissons of pleasure scurried up to her breasts and she wanted him to touch more of her. Beneath her hands, his muscles strained his jacket as he held her for a moment too long before lowering her feet to the ground. Sucking in a breath, she hoped no one noticed her reaction. Phinn gazed down at her, capturing her gaze with his clear gray eyes. And for those seconds, she felt a connection to him she'd never imagined feeling for anyone.

Swallowing, she lowered her eyes, and he released her. The rest of their party was following their hosts into the house. "We should go in as well."

As their horses were being led away, he offered her his arm. "As you wish."

The hall was three floors high with an impressive double marble staircase leading to the first floor. Two coats of arms guarded the bottom of the steps. The rest of the hall was plastered and hung with huge tapestries.

"My husband and then my son have added as many modern conveniences as possible," Lady Celje said. "Yet it refuses to give up its original design."

"Do you live here year-round?" Augusta thought it must be quite cold in winter.

"No, we have a more modern palace in the town. In summer, it is more comfortable here." Her ladyship gestured toward the staircase. "Come. You may explore to your heart's content after you have had an opportunity to change."

Following Lady Celje up the stairs, Augusta caught a whiff of horse. She'd need to bathe as well. The bed-chamber had lead-glass panes in the same diamond shape she'd seen in old Tudor houses. One stood open, giving a beautiful view of the valley and town below.

"I've ordered a bath for you, my lady," Gobert said. "Her ladyship's maid said tea will be served in an hour."

"That long?" Augusta's stomach was already growling.

"I was told fruit and cheese would be prepared and brought to the bedchamber." Sounds of water being pumped came from across the corridor. They must have a bathing chamber. Her maid started unbuttoning her riding habit. "Do you want to bathe first?"

"I had probably better." Horses only smelled good when one was in the stables or riding. "Where are Minerva and Etienne?"

"Durant is walking them."

After bathing and dressing in a muslin gown, Augusta sated her hunger and inspected the large room. Her maid had come through a small door made to look like the papered wall. Two other doors stood on either side of the chamber. Did all the rooms connect? Before she could explore, her cat dashed in and insisted on being picked up. The Dane barked, and a door near her room opened and closed. Phinn must be close by.

A footman came to guide her to the drawing room and when she stepped into the corridor, Phinn waited as well. "I believe we are the last ones to go down. At least, that's what I think the man said."

"Your Slovenian has become very good. I'm sure you're correct." She took his arm as they were led down the main staircase to a wide terrace at the back of the castle. "This reminds me of France."

"I have no doubt the castle has been remodeled any number of times over the centuries. Taking ideas from wherever its masters traveled."

"Lady Celje alluded to that earlier." The gardens beyond the terrace reached the short way to the wall where red climbing roses hid the stone. She and Phinn were, indeed, the last to arrive. "Are we late?"

"No, dear." Jane gestured to the place next to her on a sofa. Tommy had got down and was toddling around the terrace. "We did not expect to see you until now."

Her ladyship poured tea and her grandson handed around plates.

"Lady Celje thought you and Lord Phineas might like to explore the castle tomorrow. Therefore, we've decided to remain until the day after," Jane said.

"Thank you. We are extremely interested in the structures and grounds." Augusta was thankful that after helping his grandmother with tea the viscount had taken himself off.

A priest, about the same age as Count Celje, joined them. "Lady Augusta, Mrs. Addison, and Mrs. Brunning, please allow me to introduce my brother-in-law, Father Christophe," her ladyship said. "He is our castle priest."

Father Christophe gave a courtly bow. "It is always a pleasure to have visitors at the castle."

His lordship introduced the men next. The butler arrived with three footmen carrying large trays.

Phinn took the seat on the other side of Augusta. "That looks like apricot marmalade."

She picked up a spoon and tasted the confection. "It is, and it's delicious. I've never seen any of these foods. I wish I could taste them all."

"Let's share." He broke off a piece of cake and held it out to her.

That was the one thing even Walter refused to do. "Are you sure?"

"Absolutely. There are at least ten different sweets and savories. If you do not wish to ruin your dinner, it's the only way."

She took the cake. "Thank you."

"Excuse me, my lady," Father Christophe said. "I have been given to understand that you and Lord Phineas are betrothed. Have you decided when you will wed?"

Augusta thanked God she'd just swallowed the sip of tea. "No. We . . . we, er . . ."

"We have not made any plans yet," Phinn said.

"Do you intend to wait until you return home?"

"No." Augusta couldn't get the word out fast enough.

"In that case, allow me to recommend this castle. The chapel is beautiful and said to bring good luck." The priest smiled. "There is no need to answer me now. Think about it." Father Christophe bowed before entering the house.

Phinn touched her hand. "It will all be fine."

Except it wouldn't. She wanted to attend university and have him. And she couldn't.

Chapter Thirty-Four

Well, hell! Phinn wished the priest hadn't said anything. He'd like nothing better than to marry Augusta tomorrow. The last letter he'd received from his brother had effectively released Phinn from having children as immediately as possible. Helen was, indeed, pregnant again, and Dorchester hoped for an heir. The whole process was a mystery to Phinn, but apparently, she was carrying much differently than she had with the girls. Would that be enough to bring Augusta around?

He'd have to figure out a way to tell her he loved her and hope she didn't reject him again. Yet, this time he did love her, and he could promise she could attend university.

Lady Celje rose. "If you are finished with tea, I would like to show you my solar. It's beautiful at this time of day."

They were shown to Lady Celje's solar where Augusta, Phinn, Addison, and Jane were served wine.

Lady Celje drank half her glass and filled it up again. "I regret to have to inform you that your visit was my grandson's idea," she said in excellent English. "My servants are guarding this chamber to ensure he does not hear of our conversation."

Hell and the devil! It was like a medieval tale. Phinn exchanged a look with Addison.

"We were stopped on the road to Trieste, where we have a ship waiting to take us to Venice." Augusta took a sip of wine and swallowed. "I do not know what Viscount Celje has planned, but I can guess. What he refuses to understand is that I am betrothed to Lord Phineas."

She glanced at Phinn, and he took up the story. "It is a match our families have desired for a very long time." At least since he'd returned from Mexico. Damn, he might as well say it. "I can assure you I am deeply in love with Lady Augusta."

She stared at him for a brief moment, but he couldn't work out what she was thinking. "And I with Lord Phineas."

Her ladyship nodded sharply. "My grandson is an idealistic fool. He saw Lady Augusta in Paris and decided he was in love. You will forgive me, but this is what comes of reading romantic poetry." Phinn had been right. Viscount Celje had been following them. "His father has arranged a perfectly good match for him. You are in no danger of falling for his charms. Therefore, I shall serve you an excellent meal this evening. You shall have a good night's sleep, and tomorrow you will be on your way." She held up her wineglass, and they did the same. "Here is to your continued journey." They could all agree with that. "There is no reason to come to the dining room. I will arrange to have your meal served here." Her ladyship rose. "There are not sufficient bedchambers for all of you and your servants." He didn't believe that at all. She nodded to Augusta. "You and Mrs. Brunning will share a room.

Your lady's maid's bed is in a room off that chamber.
Lord Phineas, you and your secretary have the bedroom next to that of Lady Augusta. Mr. Addison, you
and your lady are on the other side of Lady Augusta.
Your child and nurse have the chamber on the other
side. There is a door connecting the rooms." She inclined her head. "I wish you a pleasant evening."

She didn't mention either his valet or Jane's maid,
but Phinn assumed their bedchambers had dressing
rooms as well.

"Well"—Jane turned to all of them—"I feel as if I am
in one of Mrs. . . . . oh, how could I forget her name! In
any event, a gothic romance story."

"I know what you mean. I must say I greatly prefer Miss
Austen's plots." Augusta pursed her lips for a moment. "I
think we should continue to use other languages. One
never knows when we are being spied upon."

"I agree." Phinn had been struck by her ladyship's
pronouncement that her people were keeping guard.
"We will be much safer."

"I understand your caution." Jane gave them a
chagrined look. "The problem is, I have only French,
German, and some Italian. I am afraid that will not
be helpful."

"Don't worry, my dear." Addison put his arm around
her. "I taught Augusta Punjabi a few years ago. All you
have to do is be beautiful and smile."

Jane punched him in the arm. "You, sir, will pay
for that."

"Yes." He gave her a warm expression and chuckled.
"I imagine I shall."

A few minutes later, Tommy and the animals were
brought in. Phinn was pleased that even though Minerva

greeted Augusta first, she came to him. Still, the Dane needed to be ready to protect her.

He stroked the dog's head and whispered, "You must stay with Augusta tonight." She leaned her head on his knee and gazed up at him. Clearly the dog didn't understand the gravity of the situation.

They picked through what was probably an excellent meal, before retiring to their own chambers. The walls of the room he was sharing with his secretary were paneled and plastered. Most likely, over the original stone. Two doors were set into the walls, one on each side of the chamber.

Musson entered the room from one of them. "I have been allotted a small bedchamber off the dressing room." He surveyed the room. "I only unpacked your night kit, my lord."

"Good man." Phinn glanced at the other door. "Do you happen to know where that door leads?"

"Indeed, my lord. Lady Augusta and Mrs. Brunning's room is on the other side."

Minerva, who had insisted on coming with Phinn, went over to the door and sniffed. Apparently satisfied, she lay down in front of the door.

"Is it locked?" There was no point having a room next to Augusta's if he couldn't get to her in the event she needed him.

Musson went to the door, presumably to assure himself that no key was in the door—why did people do that?—then began searching a desk against the wall. He held up a key. "Perhaps this will work."

Silently, he slid the key in and turned it. "Yes, this is the one."

"Leave it in the lock," Phinn instructed. "I don't want to have to go looking for it if it is needed."

Musson backed away as if he'd been tempted to take it out but was determined to disregard his instincts.

"Be ready to leave at a moment's notice." Phinn had no idea what would happen tonight, but he was sure something would. He didn't trust the viscount. The man was as knocked-in-the-cradle as Lord Lancelot. Unfortunately, Celje had armed men and a walled castle. He'd probably even read the book Jane had mentioned. Phinn rubbed the back of his head. Jane was right; the situation was too fantastical.

"As you wish, my lord." Musson retired to either the dressing room or his bedchamber.

"Damn if I wouldn't like a bottle of brandy." Boman rubbed his forehead from his nose to his hairline.

That was strange. "You barely touch spirits."

"It's this whole situation. I feel as if I've been cast back to medieval times." He opened the stained glass window and glanced out. "It's a long way down."

"I can't disagree with you there. If it wouldn't cause problems, I'd have the ladies sleep in here. It wouldn't be the first time I've slept on a stone floor. At least this one has a carpet."

"We could let them know the door is unlocked." Boman's brows drew up, wrinkling his forehead.

"Excellent idea." Phinn went to the door, turned the lock, and knocked. "Augusta, Prue, if you need us, the door will remain unlocked."

Shuffling sounded on the other side of the door. "Thank you."

Augusta. He'd recognize her voice anywhere. "If anything happens, just open the door."

"We shall leave it ajar, if you don't mind," Prue said. "I know what the countess said, but I cannot be easy."

Well, that made at least three of them. He picked up his pistol and made sure it was loaded.

"Neither am I," Augusta said. Very well, four, Phinn thought. "He lied to his grandmother."

"Some people have no sense." Phinn had learned at an early age never to be untruthful to his grandmother. It was a much greater sin than lying to one's parents.

"Or sense of shame."

That too. "Good night." By this time he was pressed up against the wall next to the door. He'd sleep there if Minerva hadn't already claimed the spot.

He imagined Etienne curled up against Augusta. Right where Phinn wanted to be.

"Good night to you. I do not think I shall sleep a wink." The door pushed in just a bit more, and a pattering of feet fled across the floor.

"Good night." *My love.* Soon he'd tell her how he felt and how much he needed her in his life.

"This is a fine mess." Boman placed his pistol on a table next to the bed, before lying down fully clothed, his hands behind his head.

"We must have been followed from Budapest." That was the only way the viscount could have known to a nicety where they were.

"That's what I think as well." Why the devil hadn't Phinn thought to post some of the outriders behind them?

"The question is, will Lady Celje be true to her word?"

"I believe she will try." However, short of drugging her grandson, he didn't know how she'd manage him. "Get some sleep. I'll take the second watch."

Boman grunted. "You sleep first. I'm not that tired."

Shortly before dawn, Minerva began a low growl, then Etienne jumped onto Phinn's chest, before dashing back into Augusta's bedchamber. Phinn reached over to Boman, but he was already out of bed, pulling on his boots.

"Hell." Why couldn't the bounder have listened to his grandmother?

A shot echoed and someone screamed.

Augusta!

It was still dark when Etienne pounced on Augusta's chest and chirped. He'd never done that before. She hadn't meant to fall asleep at all. "What?"

"Footsteps." Prue threw Augusta her robe, as the dog began to growl softly. "I locked the door."

The cat flew across the room toward Phinn's chamber. That was good. She did not want him harmed. Donning her robe, she slid her pistol from under the pillow and joined Prue. "What is taking them so long?"

"They don't want to wake anyone else."

The lock clicked, a light shone first, then the door opened fully. Augusta pointed her weapon at the door. She doubted it was the countess, so she spoke in German. "Halt or I shall shoot."

"Don't be ridiculous," Celje scoffed. "This is merely a bride kidnapping. It is a wedding tradition in my country." He swaggered into the bedchamber. "It is important for a man to be able to rescue his bride."

She didn't doubt that at all, but Augusta knew he had no intention of returning her or making it easy for Phinn to find her. Blast it all, if she was going to be married it would be to Phinn or no one.

She waited as light brightened the bedchamber. The viscount was dressed for traveling. Shifting the pistol, she leveled it at him. "Come no closer." If he was going to act as if they were characters in a book, she could too. "I will shoot."

Holding out his arms, he smiled. "No lady would shoot a gentleman coming to rescue her from a loveless marriage."

For a moment Augusta's jaw dropped. What arrogance. The man was worse than Lord Lancelot. Celje definitely needed to be taught not to argue with a lady. She clamped her mouth shut, aimed at his arm, and fired the pistol. Celje screamed. Smoke drifted up from the gun. Minerva, who'd been in the doorway growling, lunged at the cur, knocking him to the floor. Celje drew one arm back as if to punch the dog, but Etienne sprang forward, sinking his front claws into the man's hand.

"What the . . ." Before she knew it, Phinn was next to her. "Augusta?"

"I shot him." She turned her head and looked him in the eyes. *What is it about my family?* "He was going to kidnap me. I will not allow that to happen."

Hector had run in from the other door. "What the devil is going on here?"

"Well, this wasn't how we'd planned it." Prue, mumbled, still holding a large pistol leveled at the intruders. Someone was shouting in the corridor. Blood poured down the viscount's arm and hand. The viscount's screams had become raw sobs.

One of the viscount's men glanced at Augusta. "May we take him, please?"

"Minerva, Etienne, to me." She was delighted to see that both animals obeyed immediately.

"Minerva's growling woke me. Just to make sure I was up, the cat pounced on my chest. I should have slept in my clothes." Phinn put his arm around her. Her scantily dressed body soaked in his heat. She wanted to turn into him, and have him hold her. "That is a single-shot pistol, sweetheart." *Sweetheart?* Did he mean to call her that? "Give it to me and Boman will reload it."

Augusta nodded and he took the pistol. True to his word, seconds later he gave it back to her. "We must prepare to leave."

"Yes." He turned. "Musson, get our kit ready. We're going as soon as it's light."

She wanted to depart now, but he was right. The winding road to the castle was too dangerous to travel in the dark.

"I have had enough of your foolishness." Lady Celje's voice echoed from the corridor. "Gal, send for the doctor."

"Yes, my lady."

Lady Celje entered the room dressed in a colorful and elaborately embroidered robe. "I am sorry for my grandson's behavior." For a scant moment she looked exhausted, but recovered immediately. "He will be in his chambers until the doctor arrives and treats him. If he bothers you again, I will lock him in the dungeon until my son arrives."

"Thank you, my lady." Augusta managed a small smile. "I should probably apologize for shooting your grandson, but I cannot."

"You *should* not." Her ladyship's lips rose into a smile. "I think it did him a great deal of good to have his actions result in immediate consequences. Aside from that, unless you had accepted the offer to marry here, it was not the time for a wedding kidnapping."

Phinn had no idea what Lady Celje was talking about. "What is a wedding kidnapping?"

"It is an old custom, but these days, its purpose is to make the groom pay a price for a bride or give her concessions."

Addison gave Phinn a long look. "I think there are

times when it could be a very good idea. Jane, my love, we have done all we can here."

"Yes, of course." Jane—when had she arrived?—touched Prue's arm. "Will you come with us?"

"Ah, yes." She closed the door between the rooms.

This was it then. It was time for him to tell Augusta he loved her and beg her to marry him.

"We should never have pretended to be betrothed." She left his side, strode halfway across the room, turned and faced him. "Look what has come of it."

Phinn had never met such a stubborn female. Nor one who was so intrepid, intelligent, or beautiful. He ambled toward her, and she took a step back. "I'd like to make you an offer."

Despite the retreat, she stood as straight and assured as if she were in a ballroom, not in a bedroom with nothing between them but a nightgown and a robe. "What?"

"Marry me in truth." He continued to stroll forward and she continued to withdraw. Her back hit the tapestry-covered wall. "Augusta, I love you."

"No." She shook her head. Curls escaped the loose braid. He wanted to reach out and run his fingers through her sable hair. "You just said that."

"I can't believe you haven't figured it out." He dragged a hand down his face. Had he been so incompetent in showing his regard for her that she truly didn't know?

Her hands went to her hips. "If it's true, why did you not tell me?"

"I just did." His voice echoed in the chamber and he took a breath. Shouting wouldn't help. "You were the one who told me that I didn't love you because I wasn't acting like a man in love. Well, I'm not sure what you were waiting for me to do, but I *do* love you." He reached out to her, but let his hand fall.

"I cannot." She shook her head again. But her face had lost the anger. Now she just looked tired as she rubbed her heart with a fisted hand. "It still will not work. You need an heir, and having a child would hinder me from achieving what I need."

He was so close he could feel the heat rising from Augusta. Her full breasts rose and fell with each breath she took. The closer he got, the more her nipples furled into tight buds, visible through her nightgown and robe. She might not know it, but she wanted him as much as he wanted her. He had to make her understand how much they needed each other.

"You were right in London when you told me I didn't love you." Phinn was so close now her gown grazed his bare feet. "I do now, Augusta. More than I ever knew it was possible for a man to love a woman. Ever since we were at Versailles, I've been trying to show you how much I love you."

Closing her eyes, she pulled her lower lip between strong white teeth. God, how he wanted to kiss those lips. "That does not change what I need for my life."

He kept his hands at his sides. If he allowed them loose, only the Fates knew what he'd do. "I could not take that away from you. I want for you what you want for yourself."

She opened her deep blue eyes and met his gaze. "You have to go back to England and have an heir."

"That is going to be hard to do when the only woman I want to marry is right here." Her breasts rose again, begging him to take them in his mouth. "If it means leaving you, my brother can make his own heir." Her breath came faster, but neither of them moved. "We'll go to Padua, and you will attend the university. There is plenty of architecture for me to study in Italy."

He gave her a rueful grin. "You won't want me around when you are studying for your examinations."

Her eyes widened as she searched his. "You're serious?"

"Augusta." He moved his hands to the wall on either side of her. "I will do anything to make you happy. My life has no meaning without you."

Her eyes were large and dilated. If he reached for her, would she come to him? What must this be costing her?

"But marriage means children."

"There are ways not to have them until you are ready." He brushed his lips across hers. "You can attend university. Afterward, if you like, we can travel anywhere you wish. We won't have children until you're ready for them." He held her tightly, tucking her head beneath his chin. "Believe in me, please. I love you, and I will not disappoint you."

"But what if—" He took her mouth with his.

Damn. She was so sweet. He should have kissed her before. "Believe in us. Believe that we can do anything together."

Her lips softened beneath his. When he ran his tongue across the seam of her mouth, she opened for him. When her arms slid around his neck, he tilted his head, deepening the kiss. With one hand, he cupped a breast, and with the other he pressed her to him. "Will you be my partner in life and marry me?"

"Yes." She pulled his head down, leaning her forehead against his. "Yes, I will marry you."

"Thank God!" Sweeping her up into his arms, he carried her to the bed. Yet, now was the time to keep one of his promises. "Where are you in your cycle?"

She didn't even flinch. "I finished my courses a few days ago."

"Are you regular?"

"I wasn't when I first left England, but I am again. To the hour."

"In that case, we're safe."

"Not yet we are not." Augusta scurried off the bed. "You, sir, must wait until after the wedding. One of the other marriage customs is hanging the sheet."

"You want to wed here?" After what had happened, he couldn't be more surprised.

"Why not? We're not going back to England for the ceremony." She kissed the corner of his mouth, resisting when he tried to claim her lips again. "I like Father Christophe, and he did say the chapel brought one luck."

"All very valid points. Let's tell Father Christophe he can marry us." He jumped off the bed. "Musson!" Phinn shouted. "Lady Augusta and I require baths."

Peals of laughter came from the chamber bordering hers. Damn. He'd forgotten all about her family.

"The tubs are being filled in the bathing rooms, my lord."

He pulled her into his arms again and kissed her. "We'll continue this later."

It wasn't until he was dressed and ready to find the chapel that he remembered the ring. "Musson, I need my jewel box."

"I have the wedding ring here." Boman held up the ring composed of platinum and sapphires. Phinn had had it made in Paris.

"Then all I need is a bride." He started toward Augusta's bedchamber.

"You may not see her before you arrive at the church step," Prue called from beyond the closed door. "That is the castle custom. There will also be broken glass for her to step over."

He'd heard of the church steps. That dated back

centuries in various places. But broken glass was new. Still, there was no way he would allow her to stroll through the castle without him guarding her. Not with Celje about. "She needs to be protected."

Prue laughed again. "No more than you do."

At first Phinn didn't understand, but then it dawned on him, if he was missing there couldn't be a ceremony. How the devil were they going to do this? "Give me a moment."

Despite what Lady Celje said, he couldn't bring himself to trust anyone who was not in their party. Even her ladyship's guards had not been able to keep that idiot from gaining access to Augusta's chamber. He lowered his voice. "Musson, I want all of our people armed and up here immediately."

"Yes, my lord." He dashed out of the room.

"I know that look," Boman said. "You have a scheme."

Phinn nodded. "We shall go first. Augusta will follow, but we'll go as a group."

"I'll tell the others."

The dowager countess said she'd send a footman to guide them to the castle's chapel. Phinn would follow behind the servant, accompanied by Boman. Both had their pistols. According to the plan Phinn had drawn up, they'd be followed by Jane and Prue. Augusta and Addison would be last, but they'd have the rest of their servants grouped around them. Two of the grooms remained with the coaches and the outriders who'd refused to go against Celje's men in the castle proper.

A knock sounded on the door between Augusta's chamber and his bedroom. Addison walked in carrying a letter bag. "There are some details we must discuss before the ceremony." He placed the satchel on the desk, and took out a thick stack of papers. "I received these from Worthington when we were in Vienna. In the event Augusta married."

"A settlement agreement?" Phinn took them from the older man and began to read documents. "He made sure she is well protected financially."

"It is my understanding that her sisters and Lady Merton had essentially the same agreement. I know Jane does."

He continued to read until he reached the part that concerned his finances. How the hell had Worthington found out . . . Dorchester. *That devil.* The assistance he'd given Phinn, and the letter, made a great deal more sense. His brother had always intended for him to marry Augusta.

He sharpened a pen, dipped it in the inkwell, signed the document, and handed it back to Addison. What did one say now?

Thankfully, Addison slapped Phinn on the back. "Welcome to the family."

He wished his family could be here too. "Speaking of family, is Augusta ready?"

"If not quite yet, then soon. The ladies are taking care of some English traditions."

Once their servants had been assembled, Phinn gave them their positions, then he and Boman went into the corridor to find a footman standing against the wall. "Her ladyship sent me to escort you to the chapel."

Boman knocked on Augusta's door. "Are you ready for us to start down?"

"Yes," Jane replied.

Durant stepped out from Addison's room. "As soon as you pass me, her ladyship shall step into the corridor."

"Let's go." There was indeed a small pile of broken glass at the entrance to the ladies' chamber.

A few moments later, high-pitched laughter echoed from behind him. Phinn grinned to himself. The day would not be horrible after all. The footman led them down the grand stone staircase to the hall. He'd expected the chapel to be in the back of the castle somewhere; instead his senses pricked as the butler opened the front door. Once he passed through, he saw the small church positioned across the courtyard. He glanced up, almost expecting to see archers high on the crenellated roof, but there were none. This was the nineteenth century. Jane's talk of gothic novels must be affecting his thinking.

Phinn and his secretary took their places on the church steps, to the right of Father Christophe. Even though he knew a marriage performed under the laws of the country was legal in England, when they arrived in Venice, he'd make sure the marriage was registered with the British Consul.

Boman nudged Phinn with his elbow. Augusta's escorts had dispersed to form a half circle around them, as she climbed the shallow steps. She was exquisite, and all of her would soon be his. His gaze dropped to her hands. Instead of flowers, she held her pistol. He wished she could have a proper wedding with all of her family and friends, and a posy instead of a gun.

Chapter Thirty-Five

As soon as Phinn left the room, Jane, Prue, and Gobert flew into action.

"My lady," Gobert said. "You must choose a gown. I recommend the blue you had made in Paris, with the embroidery traveling up from the hem."

The dress looked as if a flower garden was growing up the skirts. The same pattern was on the puffed sleeves. It was the most beautiful gown Augusta owned, and the most sophisticated. "I agree. I shall wear my pearls."

She bathed in the dressing room, and afterward Prue took out the basket of food they had packed for yesterday's travel, and they broke their fast. Earlier a maid had come, asking if the ladies would like breakfast, but after the abduction attempt, no one trusted the castle fare.

Her cousins exchanged looks with each other. Then Jane blushed and took a breath. "I suppose we should explain what to expect when you and Phinn consummate the marriage."

Augusta decided to confess that she was not ignorant

of the details. "Dotty already told me what, when, where, and how it happened."

"Wonderful!" Jane smiled, looking relieved.

"Did she explain what happened before the actual act?" Prue asked.

That was something Augusta had not asked about. "No, I did not think it mattered."

"Ah. As it is about to happen, you might want a *bit* more information."

Once again, Jane's cheeks were painted red. "That is actually the part that makes a lady want to have the rest."

Augusta's breast tingled with the memory of Phinn touching it. "Oh! Such as kissing and the like?"

"Mm-hm." Prue nodded and began to explain all the ways a man could kiss a woman to make her want him, and other things he'd do to make relations easier for her. "It will still hurt, but, if he is careful, it won't be as painful as it could be otherwise."

During the explanation, Augusta had grown warm thinking of Phinn's mouth on her body and his hands touching her. She pressed her palms to her cheeks. "I'm not sure I will be able to look him in the eyes, knowing what will occur."

Her cousin laughed. "You'll be fine. And if you blush as prettily when you do look at him, he will love you all the more."

"Well, now that that is over"—Jane rose—"we have a few things for you." She took out a velvet pouch from her valise she had brought in with her, handing it to Augusta. "Something old from the Vivers side."

Augusta opened the bag and drew out a long strand of matched pearls. "These are beautiful! But how—?"

"Grace. She did not know if you would decide to marry, but she wanted me to be prepared."

Tears pricked Augusta's eyes and she blinked them away. "She must be the wisest person I know."

"Something borrowed," Prue said, handing Augusta a coin. "It's a Roman coin I found in Spain. It has brought me good luck."

"Something blue and new." Jane held out a ring. "This is from Hector and me. We bought it in Paris after he decided that Phinn was falling in love with you."

Augusta put it on the index finger of her right hand. "Why did he not tell me?"

Her cousin smiled indulgently. "It is always better for a man and a woman to hear it from the other person."

"Unless they are being complete idiots." Prue's tone was as dry as dust, but her eyes twinkled. "In your case, you had goals that were making marriage more complicated."

Prue's maid came into the chamber carrying a sack. "I brought the extra pistol as you asked."

"Thank you. I hope we'll not need it." She removed the weapon from the bag. "It's loaded?"

"Indeed it is." The maid looked affronted. "It's no use if it's not."

"Gobert, I'd like you to carry it."

"It would be my honor, my lady."

Augusta would take hers as well. It was a shame they could not depart directly after the ceremony.

Less than an hour later, they were all dressed and waiting on the signal to make their way to the church.

A knock came on the door. "His lordship has passed, my lady."

Prue opened the door and started to laugh. "Apparently, the dowager countess wished to give you some luck. You must step over the broken glasses."

Augusta started to laugh as well. "I hope it works."

There were so many of their servants between her

and Phinn, the first sight of him she had was on the church steps. He had dressed in a Prussian-blue jacket, over a lighter blue waistcoat with gold stripes. His linen, as always, was snowy white, and a gold pin nestled in the folds of his cravat.

His eyes locked with hers as she climbed the steps. She truly had been blind. How had she not seen before how much he loved her?

"Good morning." Father Christophe glanced at their pistols. "I do not like weapons in the church, but my nephew has gone mad, therefore I shall allow it. I promise you he will be punished. Shall we begin?"

Hector gave her hand into the priest's, who then took Phinn's hand, turning it so it held hers. "In times past, I would have tied a ribbon around your hands. It is enough that you hold each other's hands as we walk into the church." He led them into the chuch, and, after their party was settled in the pews, began the ceremony.

Phinn was in the process of saying his vows when the church door slammed against the wall, and Viscount Celje stood in the entrance, his arm in a sling and his hand bandaged. The priest glared, and Augusta pointed her pistol at the intruder. Prue and the others quickly followed suit.

"Pavle." Father Christophe's hard tone echoed in the chapel. "Remain there. If you do not, I will not blame our visitors for shooting you again." Inclining his head, he continued with the service.

"The ring." Boman handed it to Father Christophe, who blessed it before glancing at the pistols she and Phinn held.

She glanced down. "Oh, Prue, I need both hands. Will you take this for a moment?"

"Of course." Augusta handed her cousin her pistol. Phinn gave his to Boman. "Thank you."

"My pleasure." He grinned. "This has to be the most interesting wedding I've ever attended."

Turning back to the priest, Phinn nodded. "Please continue."

A few minutes later, Father Christophe pronounced them man and wife, then whispered, "I would waste no time getting her to bed."

"Don't worry, Father." Phinn grinned as Augusta's cheeks heated. "I won't."

They regained their pistols, and she took a deep breath. She'd hate to have to shoot someone on the way to her wedding bed. "Are you ready?"

"I am." Phinn sounded confident. "Be prepared to run."

"That is the reason I wore half-boots instead of slippers."

They made it to the hall before he whispered, "Now."

Pelting up the stairs, they made it to her bedchamber, closed the door, locked it, and moved a chest in front of it. From the chambers next to them, it was clear their family, friends, and servants were doing the same thing.

Suddenly a fiddler started to play.

Augusta stared at the door. "What in Heaven's name is that for?"

"It's to mask our sounds." Phinn took off his shoes and started on his cravat.

"What sounds?"

The cravat dropped to the floor. "You'll see." His lips fluttered across hers and she opened her mouth. "I can't tell you how sorry I am that we are not able to take all night for this."

She pushed his jacket over his arms. "We'll have time later."

"Should I call your maid to take your hair down?" He went to work on her buttons.

Once her bodice sagged, she removed her arms from the sleeves. "I can do it."

"Oh, God." Having removed her petticoat and stays, he cupped her breasts. "I've never seen anything so perfect."

Dipping his head, he took one nipple in his mouth, and Augusta's back arched, pressing into him. Moaning, she finally understood the fiddler's purpose. "You are still dressed."

In a trice, the rest of his clothing lay on the floor. "Come, my lady wife. Let's to bed."

Swooping her into his arms as he had earlier, he placed her gently on the bed, then followed. Their lips met again, but this time she could feel his hot skin and muscular chest. Thick light brown hair covered his chest, and she wanted to run her fingers through it.

She protested when his kisses moved from her mouth to her neck and lower, licking her breasts and stomach. Fire flowed through her veins, and her hips, knowing what they were about, lifted.

"I hope I'm not going to shock you, but this is the fastest way." His mouth covered her mons, and all the heat, all the need that had been growing, coalesced *there.*

Even to her ears, her moans grew louder. "Phinn, *Phinn!*"

Using his fingers as well as his mouth, he made the tension grow. "Come for me, my love. Come for me."

Just when she thought she'd splinter apart, her body convulsed and he rose over her and plunged into her, filling her as she had never thought possible. The pain of being stretched warred with the pleasure of her orgasm.

"Are you all right?" His voice was tight.

Opening her eyes, she saw his beautiful silver eyes filled with worry. "I'm fine."

Augusta's eyes were a brighter blue and her skin was flushed with passion. She had never been so beautiful. Phinn touched his forehead to her forehead for a moment, then took her mouth as he began to move. "Put your legs around me."

Once she had done as he'd asked, he increased his pace, willing her to come again. He loved her more and more each time they were together. Just as he was to spill, she cried out, calling his name.

Rolling off her, he held her close, their hearts beating together. "I love you."

She raised up and kissed him lightly. "I love you too."

She rested her head on his shoulder and he caressed her. If only they could stay like this forever. Or for another thirty minutes.

The fiddler stopped and a scuffle sounded from the corridor.

Hell and damnation! "We have to get dressed."

"Sorry, my lady." Gobert entered the room, one hand over her eyes, the other holding out a robe. "We need the sheet."

"Drop the wrapper. I'll be a moment." Rising, Augusta glanced at the bed. Her eyes widened in shock. "There is no blood." She gaped at him. "Why is there no blood?"

"There's no time to discuss this now. Where is a hat pin or a knife?"

Stepping to the desk, she picked up a long, pearl-tipped hat pin. "Here it is." Returning to the bed, and before he could take the pin from her, she closed her eyes and stabbed her finger. Blood welled up. "Now what do I do?"

This was the tricky part. The blood couldn't be too

strong. "Rub it against your mons, where I entered you." Once she was done, he grabbed the bottom sheet and rubbed it between her legs. Taking her finger, he pressed lightly, a drop of blood fell onto his cock, then he rubbed it around. A basin of water and a cloth stood behind the screen. Wetting the cloth, he cleaned himself and her before throwing it on the side of the stand. "There. That should do it."

She picked up her robe and donned it before glancing at him. "You might want to put something on."

The door to his bedchamber opened, and Musson entered with Phinn's robe. "My lord."

"Thank you." Someone was attempting to gain access from the corridor. He handed Augusta her pistol. "Musson, help me move the dresser if you will."

"Indeed, my lord."

No sooner had they pushed it off to the side than the door crashed against the wall. Was that the only way the man knew how to enter a room? Celje stood there breathing heavily.

A maid squeezed around him. "I've come for the sheet," she said in Slovenian. A stricken look crossed her face, and she repeated herself in German. "I must take the sheet."

Prue marched into the chamber before the maid reached the bed. "Not without one of us coming with you."

The woman gave the viscount a terrified glance, but Prue didn't wait for her. Taking hold of the sheets, she ripped them off the bed and pointed at the maid. "There is most likely a rag next to the washbasin. Get it and give it to me as well."

"Come, my lady. You need to dress." Gobert pulled Augusta away. "Mr. Addison and Mr. Boman are accompanying Mrs. Brunning."

Suddenly, Celje crumpled to the floor. Behind him, the countess stood holding a cudgel. Glancing to her side, she said, "Take him to the dungeon and bring me the key."

A shout sounded from the hall and Count Celje appeared in the corridor. "I came as quickly as I could." He looked down at his son. "The dungeon is a good place for him. Shackle him as well. He has disgraced our house and deserves no kindness." Once the viscount had been removed, Lord Celje addressed Phinn and Augusta. "I offer you my most sincere apologies. He will not bother you again. This I vow to you."

The dowager countess gave Lord Celje a letter, saying, "The *Luciana*."

"Yes, indeed, Mama, thank you for thinking of it." He offered the letter to Phinn. "I have a large yacht in Trieste. It will be much more comfortable than any vessel you could hire. This is a letter for the captain. Please make use of it. I shall also write a letter to the manager of the Hotel Locanda Grande, informing him you will be using our apartments."

"Once again I apologize for my grandson's behavior," her ladyship said.

"I am sorry to say we cannot accept." Phinn glanced at Lord Celje. "He is a man and responsible for his own actions."

"You are correct, my lord. Fortunately, there are actions I can and shall take to ensure he learns to behave as a responsible gentleman."

The dowager inclined her head and one of her men closed the door.

Less than an hour later, Phinn, Augusta, Prue, and Boman rode through the castle gates with the rest of their party following in the coaches.

"I hope never to have to go through anything like that again," Augusta said.

"I hope it's the *last* time I have to go through this type of thing." Phinn was getting damned tired of other people thinking they could do as they pleased.

Their party arrived at the Hotel Locanda Grande in Trieste in time for dinner.

The four of them entered the hotel. "I am Lord Phineas Carter-Woods." He handed the clerk at the desk the letter.

"Of course, my lord." The man bowed. "The chambers will be ready for you momentarily. Do you have anyone accompanying you?"

He gave Addison's name and discovered he'd already reserved rooms.

"We also need to speak to the captain of a private yacht called the *Luciana*," Augusta said.

"Yes, of course. I will have a messenger sent immediately."

By then, Jane and Addison strolled into the hotel, and Augusta told them the captain had been sent for.

By the time they'd washed and refreshed themselves, Captain Gasparino was shown into the parlor they'd been given. Phinn handed him the missive and waited.

"The wind will not last long. Unless you wish to remain in Trieste for several days, we must depart at daybreak."

"I am ready to visit Venice," Jane said.

"As you will." The captain frowned. "Unfortunately, I do not have the capability of carrying more than one carriage and a pair of horses."

"I have a ship waiting for us that can transport the cattle and coaches. Have you seen the *Eleanor Jane*?"

"Yes, sir, but her captain was arrested two days ago. She cannot sail while he is detained."

"They can if there is a new captain. I'm going to the harbor with you." Addison gave Jane a short kiss. "Get cleaned up and eat. Then be ready to depart. We'll sleep on board tonight. It will be easier than rousing everyone tomorrow morning."

Baiju signaled to the grooms and coachmen. "Come with us. There is sufficient light to load the horses and coaches."

"I'll stay with Jane," Prue said, "and arrange transportation to the docks."

Phinn and Augusta decided to accompany her cousin. Minerva insisted she was remaining with them as did Etienne. Fortunately, they did not have far to go.

When they reached the *Eleanor Jane*, Hector called to one of the crewmen. "I'm Addison. Get your first mate out here now."

A man, no older than Phinn, rushed down the gangway. "Sir. I'm sorry—"

"No need for you to apologize for Griffin. The man's an idiot. You're in charge now, Captain. Get the ship ready to load my coaches and cattle. We'll be sailing on a private yacht at first light and I want you to sail with us."

As if they had not already dashed across the countryside, events occurred at a dizzying speed after that. Baiju organized the horses and carriages.

Phinn took Captain Gasparino aside for a hushed conversation.

Augusta had not known he spoke Italian, but she should have, knowing the other languages in which he was fluent.

He turned to Hector. "They have sufficient cabins on the yacht for us and our personal servants. The rest will have to make the crossing on the other ship."

"Very well. Baiju?" The man looked over. "Will you sail with the equipment or with us on the yacht?"

"I'll remain with the equipment." He grinned. "With you not sailing on this ship, I will have better quarters."

The staterooms and other compartments on the *Luciana* surpassed Augusta's expectations. Not that she had much knowledge of yachts. Once they had settled in, she went in search of Prue. There was a question to which Augusta did not have an answer. She found her cousin in the salon, sipping a glass of red wine. No longer fearing succumbing easily to spirits, she poured a glass for herself. "I have a question."

"I thought you might." Prue took another sip. "I heard part of what happened."

"I do not understand what *could* have happened." The question had dogged Augusta all day.

"Not all women are born with a maidenhead. Others break them somehow. I once knew a girl who inadvisably decided to ride a half-broken horse. She bled afterward."

"Oh." That would explain it. The horse had not been wild, but she'd tried to ride a horse that had been trained only for side-saddle, on a regular saddle. It had not gone well. Her mother had been away, and Louisa had told Augusta she was most likely starting her courses. But she hadn't bled after that.

"As long as Phinn doesn't doubt you, and I have no reason to think he does, it's all well." Her cousin smiled. "You, both of you, took care of the problem in the most expeditious manner possible."

"Was that the reason you came in?"

"Partly. The other part was that I had a suspicion that if one of us did not accompany the sheet, it would have disappeared." Prue raised her glass. "May I say how delighted I am that you are finally married, and to a man who loves you as much as you love him?"

"I wish he would have told me before." Even as Augusta said the words, she knew it wouldn't have served. It was the urgency in his voice and eyes that had convinced her.

"After you rejected him?" Her cousin raised one brow. "In that case, my dear, you have a great deal to learn about male pride." She took a packet out of her reticule. "Before I forget, Jane asked me to give you this. If you truly wish to avoid pregnancy, make a tisane using this herb. She has been using it since she stopped nursing Tommy."

Augusta took the packet. "What is it?"

"*Daucus carota*. The common name is Queen Anne's lace."

"Thank you." As happy as Augusta was that Phinn had agreed they could delay having children, he'd conceded that many methods did not work all the time. With luck, the herb would.

Chapter Thirty-Six

"Augusta." Phinn had almost panicked when she wasn't in their room. Ridiculous, of course. Nothing could happen to her on the yacht. Still, he couldn't be happy until he was with her again. Striding up to her, he took her in his arms. "I love you."

"I love you too." She gazed up at him, her beautiful blue eyes shining with her love for him.

All too soon, the rest of their party joined Phinn, Augusta, and Prue in the salon. More than anything, he wanted to take her back to their room and make love to her, slowly and properly this time. But after their hasty coupling this morning, and the long ride to Trieste, he knew she would be too sore. And they were both exhausted. As was everyone else, it seemed, as they agreed to make their way to their staterooms.

Augusta entered their cabin from a small chamber to one side of it. His valet was in a similar room on the other side. Rising, Phinn took her hand and kissed it. "You are the most enchanting woman I know." As she gazed at him, it was somewhat of a shock to realize it was the same way she'd looked at him for a while now. Since Munich. What a fool he'd been.

"You are the most handsome man I've ever seen."

It was his turn to blush. "Come to bed. I just want to hold you while we sleep."

Her lips pinched together. "Is anything wrong?"

Remembering her utter shock and panic this morning, he held her tighter. "Absolutely nothing. But we are both tired, and we have time."

She curled up next to him, and he slept better than he ever had. When he woke the boat was at sea, the cat was in bed on the other side of Augusta, and Minerva was curled up on the bed at his feet. He'd never seen such a large animal make herself so small. Even without children, they had a family. Augusta sighed in her sleep and snuggled into him. Phinn never thought he'd think of a phrase like *his heart was so full*. But it was, and it was because of her.

Several hours later they docked at a port near Venice.

"I have one question," Phinn said. He and Addison were in the salon looking at a map of Italy. "How were you able to place Griffin in charge of the ship?"

"I'm the majority partner in the company that owns the *Eleanor Jane* and several other ships."

Phinn had heard from his brother that Addison had his fingers in several ventures. "That was helpful."

Addison grinned. "Indeed it was. Now"—he tapped the map—"we are only staying in Venice for a few days before traveling on to Lake Garda in the foothills of the Alps. We'll return to Venice in September, just before you and Augusta journey to Padua."

"I've heard Venice is not pleasant during the summer months."

"That's what I've been told as well." He rolled up the map. "The first stop you and I will make after taking everyone else to the palazzo is to the British Consul. There is a rector assigned there who will look over this document the priest handed me this morning, after you and Augusta sign it. I already have Boman's and Prue's signatures as witnesses."

That was backward, but if it worked, what did it matter? "And if the marriage paper is not accepted?"

"Then we do it again."

"Augusta and I will add our signatures immediately."

Once everyone and everything had been taken to the palazzo Addison had leased, the new Captain Griffin led Phinn and Addison to the British Consul in Venice, only to find that with the exception of a clerk, the entire consul had decamped to Lake Garda. Not that Phinn could blame them. The heat was already making the city reek like a sewer.

"Shall we cut our visit short and head to Lake Garda as well?" Phinn asked.

"Give the horses a day or so to rest and we'll depart." Addison rubbed his cheek. "I don't mind telling you I'll be happy to remain in one place for more than a week or two."

"As much as I enjoy traveling, I have to agree."

Ten days later, they arrived at the villa Hector had rented in Lake Garda. As soon as they'd arrived, Augusta and Phinn had spoken to the consul's chaplain and ascertained that their marriage was legal in England. After that, she had lost no time writing her family about her marriage. Phinn wrote his brother and mother as well.

One day in late August, the sun was in the west, casting shadows over the valley, while they sipped the dry white wine of the Veneto on a terrace overlooking the lake. A new acquaintance, Count von Eppan, one of the many Austrians in the area, told them of the marriage of a friend's daughter to the eldest son of the Count of Celje.

"The young man had been resistant to the idea of marrying her at first," the count said.

"Indeed." His wife picked up the story. "Apparently he had formed a violent attachment to another lady. But he is now deeply in love with his new wife."

Phinn, Augusta, and the others in their party glanced briefly at each other. She wondered what the count and countess would say if they knew it was her. Still, in a strange way, the viscount's obsession had been what caused her and Phinn to finally admit their love for each other. Who knew how long it would have taken otherwise.

"It is always the way with these young men with a romantic nature." Count von Eppan drank his wine.

The English, Venetians, and Austrians were a great source of balls and other entertainments. Phinn received quite a lot of good-natured joking about not allowing Augusta to dance with anyone but him, but she had no desire to stand up with a gentleman other than her husband. To her delight, she actually came to enjoy the events.

By early September, Phinn, Augusta, Prue, and Boman, along with their servants, had arrived at her sponsor's summer house not far from Padua and been offered a commodious town house in Padua near the university. Augusta had the feeling the couple was more than pleased not to have to sponsor her. By the time they were settled, it was still another two weeks before the term began.

One day she and Phinn were strolling in a park near

the river. "It's beautiful, but so empty. Even many of the stores are not open yet."

"Much like Oxford when the students are gone. Enjoy the peace. When they return, the streets will be worse than London during the Season."

"I'd like to see it busy." She wanted to be part of the rush to get to class. "I wrote Professor Angeloni, but even he is not here yet."

"That doesn't surprise me." Phinn stopped and kissed her. "Patience, sweetheart."

Less than a week before the term was to begin, she received a stilted letter from Professor Angeloni. "This does not have the same feel as his other letters to me. He says we have a meeting with the university chancellor. What do you suppose it means?"

Phinn shook his head. "Haven't a clue, but you'll know soon. The meeting is tomorrow."

The next day, Augusta, accompanied by her cousin, entered the house that was to have been their home for the next few years. She had rarely been so exasperated and enraged. For men who were supposed to be educated, they were as small-minded as many of the same sex.

"I'd ask how it went." Phinn's arms went around her and she had to blink back tears of frustration. "But I think I know by the look on your face."

"They will let me attend lectures, but I may not matriculate. Baron von Neumann and his friend did all that was possible, but the head of the school and his advisers would not budge. I am allowed to study literature and philosophy, but nothing more."

He led her to a small parlor overlooking their courtyard. Something didn't make sense. "Why did the baron let you come all this way, thinking you'd been accepted?"

"Professor Angeloni, the one who told me I'd been accepted, only wanted me to work as his assistant for his research and translations. I speak many more languages than he does." She bit down on her lip to stop herself from taking her anger out on her poor husband. "He knew I would not be accepted as a regular student." Augusta would dearly love to murder the man. "I do not want to think about what I would have done if I had arrived here with only Prue. By the time I could have made arrangements to travel back, it would have been too late in the year."

Wine, rather than tea, arrived along with cheese and bread. Phinn fixed her a plate, while Durant poured two glasses of chilled, dry white wine.

"What do you want to do?" Phinn's tone was full of concern for her. Augusta fell in love with him all over again.

"I do not know. If I leave, would it be seen as failing or refusing to bow down to them?" She took a sip of wine, savoring the crispness. "They obviously think they have me backed into a corner." His arm went around her shoulders. "I did not tell them I am married."

"Knowing how some men's minds work, if you'd mentioned that, they would have dismissed you out of hand." He placed a slice of cheese on the freshly baked bread and ate it. "You'll have to make a decision whether to remain and study what you already know. Or we can travel. There is a great deal of ancient architecture in Italy and all of Southern Europe. You once told me that you had first decided to attend university because you didn't think you'd be allowed to make a Grand Tour."

That had been true, until she had studied for her entrance examinations when the excitement of attending a university had replaced her original desire. "I feel as if I will have failed. You went to Oxford. Charlie is there, and Walter will go next year."

"But I didn't graduate. I doubt if Charlie will either.

Walter or Phillip might, but only if they wish to go into the church, law, medicine, or wish to be a don."

She had never heard that before. "Then why do so many young gentlemen attend?"

Phinn chuckled. "Probably to keep us out of trouble. Unlike ladies, young men are not suitable for marriage. Being in university gives us a chance to be away from the structure and protection of home and colleges such as Eton, yet still be in a safer place than Town." He drank some of his wine. "Not that it always works."

"I never knew that." Yet did it matter? This had been her *dream.*

"What would a young man do if he faced the same choice as I am facing?" Augusta felt she owed it to the women who came after her—if women would ever be allowed to attend university—to make the same decision a man would make.

Phinn leaned back against the cushions, staring up at the ceiling. After several moments, he straightened. "Obviously, the circumstances would not be the same, but, if it were me, I'd wrap myself in my pride, and tell them to keep their offer. That I had better things to do with my mind and my time." Phinn sipped his wine for a few seconds more. "Unless there was something they could teach you about Italian literature?"

"No." Augusta shook her head. "I studied literature with one of the masters who was visiting London, and we have maintained a correspondence."

"My dear, sweet, clever wife"—Phinn kissed her hair—"I am almost positive that you've learned everything a university has to teach you and more. If you wish to tell them to go to the devil, it is their loss."

"I must think about all of this. Today has been such a disappointment." It was as if something had been ripped out of her. Not her heart—Phinn held that—but something vital. She drained her glass and rose. "If you will excuse me."

Her husband stood, holding out his hand. "Of course. I'll see you at dinner. I have some business to attend to."

Phinn watched Augusta trudge slowly up the stairs. Knowing her, she had not let those rubbishing commoners see her disappointment and anger. Yet it was palpable to him. He strode into the hall. "I'm going for a walk."

"Yes, my lord." Durant bowed. "When may I say you will return?"

"In two or three hours." After he murdered the professor, then the chancellor. If there was any way possible, Augusta would attend this blasted university.

He found the administrator's office, and was admitted immediately. Phinn only hoped he could find a solution for Augusta.

"Lord Phineas," an older man said in excellent English. "I am Chancellor Balestra. It is a pleasure to meet you." The man bowed. "I also have an interest in ancient architecture, and I recently read the paper you presented to the Royal Institution. It was well thought out." He went back behind his desk and sat down.

Well, wasn't that helpful. If he weren't so angry, Phinn might have been pleased that someone in Italy had read his paper. Instead, he had to restrain himself from wrapping his hands around the man's scraggy neck. "You spoke to a lady today. Lady Augusta Vivers?"

"Ah, yes. A very beautiful young woman, but sadly mistaken in her ability to attend our university. It is true we did allow one lady, but she was truly exceptional."

Phinn was going to kill the man. "I understand she passed your examination."

"So I was told, but many do." The chancellor stared at Phinn for a second. "As a gentleman, you must agree that it is not a woman's place to attend university. Your English universities do not allow women. And for good reason. The female sex cannot withstand the rigors of academia. Why her family allowed her to travel all this way with merely a chaperone is beyond my comprehension."

Starched up, consequential prig. "Oh?" Phinn widened his eyes. "Did she swoon or resort to tears when you told her she had been lied to by one of your dons?"

"No." The man shook his head. "She was very calm."

"She's a damn sight calmer than I am right now." He leaned forward, placing his hands on the desk. "I'd like to throttle you to within an inch of your life."

Shock replaced the smug expression on Chancellor Balestra's face. "May I ask what Lady Augusta means to you that you are so exercised on her behalf?"

At last, an intelligent question. "She is my wife. Lady Phineas Carter-Woods. Sister-in-law to the Marquis of Dorchester, cousin of the Marquis of Merton, and sister to the Duke of Rothwell. She is also *the* most *intelligent* person I have ever met or with whom I have come in contact. If I know her, and I do, she not only passed your blasted entrance examination, but did better than anyone else."

Phinn couldn't help a feeling of satisfaction when the man's eyes protruded in fear. "I . . . I really couldn't say."

"Call in the don who graded the paper."

The man swallowed, his throat working with the effort. He was lying. "That will not be necessary. She did indeed exceed the requirements."

Finally, they were getting somewhere. "You might not approve her to attend the university"—unfortunately, it didn't take much for him to imagine how difficult and humiliating they'd make it for her—"but you *will* allow her to take the final examinations required for a degree.

I have no objection to the questions being in writing. Her Italian is fluent. You may choose literature if you wish."

"But, my lord,"—the man was obviously in a panic—"she has not studied the material."

"Nevertheless, you will permit her to take the examination, and if she passes, she will receive a degree certificate." Phinn was about to offer a donation to the damned place. Anything to allow Augusta to show these worthless popinjays she was better than them. "If you do not, I will contact Prince von Metternich—as head of the Habsburg foreign office, that should terrify the chancellor—and tell him the assurances he received concerning my wife's place at the university were a lie."

That threat did the trick. The man appeared stricken with dread. "Very well. It shall be as you wish."

"So we are clear"—he speared the older man with a look—"I will make a copy of both the examination and her answers and send them to England, where the foremost authority on the Italian language and literature will also read them." Phinn stood. "I shall leave our address with your secretary. I expect to hear from you within the next few days."

"Of course, my lord."

Phinn strode out of the room, stopping only to write down his address. Now he needed to find his wife a present so she wouldn't murder him when he told her what he'd done.

Chapter Thirty-Seven

Augusta spent the rest of the day trying to decide what to do. Phinn's offer of travel was more than enticing. Yet, by dinner, she had not been able to make a decision. Making her way to the courtyard, where they usually met for wine, she was surprised to see only her husband. "Where are Prue and Boman?"

"They decided to try a restaurant someone told them about." Phinn handed her a book. "I thought you might like this. It is a collection of poetry by Veronica Gambara."

Augusta opened the book to the first page and her jaw dropped. "It is not only a collection of poetry, but the first of the printings." She glanced at Phinn. "This must have set you back."

"I wish it had. It was quite reasonable, but I knew you'd love it." He poured the wine, but instead of handing her one of the goblets, he put them on the table.

Setting the book down carefully, she threw her arms around him. "What is the occasion? Or should I ask what you've done?"

His arms came around her, clasping her tightly to him, as if she might run away if he didn't hold on.

"Gave you another option." He dropped a kiss on her head. "I went to see the chancellor and told him he would allow you to take the examination, and if you passed—which you will—they had to grant you a degree certificate."

Elation such as she'd not felt since France filled her. Augusta leaned back to look at her husband. "How exactly did you convince him to agree?"

He gave her a sheepish look. "I threatened him with the full force of the Austrian Foreign Office."

Never in her life could she have imagined being married to a man who was so in tune with her. Who wanted for her what she wanted. How had she got so lucky?

"You're not angry?" He searched her eyes.

"Angry? No, not at all. Aside from the book, by a female poet, you gave me the solution to my problem." Reaching up, she kissed him. What a clever man. "You do realize that if von Metternich and not his secretary had been involved, I might not be here at all?"

"That may be true. I have to say, once I worked out that Metternich was not in Vienna for most of the year, the same thought occurred to me. He is very much a conservative. So the secretary must have written all the correspondence. But, we'll never know, will we?"

Two days later, Augusta received a letter inviting her to sit for the examination the following day. Her hand shook with excitement and anxiety. "What if I do not pass?"

"You will." Phinn gave her an encouraging smile. "I have complete trust and faith in you."

She was glad he did. Yet, was he right? Had all her studying and correspondence given her the equivalent of a university degree? She was about to find out.

The next day she sat for the examination, reading it over twice before she began to write. It was nothing she had not studied before. In fact, the test was not as demanding as her studies had been. Phinn had been correct. She already had a university education; she just hadn't realized it.

Four hours later she handed it to the proctor seated on a high platform at the end of the room. The man glanced down at her. "Do you require a pause?"

"No, I have finished."

A smug smile pulled at his lips. "So, you have given up."

Augusta raised one brow. "Not at all. I have completed the test." Walking over to the door, she opened it and a man entered. "My husband has hired a clerk who will copy my answers. They will be sent to England and reviewed."

"Yes, the chancellor said as much."

"In that case, I trust there will be no irregularities." She nodded her head. "Thank you for the opportunity."

Durant met her in the corridor.

"Let's go home. I won't have the results for a few days."

"Yes, my lady." To her surprise, he grinned.

"What is it?"

"I've picked up enough Italian to know it usually takes more than four hours to take that test. It will probably be the best one they've ever read."

The mood was quiet when they reached the house. Everyone had agreed there would be no celebration until she received the results. The dinner conversation revolved around what city they wanted to see next. Letters had arrived from England, but Augusta was too distracted to read them.

That night, Phinn made love to her slowly, kissing

and caressing every inch of her body until she was frantic with wanting him. "Now!"

"Almost." He grinned against her inner thigh.

The instant his tongue touched her mons, she shattered into a thousand pieces. When he entered her, it was one smooth motion, and she clasped her legs around him, urging him to go faster until her sheath convulsed around him.

A week later, just as Augusta was fighting to keep herself from snapping at everyone around her, including the cat and dog, and Phinn was threatening to strangle the chancellor, a messenger from the university was shown into the drawing room.

The boy handed her a large letter paper-case, bowed, and left. For a long time, she couldn't speak. "I don't think I can open it."

Prue studied the case. "It doesn't look thick enough to be the examination." She glanced at Boman. "Do they return one's paper?"

"I never got mine back." He looked at Phinn.

"Nor did I." He turned to her. "Do you want me to open it?"

"No." She shook her head. It was something she had to do. Untying the ribbon wrapped around it, she placed it on the low table in front of the sofa, and sat. No matter what happened, she did not want to be standing. She lifted the stiff, dark brown leather flap, took a breath, and drew out an ornate gold-edged certificate with seals and the words *cum laude* on the front next to her name. "I passed." Heart pounding, she glanced up and everyone else was smiling. Tears filled her eyes. Phinn hugged her, being careful not to touch the certificate. "I passed. I really did it!"

He searched her eyes as he dabbed them with his handkerchief. "I always knew you would."

Prue passed around glasses of French champagne. "Hector gave me several bottles in the event we had something to celebrate."

Augusta swiped at her eyes, unable to think of anything to say.

Holding up his glass, Phinn said, "To the most intelligent lady I know."

"Here, here!"

Minerva barked and ran around the parlor in a circle, and Etienne jumped onto Augusta's lap. She saved her drink from being knocked over by the Dane's tail. "I think they feel the happiness too."

Phinn took the certificate, placing it back in the letter-case. "What's next?"

"How would everyone like to travel down to the south of Italy and take a ship to Egypt?" Augusta glanced at the smiles on everyone's faces.

"I think that sounds like an excellent idea. You can study hieroglyphics and I'll—"

"Study the pyramids."

AUTHOR NOTES

By the early 19th century, there were three universities in Europe that had allowed women to attend and attain degrees. Utrecht, Holland, the closest had been lowered to the status of a college. Not like a US college but a school such as Eton. Bologna allowed a lady attend the university in the 18th century. She also remained there and taught. That was my first choice. Unfortunately, after the Congress of Vienna, the city was put under Papal jurisdiction and did not accept another female for almost a hundred years. Padua, also one of the best universities in Europe, was the only one left. They'd had a lady attend in the 17th century. But in 1818 they came under the Habsburg Empire. I corresponded with them and was told that the lady in question had been extremely special. Naturally, I wrote back asking if an English lady from a noble house who was also extremely special and who had the backing of dignitaries of the Habsburg Empire and one of the professors at Padua would have been accepted. They declined to reply, so I decided she would have been allowed to attend.

One of the issues I had was getting my characters to Vienna. The roads really were as bad as I've portrayed them. Then I discovered that most goods and people traveled by water. But I knew that today, the Isar river from Munich to the Danube at Regensburg is not navigable. Further research revealed that in the early 19th century a series of canals and locks had been built to facilitate river traffic.

According to accounts written by English travelers in the early 19th century, Vienna's streets, indeed, had no sidewalks (pavements) and were hazardous to tourists. English coachmen frequently came to grief. Therefore, local coachmen were hired.

In England betrothal rings that were also used as wedding rings were common among the aristocracy. However, in the Austrian Empire engagement rings as we know them were used with regularity.

In parts of the Austrian Empire, such as Slovenia, Hungary, and Croatia, many noblemen maintained a household troop.

The marriage customs mentioned were and, in some places, still are common.

If you ever have a question about something in one of my books, please ask. My website is www.ellaquinn author.com. By signing up for my newsletter (the link is on my website) you can find out more about my books as well as promotions and sales.

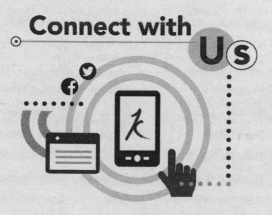

Books by Bestselling Author
Fern Michaels

Available Wherever Books Are Sold!
Check out our website at www.kensingtonbooks.com